THE BETTY NEELS COLLECTION

Betty Neels's novels are loved by millions of readers around the world, and this very special ***2-in-1 collection*** offers a unique opportunity to relive the magic of some of her most popular stories.

We are proud to present these classic romances by the woman who could weave an irresistible tale of love like no other.

So sit back in your comfiest chair with your favorite cup of tea and enjoy these best of Betty Neels stories!

BETTY NEELS

Romance readers around the world were sad to note the passing of Betty Neels in June 2001. Her career spanned thirty years, and she continued to write into her ninetieth year. To her millions of fans, Betty epitomized the romance writer, and yet she began writing almost by accident. She had retired from nursing, but her inquiring mind still sought stimulation. Her new career was born when she heard a lady in her local library bemoaning the lack of good romance novels. Betty's first book, *Sister Peters in Amsterdam,* was published in 1969, and she eventually completed 134 books. Her novels offer a reassuring warmth that was very much a part of her own personality, and her spirit and genuine talent live on in all her stories.

BETTY NEELS

A Suitable Match

and

A Gentle Awakening

HARLEQUIN® THE BETTY NEELS COLLECTION

Recycling programs for this product may not exist in your area.

ISBN-13: 978-0-373-60658-0

A SUITABLE MATCH AND A GENTLE AWAKENING

This edition published by arrangement with Harlequin Books S.A.

For questions and comments about the quality of this book, please contact us at CustomerService@Harlequin.com.

Printed in U.S.A.

Resisting Mr. Off-Limits!

Owner of Obsidian Studios, Garrett Black might be scarred both inside and out, but with the Hollywood Hills Film Festival fast approaching, there's no time for distractions. Especially not those as tempting as event coordinator Tori Randall….

Who cares if he's gorgeous? Tori's frustrated by this brooding CEO's aloof attitude and near impossible demands. Even if Garrett wasn't her boss, she'd never risk her heart to another emotionally closed man. Normally she'd run in the opposite direction…so why does she feel so compelled to stay?

Her Boss by Arrangement

by

Teresa Carpenter

Available September 2014 from Harlequin Romance, wherever books and ebooks are sold.

www.Harlequin.com

HR74305

CONTENTS

A SUITABLE MATCH

Chapter 1

Eustacia bit into her toast, poured herself another cup of tea, and turned her attention once again to the job vacancies in the morning paper. She had been doing this for some days now and it was with no great hope of success that she ran her eye down the columns. Her qualifications, which were few, didn't seem to fit into any of the jobs on offer. It was a pity, she reflected, that an education at a prestigious girls' school had left her quite unfitted for earning her living in the commercial world. She had done her best, but the course of shorthand and typing had been nothing less than disastrous, and she hadn't lasted long at the boutique because, unlike her colleagues, she had found herself quite incapable of telling a customer that a dress fitted while she held handfuls of surplus material at that lady's back, or left a zip undone to accommodate surplus flesh. She had applied for a job at the local post office too, and had been turned down because she didn't wish to join a union. No one, it seemed, wanted a girl with four A levels and the potential for a university if she had been able to go to one. Here she was, twenty-two years old, out of work once more and with a grandfather to support.

She bent her dark head over the pages—she was a pretty girl with eyes as dark as her hair, a dainty little nose and a rather too large mouth—eating her toast absentmindedly as she searched the pages. There was nothing… Yes, there was: the path lab of St Biddolph's Hospital, not half a mile away, needed an assistant bottle-washer, general cleaner and postal worker. No qualifications required other than honesty, speed and cleanliness. The pay wasn't bad either.

Eustacia swallowed the rest of her tea, tore out the advertisement, and went out of the shabby little room into the passage and tapped on a door. A voice told her to go in and she did so, a tall, splendidly built girl wearing what had once been a good suit, now out of date but immaculate.

'Grandpa,' she began, addressing the old man sitting up in his bed. 'There's a job in this morning's paper. As soon as I've brought your breakfast I'm going after it.'

The old gentleman looked at her over his glasses. 'What kind of a job?'

'Assistant at the path lab at St Biddolph's.' She beamed at him. 'It sounds OK, doesn't it?' She whisked herself through the door again. 'I'll be back in five minutes with your tray.'

She left their small ground-floor flat in one of the quieter streets of Kennington and walked briskly to the bus-stop. It wasn't yet nine o'clock and speed, she felt, was of the essence. Others, it seemed, had felt the same; there were six women already in the little waiting-room inside the entrance to the path lab at the hospital, and within the next ten minutes another four turned up. Eustacia sat there quietly waiting, uttering silent, childish prayers. This job would be nothing less than a godsend—regular hours, fifteen minutes from the flat and the weekly pay-packet would be enough to augment her grandfather's pension—a vital point, this, for they had been eating into their tiny capital for several weeks.

Her turn came and she went to the room set aside for the interviews, and sat down before a stout, elderly man sitting at a desk. He looked bad-tempered and he sounded it too, ignoring her polite 'Good morning' and plunging at once into his own questions.

She answered them briefly, handed over her references and waited for him to speak.

"You have four A levels. Why are you not at a university?'

'Family circumstances,' said Eustacia matter-of-factly.

He glanced up. 'Yes, well…the work here is menial, you understand that?' He glowered across the desk at her. 'You will be notified.'

Not very hopeful, she considered, walking back to the flat; obviously A levels weren't of much help when applying for such a job. She would give it a day and, if she heard nothing, she would try for something else. She stopped at the baker's and bought bread and then went next door to the greengrocer's and chose a cauliflower. Cauliflower cheese for supper and some carrots and potatoes. She had become adept at making soup now that October was sliding into November. At least she could cook, an art she had been taught at her expensive boarding-school, and if it hadn't been for her grandfather she might have tried her luck as a cook in some hotel. Indeed, she had left school with no thought of training for anything; her mother and father had been alive then, full of ideas about taking her with them when they travelled. 'Plenty of time,' they had said. 'A couple of years enjoying life before you marry or decide what you want to do,' and she had had those two years, seeing quite a lot of the world, knowing only vaguely that her father was in some kind of big business which allowed them to live in comfort. It was when he and her mother had been killed in an air crash that she'd discovered that he was heavily in debt, that his business was bankrupt and that any money there was would have to go to creditors. It had been frightening to find herself without a penny and an urgent necessity to earn a living, and it had been then that her grandfather, someone she had seldom met for he'd lived in the north of England, had come to see her.

'We have each other,' he had told her kindly. 'I cannot offer you a home, for my money was invested in your father's business, but I have my pension and I believe I know someone who will help us to find something modest to live in in London.'

He had been as good as his word; the 'someone' owned property in various parts of London and they had moved into the flat two years ago, and Eustacia had set about getting a job. Things hadn't been too bad at first, but her typing and shorthand weren't good enough to get a job in an office and her grandfather had developed a heart condition so that she had had to stay at home for some time to look after him. Now, she thought hopefully, perhaps their luck had changed and she would get this job, and Grandfather would get better, well enough for her to hire a car and take him to Kew or Richmond Park. He hated the little street where they lived and longed for the country, and so secretly did she, although she never complained. He had enough to bear, she considered, and felt nothing but gratitude for his kindness when she had needed it most.

She made coffee for them both when she got in and told him about the job. 'There were an awful lot of girls there,' she said. 'This man said he would let me know. I don't expect that means much, but it's better than being told that the job's been taken—I mean, I can go on hoping until I hear.'

She heard two days later—the letter was on the mat when she got up, and she took it to the kitchen and put on the kettle for their morning tea and opened it.

The job was hers—she was to present herself for work on the following Monday at eight-thirty sharp. She would have half an hour for her lunch, fifteen minutes for her coffee-break and tea in the afternoon, and work until five o'clock. She would be free on Saturdays and Sundays but once a month she would be required to work on Saturday, when she would be allowed the following Monday free. Her wages, compared to Grandfather's pension, seemed like a fortune.

She took a cup of tea to her grandfather and told him the news.

'I'm glad, my dear. It will certainly make life much easier for you—now you will be able to buy yourself some pretty clothes.'

It wasn't much good telling him that pretty clothes weren't any use unless she had somewhere to go in them, but she agreed cheerfully, while she did sums in her head: the gas bill, always a formidable problem with her grandfather to keep warm by the gas fire in their sitting-room—duvets for their beds, some new saucepans… She mustn't get too ambitious, she told herself cautiously, and went off to get herself dressed.

She got up earlier than usual on Monday, tidied the flat, saw to her grandfather's small wants, cautioned him to be careful while she was away, kissed him affectionately, and started off for the hospital.

She was a little early, but that didn't matter, as it gave her time to find her way around to the cubby-hole where she was to change into the overall she was to wear, and peep into rooms and discover where the canteen was. A number of people worked at the path lab and they could get a meal cheaply enough as well as coffee and tea. People began to arrive and presently she was told to report to an office on the ground floor where she was given a list of duties she was to do by a brisk lady who made no attempt to disguise her low opinion of Eustacia's job.

'You will wear rubber gloves at all times and a protective apron when you are emptying discarded specimens. I hope you are strong.'

Eustacia hoped she was, too.

By the end of the first day she concluded that a good deal of her work comprised washing-up—glass containers, dishes, little pots, glass tubes and slides. There was the emptying of buckets, too, the distribution of clean laundry and the collecting of used overalls for the porters to bag, and a good deal of toing and froing, taking sheaves of papers, specimens and the post to wherever it was wanted. She was tired as she went home; there were, she supposed, pleasanter ways of earning a living, but never mind that, she was already looking forward to her pay-packet at the end of the week.

She had been there for three days when she came face to face with the man who had interviewed her. He stopped in front of her and asked, 'Well, do you like your work?'

She decided that despite his cross face he wasn't ill-disposed towards her. 'I'm glad to have work,' she told him pleasantly, 'you have no idea how glad. Not all my work is—well, nice, but of course you know that already.'

He gave a rumble of laughter. 'No one stays for long,' he told her. 'Plenty of applicants when the job falls vacant, but they don't last…'

'I have every intention of staying, provided my work is satisfactory.' She smiled at him and he laughed again.

'Do you know who I am?'

'No. I don't know anyone yet—only to say good morning and so on. I saw Miss Bennett when I came here—she told me what to do and so on—and I've really had no time to ask anyone.'

'I'm in charge of this department, young lady; the name's Professor Ladbroke. I'll see that you get a list of those working here.'

He nodded and walked away. Oh, dear, thought Eustacia, I should have called him 'sir' and not said all that.

She lived in a state of near panic for the rest of the week, wondering if she would get the sack, but pay-day came and there was nothing in her envelope but money. She breathed a sigh of relief and vowed to mind her Ps and Qs in future.

No one took much notice of her; she went in and out of rooms peopled by quiet, white-coated forms peering through microscopes or doing mysterious things with tweezers and pipettes. She suspected that they didn't even see her, and the greater part of her day was concerned with the cleansing of endless bowls and dishes. It was, she discovered, a lonely life, but towards the end of the second week one or two people wished her good morning and an austere man with a beard asked her if she found the work hard.

She told him no, adding cheerfully, 'A bit off-putting sometimes, though!' He looked surprised, and she wished that she hadn't said anything at all.

By the end of the third week she felt as though she had been there for years—she was even liking her work. There actually was a certain pleasure in keeping things clean and being useful, in however humble a capacity, to a department full of silent, dedicated people, all so hard at work with their microscopes and pipettes and little glass dishes.

She was to work that Saturday; she walked home, shopping on her way, buying food which her grandfather could see to on his own, thankful that she didn't have to look at every penny. In the morning she set out cheerfully for the hospital. There would be a skeleton staff in the path lab until midday, and after that she had been told to pass any urgent messages to whoever was on call that weekend. One of the porters would come on duty at six o'clock that evening and take over the phone when she went.

The department was quiet; she went around, changing linen, opening windows, making sure that there was a supply of tea and sugar and milk in the small kitchen, and then carefully filling the half-empty shelves with towels, soap, stationery and path lab forms and, lastly, making sure that there was enough of everything in the sterilisers. It took her until mid-morning, by which time the staff on duty had arrived and were busy dealing with whatever had been sent from the hospital. She made coffee for them all, had some herself and went to assemble fresh supplies of dishes and bowls on trays ready for sterilising. She was returning from carrying a load from one room to the next when she came face to face with a man.

She was a tall girl, but she had to look up to see his face. A handsome one it was too, with a commanding nose, drooping lids over blue eyes and a thin mouth. His hair was thick and fair and rather untidy, and he was wearing a long white coat—he was also very large.

He stopped in front of her. 'Ah, splendid, get this checked at once, will you, and let me have the result? I'll be in the main theatre. It's urgent.' He handed her a covered kidney dish. 'Do I know you?'

'No,' said Eustacia. She spoke to his broad, retreating back.

He had said it was urgent; she bore the dish to Mr Brimshaw, who was crouching over something nasty in a tray. He waved her away as she reached him, but she stood her ground.

'Someone—a large man in a white coat—gave me this and said he would be in the main theatre and that it was urgent.'

'Then don't stand there, girl, give it to me.'

As she went away he called after her. 'Come back in ten minutes, and you can take it back.'

'Such manners,' muttered Eustacia as she went back to her dishes.

In exactly ten minutes she went back again to Mr Brimshaw just in time to prevent him from opening his mouth to bellow for her. He gave a grunt instead. 'And look sharp about it,' he cautioned her.

The theatre block wasn't anywhere near the path lab; she nipped smartly in and out of lifts and along corridors and finally, since the lifts were already in use, up a flight of stairs. She hadn't been to the theatre block before and she wasn't sure how far inside the swing-doors she was allowed to go, a problem solved for her by the reappearance of the man in the white coat, only now he was in a green tunic and trousers and a green cap to match.

He took the kidney dish from her with a nice smile. 'Good girl—new, aren't you?' He turned to go and then paused. 'What is your name?'

'Eustacia Crump.' She flew back through the swing-doors, not wanting to hear him laugh—everyone laughed when she told them her name. Eustacia and Crump didn't go well together. He didn't laugh, only stood for a moment more watching her splendid person, swathed in its ill-fitting overall, disappear.

Mr Brimshaw went home at one o'clock and Jim Walker, one of the more senior pathologists working under him, took over. He was a friendly young man and, since Eustacia had done all that was required of her and there was nothing much for him to do for half an hour, she made him tea and had a cup herself with her sandwiches. She became immersed in a reference book of pathological goings-on—she understood very little of it, but it made interesting reading.

It fell to her to go to theatre again a couple of hours later, this time with a vacoliter of blood.

'Mind and bring back that form, properly signed,' warned Mr Walker. 'And don't loiter, will you? They're in a hurry.'

Eustacia went. Who, she asked herself, would wish to loiter in such circumstances? Did Mr Walker think that she would tuck the thing under one arm and stop for a chat with anyone she might meet on her way? She was terrified of dropping it anyway.

She sighed with relief when she reached the theatre block and went cautiously through the swing-doors, only to pause because she wasn't quite sure where to go. A moot point settled for her by a disapproving voice behind her.

'There you are,' said a cross-faced nurse, and took the vacoliter from her.

Eustacia waved the form at her. 'This has to be signed, please.'

'Well, of course it does.' It was taken from her and the nurse plunged through one of the doors on either side, just as the theatre door at the far end swished open and the tall man she had met in the path lab came through.

'Brought the blood?' he asked pleasantly, and when she nodded, 'Miss Crump, isn't it? We met recently.' He stood in front of her, apparently in no haste.

'Tell me,' he asked, 'why are you not sitting on a bench doing blood counts and looking at cells instead of washing bottles?'

It was a serious question and it deserved a serious answer.

'Well, that's what I am—a bottle-washer, although it's called a path lab assistant, and I'm not sure that I should like to sit at a bench all day—some of the things that are examined are very nasty...'

His eyes crinkled nicely at the corners when he smiled. 'They are. You don't look like a bottle-washer.'

'Oh? Do they look different from anyone else?'

He didn't answer that but went on. 'You are far too beautiful,' he told her, and watched her go a delicate pink.

A door opened and the cross nurse came back with the form in her hand. When she saw them she smoothed the ill humour from her face and smiled.

'I've been looking everywhere for you, sir. If you would sign this form...?' She cast Eustacia a look of great superiority as she spoke. 'They're waiting in theatre for you, sir,' she added in what Eustacia considered to be an oily voice.

The man took the pen she offered and scrawled on the paper and handed it to Eustacia. 'Many thanks, Miss Crump,' he said with grave politeness. He didn't look at the nurse once but went back through the theatre door without a backward glance.

The nurse tossed her head at Eustacia. 'Well, hadn't you better get back to the path lab?' she wanted to know. 'You've wasted enough of our time already.'

Eustacia was almost a head taller, and it gave her a nice feeling of superiority. 'Rubbish,' she said crisply, 'and shouldn't you be doing whatever you ought instead of standing there?'

She didn't stay to hear what the other girl had to say; she hoped that she wouldn't be reported for rudeness. It had been silly of her to annoy the nurse; she couldn't afford to jeopardise her job.

'OK?' asked Mr Walker when she gave him back the signed form. He glanced at it. 'Ah, signed by the great man himself…'

'Oh, a big man in his theatre kit? I don't know anyone here.'

Mr Walker said rather unkindly, 'Well, you don't need to, do you? He's Sir Colin Crichton. An honorary consultant here—goes all over the place—he's specialising in cancer treatment—gets good results too.' He looked at his watch. 'Make me some tea, will you? There's a good girl.'

She put on the kettle and waited while it boiled and thought about Sir Colin Crichton. He had called her Miss Crump and he hadn't laughed. She liked him, and she wished she could see him again.

However, she didn't, the week passed and Saturday came again and she was free once more. Because it was a beautiful day—a bonus at the beginning of the winter—she helped her grandfather to wrap up warmly, went out and found a taxi, and took him to Kew Gardens. Supported by her arm and a stick, the old gentleman walked its paths, inspected a part of the botanical gardens, listened to the birds doing their best in the pale sunshine and then expressed a wish to go to the Orangery.

It was there that they encountered Sir Colin, accompanied by two small boys. Eustacia saw him first and suggested hastily to her grandfather that they might turn around and stroll in the opposite direction.

'Why ever should we do that?' he asked testily, and before she could think up a good reason Sir Colin had reached them.

'Ah—Miss Crump. We share a similar taste in Chambers' work—a delightful spot on a winter morning.'

He stood looking at her, his eyebrows faintly lifted, and after a moment she said, 'Good morning, sir,' and, since her grandfather was looking at her as well, 'Grandfather, this is Sir Colin Crichton, he's a consultant at St Biddolph's. My Grandfather, Mr Henry Crump.'

The two men shook hands and the boys were introduced—Teddy and Oliver, who shook hands too, and, since the two gentlemen had fallen into conversation and had fallen into step, to stroll the length of the Orangery and then back into the gardens again, Eustacia found herself with the two boys. They weren't very old—nine years, said Teddy, and Oliver was a year younger. They were disposed to like her and within a few minutes were confiding a number of interesting facts. Half-term, they told her, and they would go back to school on Monday, and had she any brothers who went away to school?

She had to admit that she hadn't. 'But I really am very interested; do tell me what you do there—I don't mean lessons…'

They understood her very well. She was treated to a rigmarole of Christmas plays, football, computer games and what a really horrible man the maths master was. 'Well, I dare say your father can help you with your homework,' she suggested.

'Oh, he's much too busy,' said Oliver, and she supposed that he was, operating and doing ward rounds and out-patients and travelling around besides. He couldn't have much home life. She glanced back to where the two men were strolling at her grandfather's pace along the path towards them, deep in talk. She wondered if Sir Colin wanted to take his leave but was too courteous to say so; his wife might be waiting at home for him and the boys. She spent a few moments deciding what to do and rather reluctantly turned back towards them.

'We should be getting back,' she suggested to her grandfather, and was echoed at once by Sir Colin.

'So must we. Allow me to give you a lift—the car's by the Kew Road entrance.'

Before her grandfather could speak, Eustacia said quickly, 'That's very kind of you, but I daresay we live in a quite opposite direction to you: Kennington.'

'It couldn't be more convenient,' she was told

smoothly. 'We can keep south of the river, drop you off and cross at Southwark.' He gave her a gentle smile and at the same time she saw that he intended to have his own way.

They walked to the main gate, suiting their pace to that of her grandfather, and got into the dark blue Rolls-Royce parked there. Eustacia sat between the boys at the back, surprised to find that they were sharing it with a small, untidy dog with an extremely long tail and melting brown eyes. Moreover, he had a leg in plaster.

'This is Moses,' said Oliver as he squashed in beside Eustacia. 'He was in the water with a broken leg,' he explained and, since Eustacia looked so astonished, said it for a second time, rather loudly, just as though she were deaf.

'Oh, the poor little beast.' She bent to rub the unruly head at their feet and Sir Colin, settling himself in the driving-seat, said over his shoulder, 'He's not quite up to walking far, but he likes to be with us. Unique, isn't he?'

'But nice,' said Eustacia, and wished she could think of a better word.

It was quite a lengthy drive; she sat between the boys, taking part in an animated conversation on such subjects as horrendous schoolmasters, their favourite TV programmes, their dislike of maths and their favourite food. She found them both endearing and felt regret when the drive was over and the car drew up before their flat. Rolls-Royces were a rarity in the neighbourhood, and it would be a talking-point for some time—already curtains in neighbouring houses were being twitched.

She wished the boys goodbye and they chorused an urgent invitation to go out with them again, and, conscious of Sir Colin's hooded eyes upon her, she murmured non-committally, bending to stroke Moses because she could feel herself blushing hatefully.

She waited while her grandfather expressed his thanks for the ride, and then she added her own thanks with a frank look from her dark eyes, to encounter his smiling gaze.

'We have enjoyed your company,' he told her, and she found herself believing him. 'The boys get bored, you know; I haven't all that time at home and my housekeeper is elderly and simply can't cope with them.'

'Housekeeper? Oh, I thought they were yours.'

'My brother's. He has gone abroad with his wife, a job in Brunei for a few months. They are too young for boarding-school…'

They had shaken hands and he still held hers in a firm grasp.

'They like you,' he said.

'Well, I like them. I'm glad I met them and Grandfather has enjoyed himself. He doesn't get out much.'

He nodded and gave her back her hand and went to open the rickety gate, and waited while they went up the short path to the front door and opened it. Eustacia turned as they went inside and smiled at them all, before he closed the gate, got back into his car and drove away.

'A delightful morning, my dear,' said her grandfather. 'I feel ten years younger—and such an interesting conversation. You are most fortunate to be working for such a man.'

'Well, I don't,' said Eustacia matter-of-factly. 'I only met him because he came down to the path lab for something. He goes to St Biddolph's once or twice a week to operate and see his patients, and as I seldom leave the path lab except when there is a message to run we don't meet.'

'Yes, yes,' her grandfather sounded testy, 'but now that you have met you will see more of each other.'

She thought it best not to argue further; she suspected that he had no idea of the work she did. Sir Colin had been charming but that didn't mean to say that he wished to pursue their acquaintance; indeed it was most unlikely. A pity, she reflected as she went to the kitchen to get their lunch, but they occupied different worlds—she would probably end up by marrying another bottle-washer. A sobering thought even while she laughed at the idea.

It was December in no time at all, or so it seemed, and the weather turned cold and damp and dark, and the shops began to fill with Christmas food and a splendid array of suitable presents. Eustacia did arithmetic on the backs of envelopes, made lists and began to hoard things like chocolate biscuits, strawberry jam, tins of ham and a Christmas pudding; she had little money over each week and she laid it out carefully, determined to have a good Christmas. There would be no one to visit, of course. As far as she knew they had no family, and her grandfather's friends lived in the north of England and her own friends from school days were either married or holding down good jobs with no time to spare. From time to time they exchanged letters, but pride prevented her from telling any of them about the change in her life. She wrote cheerful replies, telling them nothing in a wealth of words.

On the first Saturday in December it was her lot to work all day. Mr Brimshaw arrived some time after she did, wished her a grumpy good morning and went into his own office, and she began on her chores. It was a dismal day and raining steadily, but she busied herself with her dishes and pots, made coffee for Mr Brimshaw and herself and thought about Christmas. She would have liked a new dress but that was out of the question—she had spent more than she could afford on a thick waistcoat for her grandfather and a pair of woollen gloves, and there was still something to be bought for their landlady, who, although kindly disposed towards them as long as the rent was paid on time, needed to be kept sweet. A headscarf, mused Eustacia, or perhaps a box of soap? She was so deep in thought that Mr Brimshaw had to bawl twice before she heard him.

'Hurry up, girl—Casualty's full—there's been an accident in Oxford Street and they'll be shouting for blood before I can take a breath. Get along with this first batch and then come back as fast as you can.'

He had cross-matched another victim when she got back, so she hurried away for a second time with another vacoliter and after that she lost count of the times she trotted to and fro. The initial urgency settled down presently and Mr Brimshaw, crosser than ever because he was late for his lunch, went home and Mr Walker took over, and after that things became a little more settled. All the same, she was tired when the evening porter came on duty and she was able to go home. It was still raining; she swathed her person in her elderly raincoat, tied a scarf over her hair and made for the side entrance. It being Saturday, there wouldn't be all that number of buses which meant that they would be full too. She nipped smartly across the courtyard, head down against the rain, and went full tilt into Sir Colin, coming the other way. He took her considerable weight without any effort and stood her on to her feet.

'Going home?' he wanted to know gently.

She nodded and then said, 'Oh…' when he took her arm and turned her round.

'So am I. I'll drop you off on my way.'

'But I'm wet, I'll spoil your car.'

'Don't be silly,' he begged her nicely. 'I'm wet too.'

He bustled her to the car and settled her into the front seat and got in beside her.

'It's out of your way,' sighed Eustacia weakly.

'Not at all—what a girl you are for finding objections.'

They sat in a comfortable silence as he turned

the car in the direction of the river and Kennington. That he had only just arrived at the hospital intent on having a few words with his registrar, when he saw her, was something he had no intention of revealing. He wasn't at all sure why he had offered to take her home; he hardly knew her and although he found her extremely pretty and, what was more, intelligent, he had made no conscious effort to seek her out. It was a strange fact that two people could meet and feel instantly at ease with each other—more than that, feel as though they had known each other all their lives. Eustacia, sitting quietly beside him, was thinking exactly the same thing.

He smiled nicely when she thanked him, got out of the car and opened the gate for her and waited until she had unlocked the door and gone inside before driving himself back to the hospital, thinking about her. She was too good for the job she was doing, and like a beautiful fish out of water in that depressing little street.

He arrived back at St Biddolph's and became immersed in the care of his patients, shutting her delightful image away in the back of his mind and keeping it firmly there.

Chapter 2

The path lab would be open over Christmas; accidents and sudden illness took no account of holidays. Eustacia was to work on Christmas Day morning and again on Boxing Day afternoon, sharing the days with the two porters. She went home on Christmas Eve much cheered by the good wishes and glass of sherry she had been offered before everyone left that evening. Once there, she opened the bottle of claret she had been hoarding and she and her grandfather toasted each other before they sat down to supper. She had bought a chicken for their Christmas dinner, and before she went to bed she prepared everything for the meal so that when she got back home the next day she would need only to put the food in the oven. In the morning she got up earlier than usual, laid the table and put the presents they had for each other beside the small Christmas tree, took her grandfather his breakfast and then hurried off to work. There was no one there save the night porter, who wished her a hasty 'Merry Christmas' before hurrying off duty. He hadn't had to call anyone up during the night, he told her, and hoped that she would have a quiet morning.

Which indeed she did. Mr Brimshaw, arriving shortly afterwards, wished her a mumbled 'Happy Christmas' and went along to his office to deal with the paperwork, and Eustacia set about putting the place to rights, turning out cupboards and then making coffee. The telephone went incessantly but there were no emergencies; at one o'clock the second porter took over and Mr Brimshaw handed over to one of the assistants. Eustacia went to get her outdoor things, wished the porter a civil goodbye and made for the door just as one of the hospital porters came in with a parcel.

'Miss Crump?' he enquired. 'I was to deliver this before you left.'

'Me?' Eustacia beamed at him. 'You're sure it's for me?'

'Name's Crump, isn't it?'

He went away again and she tucked the gaily packed box under her arm and went home, speculating all the way as to who it was from.

But first when she got home there was her present from her grandfather to open—warm red slippers; just what she needed, she declared, during the cold months of winter. After he had admired his waistcoat and gloves she opened her package. It had been wrapped in red paper covered with robins and tied with red ribbons, and she gave a great sigh of pleasure when she saw its contents: an extravagantly large box of handmade chocolates, festooned with yet more ribbons and covered in brocade. There was a card with it, written in a childish hand, 'With Love from Oliver and Teddy.'

'Well, really,' said Eustacia, totally surprised. 'But I only met them once, remember, Grandfather, at Kew…'

'Children like to give presents to the people they like.'

'I must write and thank them—only I don't know where they live.'

'They're with their uncle, aren't they? And with luck someone at the hospital will surely know his address.'

'Yes, of course. What a lovely surprise. Have one while I start the dinner.' She paused on her way to the kitchen. 'It must have cost an awful lot, and they're only children.'

'I dare say they've been saving up—you know what children are.' Her grandfather chose a chocolate with care and popped it into his mouth. 'They're delicious.'

They had their dinner presently and afterwards Eustacia went to church, and went back home to watch television until bedtime. Without saying anything to her grandfather she had hired a set, to his great delight, for he spent a good part of the day on his own and she guessed that he was sometimes lonely. If, later on, she couldn't afford it, she could always return it—although, seeing the old man's pleasure in it, she vowed to keep it at all costs. It was an extravagance, she supposed, and the money should perhaps be saved against a rainy day or the ever-worrying chance that she might lose her job. On the other hand, it was their one extravagance and did much to lighten their uneventful lives.

She went back to work the next day after their lunch. There were two of the staff on duty, cross-matching blood for patients due for operations the following day, doing blood counts and checking test meals. Eustacia made tea for them both, had a cup herself and busied herself restocking the various forms on each bench. That done, she put out clean towels, filled the soap containers and cleaned the sinks which had been used. She was to stay until six o'clock when the night porter would take over, and once the others had gone it was very quiet. She was glad when he came to spend a few minutes in cheerful talk before she took herself off home.

Everyone was short-tempered in the morning—too much to eat and drink, too little sleep and a generally jaundiced outlook on life cast gloom over the entire department. Miss Bennett found fault with very nearly everything, until Eustacia felt like flinging a tray of dishes and bottles on to the floor and walking out for good. She held her tongue and looked meek, and to her great surprise at the day's end Miss

Bennett rather grudgingly admitted that on the whole her work was quite satisfactory, adding sternly that there was to be no more slackness now that the festive season was over. 'And a good thing it is,' she observed. It was obvious to Eustacia that the poor woman found no joy in her life. Such a pity, one never knew what was round the corner.

It was halfway through January when she got home one evening to find, to her great astonishment, Sir Colin Crichton sitting all at ease opposite her grandfather's armchair by the open fire. He got up when she went in and wished her a polite good evening, and she replied with a hint of tartness. She wasn't looking at her best; it had been a busy day and she was tired, and, conscious that her hair was untidy and her face badly needed fresh make-up, the frown she turned upon him was really quite fierce and he smiled faintly.

'I came to talk to you,' he said to surprise her, 'but if you are too tired…?'

She took up the challenge. 'I am not in the least tired,' she assured him, and then said suddenly, 'Oh—is it about my job?'

He had sat down again and she glanced at her grandfather, who, beyond smiling at her when she kissed him, had remained silent.

'Er—yes, to a certain extent.'

She took an indignant breath. She had worked hard at a job she really didn't like and now she supposed she was to get the sack, although why someone as exalted as Sir Colin had to do it was beyond her.

He said in his quiet, deliberate voice, 'No, it is not what you think it is, Miss Crump, but it would please me very much if you would give up your job in the path lab and come to work for me.'

'Come to work for you?' she echoed his words in a voice squeaky with surprise. And then added, 'Why?'

'My nephews,' he explained. 'They have both had flu, tonsillitis and nasty chests. It is obvious that London doesn't agree with them, at least until they are fit again. I feel responsible for them while their mother and father are away, but I am rarely at home during the day and there is no question of their going back to school for several weeks. I have a home at Turville, just north of Henley. A very small village and quiet—I don't go there as often as I would wish. I should like the boys to go there and I would be glad if you would go with them. They have taken to you in a big way, you know.' He smiled his charming smile. 'There is a housekeeper there, her husband does the garden and the odd jobs but they are both elderly and the boys need young company—a kind of elder sister? I think that you would fill that role exactly…'

Eustacia had her mouth open to speak and he went on calmly, 'No, don't interrupt—let me finish… I am not sure how long it might be before my brother returns—but at least two months, and at the end of that time you would have sufficient experience to get a post in a similar capacity. There is plenty of room for everyone; the Samwayses have their own quarters on the ground floor at the back of the house and adjoining it is a bedroom which Mr Crump could use. You yourself, Miss Crump, would have a room next to the boys on the first floor. Now as to salary…' He mentioned a sum which made Eustacia gape at him.

'That's twice as much as I'm getting,' she told him.

'I can assure you that you will earn every penny of it. Do you know anything about little boys?'

'No, I'm afraid not.'

He smiled. 'But I believe that you would do very well with them. Will you consider it?'

She looked at her grandfather, and although he didn't say anything she saw the eagerness in his face. 'This flat?' she asked. 'It's—it's our home.'

'You could continue to rent it. Naturally I do not expect you to pay for your rooms and food at Turville.' He sounded disapproving and she blushed.

'It is a very generous offer…' she began, and he laughed then.

'My dear girl, this is no sinecure. The boot will be on the other foot if you agree to take charge of the boys. Would you like time to think it over?'

She caught sight of her grandfather's face again. 'No, thank you, sir, I shall be glad to come.' She was rewarded by the look on the old man's face. 'I shall have to give my notice. I don't know how long…?'

'Give in your notice and I'll have a word. And don't call me sir, it makes me feel old.' He got to his feet. 'I am most grateful for your help. You will hear from me as soon as the details are settled.'

She saw him to the door. 'You're quite sure…?' she began as she opened it.

'Quite sure. The boys will be delighted.'

She stood in the doorway and watched him drive away and then went back to her grandfather.

He quickly dispelled any vague doubts floating around in her head. 'It couldn't be better,' he declared. 'It is a splendid start; when you leave the boys you will have a good reference and plenty of experience. You will be qualified for an even better post.'

'But Grandfather, what about you?' She sat down at the table.

'We still have this flat—there must be a job such as this one where one can live out.' He allowed himself to dream a little. 'You might even get a post in the country where there is a cottage or something similar where we might live.'

She had her doubts, but it would be unkind to throw cold water over his pleasure. She let him ramble on happily and hoped that she had done the right thing. After all, her job, although not to her liking, was, as far as she knew, safe enough, and she had earned enough to make their life a good deal easier than it had been. On the other hand, she wouldn't need to buy food, they would live rent-free and she would be able to save a good deal of the money she earned.

'I hope I'm doing the right thing,' she muttered as she went to the kitchen to get their supper.

She went to see Miss Bennett the next morning and was surprised to find that that lady knew all about it. 'You will have to work out your week's notice,' she told Eustacia, and her usually sharp voice was quite pleasant. 'There will be no difficulty in replacing you—I have a list of applicants ready to jump into your shoes.' She added even more surprisingly, 'I hope you will be happy in your new job. You will have to see the professor before you go. You are on Saturday duty this week, are you not?' And when Eustacia nodded, 'So you will leave at six o'clock on that day.'

She nodded dismissal and Eustacia escaped to the quiet of the little cubby-hole where she washed the bottles and dishes and, while she cleaned and polished, she allowed her thoughts to wander. Sir Colin hadn't said exactly when they were to go, but she hoped it wouldn't be until Monday so that she would have time to pack their things and leave the flat pristine.

There was a letter for her the following morning. If her grandfather and she could be ready by Sunday afternoon directly after lunch, they would be fetched by car and driven to Turville; he trusted that this arrangement would be agreeable to her. The letter was typewritten, but he had signed it with a scrawl which she supposed was his signature.

She could see no reason why they should not go when it was suggested, so she wrote a polite little note saying that they would be ready when the car came, and went off to tell her grandfather.

She packed their clothes on Saturday evening, got up early on Sunday morning and did some last-minute ironing, shut the cases and set about seeing that the flat was left clean. There wasn't time to cook lunch, so she opened a can of soup and made some scrambled eggs and was just nicely ready when the doorbell was rung.

She was surprised to find Sir Colin on the doorstep. He wished her good-day in his placid voice, exchanged a few words with her grandfather, helped him into the front seat and put their luggage in the boot, ushered her into the back and, without more ado, set off.

There was little traffic on the road. Just before they reached Henley, Sir Colin turned off on to a narrow road running between high hedges which led downhill into Turville. Eustacia saw with delight the black and white timbers of the Bull and Butcher Inn as they reached the village, drove round the small village green with its fringe of old cottages, past the church and down a very narrow lane with meadows on one side and a high flint wall on the other. The lane turned abruptly and they drove through an open gateway into a short, circular drive leading to a long, low house with many latticed windows and a stout wooden door, the whole enmeshed in dormant Virginia creeper, plumbago and wistaria. It would be a heavenly sight in the summer months, she thought; it was a delightful picture in mid-winter with its sparkling white paint and clay-tiled roofing. Sir Colin stopped the car before the door and it was immediately thrown open to allow the two boys to rush out, shouting with delight.

Sir Colin got out, opened Eustacia's door and helped her out, and left her to receive the exuberant greetings of the little boys while he went to help her grandfather. A grey-haired man came out of the door to join him. 'Ah, Samways, here are Mr and Miss Crump.' And, as he smiled and bowed slightly, Sir Colin went on, 'Pipe down, you two, and give a hand with the luggage.'

He had a quiet, almost placid voice and Eustacia saw that they did as they were told without demur. They all went indoors to the hall, which was wide and long with pale walls and a thick carpet underfoot. The graceful curved staircase faced them, flanked by a green baize door on the one side and on the other a glass door with a view of the garden beyond. It was pleasantly warm and fragrant with the scent of the hyacinths in the bowl on a delicate little wall-table.

Sir Colin said in his quiet voice, 'Samways, if you would show Mr Crump to his room…' He paused as the baize door opened and a small, stout woman bustled through. 'Ah, Mrs Samways, will you take Miss Crump to her room? And if we all meet for tea in ten minutes or so?'

Eustacia watched her grandfather go off happily with Samways and then, with Mrs Samways leading the way and the two boys following behind, she went up the staircase. There was a wide landing at its top with passages leading from it, and Mrs Samways took the left-hand one, to open a door at its end. 'The boys are just next door,' she explained. 'They have their own bathroom on the other side.' She led the way across the large, low-ceilinged room and opened another door. 'This is your bathroom, Miss Crump.'

It was all quite beautiful, its furniture of yew, the walls and carpets the colour of cream, the curtains and bedspread of chintz in pale, vague colours. Eustacia was sure that she would sleep soundly in the pretty bed, and to wake up each morning with such a glorious view from her windows…

'It's lovely,' she murmured, and peeped into the bathroom, which was as charming in its way as the bedroom with its faintly pink tiles and piles of thick towels. She gave a sigh of pure pleasure and turned to the boys. 'I'm glad you're next door. Do you wake early?'

'Yes,' said Oliver, 'and now you're here, perhaps we can go for a walk before breakfast?'

'Just listen to the boy,' said Mrs Samways comfortably, 'mad to go out so early in the day. Not that I've anything against that, but what with getting the breakfast and one thing and another I've not had the time to see to them…'

'I'm sure you haven't,' said Eustacia, 'but if Sir Colin doesn't mind and we won't be bothering you, we might go for a quick walk as long as it doesn't upset the way you like to run the house, Mrs Samways.'

'My dear life, it'll be a treat to have someone here to be with the boys. Now I'll just go and fetch in the tea and you can come down as soon as you're ready.' She ushered the boys out ahead of her and left Eustacia, who wasted five minutes going round her room, slowly this time, savouring all its small luxuries: a shelf of books, magazines on the bedside table with a tin of biscuits and a carafe of water, roomy cupboards built into the wall, large enough to take her small wardrobe several times over, a velvet-covered armchair by the window with a bowl of spring flowers on a table by it. She sat down before the triple mirror on the dressing-table and did her face and hair and then, suddenly aware that she might be keeping everyone waiting, hurried down the stairs. The boys' voices led her to a door to one side of the hall and she pushed it open and went in. They were all in there, sitting round a roaring fire with Moses stretched out with his head on his master's feet, and a portly ginger cat sitting beside him.

Sir Colin and the boys got to their feet when they saw her, and she was urged to take a chair beside her grandfather.

'You are comfortable in your room?' asked Sir Colin.

'My goodness, yes. It's one of the loveliest rooms I've ever seen.' She beamed at him. 'And the view from the window…'

'Delightful, isn't it? Will you pour the tea, and may I call you Eustacia? The boys would like to call you that too, if you don't mind?'

'Of course I don't mind.'

She got up and went to the rent table where the tea things had been laid out, and her grandfather said,

'This is really quite delightful, but I feel that I am imposing; I have no right to be here.'

'There you are mistaken,' observed Sir Colin. 'I have been wondering if you might care to have the boys for an hour each morning. Not lessons, but if you would hear them read and keep them up to date with the world in general, and I am sure that there have been events in your life well worth recounting.'

Mr Crump looked pleased. 'As a younger man I had an eventful life,' he admitted. 'When I was in India—'

'Elephants—rajas,' chorused the boys, and Sir Colin said blandly,

'You see? They are avid for adventure. Will you give it a try?'

'Oh, with the greatest of pleasure.' Mr Crump accepted his tea and all at once looked ten years younger. 'It will be a joy to have an interest...'

Eustacia threw Sir Colin a grateful glance; he had said and done exactly the right thing, and by some good chance he had hit on exactly the right subject. Her grandfather had been in India and Burma during the 1940-45 war, and as a young officer and later as a colonel he had had enough adventures to last him a lifetime. He had stayed on in India for some years after the war had ended, for he had married while he'd been out there, and when he and her grandmother had returned to England her father had been a small schoolboy.

'I am in your debt—the boys won't be fit for school for a week or two. I hope they won't be too much of a handful for you both. It is a great relief to me that they can stay here in the country.' He looked at Eustacia. 'You won't find it too quiet here?'

She shook her head. 'Oh, no, there's such a lot to do in the country.'

They finished their tea in an atmosphere of friendly agreement, and when the tea things had been cleared away by Samways they gathered round the table and played Scrabble until Sir Colin blandly suggested that the boys should have their supper and go to bed. A signal for Eustacia to go with them, to a small, cosy room at the back of the rambling house and sit with them while they ate it. It seemed obvious to her that she was expected to take up her duties then and there, and so she accompanied them upstairs to bed after they had wished their uncle and her grandfather goodnight. Getting ready for bed was a long-drawn-out business with a great deal of toing and froing between the bathroom and their bedroom and a good deal of laughing and scampering about. But finally they were in their beds and Eustacia tucked them in, kissed them goodnight and turned off all but a small night-light by the fireplace.

'We shall like having you here,' said Oliver as she went to the door. 'We would like you to stay forever, Eustacia.'

'I shall like being here with you,' she assured him. To stay forever would be nice too, she reflected as she went to her room and tidied her hair and powdered her flushed face. She was a little surprised at the thought, a pointless one, she reminded herself, for as soon as the boys' parents returned she would have to find another job. It would be a mistake to get too attached to the children or the house. Perhaps it would be a good idea if she didn't look too far ahead but just enjoyed the weeks to come.

She went back to the drawing-room and found Sir Colin alone, and she hesitated at the door. 'Oh, I'll go and help my grandfather unpack…'

'Presently, perhaps? I shall have to leave early to-morrow morning, so we might have a little talk now while we have the opportunity.'

She sat down obediently and he got up and went over to a side-table. 'Will you have a glass of sherry?' He didn't wait for her answer, but poured some and brought it over to her before sitting down again, a glass in his hand.

'You are, I believe, a sensible young woman—keep your eye on the boys, and if you aren't happy about them, if their coughs don't clear up, let me know. Make sure that they sleep and don't rush around getting too hot. I'm being fussy, but they have had badly infected chests and I feel responsible for them. You will find the Samwayses towers of strength, but they're elderly and I don't expect them to be aware of the children's health. They are relieved that you will be here and you can call upon them for anything you may need. I shall do my best to come down at weekends and you can always phone me.'

He smiled at her, and she had the feeling that she would put up with a good deal just to please him. She squashed it immediately, for she strongly suspected that he was a man who got his own way once he had made up his mind to it.

She said in her forthright way, 'Yes, Sir Colin, I'll do my best for the boys too. Is there anything special you would want me to know about them?'

He shook his head. 'No—they're normal small boys, full of good spirits, not over-clean, bursting with energy and dreadfully untidy.'

'I've had no experience—' began Eustacia uncertainly.

'Then here is your chance. They both think you're smashing, so they tell me, which I imagine gives you the edge.'

He smiled at her very kindly and she smiled back, hoping secretly that she would live up to his good opinion of her.

Her grandfather came in then and presently they crossed the hall to the dining-room with its mahogany table and chairs and tawny walls hung with gilt-framed paintings. Eustacia sat quietly, listening to the two men talking while she ate the delicious food served to her. Mrs Samways might not be much to look at but she was a super cook.

They went back to the drawing-room for their coffee and presently she wished them goodnight and took herself off to bed, first going in search of her grandfather's room, a comfortable apartment right by the Samwayses' own quarters. He hadn't unpacked so she did that quickly, made sure that he had everything that he might need and went upstairs to her own room.

The boys were asleep; she had a bath and got into bed and went to sleep herself.

She was wakened by a plump, cheerful girl, who put a tray of tea down by the bed, told her that it was going to be a fine day and that her name was Polly, and went away again. Eustacia drank her tea with all the pleasure of someone to whom it was an unexpected luxury, put on her dressing-gown and went off to see if the boys were awake.

They were, sitting on top of their beds, oblivious to the cold, playing some mysterious game with what she took to be plastic creatures from outer space. Invited to join them, she did so and was rewarded by their loud-voiced opinions that for a girl she was quite bright, a compliment she accepted with modesty while at the same time suggesting that it might be an idea if they all had their breakfast.

She made sure that their clothes were to hand and went away to get herself dressed, and presently returned to cast an eye over hands and hair and retie shoelaces without fuss. They looked well enough, she decided, although they were both coughing. 'I'd quite like to go for a walk after breakfast,' she observed casually. 'I mean a proper walk, not on the road.'

Breakfast was a cheerful meal, with Samways hovering with porridge, bacon and scrambled eggs, and her grandfather, after a good night's sleep, willing to recount some of his youthful adventures. Eustacia left them presently, went upstairs and made their beds and tidied the rooms, did the same for her grandfather and then went to remind the boys that they were going to take her for a walk.

'There's a windmill,' she reminded them. 'It doesn't look too far away—I'd love to see it.'

She had hit on something with which to interest them mightily. Had she seen the film *Chitty Chitty Bang Bang*? they wanted to know, because that was the very windmill in it. They walked there briskly and returned to the house for hot cocoa and an hour's reading before lunch. The afternoon was spent with her grandfather and she was able to spend an hour on her own until Mrs Samways suggested that she might like to look round the house. It was quite large and rambled a good deal. 'Rather a lot to look after,' observed Eustacia, peering at family portraits in the library.

'Ah, but there's two good girls who come up from the village each day, and Sir Colin comes mostly at weekends and then not always... He brings a few guests from time to time and we have Christmas here, of course. He's not all that keen on London. But there he's a clever gentleman and that's where he works. I dare say if he were to marry—and dear knows I hope and pray he does, for a nicer man never stepped—he'd live here most of the time. London isn't a place for children.'

Eustacia murmured gently; she realised that Mrs Samways was doing her an honour by talking about her employer and she was glad that the housekeeper seemed to like her. It hadn't entered her head that making the beds and tidying up after the boys had endeared her to Mrs Samways' heart. 'That's a nice young lady,' she had informed her husband. 'What's more she gets on with the boys and they listen to her, more than they ever did with me.'

They had their tea in a pleasant little room at the back of the house and gathered round the table afterwards to play cards until the boys' supper and bedtime. Eustacia tucked them in finally, listening rather worriedly to their coughs, although neither of them were feverish. They had certainly eaten with youthful gusto and, by the time she had got out their clean clothes for the morning and gone to her own room to tidy herself, they were sound asleep, their nice, naughty-little-boy faces as peaceful as those of small angels.

After dinner she sat with her grandfather in the drawing-room, listening to his contented talk. He hadn't been so happy for a long time, and it reminded her of his dull existence at their flat in London; this was like a new lease of life to him. Her thoughts flew ahead to the future when the boys' parents would return and she would know that she was no longer needed. Well, she reflected, she would have to find another job similar somewhere in the country and never go back to London. She had said goodnight to her grandfather and had seen him to his room and was on the point of going upstairs when the phone rang as she was turning out the drawing-room lights.

She picked it up hesitantly, not sure if this was something the Samwayses would consider to be their prerogative, and indeed Mr Samways appeared just as she was lifting the receiver.

'I'm sorry—I should have left it for you.'

He smiled at her in a fatherly fashion. 'That's all right, miss, I dare say it will be Sir Colin.' He took the receiver from her and said in a different, impersonal voice, 'Sir Colin Crichton's residence,' and then, 'Good evening, sir. Yes, Miss Crump is here.'

He smiled again as he handed her the phone.

Sir Colin's voice came very clearly over the line. 'Eustacia? You don't mind if I call you that? The day has gone well?'

'Yes, thank you, sir. They have been very good and they went to bed and to sleep at once.' She gave him a brief, businesslike résumé of their day. 'They both cough a great deal...'

'Don't worry about that, that should clear up now they're away from London. I'll look them over when I come down. You and your grandfather have settled in?'

'Yes, thank you. Grandfather has just gone to his room. I think that he is a very happy man, sir...'

'And you, Eustacia?'

'I'm happy too, thank you, sir.'

'Good, and be kind enough to stop calling me sir with every breath.'

'Oh, very well, Sir Colin. I'll try and remember.'

He sounded as though he was laughing as he wished her goodnight and rang off.

The week went by, delightful days filled with walks, visits to the village shop, an hour or so of what Eustacia hoped was useful study with the boys and afternoons spent helping Mrs Samways with the flowers, the linen and such small tasks that the housekeeper didn't allow the maids to do, while the boys spent a blissful hour with her grandfather.

It was, thought Eustacia, too good to be true. And she was right.

Sir Colin had phoned on the Saturday morning to say that since he had an evening engagement he wouldn't be down until Sunday morning.

'I expect he's going to take Gloria out to dinner,' said Oliver. 'She's keen on him…'

Eustacia suppressed a wish to know more about Gloria and said quellingly, 'I don't think we should discuss your uncle's friends, my dear. You can stay up an hour later this evening because you always do, don't you? But no later. I dare say he'll be here quite soon after breakfast.'

The boys complained, but only mildly; she swept them upstairs to bed with only token arguments against the harshness of her edict and, with the promise that she would call them in good time in the morning just in case their uncle decided to come for breakfast, she left them to go to sleep. Her grandfather went to bed soon after them and, since there was no one to talk to and the Samwayses had gone out for the evening and wouldn't be back until late, she locked up carefully, mindful of Mr Samways' instructions about leaving the bolts undone on the garden door so that he could use his key to get in, and took herself off to bed.

She didn't hurry over her bath, and finally when she was ready for bed she opened one of the books on her bedside table, got into bed, and settled down for an hour of reading. It was an exciting book, and she was still reading it an hour later when she heard the telephone ringing.

It was almost midnight and the Samwayses weren't back yet; she bundled on her dressing-gown and went silently downstairs to the extension in the hall. She was in two minds as to whether to answer it—it was too late for a social call and it could be one of those heavy-breathing types… She lifted the receiver slowly and said austerely, 'Yes?'

'Got you out of bed?' enquired Sir Colin. 'Eustacia, I'm now on my way to Turville. I'll be with you in half an hour. Are the Samwayses back?'

'No.' There had been something about his voice. 'Is there something the matter? Is something wrong?'

'Very wrong. I'll tell you when I get home. If you have locked up I'll come in through the garden door.'

He hung up before she could say anything more.

She left the light on in the hall and went along to the kitchen, where she put the coffee on the Aga and laid up a tray with a cup and saucer, sugar and cream, and while she did that she wondered what could have happened. An accident with his car? A medical report about one or both of the boys?

She shuffled around the kitchen, peering in cupboards looking for biscuits—he would probably be hungry. She had just found them when she heard the car, and a moment later his quiet footfall coming along the passage towards the kitchen.

He was wearing a dinner-jacket and he threw the coat he was carrying on to a chair as he came in. He nodded to her without speaking and went to warm his hands at the Aga, and when she asked, 'Coffee, Sir Colin?' he answered harshly,

'Later,' and turned to face her.

It was something terrible, she guessed, looking at his face, calm and rigid with held-back feelings. She said quietly, 'Will you sit down and tell me? You'll feel better if you can talk about it.'

He smiled a little although he didn't sit down. 'I had a telephone call just as I was about to leave my London house this evening. My brother and his wife have been killed in a car accident.'

Chapter 3

Eustacia looked at Sir Colin in horror. 'Oh, how awful—I am sorry!' Her gentle mouth shook and she bit her lip. 'The boys…they're so very small.' She went up to him and put a hand on his arm. 'Is there anything that I can do to help?'

She looked quite beautiful with her hair loose around her shoulders, bundled into her dressing-gown—an unglamorous garment bought for its long-lasting capacity—her face pale with shock and distress, longing to comfort him.

He looked down at her and then at her hand on his arm. His eyes were hard and cold, and she snatched her hand away as though she had burnt it and went to the Aga and poured the coffee into a cup. She should have known better, of course; she was someone filling a gap until circumstances suited him to make other arrangements. He wouldn't want her sympathy, a stranger in his home; he wasn't a man to show his feelings, especially to someone he hardly knew. She felt the hot blood wash over her face and felt thankful that he wouldn't notice it.

She asked him in her quiet voice, 'Would you like your coffee here or in your study, Sir Colin?'

'Oh, here, thank you. Go to bed, it's late.'

She gave a quick look at his stony face and went without a word. In her room she sat on the bed, still in her dressing-gown, going over the past half-hour in her mind. She wondered why she had been telephoned by him; there had been no need, it wasn't as if he had wanted to talk to her—quite the reverse. And to talk helped, she knew that from her own grief and shock when her parents had died. It was a pity that he had no wife in whom he could confide. There was that girl the boys had talked about, but perhaps he had been on his own when he'd had the news.

She sighed and shivered a little, cold and unhappy, and then jumped with fright when there was a tap on the door and, before she could answer it, Sir Colin opened it and came in.

He looked rigidly controlled, but the iciness had gone from his voice. 'You must forgive me, Eustacia—I behaved badly. I am most grateful for your sympathy, and I hope you will overlook my rudeness—it was unintentional.'

'Well of course it was, and there's nothing to forgive. Would you like to sit down and talk about it?'

Her voice was warm and friendly, but carefully unemotional. 'It's the suddenness, isn't it?'

She was surprised when he did sit down. 'I was just leaving the house—I had a dinner date—we were standing in the hall while Grimstone, my butler, fetched my—my companion's handbag. When the phone rang I answered it but I wasn't really listening; we had been laughing about something or other. It was a long-distance call from Brunei. Whoever it was at the other end told me twice before I realised…' He paused, and when he went on she guessed that he was leaving something out. 'I had to get away, but I wanted to talk about it too. I got into the car and drove here and I'm not sure why I phoned you on the way.'

'Tell me about it,' said Eustacia quietly, 'and then you can decide what has to be done. Once that's settled you can sleep for a little while.'

'I shall have to fly there and arrange matters.' He glanced at his watch. 'It is too late now…'

'First thing in the morning.'

His smile shook her. 'What a sensible girl you are. I have to tell the boys before I go.' He looked at her. 'You'll stay?'

'As long as I'm needed. Tell me about your brother and his wife.'

'He was younger than I, but he married when he was twenty-three. He was an architect, a good one, with an international reputation. He and Sadie, his wife, travelled a good deal. The boys usually went with them, but this time they weren't too happy about taking them to the Far East. They were to go for three months and I had the boys—their nanny came with them but her mother was taken ill and she had to leave. Mrs Samways has done her best and so has my cook, Miss Grimstone. It was most fortunate that we made your acquaintance and that the boys took to you at once.'

'Yes. It helps, I hope. Now, we are going to the kitchen again and I'm going to make a pot of tea and a plate of toast and you will have those and then go to bed. When you've slept for a few hours you will be able to talk to the boys and arrange whatever has to be arranged.'

'You are not only sensible but practical too.'

It was after two o'clock by the time she got to bed, having made sure that Sir Colin had gone to his room. She didn't sleep for some time, and when she got up just after six o'clock she looked a wreck.

The boys were still sleeping and the house was quiet. She padded down to the kitchen and put the kettle on. A cup of tea would help her to start what was going to be a difficult day. She was warming the teapot when Sir Colin joined her. He was dressed and shaved and immaculately turned out, and he looked to be in complete control of his feelings.

'Did you sleep?' asked Eustacia, forgetting to add the 'Sir Colin' bit. And when he nodded, 'Good—will you have a cup of tea? The boys aren't awake yet. When do you plan to tell them?'

He stood there, drinking his tea, studying her; she was one of the few girls who could look beautiful in an old dressing-gown and with no make-up first thing in the morning, and somehow the sight of her comforted him. 'Could we manage to get through breakfast? If I tell them before that they won't want to eat—we must try and keep to the usual day's routine.'

'Yes, of course. May I tell Grandfather before breakfast? He is a light sleeper and there's just the chance he heard the car last night and he might mention it and wonder why you came.'

'A good point; tell him by all means. Samways will be down in a few minutes, and I'll tell him. He was fond of my brother…' He put down his cup. 'I shall be in the study if I'm wanted.'

She did the best she could to erase the almost sleepless night from her face, thankful that her grandfather had taken her news quietly and with little comment save the one that he had heard the car during the night and had known that someone was up and talking softly. Satisfied that she couldn't improve her appearance further, she went to wake the boys.

'Have you got a cold?' asked Teddy.

'Me? No. I never get colds. But I didn't go to sleep very early. I had such an exciting book…'

They discussed the pleasures of reading in bed as they dressed, and presently the three of them went downstairs and into the dining-room.

Sir Colin was sitting at the table, a plate of porridge before him, reading his post; her grandfather was leafing through the Guardian. The scene was completely normal and just for a moment Eustacia wondered if she had dreamed the night's happenings.

The boys rushed over and hugged their uncle, both talking at once. When he had come? they wanted to know. And how long was he going to stay and would he go for a walk with them?

He answered them cheerfully, begged them to sit down and eat their breakfast, bade Eustacia good morning, asked her if she would like coffee or tea and got up to fetch it for her.

Eustacia, pecking away at a breakfast she didn't want, wondered how he did it. That he was grief-stricken at the death of his brother and sister-in-law had been evident when he had talked to her but now, looking at his calm face, she marvelled at his self-control. The meal was a leisurely one and it wasn't until they had all finished that Sir Colin said, 'Eustacia, bring the boys along to the study, will you? We'll leave Mr Crump to read his paper in peace.'

He told them very simply; she marvelled at the manner in which he broke the awful news to them with a gentle gravity and a simplicity which the boys could understand. Teddy burst into tears and ran and buried his head in her lap and she held him close, but Oliver asked, 'Will they come home, Uncle?'

'Yes. I am going to fetch them.' He smiled at the child and Oliver went to him and took his hand. 'Will you look after us, Uncle? And Eustacia?'

'Of course. This will be your home and we shall be a family…'

'Mummy and Daddy wouldn't mind if you and Eustacia look after us?'

'No.' The big man's voice was very gentle. 'I think they would like that above all things.'

He put an arm round the little boy and held him close, and Eustacia, unashamedly crying while she comforted Teddy, accepted the future thrust upon her. The boys liked her, and for a time at least she could in some small way fill the immense gap in their lives. Further than that she wouldn't look for the moment.

Presently Sir Colin said, 'You know, I think a walk would do us all good. Don't you agree, Eustacia? I must get to Heathrow by two o'clock, so we can have an early lunch. I shall be gone perhaps two or three days, but you will be quite safe with Eustacia and when I get back we will have a family discussion.'

'They're safe in heaven?' Teddy wanted to know.

'Of course they are,' Sir Colin answered promptly. 'It's rather like going into another room and closing the door, if you see what I mean.'

They walked briskly up to the windmill and back again and he kept the talk deliberately on their mother and father, using a matter-of-fact tone of voice which somehow made the sadness easier to bear. Presently they sat down to an early lunch and then they waved him off in his car.

He had taken a few minutes of his time to speak to Eustacia. 'You can manage?' It was more a statement than a question. 'Very soon it will hit them hard.' His eyes searched her face. 'I believe you will be able to cope.'

She said steadily, 'Oh, yes. My parents died in a plane crash a few years ago, so I do know how they feel.'

'I didn't know. I'm sorry. You are sure...?'

'Quite sure, Sir Colin. I hope your journey will go well.'

He said softly, 'You are not only beautiful, you are a tower of strength.'

She reminded herself of that during the next few days, for just as he had warned her the boys were stricken with a childish grief, with floods of tears and wakeful nights, sudden bursts of rage and no wish to eat. It was on the third day after he had gone that he telephoned while they sat at lunch. Samways had brought the telephone to the table and given her a relieved smile. 'It's Sir Colin, Miss Crump.'

She hadn't realised just how much she had been hoping to hear from him. His voice was calm in her ear. 'Eustacia? I'm flying home in an hour's time. I'll be with you some time tomorrow. How are the boys?'

'Absolute Trojans. You'd be proud of them. Can you spare a moment to say hello?'

When they had spoken to their uncle and he had rung off, Oliver asked, 'What's a Trojan, Eustacia?'

'A very brave, strong man, my dear.'

'Like Uncle Colin?'

'Exactly like him. Aren't you lucky to have him for an uncle?'

'When I grow up,' said Teddy, 'I shall be just like him.'

'What a splendid idea, darling.'

'And I shall be like Daddy,' said Oliver, and although his lip trembled he didn't cry.

'Of course, he'll be proud of you.' She glanced at her grandfather. 'It's still raining, so how about a game of Scrabble? Let's see if we can beat Grandfather.'

She was becoming adept at keeping the boys occupied and interested. Walking, she had quickly found out, was something they liked doing, and since she had spent a good deal of her childhood in the country she was able to name birds, tell weeds from wild flowers and argue the difference between a water-vole's hole and that of a water-rat. Even on a wet morning such as it had been she managed to keep them amused, first with Scrabble and then after lunch with painting and drawing until teatime. They spent the time before bed cleaning their bikes while Eustacia did the same to Mrs Samways' elderly model, which she had been allowed to borrow. She wasn't too keen on cycling—it was years since she had ridden a bike and, although Samways had assured her that once one had learned to ride one never forgot, she wasn't too happy about it. She wasn't too happy about the skateboards either; if it was a fine morning, she had promised to try one out under the expert eyes of the boys and, although she was prepared to do anything to keep them from the grief which threatened to engulf them from time to time, she wasn't looking forward to it. But there would be no one to see her making a fool of herself, she reflected, and if she made the boys laugh so much the better.

As it turned out, she did rather better than she had expected; the boys were experts, turning and twisting with the fearlessness of the young, but they were patient with her while she wobbled her way down the slope at the back of the house, waving her arms wildly and tumbling over before she reached the bottom. They yelled and shrieked and laughed at her and did a turn themselves, showing off their expertise, and then finally she managed to reach the end of the slope still upright on her board and puffed up with pride. She did it again, only this time she began to lose her balance as she reached the end of the slope. Waving her arms wildly with the boys shouting with laughter, she fell into the arms of Sir Colin, who most fortuitously appeared at that moment to block her path. He received her person with ease, set her upright and said, 'What a nice way to be welcomed home.'

Eustacia disentangled herself, red in the face. 'Oh, we didn't know—good afternoon, Sir Colin, we're skateboarding…' She stopped, aware of a pleasant surge of delight at the sight of him and, at the same time, of the inanity of her remarks.

He didn't answer her, for the boys had rushed to meet him, and thankfully she collected the skateboards and started to walk back to the house. They would have a lot to say to each other and it would give her time to regain her normally calm manner.

Sir Colin left again on the following day; his

brother had lived in London when he hadn't been travelling abroad, and his affairs had to be set in order and the funeral arranged. He told Eustacia this in an impersonal manner which didn't allow her to utter anything warmer than a polite murmur. In his calm face there was no trace of the man who had come to her room and talked as though they were friends.

'When I return we must have a talk,' he told her. 'The boys' future must be discussed.'

She was surprised that he should wish to discuss it with her; she had already said that she was willing to stay with the boys until such time as permanent arrangements had been made. Perhaps he no longer wanted her and her grandfather to remain at his house; it had been a temporary arrangement and he could hardly have envisaged their permanent residence there.

She said, 'Very well, Sir Colin,' and watched him drive away in his Rolls-Royce. There was no point in speculating about the future until he chose to tell her what he intended to do.

He returned three days later, and not alone. A middle-aged couple, his sister-in-law's parents, were with him as well as an older lady who greeted the boys with affection and then held out her hand to Eustacia.

'You must be Eustacia. My son has told me what a great help you have been to him during these last few days.'

She was tall and rather stout, but not as tall as

Eustacia. She was elegantly dressed and good-looking and her eyelids drooped over eyes as blue as her son's. Eustacia liked her, but she wasn't sure that she liked the other guests. They greeted the boys solemnly and the woman burst into tears as she embraced Teddy, who wriggled in her arms.

'Mother, you have already introduced yourself—Mrs Kennedy and Mr Kennedy, my sister-in-law's parents. They will be spending a day or so here before they go back to Yorkshire.'

Clearly they regarded her as a member of the staff, nodding hastily before they turned back to the boys. Mrs Kennedy uttered little cries of, 'My poor darling boys, motherless. Oh, my dearest Sadie—the awful shock—how can I go on living? But I must, for someone must look after you…'

Mrs Crichton tapped her briskly on the shoulder. 'Dry your eyes, Freda, and endeavour to be cheerful.' She eased the two boys away from their maternal grandparents and marched them into the house. 'I'd like my tea,' Eustacia heard her say and Samways, as if on cue, appeared with a loaded tray.

Mrs Samways led the ladies away to their rooms and then Eustacia, bidden by Sir Colin, poured the tea, settled the boys with sandwiches and cake and handed plates. Mrs Crichton evinced no surprise at the sight of Eustacia sitting behind the teapot, but Mrs Kennedy raised her eyebrows and made a moue of disbelief. 'I thought this was to be a family conference,' she observed.

Sir Colin glanced at her, his face blandly polite,

his eyes hidden by the heavy lids. 'Which it is, but I think we might have tea first. Mr Baldock will be here very shortly with Peter's will. In the meanwhile shall we hear what the boys have been doing with themselves?' He glanced at Eustacia. 'Any more walks to the windmill?'

She nodded. 'Oliver, do tell about the rabbits...'

He embarked on a long account of the animals they had seen and Teddy, his tears forgotten, joined in. 'And we had another go with the skateboards,' said Oliver. 'Eustacia stayed on twice, she's not bad for a girl.'

Mrs Kennedy drew a deep breath. 'But surely, today of all days, they should have been—?'

She wasn't allowed to finish—Mrs Crichton said rapidly, 'I've always wanted to go on one of those things. Is it difficult, Eustacia?'

'Very, Mrs Crichton, but such fun. The boys are very good, I don't know who showed them how—Sir Colin, perhaps?'

She hadn't meant the question seriously, but he answered at once. 'Indeed I did. I consider myself pretty good. Once we have perfected Eustacia's technique I think we must persuade Mr and Mrs Samways...'

A remark which set the boys rolling around with laughter, and Mrs Kennedy's expression became even more disapproving. She looked at her husband, who cleared his throat and began, 'The boys—' but got no further, for Samways announced Mr Baldock.

He was elderly, tall and thin and wore old-fashioned pince-nez attached to his severe black coat by a cord, but his eyes were very alive and he had a surprisingly loud voice. Sir Colin got up to greet him while Samways fetched fresh tea. 'You know everyone, I believe, except Miss Eustacia Crump, who is my right hand and a tower of strength and common sense.'

He shook her hand and took a good look at her. 'A very pretty name and certainly a very pretty girl,' he observed. 'You are indeed fortunate.' He added thoughtfully, 'Small boys can be the very devil.'

She agreed composedly. 'But they are great fun too—they see things one overlooks when one is grown-up.'

'Intelligent, too.' He sat down, accepted a cup of tea and made light conversation about this and that, never once alluding to the funeral they had all attended earlier that day. Not an easy matter, for Mrs Kennedy tried her best to turn the cheerful tea-party into a wake.

Tea things cleared, Eustacia rose, intent on making an unobtrusive exit with the boys. She was hindered, however, by Sir Colin. 'Take the boys along to Mrs Samways, Eustacia, and come back here, will you?'

She gave him an enquiring look and he smiled and added, 'Please?'

She slipped back into the room and Sir Colin looked round and smiled again as she sat down a little to one side of the gathering.

'Good. Will you start, Mr Baldock?' Sir Colin

sat back, his long legs stretched out before him, and smiled at his mother.

The will was brief and very much to the point. Sir Colin was to be the legal guardian of Oliver and Teddy, assisted as he might think fit by some suitable person or persons and should he marry it was hoped that his wife would become a guardian also. The bulk of the estate went to the boys in trust, but there were legacies for members of the family and various directions as to the selling of property.

Mr Baldock smoothed the pages neatly and took off his pince-nez. 'A very sensible document, if I may be allowed to say so. And quite straightforward.'

'But it's ridiculous,' exclaimed Mrs Kennedy. 'I have every right to have the boys, they are my grandchildren—'

'They are also mine,' said Mrs Crichton briskly, 'but I don't consider that any of us has a right to them. Colin is very well fitted to bring them up, and if he should marry they will have brothers and sisters as any normal child would like to have.'

'But Colin has no time—he's at that hospital all hours of the day and he's always travelling from one place to another; the boys will be left to servants—'

'They will be in the care of Eustacia, whom they happen to have developed a deep affection for. She has promised to stay and care for them and, despite my work, I do spend my evenings and nights at home. As soon as they are perfectly fit they will go back to school like any other small boys, and if it is possible they will come with me should I have a lecture tour or seminars.'

'And this—this Eustacia? Will she go with you?' Mrs Kennedy was plum-coloured with temper.

He gave her a cold look from eyes suddenly icy. 'Of course. Much as I enjoy their company, I am not conversant with their wants. If Mr Baldock agrees to this arrangement as the other executor of the will, I think that it will work perfectly.'

'Do you intend to marry in the foreseeable future?' asked Mr Kennedy.

Sir Colin said, 'Yes,' without a moment's hesitation, and Eustacia felt a distinct pang of regret. And very silly too—she gave herself a metaphorical shake—there was no earthly reason why she should concern herself with Sir Colin's private life.

'And until such time as this should occur,' said Mr Baldock, 'you are willing to remain as surrogate mother to Oliver and Teddy?' He studied her over his glasses and gave a little nod of approval.

'Yes, I told Sir Colin that I would stay as long as I am needed, and if you wish me to do so I will repeat my promise.'

'No need, my dear young lady. I perceive that you are eminently suitable for the post.' He glanced across to Mrs Crichton. 'You agree with me, Mrs Crichton?'

'Absolutely. And I am sure that Mr and Mrs Kennedy will give their approval. The boys are fortunate in having grandparents living in such a lovely part of Yorkshire—think of the holidays they will enjoy…'

Mrs Kennedy dabbed her eyes with a handkerchief. 'I still think that it is against human nature...'

Everyone looked rather puzzled until Sir Colin said kindly, 'But you must agree that Peter—and I'm sure that Sadie would have agreed with him—was thinking of the boys and their future. I must state the obvious and point out that when they are still young men I shall, hopefully, be here to act as their guardian, whereas you may no longer be with us.'

'Well, really,' exclaimed Mrs Kennedy, 'what a thing to say.' She caught her husband's eye. 'Though that may be true enough. They must come to us for holidays.'

'Of course, and you both know that you are always welcome at my home. I was fond of Sadie and it is a consolation to know that they were devoted to each other and the boys. We must all do our best to continue that devotion.'

From anyone else it would have sounded pompous, reflected Eustacia, but Sir Colin had uttered the words in a calm and unhurried voice and moreover had sounded quite cheerful.

'Eustacia, would you fetch the boys here, please? And how about a drink before dinner? You'll stay, of course, Mr Baldock? Samways will drive you back to town.'

Eustacia ushered the boys into the drawing-room and slid away to find her grandfather. He was in his room, sitting before a cosy little fire, enjoying a late tea. He bent a patient ear to her account of the family gathering and agreed with her that she had no option but to stay with the boys.

'Their granny and grandpa from Yorkshire don't like the idea,' she explained, 'they don't like me; they want the boys with them but they had to agree to the will. I don't think Sir Colin's mother minds; she's nice and she's sad, but she didn't let the boys see that…'

She went away presently to be told that as a great treat the boys were to stay up for dinner. Sir Colin, when he told her, didn't mention that Mrs Kennedy had expressed annoyance at the idea of Eustacia's dining with them; she had made the mistake of saying so in front of the boys, who had instantly chorused that if Eustacia couldn't be there, they didn't want to be there either.

Sir Colin, a tactful man, smoothed frayed tempers and presently they all sat down to dinner, during which he kept the conversation firmly in his hands, aided by his mother, not allowing Mrs Kennedy to dwell on the unhappy circumstances which had brought them together that day. And after the meal, when Eustacia had bidden everyone goodnight and borne the boys off to their beds, he played the perfect host until Mr Baldock declared that he must go home and Mr and Mrs Kennedy retired to bed, for they were to stay the night. Only when he was alone with his mother did Sir Colin allow his bland mask to fall.

'Not the happiest of days, my dear,' he observed. 'I would wish that we could have been alone—there has been no chance to talk about Peter. I shall miss him and so will you. You have been very brave, Mother, and a great help. It is a pity that the Kennedys can't see that the boys are more important than anything else.'

'I never liked the woman,' said Mrs Crichton forthrightly. 'I like that young woman, Eustacia, and the boys like her too. She will be able to give them the comfort they'll need. I must get to know her.' She stood up. 'I'm going to bed now, my dear—don't sit here grieving.'

He stood up and kissed her cheek. 'You'll stay a few days? I'll be free at the weekend, and I'll run you back to Castle Cary—the boys will enjoy the ride.'

At breakfast he was his usual pleasant self, joking with the boys, exchanging opinions with Mr Kennedy about the day's news and listening courteously to Mrs Kennedy's advice about the boys' coughs. Eustacia, watching him when she could, saw the tired lines in his face and the tiny muscle twitching in his cheek. Probably he had slept badly and no wonder, he had had a wretched week and hadn't complained once. That bland, cheerful manner must have cost him something... He looked up and caught her eye and smiled warmly and her heart gave a lurch and she glanced away, feeling uncertain and not knowing why.

The Kennedys went presently after a protracted farewell to the boys, a chilly one to Sir Colin and his mother and a frosty nod to Eustacia. Quite definitely she wasn't liked.

With their departure it was as though a cloud had lifted from the house. Sir Colin stayed for lunch and then went back to the hospital, saying as he went that he would be back at the weekend. 'We'll take Granny back home and see about Moses's leg on Sunday—that plaster is due to come off.'

He kissed his mother, gave the boys an avuncular hug and opened his car door, then turned back to where they were standing outside the door to wave him on his way.

'You will phone me if you are in the least worried about anything, Eustacia.' She was surprised when he went and kissed her swiftly, then he got into his car and drove away.

Eustacia had gone delightfully pink, but a quick glance at her companions showed her that they had either not noticed or they found nothing strange in Sir Colin's behaviour. They went into the house and she told herself that he had been acting out of kindness, not wishing her to feel left out. He had certainly noticed Mrs Kennedy's coldness towards her although he had said nothing.

Mrs Crichton took the boys to the village shop to buy sweets, and Eustacia went along to see her grandfather. He looked up with a smile as she joined him.

'Sir Colin gone? But back at the weekend, he tells me. You are quite happy about this job, my dear? I must say that Mrs Kennedy didn't seem too pleased about it, but really it is a most sensible arrangement at least until such time as the boys are over their grief. Thank heaven that children are so resilient. Am I to continue with our little sessions or are they to be free?'

Eustacia sat down beside him. 'I should think that an hour in the afternoon would be a good idea. Mrs Crichton will be here for the rest of the week and I think she might like to have them to herself in the mornings. She's very fond of them and they love her.'

'A fine woman, and she has a fine son.'

The week passed pleasantly and Eustacia took care to fill the days so that the boys had no time to mope. There were moments of sadness, but comforting and some small treat mitigated those and Mrs Crichton was a great help; she had her son's calmness and a capacity for inventing interesting games. She and Eustacia liked each other and, with her grandfather and the faithful Samways backing them up, Eustacia felt that they had come through a trying two weeks very well.

Sir Colin arrived home on Friday evening. The boys were already in bed but Eustacia, crossing the hall on the way to the dining-room with a tray of glasses as he came in, paused to say that they were still awake and waiting for him.

He crossed the hall, took the tray from her and said, 'Good. How are they?'

'Recovering well. Mrs Crichton has been marvellous with them and they love her very much, don't they?'

'Yes. Why are you carrying trays?'

'Just one tray, Sir Colin. Samways is in the cellar

and Mrs Samways can't leave the stove just at the moment.' She took the tray back. 'Your mother is in the drawing-room.'

He nodded and looked faintly amused. 'You will join us with your grandfather? He is well?'

'Yes. Thank you. The boys have had their reading lessons and they're starting on a map of India.'

'Splendid.'

He let her go then and went unhurriedly into his drawing-room where his mother and Moses waited for him.

She was told at breakfast the next day that she would be going to Castle Cary with the boys—something she hadn't expected. 'We'll leave directly after we have had coffee, stop for lunch on the way, have tea there and drive back in the early evening.'

An announcement hailed with delight by the boys and uncertainty by Eustacia.

'Oh, very well, Sir Colin, but I thought you might like to have the boys…'

He smiled his kind smile. 'I'm delighted to have the boys; I'm not sure if I'm qualified to cope with their various needs. Your grandfather assures me that he will very much enjoy a day on his own. The Samwayses will take good care of him.'

They drove down to Henley-on-Thames, through Wokingham and on to the M3, and presently they were on the A303. At Amesbury they stopped for lunch at the Antrobus Hotel, a pleasantly old-fashioned hotel where the boys were listened to with sympathy when they requested sausages and some chips in preference to the more sophisticated menu.

It was a cheerful meal, and they drove on in high spirits until they reached Wincanton and turned off to Castle Cary. Eustacia had never been there and she was enchanted by the mellow stone cottages and the narrow high street lined with small shops.

Mrs Crichton lived in the centre of the small town, in a large Georgian house with a vast front door with its brass knocker and bell. There was no garden before it but the windows were just too high for passers-by to peer in. In any case, Eustacia thought, it was such a dignified house, no one would dare to stare in even if they could.

The door was opened as they got out of the car and a small, stout woman ushered them in, beaming from a rosy-cheeked elderly face.

'Well, madam dear, it's nice to see you back and no mistake. And the two young gentlemen too, and how is Mr Colin?'

'All the better for seeing you, Martha.' He placed a kiss on her cheek. 'This is Eustacia Crump, who is looking after the boys. Eustacia, this is Martha, who has lived with us forever.'

They shook hands and liked each other at once. 'Now, isn't that nice?' observed Martha in her soft Somerset voice.

The house was warm and very welcoming; it was furnished with some lovely old pieces and yet it was lived in and comfortable. Mrs Crichton led the way into a high-ceilinged room overlooking the street.

'I know you can't stay long, but tea will only be a few minutes.'

Eustacia took the boys' coats and caps, took off her own coat and went with them to look at the garden from the big bay window of a room leading out of the sitting-room. It was rather grandly furnished and a Siamese cat was sitting on the rent table by the window. It got up sedately and went to meet Mrs Crichton and they all gathered by the window to look at the garden. It was large, charmingly laid out and walled. Even with local traffic going to and fro the house was very quiet.

'You must come and stay when the weather is warmer,' said Mrs Crichton. 'The Easter holidays, perhaps?' An invitation accepted with enthusiasm by the boys. Eustacia shared their enthusiasm but she didn't say so—she wasn't sure if she was included in the invitation.

They had their tea in a small room at the back of the hall, at a round table near the open fire. The kind of tea little boys liked: muffins swimming in butter, Marmite on toast cut in little fingers, fruit cake and sandwiches and a plate of chocolate biscuits to finish. The boys ate with gusto and so, for that matter, did Sir Colin.

They left soon after tea and this time the boys were strapped into the back seats and Eustacia was bidden to sit in front.

The boys were sleepy by the time they got back; they ate their supper quickly, full of their day and the pleasure of taking Moses to the vet in the morning, but they were too tired to protest when Eustacia bade them say goodnight to their uncle and whisked them upstairs to baths and bed. When she got down again, it was to find Sir Colin gone. An urgent call from St Biddolph's, Samways told her, and he would see her at breakfast. She dined with her grandfather, recounting details of their trip while they ate.

'You didn't mind being on your own, Grandfather?'

'My dear child, it was delightful. I had the leisure to read and write and eat the delicious meals Mrs Samways cooked. I have never been more content. I realise that it cannot last forever, but I am grateful for these weeks of pleasant living.'

They went to the vet's in the morning and Moses had his plaster removed and was allowed, cautiously, to walk on all his legs. After lunch, since Sir Colin said that he had work to do in his study, Eustacia took the boys for a ride on their bikes, mounting guard upon them from the elderly bike which Mrs Samways had lent to her.

They all had tea round the fire and then a rousing game of Snap before the boys had supper and went to bed. Eustacia came down presently to find Sir Colin and her grandfather discussing the boys' schooling, but they broke off when she joined them and Sir Colin got up to fetch her a drink.

'I think that the boys might go back to school in another two weeks,' he told her. 'There is a good prep school on the other side of Turville Heath, only a mile or so away. Can you drive, Eustacia?'

'Yes, but I haven't for several years.'

'Well, there is a Mini in the garage—take it out once or twice and see how you get on. Samways will go with you if you like.'

'I'd rather go alone.'

'I shall be away all this next week but here for the weekend. The following week I have to go to Leiden to give a series of lectures. I'll leave a phone number in case of an emergency but you will find Samways a tower of strength. Your grandfather has most kindly suggested that he should have the boys each morning for easy-going lessons so that they won't feel too strange when they start school.'

They dined in a leisurely fashion, and later when she said goodnight he said, 'I shall be gone by the time you get down in the morning. Enjoy your week, Eustacia.'

She did; the boys had recovered their good spirits and she kept them occupied when they weren't at their lessons. She thought the lessons weren't very serious, for she heard gales of laughter coming from the room where they studied with her grandfather. She told Samways that she was to drive the Mini and he got it from the garage for her and told her of the quietest roads. After the first uncertain minutes, she found that she was enjoying herself hugely. After the first day or two she ventured on to a nearby main road and then drove to the school where the boys were to go, quite confident now.

When Sir Colin came at the weekend she assured him that she felt quite capable of driving the boys, and he said at once, 'Good. Get your coat, we'll go over to the school—I want to see the headmaster.'

Something she hadn't bargained for, but she got into the driver's seat, and since she was a big girl and he was an extremely large man the journey was a cramped one—indeed she found it rather unsettling.

At Sir Colin's request, she went with him and was introduced. 'So that you are known here when you come to fetch the boys,' explained Sir Colin. They went back home presently; the boys were to start school in two weeks' time—after half-term—and she would fetch them each day and ferry them to and fro.

The weekend went too quickly and on Monday morning Sir Colin left again. 'I'll be away for a week, perhaps a little longer—I have friends in Holland and I may stay a day or two with them.'

He hugged the boys, promised that he would bring them something Dutch when he got back, shook Mr Crump's hand and, rather as an afterthought, kissed Eustacia's cheek before he drove himself off.

The house seemed empty without him; he was a quiet man but somehow, reflected Eustacia, one felt content and secure when he was there. The days ahead looked empty. She was vexed with herself for feeling discontented—the calm routine of their days was something to be thankful for.

It was towards the middle of the week that the calm was disrupted.

Mrs Kennedy telephoned quite late one evening; the boys were long since in bed and her grandfather had gone to his room.

'I wish to speak to Sir Colin,' said Mrs Kennedy. 'Is that the maid?'

'Eustacia,' said Eustacia with polite coolness.

Mrs Kennedy gave a nasty little laugh. 'Well, fetch him, will you?'

'He isn't here, Mrs Kennedy.'

'Oh, where is he? In town?'

'He's abroad.' The moment she had said it, Eustacia would have given anything to recall her words.

'Do you mean to say that he has left you in charge of my grandsons? You're not capable of looking after them. I simply won't have it.' She was fast working herself into a temper. 'I don't know how long he will be away but I intend fetching them to stay with us until such time as he returns. It was made clear in my son-in-law's will that they should live with their guardian, but obviously Sir Colin chose to ignore that. Expect me some time tomorrow and have the boys ready to leave with us.'

She hung up abruptly and Eustacia replaced the receiver.

It was time-wasting to call herself a fool, but she undoubtedly was. What was more she was shaking with fright and rage. She must do something about it, and quickly. She went to Sir Colin's study and took the slip of paper from his desk, and picked up the phone and dialled the number on it.

She was answered very quickly but she had to wait until he was found. His 'Yes, Eustacia?' was uttered in a calm voice which checked her wild wish to burst into tears and, while she was struggling for a normal voice, he said, 'Take your time and try not to cry.'

She took a deep breath and, in a voice squeaky with battened-down emotions, began to speak.

Chapter 4

'Mrs Kennedy,' said Eustacia in a voice she was pleased to hear sounded normal. 'She telephoned about ten minutes ago; she asked to speak to you and I said you weren't here, so she asked where you were.' She gulped. 'I said that you were abroad, and do call me fool if you want to because that's what I am… She said that I wasn't fit to look after the boys and they should be living with her because you weren't at home, and she is coming to fetch them tomorrow…'

'Dear me, what a tiresome lady, and don't reproach yourself, Eustacia, you weren't to know that she was going to turn nasty. Now please stop worrying about it; I'll be home in time to deal with the matter. Go to bed, there's a good girl.' He sounded just as he did when he was talking to his nephews: firm but kind.

'But you're in Holland—it's miles away…'

'Have you never heard of aeroplanes, Eustacia? Are you crying?'

'Well, a bit—I've let you down.'

'Don't be silly; now go to bed. Oh, and unbolt the garden door again, will you? Leave it locked and take the key out of the lock.'

She dealt with the door and went obediently to bed where, surprisingly, she slept until the early morning. She lay and worried for a while and then got up, showered and dressed and crept downstairs with the vague idea that, if Mrs Kennedy should arrive unexpectedly, she would at least be ready for her. She gained the bottom of the staircase and the study door opened and Sir Colin came out. He was dressed with his usual elegance and from where she was standing he appeared to be a man who had had a good night's sleep in his bed.

She surged across the hall, delight and relief making her beautiful face a sight to linger over. 'Oh, you're here, I'm so very glad to see you.'

He smiled down at her. 'Good morning, Eustacia. Why are you up and dressed at six o'clock in the morning?'

She answered him seriously. 'Well, I thought if Mrs Kennedy arrived unexpectedly I'd be ready for her.'

'I told you I would be home in time to see her.'

'Yes, and I believed you, but you might need help.'

His eyes gleamed with amusement but he said gravely, 'That was most thoughtful of you. Do you suppose we might have a cup of tea?'

'Of course, I'll bring you a tray. Would you like some toast with it?'

'Yes, I would. We will have it in the kitchen while we make our plans.'

The kitchen was warm, and Moses opened a sleepy eye and thumped his tail with pleasure at seeing his master. Eustacia put the kettle on the Aga and fetched cups and saucers while Sir Colin cut the bread.

'Is there any of Mrs Samways' marmalade?' he wanted to know, and loaded the toaster. She found the marmalade and the butter and got plates and knives and presently they sat down opposite each other at the big scrubbed table with Moses sitting as close as he could get to Sir Colin.

'How did you get here so quickly? There aren't any planes during the night, are there?'

'I chartered one.' He took a bite of toast.

'Oh, I see. You didn't mind me phoning you, Sir Colin? It hasn't made a mess of your seminar—or was it lectures?'

He smiled. 'Both, and the lectures were finished—the seminar isn't all that important.' He passed his cup for more tea. 'No, I didn't mind your phoning, Eustacia; indeed, I would have been very angry if you hadn't.'

'It was silly of me…'

'Why? You were not to know what Mrs Kennedy intended.'

'What shall you do?' She passed the marmalade. 'She can't take the boys away, can she?'

'Of course not.' He sounded placid. 'And there is a simple solution to the problem.'

'Oh—good.' She bent to give Moses a piece of buttered toast.

'We could marry.'

She almost choked on her toast. 'Marry? You and me? Me? Marry you?'

'A very sensible idea,' he pointed out smoothly. 'You will then be a guardian of the boys and there can never be a question of their being taken away from us.'

'But I don't—that is, you don't…' She came to a stop searching for the right words.

'I hardly see that that comes into it. We get on well together, do we not? We should be able to provide a secure background for the boys without getting emotionally involved with each other. After all, there won't be any difference if you become my wife; we get along well, as I have just said, and I see no reason why we shouldn't continue to do so. I am a good deal older than you and there is always the hazard that you may meet someone with whom you will fall in love, in which case the situation can be dealt with reasonably. I assure you that I wouldn't stand in your way.'

It sounded very cold and businesslike. 'Supposing you fall in love?' she asked him.

'But I already have, so you need not concern yourself with that.'

'Grandfather…?'

'A delightful old gentleman, welcome to live here for the remainder of his days.'

'I—I would like to think about it.' There was a panicky excitement inside her.

'By all means,' he glanced at his watch, 'I doubt if the Kennedys will get here for another two hours at the earliest.'

'You mean I have to decide before then?'

'It would make things much easier.' He smiled across the table; he was tired but he knew exactly what he was doing. 'Do you suppose your grandfather is up yet? I should like to talk to him.'

She was glad to have an excuse to get away. Her head was in a turmoil and she simply had to have time to think. 'I'll go and see. I think he may be in the library—he likes to read before breakfast.'

She left the two men there and went to get the boys out of their beds.

'You look funny,' said Oliver as she brushed his hair. In case she hadn't understood, he added, 'You're pretty, I don't mean that—you look excited.'

'Probably the thought of breakfast. I'm hungry, aren't you?'

'Yes!' shouted Teddy. 'Bacon and eggs and sausages and mushrooms and toast and marmalade…'

The three of them hurried downstairs.

Over breakfast Mr Crump suggested that since their uncle was home and might want to take them out later it would be a good idea if they did some reading first.

'What a splendid idea,' observed Sir Colin, for all

the world as though he hadn't just arranged that, and smiled at Eustacia. He looked pleased with himself and confident, as though he was certain that she would consent to his preposterous idea. She would have to talk to him about it once the boys had gone with her grandfather, but as it turned out she had no chance—they had left the table, the boys and Mr Crump to go to the library, she to make the beds upstairs, Sir Colin presumably to go about his own business, when there was a demanding peal on the doorbell.

Sir Colin caught her by the arm as Samways went to answer it.

'Mrs Kennedy?' she heard him say to Samways, who nodded with dignity and a knowing look. So Sir Colin had found time to tell Samways too… Eustacia allowed herself to be drawn into the drawing-room. 'Sit there,' said Sir Colin and urged her into a small easy-chair facing the door, 'and don't say a word unless I ask you something.' He smiled suddenly. 'Will you marry me, Eustacia?'

She opened her mouth to explain that she must have time to think about it, but now there were voices, rather loud, in the hall—any moment Mrs Kennedy and Mr Kennedy with her would be in the room. She said snappily, 'Oh, all right, but I haven't—' She felt the quick kiss on her cheek and then he was gone, to the other end of the room away from the door, where he wouldn't be seen at once.

Samways opened the door and Mrs Kennedy and her husband surged past him, ignoring his announcement.

'It has been no easy matter driving here, Miss—er—Crump, but I know my duty. If Sir Colin feels unable to make a suitable home for the boys then I must sacrifice my time and leisure and bring them up as befits my daughter's children. Be good enough to send for Oliver and Teddy at once; they will return with us. When Sir Colin chooses to return we can discuss the matter further. For them to remain here with nothing but a parcel of servants is quite—' She stopped, her cross face assuming a look of utter astonishment, her eyes popping.

Sir Colin had advanced a few steps so that he had come into her line of vision. His voice was blandly polite. 'Mrs Kennedy, you must have had a very tiring journey—you travelled through the night? May I offer you both breakfast?'

Mrs Kennedy made a gobbling noise. 'She,' she nodded at Eustacia, 'told me that you were abroad.'

'Eustacia spoke the truth; when you telephoned I was. It seemed to me to be necessary to come home and put your mind at rest about the boys. Let me allay your doubts—Eustacia and I are to be married very shortly so that, when I need to be away from home, they will have a guardian in her.'

'Marry her?' Mrs Kennedy had gone an unbecoming plum colour.

Sir Colin's voice was as steely as his eyes. 'Eustacia has done me that honour.'

'It's a put-up job, she's no more—'

'I beg your pardon, Mrs Kennedy?'

Mr Kennedy spoke for the first time. 'My wife

didn't mean that,' he said hastily. 'I did explain to her that everything was quite satisfactory as regards the boys.' He added awkwardly, 'My congratulations, I hope you will be very happy.'

Mrs Kennedy had pulled herself together. 'Yes, yes indeed. I spoke hastily. One forgets how quickly one can travel these days. Aeroplanes, you know, and hovercraft and so on.' She looked around her a little wildly and Eustacia, much as she disliked her, decided that it was time to rescue her from an awkward situation.

'Won't you sit down, Mrs Kennedy and Mr Kennedy? And shall I fetch the boys, Colin?'

She uttered this in what she hoped was a sufficiently loving voice and got answered in her own coin.

'Will you, darling? And ask Samways to bring coffee, would you?'

The smile which went with it was full of tender charm as he went to open the door for her. She didn't dare to look at him. He must be a splendid actor, she reflected, hurrying across the hall; she had read somewhere that surgeons very often had a strong artistic streak, and his must be acting.

The boys weren't exactly enthusiastic. 'Must we?' asked Oliver. 'Mr Crump was just telling us about the Aztecs and it's really very interesting.'

'Yes, I'm sure it is,' agreed Eustacia, 'and you won't need to stay long. I'm sure Grandfather will be delighted to continue when you get back. He's going to have a cup of coffee now.'

The boys behaved beautifully, offering hands and cheeks and answering politely when they were questioned. They pretended not to notice when their grandmother started crying, and Eustacia suggested that she might like to freshen up after her drive. A sudden imp of mischief prompted her to add, 'Perhaps you would like to stay the night?' She turned her beautiful face towards Sir Colin. 'Don't you think that is a good idea, Colin?' She gave him an innocent look, and he turned a sudden laugh into a fit of coughing.

'By all means, darling.' He sounded the perfect host, anxious to do all he could for his guests.

However, the Kennedys didn't wish to stop. Mrs Kennedy was shepherded away to repair her face and tidy herself, and presently they made their farewells and drove away with the assurance, not over-enthusiastically received by them, that Sir Colin, Eustacia and both the boys would spend a day or two with them as soon as the warmer weather arrived.

They stood on the steps, waving, and the two boys scampered back to Mr Crump. 'I had no idea that you had it in you, Eustacia,' said Sir Colin.

'Had what, Sir Colin?'

'This ability to be a loving fiancée at a moment's notice, although I could have wished for a few more melting glances.'

'Well, I didn't want to overdo it.'

'That would be impossible.' He turned her round and took her arm and walked her into the house. 'Now, when shall we get married?'

She turned to face him. 'You aren't serious?' She studied his face and decided that he was.

'Am I to be jilted before we are even engaged? I had thought better of you, Eustacia.'

She stammered a little. 'I thought—well, I thought that it was just an emergency.'

'Certainly not—an expediency, perhaps. You must see, since you are a sensible girl, that if we marry it ensures a secure and happy future for the boys with no further interference from the Kennedys. Of course, they have every right to see the boys as often as they wish, and have them to stay for holidays, but this will be their home and you and I will be, in effect, their parents.'

She had nothing to say; it all sounded so logical and businesslike.

Sir Colin eyed her thoughtfully. 'Naturally our marriage will be one of convenience. We have, I think, a mutual liking for each other which is more than can be said of a good many marriages these days. Should you meet a man you truly love, then I will release you—'

'And what about you?' asked Eustacia sharply. 'You're just as likely to meet another woman.'

He said seriously, 'I'm thirty-six, my dear, I have had every opportunity to meet another woman…'

'What about Gloria?'

She wished she hadn't said it, for his face became as bland as the voice with which he echoed her. 'Gloria?'

She muttered, 'It was something I heard, and I thought that she was—'

'Set your mind at rest, Eustacia. Gloria was—still is—a friend of long standing and the very last woman I would marry.'

She went pink but met his look candidly. 'I'm sorry, it isn't my business—it was impertinent of me.'

The bland look which she didn't much care for disappeared and he smiled at her, the kind smile which made her feel that everything was all right between them. He said gently, 'I am a good deal older than you, Eustacia—if you do have second thoughts I shall understand.'

'Well, I hadn't thought about it,' she told him, 'and it doesn't matter. I do like you very much and I think that I could love the boys, really love them, and I should be very happy living here with them…'

He chuckled. 'I do come home at weekends and sometimes during the week. Besides, from time to time I should like you to come up to town. I have many friends and I like to entertain them occasionally. Have you any objection to that?'

'Me? No, it sounds exciting. You don't mind Grandfather being here? Would you like him to go back to the flat? I dare say—'

'Certainly not. I find him a delightful man and the boys like the time they spend with him and are fond of him. I believe he is happy here, is he not? And he is performing a yeoman service teaching them to play chess and answering all their questions, and I suspect that when they go to school he will be roped in to help them with their homework.'

They had been standing in the hall, and at Samways' little cough they both looked round.

'I thought perhaps some fresh coffee, sir?'

'Excellent, Samways. And please fetch up a couple of bottles of champagne—we will have some at lunch. Miss Crump and I have just become engaged.'

Samways was delighted; he offered congratulations with suitable gravity, mentioned that Mrs Samways would be more than pleased to hear the news, and went away to fetch the coffee.

'I think,' said Sir Colin, sitting in his chair with a coffee cup in his hand, 'that you had better come up to town with me; I have a small house there, and I should like you to meet Grimstone who runs it for me—his sister does the cooking. We must decide on a date for the wedding too.' He sat thinking. 'I'm rather busy for the next few days but I will send Samways down to fetch my mother—she can stay here and help your grandfather to keep an eye on the boys so that you may spend a few days shopping. Would you object to marrying here in the village? The church is rather nice…'

Really, thought Eustacia, he's arranged everything in a couple of sentences. She said calmly, 'I think that would be delightful—being married here, I mean. And if you want me to come up to London with you then I will. The boys will be all right?'

'Perfectly all right. We will drive up this afternoon and I'll bring you back this evening. I have a list in the morning but not until ten o'clock, so I can spend the night.' He glanced at her. 'Am I going too fast for you?'

'Yes, but I'll catch up. Will your mother mind?'

'No. She likes you. Shall we go and tell your grandfather and the boys?'

Their news was received with boisterous delight by the boys and quiet satisfaction by her grandfather.

'You'll never go away?' asked Teddy. 'You'll look after us?'

She hugged him. 'Of course I will, we'll all have such fun…'

'And when you're an old lady,' said Oliver, 'if you need looking after, you and Uncle Colin, we'll take care of you both.'

'I think we shall both be very glad to have you around and it is very kind of you to think of us, my dear.'

'We call Uncle Colin Uncle—do we have to call you Aunt?'

'Only if you would like to.'

'You won't mind if we call you Eustacia?'

'I should like it above all things.'

She had sat down at the table with the boys on either side of her, and Sir Colin turned round from the conversation he was having with her grandfather.

'Uncle Colin, we think you are a very lucky man,' said Oliver.

'I know I am, old chap. We shall be married here quite soon and have all our friends at the church.'

'And a cake, and Eustacia will be a bride in a white dress?'

Before she could answer, Sir Colin said positively, 'Yes, to both questions.'

'A party?' asked Teddy, happily.

'A party it shall be.' He spoke to his small nephew but he looked at Eustacia, smiling faintly. Quite carried away by the excitement of the moment, she smiled back, her cheeks pink and her eyes sparkling.

The next hour or so seemed a little hazy, partly due to the champagne and the children's excitement, which made sensible conversation, or sensible thought for that matter, impossible. Presently she found herself sitting beside Sir Colin, in the Rolls, waving goodbye to the little group at the front of the house, and when they were out of sight she sat back composedly, very neat in the elderly suit. There was still a great deal she wanted to know and she supposed she would be told sooner or later; meanwhile there seemed little point in aimless chatter.

Presently Sir Colin said, 'It is the prerogative of the bride to decide what kind of wedding she wants, is it not? There was no chance to explain my high-handed plans, but perhaps you understood?'

'Yes. It's for the boys, isn't it? It will help them to adjust, won't it? If they have something positive to hang on to.'

'Exactly. This afternoon we are going to visit an old friend of my father's. He is a bishop and I hope he will be able to advise us about a special licence and the quickest way to get one. I shall put an announcement in the *Telegraph* tomorrow and invite friends to the wedding. I haven't many relations, but they will come, I'm sure of that. So will colleagues I work with. Is there anyone you would like to invite? I know that you have no family…'

'There isn't anyone—I had friends, but during the last two years I've lost touch.'

'I dare say one or two people from the path lab will want to come.'

They were in London by now, going through Chiswick and Kensington and skirting Hyde Park, up Park Lane and then into the elegant, quiet streets around Portman Square. The street they turned into was short, tree-lined and bordered by narrow, bow-windowed Regency houses. Sir Colin stopped at the end of the terrace where there was an archway leading to a mews behind the houses.

Eustacia studied it from the car window. 'You live here?'

'Yes. It's not too far from St Biddolph's and I've consulting-rooms in Wimpole Street.'

He got out and opened her door and they crossed the narrow pavement together. He let himself in with his key and ushered her into the narrow hall, and at the same time a tall, very thin man came up the stairs at the back.

He answered Sir Colin's cheerful greeting solemnly and then bowed to Eustacia as Sir Colin said, 'This is Grimstone, Eustacia, he runs this house on oiled wheels and his sister is my cook. Grimstone, Miss Cramp has done me the honour of promising to marry me in the very near future.'

Grimstone bowed again. 'I'm sure we are delighted to hear the news, Sir Colin and Miss Crump. My felicitations.'

Sir Colin swept Eustacia across the hall and into a charming room overlooking the street. 'Take Miss Crump's coat, will you, Grimstone, and may we have some tea? We have to go out very shortly but shall be back for dinner if Rosie can manage something. I'll be down at Turville tonight.'

'Very good, sir, I will speak to Rosie.'

When he had gone Sir Colin sat her down in a small armchair by the brisk fire, sat himself down opposite her and observed, 'Grimstone appears severe, but in fact he has a heart of gold and a very wise old head. He'll be your slave but he will never admit to it.'

'He's been with you for a long time?'

'He was with my father and mother. They lived here when my father was alive; when my mother moved to Castle Cary, Grimstone elected to stay here and run the house for me. He doesn't like the country.'

While they had their tea she looked around her. The room wasn't very large but the furniture, mostly Regency and comfortable chairs and sofas, suited it very well for there wasn't too much of it.

'I've hardly altered anything,' observed Sir Colin, almost as though he had read her thoughts. 'My father inherited this house from an aunt and it had been in her family for a very long time. I loved living here when I was a child, although I'm just as fond of the house at Turville. The best of both worlds—it hardly seems fair…'

'If you idled away your days it wouldn't be fair, but you work hard and you help people—save their lives—take away their pain.'

He said without conceit, 'I do my best; my father was a physician, so was his father, and I don't think they ever quite forgave me for taking up surgery.' He put down his cup. 'Shall we go and see this bishop and see what he can do for us?'

He took her to a nice old house in Westminster and the bishop, an old man with bright blue eyes which missed nothing, approved of her. There were certain formalities, he explained, which he would be delighted to arrange, and he could see no reason why they shouldn't marry within about a couple of weeks in Turville Church. 'And I hope I shall be invited to the wedding.'

Eustacia glanced at Sir Colin and saw his faint smile. 'I don't suppose you would marry us?' she ventured.

'My dear young lady, I hoped that you might ask that. I shall be delighted. I will get in touch with your rector, and you of course will be going to see him.'

'It will have to be tomorrow evening…'

They left presently and, as they drove back to the house, Sir Colin said, 'I'll leave you to choose the day, Eustacia. If you could let me know by the weekend I can organise a couple of days free.'

No honeymoon, she reflected, but a honeymoon would be silly in the circumstances; they were entering a kind of business partnership for the sake of the boys, and she mustn't forget that. She agreed pleasantly and later, sitting in the drawing-room drinking her sherry before dinner, she followed his lead and kept the talk impersonal.

They dined deliciously; tomato and basil soufflé, roast lamb with new potatoes and purée of broccoli and a syllabub with ginger biscuits. The white burgundy she was offered pleased her and loosened her tongue too, so that her host sat back with a glint in his eyes, encouraging her to talk.

She was taken aback when, instead of Grimstone, his sister Rosie came in with the coffee-tray. She beamed at Eustacia as she put the tray on the table. 'I'm sorry that I hadn't the time to plan a good dinner for you, seeing as how you're engaged and that. And I'm sure I wish you both very happy. I did the best I could but there weren't no time.'

'It was a delicious dinner,' said Eustacia, and she meant it. 'Those ginger biscuits—you made them yourself, of course.'

Rosie's smile became even wider. 'Indeed I did, Miss Crump. I don't allow Sir Colin to eat any of those nasty cakes and biscuits from the shops. Sawdust and sugar, I always say.'

'I'm sure you look after him beautifully, Rosie, and it really was a super dinner.'

Rosie retired, still smiling, and Sir Colin, who hadn't said a word, drank his coffee and she said uneasily, 'I've annoyed you, haven't I?'

'Now why should you say that, Eustacia? On the

contrary, I have been thinking that you have the gift of instant empathy.'

'Oh, have I? I like people—well, most people.' She thought of Mrs Kennedy and hoped that next time they met the meeting would be a happier one, though she doubted it.

They drove back to Turville very shortly afterwards, to discuss their plans with her grandfather, but not before Eustacia had nipped up to the boys' room and made sure that they were sleeping. Oliver opened an eye as she peered at them both by the light of the dim night-light she thought it prudent to allow them.

'You're back? Is Uncle with you?'

She tucked him up and dropped a kiss on the top of his head. 'Yes, dear, but he has to go again after breakfast. Now go to sleep like a good boy.'

She went to bed herself shortly afterwards—the day had been full of surprises and she hadn't been given time to think about them. Once in bed, she allowed her thoughts to wander. Her grandfather and Sir Colin had been so matter-of-fact about the whole thing, she thought peevishly, as though the kind of upheaval she had experienced that morning was a perfectly normal happening—and now she came to think about it, perhaps she had been too hasty. It had all sounded so sensible when Sir Colin had suggested that they should marry, but now a hundred and one reasons why she should cry off reared their heads. An hour later, from whichever angle she looked at it, the reason for marrying Sir Colin more than cancelled out her own against. The Kennedys, she felt sure, were quite capable of doing their utmost to have the care of the boys unless Sir Colin could provide them with a stable background. And, of course, if she married him the background would be just that. They were dear children and they had been dealt a bitter blow, and Sir Colin was so obviously the right person to give them a home. She slept on the thought.

Sir Colin left after breakfast with the promise of a speedy return, and it was left to Eustacia to enlarge upon the plans for the wedding. The rest of the week was largely taken up with discussions involving the actual wedding, the prospect of school and what Eustacia was to wear. It must be white, they told her, but she drew the line at a train, six bridesmaids and a diamond tiara. 'Would a pretty hat do?' she wanted to know. 'And no bridesmaids, but I promise you that I'll wear white,'

In the quiet of her room she did anxious sums; she had saved her salary and there was a small amount in the bank. It wasn't just the wedding dress—she simply had to have a suit and some shoes and a dress—one which she could wear if by any chance someone came to dinner or they went out. It didn't seem very likely; she envisaged a quiet future, with her living with the boys at Turville, making a home for them. That was why she was marrying Sir Colin, wasn't it?

He came home at the weekend, swept them all off to church on Sunday morning, took the boys for a walk after lunch and drove her back to London after tea. Over dinner he told her that he would be at the hospital for the next two days, going from there to his consulting-rooms and getting back for dinner in the evening. 'I'll drive you back on Wednesday evening,' he told her. 'Can you get your shopping done in that time?' He smiled his gentle smile. 'Have you enough money?'

'Oh, yes, I think so.'

'How much?'

And when she told him, 'You will have an allowance when we are married. I think it might be a good idea if I give it to you before you start your shopping.' And when she demurred, 'No, please don't argue, Eustacia. I have a number of friends and we shall have social occasions to attend together as well as the occasional weekend when we are away or entertaining guests at Turville. Buy all the clothes you will need and, if you run out of money, let me know.'

She thanked him quietly; there was no point in arguing about it for he made sense—her wardrobe was scanty, out of date and quite unsuitable for the wife of an eminent surgeon.

They didn't talk about it again. He told her that he had arranged for the wedding to take place on the day she had wanted, and there would be fifty or sixty guests coming. 'Short notice, I know, but I know most of them well enough to phone them.'

She went to bed soon after dinner and he made no attempt to keep her up. He opened the door for her and put a hand on her arm as she passed him. 'Don't worry, it will work out perfectly.'

He kissed her cheek and wished her goodnight,

and she wondered if he had meant the wedding or their future together.

He had gone when she went down in the morning. She had slept peacefully in the charming room with its pastel colours and silk curtains, and it had been bliss to be roused by Rosie with early-morning tea. There was an envelope on the tray with a note from Sir Colin hoping that she had had a good night's sleep. There was a roll of notes too. Her eyes almost popped from her head when she counted them—she could never spend that in a year… The note bore a postscript: he hoped there was sufficient for her to get the wedding clothes, and he would see that she had the same amount before the following day. 'Well,' said Eustacia, and counted the notes again just to make sure and then, over breakfast, fell to making a list of suitable clothes for every occasion. She glanced down at her well-worn skirt and wondered if he had minded her shabbiness; never by a glance had he betrayed that fact. He was a kind man and they got on well now that she had got to know him better. She wondered if he had been in love and decided that he had, quite a few times probably—he might still be for all she knew, but that was not her concern—she must remember that they were marrying for the boys' sake and for no other reason. She shook off a sudden feeling of sadness and applied herself once more to her list.

Chapter 5

Eustacia hadn't had the chance to shop with almost unlimited money in her purse for several years—her venue had been the high street stores at sale-time, and even then it had been a question as to whether it was a garment which would stand up to a good deal of wear and still remain at least on the fringe of fashion. Now, clutching what she considered to be a small fortune, she took a bus to Harrods.

She paused for an early lunch, surrounded by dress-boxes and elegant packages, the possessor of a wedding dress, a charming hat to go with it, elegant shoes she felt she would never wear again after the wedding-day, a beautifully tailored suit in a rich brown tweed, sweaters and blouses to wear with it, and two dresses which she hoped would be suitable for any minor social occasion. She scanned her list as she ate her asparagus flan and decided what to buy next. A decent raincoat and stout shoes, and, if there was any money left, a pretty dressing-gown and slippers, and even if there was any money left after that she doubted whether she would be able to carry any more parcels, even as far as a taxi.

It was teatime when she arrived back at Sir Colin's house. Grimstone must have been on the look-out for her for he opened the door as she got out of the taxi, paid the driver and carried her packages inside.

'A successful day, Miss Crump?'

'Oh, very, thank you, Grimstone, I've had a lovely time.'

'I will convey these to your room, miss, and tea will be served in the drawing-room in ten minutes' time if that is suitable to you?'

There seemed an awful lot of boxes and bags, but she resisted the desire to open them and take a look, tidied herself in a perfunctory fashion and went downstairs. Tea had been arranged on a small table before the fire; tiny sandwiches, strips of toast, little iced cakes arranged on paper-thin china, and, to keep her company, Moses and Madam Mop the cat. There was no sign of Sir Colin, so presently she went upstairs and opened the purchases. The wedding dress she hung away in the wardrobe, resisting the temptation to try it on once more. It was of very fine white wool with a satin collar and cuffs and of an exquisite cut, worth every penny of its exorbitant price. Then she took the hat out of its box; it was white mousseline and satin with a wide brim and a satin bow to trim it, not, perhaps, quite what the boys had wanted but definitely bridal. She was head and shoulders in the wardrobe arranging the shoes just so when there was a knock on the door, and she called, 'Come in.'

She backed away, expecting to see Rosie intent on drawing the curtains and turning down the bed, but Sir Colin was standing there, leaning against the door. She said, 'Oh, hello,' and then, stupidly, 'You're home.'

He smiled and agreed; he had started his day just after eight o'clock with a ward round, operated until the early afternoon, eaten a sandwich, spent an hour in Outpatients and then gone to his rooms to keep appointments with his private patients and presently, after dinner, he would go back to St Biddolph's to check on the patients he had operated upon that morning. A long, hard day and he was tired. It struck him that the sight of Eustacia, standing there surrounded by tissue paper and cardboard boxes, was somehow very soothing.

'Had a good day?' he asked, and when she said yes in a shy voice, 'Then let's go down and have a drink and you can tell me all about it.'

The evening, for Eustacia, was quite perfect. They discussed the wedding over dinner in a matter-of-fact manner and later, when she said goodnight, he bent to kiss her cheek again. 'I hope to be home soon after tea tomorrow, so buy a pretty dress and we will go out to dinner.' He smiled down at her and then kissed her again, and when she looked surprised, 'We should put in some practice,' he told her blandly, 'the boys will expect it.'

There was another envelope on her tea-tray in the morning, and this time the money was almost double the amount she had been given on the previous day. She counted it and wondered if she should save some of it, but on the other hand he had told her to buy all the clothes she needed...

She made another list and presently went back to Harrods. A winter coat was a must, even though it was the tail-end of winter. There were still cold days ahead and her coat was old and very shabby—and a pretty dress... She found a brown top-coat which went well with the tweed of her suit, and then she began her search for a dress. She found what she wanted—amber satin swathed in chiffon with very full chiffon sleeves to the elbow and a low neckline, partly concealed by a swathing of chiffon. At the saleswoman's suggestion, she bought an angora wrap to go over it.

There was still plenty of money; she found slippers and a small evening-bag and took herself off to the undies department where she spent a good deal more money on wisps of silk and lace, to her great satisfaction. Gloves and a leather handbag took almost all the money which was left in her purse; she collected her purchases and got into a taxi.

She had forgotten lunch although she had stopped for a cup of coffee, and, since it was three o'clock in the afternoon and Grimstone had doubtless taken it for granted that she had had a meal while she was out, she went to her room, ate all the biscuits in the tin by her bed and examined her new purchases and then put them away tidily. By that time it was after four o'clock and she went downstairs, her thoughts on a cup of tea and some of Rosie's dainty sandwiches. Sir Colin had said that he would be back after tea, and that small meal would fill in the time nicely until he came.

Grimstone was in the hall and went to open the drawing-room door for her, murmuring in his dignified way that tea would be brought at once, and shutting the door firmly behind her.

Sir Colin was sitting beside the fire with Moses beside him and Madam Mop curled up at his feet. He got up as she paused halfway across the room and said, pleasantly, 'Come and sit down. Outpatients wasn't as heavy as usual so I came home early. Have you had a good day?'

She sat down opposite him. 'Heavenly, thank you. And thank you for all that money. I—I've been very extravagant…!'

'Good. There's still tomorrow if you haven't finished getting all you need.'

'Well,' said Eustacia with disarming honesty, 'I've bought all I need and a lot of things I don't, but they were so exactly what I've been wanting, if you see what I mean.'

'Indeed I do. Do you like dancing? I have booked a table at Claridge's for eight o'clock.'

Eustacia beamed at him. 'Oh, how lovely—I bought a dress—I do hope it will do.'

He smiled. 'I'm quite sure it will. I look forward to seeing it. I think we might go back to Turville tomorrow evening. I've one or two patients to see in the late afternoon but I think we might get back in time for dinner there, and to see the boys before they go to bed.'

'They will be pleased. They wanted to know when we would be coming home.' She blushed. 'That is, when we would be going back to Turville.'

'I'll phone them presently. Your grandfather is all right?'

'He's so happy... You're sure, aren't you? I mean, about me and him?'

'Quite sure, Eustacia.' He put down his cup. 'I'm going to take Moses for a gentle trot and then I must do some work. Shall we meet down here a little after half-past seven?'

It was as though he had closed a door between them, very gently, but closed just the same. She said, 'Very well,' and watched him, with Moses walking sedately beside him, go out of the room. She really must remember, she reflected a little sadly, that their marriage was for the boys' sakes and personal feelings wouldn't come into it. Perhaps later on—he was an easy man to like. A small voice at the back of her head added that he would be an easy man to love too, but she refused to hear it.

Not having had lunch, she polished off the rest of the sandwiches and a slice of Rosie's walnut cake and took herself back to her room, where she sat and thought about nothing much in particular until it was time to have her bath and dress. She wanted very much to think about Sir Colin, but it might be wiser not to allow him to loom too large in her thoughts.

The dress did everything asked of it; she had a splendid figure and the satin and chiffon did it full justice. Excitement had given her pretty face a delicate colour and her hair, confined in a French pleat, framed it with its rich dark brown. She took up the wrap and little bag, slid her feet into the high-heeled slippers she had very nearly not bought because of their wicked price, and went downstairs to the drawing-room.

She was surprised to find Sir Colin already there in the subdued elegance of a dinner-jacket, and she said breathlessly, 'Oh, am I late? I'm sorry, I thought you said just after—'

'I am early, Eustacia. How delightful you look; that is a charming gown.' He studied her smilingly and she stood quietly while he did so. 'You are also beautiful—I have already told you that, haven't I?'

She said seriously, 'Yes, at St Biddolph's—but it's this dress, you know.'

'If I remember rightly, you were wrapped in a very unbecoming overall.'

'Oh, yes, well…' She could think of nothing to say and she suspected that he was amused. 'Clothes make a difference,' she added, and her eyes sparkled at the thought of her well-stocked wardrobe.

Sir Colin silently admired the sparkle. 'If you are ready, shall we go?'

As they reached the door he put out a hand to detain her. 'Before we go, I have something for you. I should have given it to you before this, but there has been no opportunity.'

He took a small velvet box from his pocket and opened it. The ring inside was a sapphire surrounded with diamonds and set in gold. 'It has been in the family for a very long time, handed down from one bride to the next.' He picked up her left hand and slipped the ring on her finger—it fitted exactly.

Eustacia gave a gulp of delight—it was a ring any girl would be proud of. She said slowly, 'It is absolutely beautiful. Thank you very much, Sir Colin—only wouldn't you rather I had a ring that wasn't meant for a—a bride?' She was aware that she wasn't making herself clear. She must try again. 'What I mean is,' she began carefully, 'this ring must have been a token...' She paused—there were pitfalls ahead and this time he came to her rescue.

'In plain words, my dear, you feel that it isn't right to accept a ring which should be given as a token of love.'

'Now why couldn't I have put it as plainly as that?' she wanted to know.

'And another thing—do in heaven's name stop calling me Sir Colin. Colin sounds much nicer, and as for the ring, there is no one else I would wish to give it to, Eustacia.' He bent and kissed her and he took her arm. 'That having been settled, let us go.'

Perhaps it was the ring or the dress or the elegance of Claridge's, but the evening was a success. They dined superbly: mousseline of lobster, noisettes of lamb, biscuit glacé with raspberries and praline, accompanied by champagne and finally coffee, and in between they danced. Eustacia, big girl though she was, was as light on her feet as thistledown, and Sir Colin danced as he did most other things, very well indeed. They made a handsome couple and she, aware that she looked her best, allowed herself, just for once, to pretend that the future would be like this too, happy in each other's company, content and secure. It was one o'clock when they arrived at his home but she felt wide awake, wanting to prolong the evening's pleasure. She stood in the hall, hoping that he would suggest that they talked for a little while, but as he shrugged off his coat he said pleasantly, 'A delightful evening, Eustacia.' He glanced at his watch. 'I have half an hour's work to do and I shall be gone before you are down in the morning. Only I'll see you tomorrow afternoon—I thought that we might try to get to Turville in time to see the boys before they go to bed.'

He crossed the hall to his study. 'Goodnight, Eustacia, sleep well.' The smile he gave her was what she described as businesslike; the warmth of the evening had gone—perhaps it had never been there, perhaps she had imagined it. She went sadly to her room, hung the lovely dress carefully in the wardrobe, put the ring carefully back into its little box and finally got into bed.

It took her a long time to get to sleep. It was too late for her to back out of their bargain now, and she wasn't sure that she wanted to. What worried her was that perhaps Colin had had second thoughts. But he had seemed so certain that everything would be all right, and he wasn't a man to change his mind once it was made up. What had she expected, anyway?

She slept on the thought.

The boys were delighted to see them home again and Eustacia slipped back into the quiet routine as though she had never been away—only the lovely clothes hanging in the wardrobe were there to remind her. She saw very little of Sir Colin; he spent his weekends at Turville and came there once or twice in the week but never long enough for them to talk for any length of time. That week went by and the boys started school and she drove them there and back each day, missing their company although she had enough to do now, for wedding presents were arriving and she needed to keep a list so that Colin could see it when he came home. There were discussions with Samways about the reception. The caterers would come on the day before the wedding, but furniture would have to be moved then the flowers would have to be arranged.

Sir Colin came home on the evening before the wedding, apparently unmoved by the thought of getting married. He approved of the flowers, conferred with Samways about the caterers and the drinks, teased the boys and settled down to a rambling discussion about the early English poets with her grandfather. His manner towards her was exactly as it always was, and she told herself that she was silly to expect anything else.

That evening his mother arrived and so did the bishop. The wedding was to be at noon with a reception directly afterwards and, as he had told Eustacia, he intended to return to London in two days' time. 'We will have a holiday later in the year,' he'd observed, 'and I'm sorry if you are disappointed, but my lists are made out weeks in advance and I have a backlog of private patients.'

She had told him matter-of-factly that she hadn't expected to go away. 'The boys have only just started school and they're a bit unsettled, although they are happy there.'

She wore one of her pretty dresses at dinner that evening and the meal turned into quite an occasion. The boys were allowed to stay up, and since Mrs Crichton and the bishop were there too there was a good deal of animated conversation. She went with the boys when the meal was finally finished and stayed a while, pottering around until, despite their excitement, they slept. When she went back to the drawing-room she found Mrs Crichton alone.

'The men are in the library,' she observed, 'looking up something or other legal, and I'm glad, for we haven't had a chance to talk, have we?' She smiled at Eustacia. 'Come and sit down, my dear, and tell me what you think of Colin.'

Eustacia sat and did her best to answer sensibly. 'He's a very kind man and good too. He's also generous—I've never had so much money to spend on clothes in my life before, I'm not sure that it's—'

She was cut short. 'Colin is a leading figure in his profession, and besides that he is a rich man. He would expect you to dress in a manner befitting his wife. You are a very pretty girl, my dear, and I am sure that you will make him proud of you.' She shot a glance at Eustacia's doubtful face. 'I dare say you will spend most of your time here. He would prefer to live here himself, I know, but he has always come here for his weekends and any evening that he can spare. I expect you will go up to town sometimes for he has any number of friends and entertains from time to time. I hope that during the Easter holidays he will agree to the boys coming to stay with me, in which case you will be able to go to town and stay there with him. A chance to go to the theatre and do some shopping. The boys are very happy—of course they grieve for their mother and father, but they love Colin and I believe that they begin to love you too.'

'I hope so, for I'm very fond of them both; besides, it will make it all worthwhile, won't it?'

'You have no doubts? No regrets?'

Eustacia shook her head. 'Oh, no. Not any more. I did for a while, you know, but Colin is quite right, it's the boys we have to think about.'

Mrs Crichton agreed placidly.

The men came back presently and after an hour's desultory conversation Mrs Crichton went to bed, and soon after that Eustacia said her goodnights and went to the door. Sir Colin opened it and to her surprise followed her into the hall.

'Cold feet?' he asked blandly.

'Yes—haven't you?'

'No.' His voice was kind now. 'It will be all right, I promise you, Eustacia.'

'Yes, I know that. I'll do my best, Colin, truly I will.'

He put his hands on her shoulders. 'Yes, I know that too, my dear.' He smiled his kind smile. 'Goodnight.' He bent and kissed her lightly, and she started up the stairs. She looked back when she reached the curve in the staircase. He was standing there still, watching her, this large, quiet man who was so soon to be her husband. And quite right and proper too, she thought absurdly, for I love him and even if he never loves me it will be quite all right to marry him. The upsurge of excitement and delight and relief was so great that she actually took a step down again in order to tell him so, but common sense stopped her just in time. It would never do for him to know; the very fact that they were good friends and nothing more had made it easy for him to suggest that they should marry. She managed to smile at him and ran up the rest of the staircase.

Sir Colin stood where he was for a few moments. Eustacia, usually so serene and practical, had looked as though she had just had a severe shock. He must remember to ask her about it.

They were all at breakfast, although Mrs Samways protested vigorously when she saw Eustacia sitting in her usual place. 'You didn't ought to be here,' she objected. 'The bridegroom shouldn't see the bride until she goes to church.'

'I won't look at her,' promised Sir Colin, and everyone laughed. 'Although I was under the impression that the bride took hours to dress.'

'Well, I shan't. I must see to the boys first...'

'What about taking Moses for a walk?' Sir Colin glanced across the table to his mother. 'Will you and Mr Crump keep each other company while we take the bishop as far as the church?'

It wasn't the usual way for a bride and groom to behave. Mrs Samways, clearing the breakfast things, shook her head and muttered darkly and went to the window to watch the pair of them with the two boys and Moses escorting the bishop as far as the church gate.

'And them in their old clothes,' observed Mrs Samways to the empty room.

However, she had to admit a few hours later that there was no fault to find with the bridal pair. Eustacia, walking down the aisle with her grandfather, made a delightful picture; the wide-brimmed hat was a splendid foil for her dark hair and the elegant simplicity of her dress was enhanced by the double row of pearls around her neck. She had found them on her dressing-table when she had gone to her room to dress with a note from Colin, begging her to wear them. There was a bouquet for her too, cream roses and lilies of the valley, freesias in the faintest pink and orange-blossom. Sir Colin was well worth a second look too, thought his devoted housekeeper. He stood, massive and elegant in his grey morning-coat and pale grey stock, and Mrs Samways wiped a sentimental eye and exchanged eloquent glances with Rosie, who had come for the wedding with Grimstone.

Eustacia walked back down the aisle, her hand tucked under Colin's arm, smiling at the rows of faces, his family and friends, of whom she knew absolutely nothing. She had expected to feel different now that she was married, although she wasn't sure why. The calm man beside her showed no sign of overwhelming happiness—indeed, he looked as he always looked: placid, self-assured and kind. She took a quick look at his profile and thought it looked stern too, but then he glanced down at her and smiled. A friendly smile and comforting, although why she needed to be comforted was a puzzle to her. She should be riotously happy, she had married the man she loved…

Photos were taken amid a good deal of cheerful bustle and presently they were driven back to the house, heading the steady flow of guests.

The next hour or two were like a dream; Eustacia shook hands with what seemed to be an unending stream of people, forgetting names as fast as they were mentioned. It was towards the end of the line of guests that she found herself facing a girl not much older than herself and as tall as she was and as splendidly built. She was pretty too, and dressed with great elegance. 'I'm Prudence,' she said cheerfully, 'I'll introduce myself while these two men talk. Haso has known Colin for years; he stays with us when he comes over to Holland, so I hope we shall see a lot of each other...'

'Haso and Prudence ter Brons Huizinga,' said Colin, 'my very good friends and I'm sure yours as well, my dear.'

Haso offered a hand. He was a tall man, fair-haired and blue-eyed and with commanding features, but his smile was nice. 'We are so pleased that Colin has married. I think that he is a very fortunate man, although I do not need to tell him that. When he comes to Holland you must come with him and stay with us.' He looked at Colin. 'There is a seminar in May, is there not?'

They made their way into the drawing-room and Eustacia said, 'I liked her; have they been married long?'

'Nearly two years. A well-matched pair, aren't they?'

They cut the cake presently and toasts were drunk, and after a while they found the guests began to leave. Eustacia started shaking hands all over again. All the people from the path lab had come; Miss Bennett in an awesome hat bade her a severe goodbye and observed, 'Of course it was obvious that you were quite unsuited for the job.' A remark which left Eustacia puzzled. Professor Ladbroke, on the other hand, gave her a hearty kiss, told her that she might find being married to Colin a good deal more exacting than cleaning bottles, and went on his way with a subdued roar of laughter.

As for Mr Brimshaw, she was touched when he said grumpily, 'Hope you'll be happy, Eustacia, you deserve to be.'

She thanked him, echoing the wish silently.

Prudence and Haso were among the last to leave and Colin and Eustacia accompanied them to their car, a dark grey Daimler. 'We're going back on the night ferry,' said Prudence. 'A bit of a rush, but I wouldn't have missed your wedding for the world.' She kissed Eustacia. 'I'm sure you'll both be very happy, just like us.'

Eustacia saw the tender look that Haso gave his wife and felt a pang of sorrow and a great wave of self-pity, instantly dismissed. She was Colin's wife now and all she had to do was to give him every opportunity to fall in love with her.

He showed no signs of doing so that evening though. They sat around, the bishop, Mrs Crichton, Mr Crump, Colin and herself, drinking tea and discussing the wedding until they dispersed to get ready for dinner, a meal Mrs Samways and Rosie had planned between them. Colin's best man, a professor of endocrinology from St Biddolph's, had driven back to town but would return for dinner and the party would be increased by the rector and his wife. The boys were to stay up and Eustacia urged them upstairs to wash their faces and brush their hair before going to her room to tidy herself. Even without the hat and the bouquet the dress looked charming.

She did her hair and her face and sat studying the plain gold ring under the sapphire and diamonds. At the moment she didn't feel in the least married.

They were all there in the drawing-room when she went down, drinking champagne cocktails, and the dinner which followed was a leisurely, convivial one. Rosie and Mrs Samways had excelled themselves: artichoke hearts, roast duck with ginger, followed by Cointreau mousse and a chocolate sauce and a splendid selection of cheeses. They drank champagne while the boys quaffed sparkling lemonade and then, pleasantly relaxed, they went back to the drawing-room where, after a short while, the boys said goodnight.

'I'll just go up with them,' said Eustacia, conscious of their wistful, sleepy faces as she ushered them to the door.

Colin opened it. 'Come down again, won't you?' he asked.

She gave him a quick smile. 'Of course.'

The boys were lively and still excited, but once they were in their beds they were asleep within minutes. She stood looking at them for a moment, the sight of their guileless, sleeping faces making sense of Colin and her marrying; they had lost the two people closest to them in their short lives and now they deserved some kind of recompense.

They sat around talking until late. The Samways and Grimstone and Rosie had been brought in to have a glass of champagne and to be complimented upon the dinner, and no one noticed the time after that. The rector and his wife were the first to go and after that the party broke up slowly until there was only Eustacia and Colin left.

Now, perhaps, thought Eustacia, we can sit quietly for half an hour and talk and get to know each other. She sat down opposite Colin and Moses pottered over to have his ears gently pulled. She was glad of that for she could think of nothing to say for the moment and Colin didn't seem disposed to speak. Presently she said brightly, 'It was a very nice day, wasn't it?'

Hardly the beginning of a scintillating conversation, but the best she could do.

'Delightful. You were a beautiful bride, Eustacia—the boys were enchanted. And it was pleasant to meet friends again; normally there isn't much time… I'm glad Prudence and Haso came; she's a darling.'

'And very pretty,' commented Eustacia, determined to be an interesting companion.

'You must be very tired—don't let me keep you up. Would you like anything else before you go to bed? A drink? Tea?' He gave her an impersonal, kindly smile and she managed to smile back, although her face almost cracked doing it.

'Nothing, thank you, and I am tired; you won't mind if I go to bed?'

He was already on his feet. 'Of course not. I must dictate a couple of letters and ring my registrar, something I should have done earlier.'

She swallowed chagrin. 'Oh, that would never do,' she said, her voice high with suppressed and sudden rage. 'You shouldn't let a little thing like getting married interfere with your work.'

She marched out of the room, whisking past him at the door. She was half-way up the staircase when he caught up with her.

'Now just what did you mean by that?' he wanted to know silkily.

'Exactly what I said; but don't worry, I'll be careful never to repeat it. But that is what I think and what I shall always think, although I promise you I'll not let it show.'

She went on up the stairs and he stayed where he was. At the top she turned round and went back to him. 'I'm sorry. I'm grateful to you for all that you have done for grandfather and me—I wouldn't like you to think that I'm not. But I did mean what I said, though it's my fault; you see, I thought we could be friends, share things… I'm making a muddle of it, though—I should have realised that there's nothing personal—it's as you said, an expediency. I'll remember that and I'll do my best to be a mother to the boys. That's what you want, isn't it?'

She didn't wait for his answer but ran back to the gallery and went into her room, where she stood looking at her trembling person in the pier-glass. For a girl who had set out to attract the man she loved, she had made a poor beginning. She took the pins out of her hair with shaking fingers, unfastened the pearls and took off the sapphire ring. She had made a mistake, she should never have consented to marry Colin, she should have turned and run at the sight of him. She undressed and lay in the bath for a long time; her usual common sense had deserted her, and all she could think of was how much she loved Colin and what she was going to do about it.

The cooling water brought her back to reality. 'Nothing,' she told herself loudly, and got out of the bath. She hadn't expected to sleep, but strangely enough she did.

Breakfast was reassuringly normal in the morning; the boys didn't go to school on a Saturday and they were excited at their uncle being at home until Monday morning and full of ideas as to what they should do.

'Shall we let Eustacia choose?' suggested their uncle and smiled across the table at her, quite at his ease. Not to be outdone, she smiled back.

'Oh, may I?' She glanced out of the window. It was a surprisingly mild morning. Do you suppose we might drive out to Cliveden and go for a walk in the grounds? I went once, years ago, and I loved it—we could take Moses too.' She looked round her, rather diffidently.

'Splendid,' said Sir Colin without hesitation, 'there are some lovely woods there, I could do with stretching my legs.'

The boys echoed him and Mrs Crichton said, 'It sounds lovely, but you won't mind if I stay here and do nothing?'

Mr Crump nodded at that. 'Yesterday was delightful, but a little tiring; I too would like to remain here.'

The professor was driving the bishop back to London during the morning; they expressed envy, agreed that it sounded a delightful way to spend a morning and accepted invitations to spend a weekend later on so that they could stretch their legs too, and everyone went their various ways.

They left half an hour later, having seen the bishop and the professor on their way, and made sure that Mrs Crichton and Grandfather were comfortably settled until lunchtime, and wrestled the boys into their outdoor things.

Eustacia, determined to fulfil the role she had promised to adopt, joined in the cheerful talk, and if she laughed rather more than usual no one noticed. It wasn't a long drive to Taplow. They parked the car in the grounds of Cliveden, got their tickets and a map of the routes they could take through the woods and set off with Moses on his lead and the boys running off the path to explore. Eustacia, walking beside Colin, kept up a cheerful chatter about nothing in particular—it was more of a monologue, actually, for he had very little to say in reply. Only when she paused for breath did he say quietly, 'I'm sorry if I upset you yesterday. It wasn't my intention. We have had no time to talk, have we? Perhaps this evening…? If we could start again with the same intention we had when we first knew about my brother and his wife?'

He had stopped for a moment, standing very close to her, and she longed to tell him that she had fallen in love with him and ask what she was to do about it. But of course she couldn't. Perhaps they could grow closer to each other through the shared aim of making the boys happy and making a home for them. She looked up into his face and saw that he was tired and worried.

She put a hand on his arm. 'We'll start again,' she told him, 'and I'm sorry too; I dare say it was getting married—it's unsettling.'

He smiled then. 'That is the heart of the matter,' he agreed. 'Perhaps we should forget about being married and return to our friendly relationship, for it *was* that, wasn't it?'

She nodded. 'Oh, yes.' She wanted to say a good deal more but she didn't, and after a moment he bent and kissed her. 'To seal our everlasting friendship,' he told her, and took her arm and walked on to where they could hear the boys calling to each other.

Chapter 6

Monday came too soon after a delightful weekend. Eustacia, conscious of her wifely status, got up early in order to breakfast with Colin. He was already at the table when she joined him, immersed in a sheaf of papers, and although he got to his feet and wished her good morning she saw at once that he would have preferred to be alone. She sat silently, drinking coffee, until he gathered up his papers and got to his feet.

'You have no need to come down early to share my breakfast,' he told her kindly. 'I'm poor company, I'm afraid. You've only had coffee, haven't you? You will be able to breakfast with the boys. I'll try and get down tomorrow evening and I'd be glad if you would come back with me—we have to see Mr Baldock and arrange for you to be made the boys' guardian.'

'Very well. How do I get back here?'

'I'll drive you back.' He laid a large hand on her shoulder and gave her an avuncular pat. 'I'll give you a ring this evening before the boys go to bed.'

Her 'very well, Colin' was uttered in what she hoped was the kind of voice a wife would use. 'I hope you have a good day; goodbye.'

His hand tightened on her shoulder for a moment and then he was gone.

The boys were full of good spirits, and she saw to their breakfast, drove them to school, assured them that she would collect them at four o'clock and drive them home, and then she went back to spend an hour with her grandfather before being led away by Mrs Samways, who, with an eye to the fitness of things, considered that Eustacia should inspect every cupboard in the house.

Colin phoned after tea and the boys talked for some time before calling her to the phone. 'Uncle's coming home tomorrow evening,' said Teddy. 'He wants to talk to you now.'

'It's me,' said Eustacia with a sad lack of grammar.

'The boys sound very happy. You've had a good day?'

'Yes, thank you.' Her loving ear caught the note of weariness in his voice. 'You're tired—you've had a lot to do?'

His chuckle was reassuring. 'No more than usual, and remember that I like doing it.'

She remembered something. 'Shall I have time to do any shopping when I'm in London? Mrs Samways wants some things from Fortnum and Mason…'

'We shouldn't be too long with Mr Baldock, so there should be time enough.' He added, 'I shall be home about six o'clock, Eustacia.'

'Oh, good.' She had no idea how delighted she sounded.

It was nearer seven o'clock by the time he arrived the next day, but the boys, bathed and ready for bed, had their supper while he talked to them until Eustacia shooed them upstairs, to tuck them up and potter quietly around the room until they were asleep.

They drove up to London directly after breakfast, taking the boys to school first, and they went straight to Mr Baldock's office. Eustacia signed papers, listened to what seemed to her to be a long-winded explanation of their guardianship by Mr Baldock, and presently left with Colin.

It was a fine morning even if chilly, and outside the office she paused. 'I can walk from here, it isn't far and it's a lovely day.'

He took her arm. 'I'm coming with you. I can park the car close by and I haven't any patients until eleven o'clock at my rooms.'

'Oh, that'll be nice.' She skipped into the car, feeling happy. It was going to be a lovely day…and not just the weather.

They strolled around Fortnum and Mason and

she bought the particular brand of marmalade and the special blend of tea Mrs Samways had asked for, and when her eye caught a box of toffees she bought them too. 'Teddy has a loose tooth,' she explained to Colin, 'and it's the best way of getting it out almost painlessly.'

They were going unhurriedly to the door when they were confronted by a small, slender woman with blonde hair, very blue eyes and a pretty, rather discontented face. She was dressed in the height of fashion and Eustacia thanked heaven that she had chosen to wear the tweed suit with a silk blouse and a pert little hat, all of them in the very best of taste and very expensive in an understated way.

Colin had stopped. 'Why, Gloria, how delightful to see you.'

He sounded far too pleased, thought Eustacia. 'I was so sorry you couldn't come to our wedding.' He smiled with charm. 'This is Eustacia, my wife; my dear, this is Gloria Devlin.'

They shook hands and smiled, and disliked each other at once. Gloria stared at Eustacia with cold eyes. 'My dear, how exceedingly nice to meet you, I have wondered what you would be like. Not in the least like me, but then it wouldn't do to marry an imitation of me, would it?' She laughed and Eustacia said gently,

'I should think it would be very difficult to imitate you, Gloria.' She allowed her gaze to roam over the woman's person, at the same time allowing her eyebrows to arch very slightly and her mouth to droop in a doubtful fashion. It had the effect she had hoped for—Gloria glanced uneasily at her flamboyant outfit and, since Eustacia's eyes had come to rest on her scarlet leather boots, bent her gaze on them.

Colin stood between them, a ghost of a smile on his bland face. He said now, 'You must come and see us soon, Gloria, must she not, Eustacia? We shall be up here from time to time—dinner one evening, perhaps?'

Eustacia smiled brilliantly. 'Oh, yes, do say you will come. Colin has your phone number, of course, and I'll give you a ring.' She glanced at her watch. 'Colin, you'll be late for your patient, we must go. It *has* been nice meeting you, Gloria—goodbye.'

'What a very pretty woman,' observed Eustacia, getting into the car. 'I'm only surprised that you didn't marry her.'

'The boys didn't like her.' His reply was most unsatisfactory. 'She is an old friend.'

'So I gather,' said Eustacia coldly.

She didn't see his smile. 'Perhaps you would like to come to my rooms and have a cup of coffee while I see my patients? Miss Butt, my receptionist, and Mrs Cole the nurse were at our wedding, and they would like to see you again.'

So Gloria was a closed book, was she? mused Eustacia, agreeing with every sign of pleasure.

The rooms were on the ground floor of a large Georgian house with several brass name-plates beside its elegant front door. He ushered her inside and Miss Butt, middle-aged, neat and self-effacing, and exuding a vague sympathy which must have been balm to such of his patients who were nervous on arriving or upset on leaving, darted forward to meet them.

'Sir Colin, will you phone the hospital—your registrar? Lady Malcolm is due in five minutes.'

Colin started for the door leading to his consulting-room. 'Thank you, Miss Butt; give Lady Crichton a cup of coffee, will you? And sneak one in to me after the first patient.'

There was a little room behind the waiting-room and Miss Butt ushered Eustacia into it. There was a small table and two comfortable chairs, a minute fridge and a shelf with an electric kettle and a coffee-making machine on it. Miss Butt got cups and saucers, sugar and milk and put them on the table and found a tin of biscuits.

'This is a pleasure, Lady Crichton, Mrs Cole and I did so enjoy your wedding, and, if I say so, you made a beautiful bride. Mrs Cole will be here in a minute or two but she won't be able to stay: she attends the patients while Sir Colin examines them.'

She poured their coffee and got up again. 'There's Lady Malcolm now. I won't be a tick.'

'I expect you have a very busy life here,' said Eustacia as Miss Butt sat down again.

'Indeed I do, and Mrs Cole too. Sir Colin works too hard, but I'm sure you know that. Going from a busy morning here to operate at St Biddolph's and then flying off heaven knows where to lecture or consult or address a seminar… There is no end to it.' She beamed at Eustacia over her spectacles. 'I dare say now that he is a married man he will cut down on some of these since he will want to be at home with you.'

'And Oliver and Teddy,' said Eustacia. 'They adore him and he's very fond of them.'

'The poor little boys. What a terrible thing to happen, but how wonderful that they have a home and two people to love them.'

She got up again as Lady Malcolm was shown out by the nurse, saying, 'I'll just pop in with Sir Colin's coffee,' and as she went out Mrs Cole came in. A small, stout lady in an old-fashioned nurse's uniform and apron, a starched cap on her greying hair.

'Well, this is nice,' she declared. 'We saw you at the wedding, of course, but there were such a lot of people there—Sir Colin has so many firm friends...'

The next patient came and went and Colin put his head round the door and said, 'Come and see my consulting-room, Eustacia.'

It was a restful place, like the waiting-room, soothing greys and a gentle green with a bowl of spring flowers by the window. His desk was large and piled with papers and she imagined him sitting at it, listening patiently to whomever was sitting in the chair on the other side of it.

This was a side of him she didn't know and she suddenly wished that she did. 'May I come to St Biddolph's one day—just to see where you work? The wards and the outpatients and the operating theatre, if that's allowed.'

'Of course it's allowed, if I say so.' He gave her a thoughtful look. 'You would really like to see everything there?'

She nodded. 'Yes, please. You see, if I know where you are, I can—' She stopped; it wouldn't do to let him think that she was deeply interested in everything he did.

He smiled a little. 'It is a strange thing, but I feel as though you have been my wife for a long time…'

'Oh, why do you say that?'

He grinned, sitting on the edge of his desk, his long legs stretched out before him. 'You behave absolutely exactly as one imagines a wife would behave. You have slipped into the role very neatly, Eustacia.'

That brought her up short. Of course, to him it was a role, not the real thing. She couldn't think of the right answer to that and presently he went on, 'We're invited to drinks at St Biddolph's—the medical staff and the cream of the nursing staff. Next Saturday—I accepted for us both. I thought we might bring the boys up in the morning and stay the night.'

'They would love that.'

'And you, Eustacia? Will you love it too?'

'Oh, yes. Although I am a bit nervous about meeting your colleagues.'

'Don't be. I'm sorry I can't take you to lunch. I'm operating this afternoon. Do you want a dress for the party on Saturday? I'll drop you off wherever you want to go…'

'Oh—well, yes, perhaps I'd better get something. Will it be very formal?'

'If you mean black ties, no, but the women will be wearing short party dresses. You know what I mean?'

She nodded, remembering the few happy years she had had after she had left school and travelled with her parents. There had been parties then…

'You will need some money. I'll arrange with Harrods so that you have a charge account, but perhaps you have some other shop in mind?' He gave her a roll of notes.

'I'm costing you an awful lot,' said Eustacia guiltily.

He smiled. 'Get something pretty, you have excellent taste.' He waited while she stowed the money away. 'Shall we go?'

She elected to get out at Harrods. It was a shop which had everything and she was sure to find something she liked; besides, she could have a snack lunch there.

'I'll be home around five o'clock,' said Colin as she got out of the car.

'Will you have had tea?'

'Oh, I'll get a cup at the hospital. Have yours when you like.'

He drove away without a backward glance and she had the lowering feeling that he had already forgotten her.

She took her time looking for a dress. It was after her lunch that she found it. Coppery autumn leaves scattered over a misty grey silk, its full skirt cleverly cut so that it swirled around her as she walked, the bodice close-fitting with a simple round neckline cut low, and very full elbow-length sleeves. It took almost all the money Colin had given her and was worth every penny of it. She bore it back to the house, tried it on once more, packed it carefully into its tissue paper, and went down to have her tea. Grimstone had set it on a small table by the fire and Rosie had made some little chocolate cakes to follow the strips of buttered toast.

She eyed everything happily. 'What a lovely tea, Grimstone, and how delightful those little cakes look.'

Grimstone allowed himself the luxury of a smile. 'Rosie thought you might like them, my lady. I'm told you will be here for the weekend with the young gentlemen. If there is anything special you would like to have you have only to say.'

'I'm sure Rosie must know better than I do what the boys like to eat, but I'll come and see her presently, shall I?'

She spent half an hour in the delightful kitchen, sitting at the table with Rosie while they discussed the merits of potatoes roasted in the oven and those baked in their skins. 'I'm sure the boys will eat them if they're smothered in butter,' said Eustacia. 'How about Sir Colin?'

'Well, he likes a nice roast potato, my lady, but I could do some of each…' They settled on a menu to suit everybody and Eustacia went back to the drawing-room, reflecting that, although she had found being called 'my lady' very strange at first, now she hardly noticed it. One could get used to everything, given time, even being married to a man who didn't love one.

Colin got back just before six o'clock. 'Give me fifteen minutes to shower and change,' he begged her. 'You're ready to leave?'

The traffic was heavy, but they got back to Turville before the boys' bedtime. Eustacia took her purchases to her room, did things to her face and hair and went downstairs to find Colin playing Snakes and Ladders with the boys and her grandfather. They looked up and smiled as she went in but returned to the game immediately, so that after a minute or two she went to the kitchen to see Mrs Samways and take her the things she had wanted.

'I'll keep dinner back until Sir Colin has gone, shall I?' asked Mrs Samways. 'Pity he can't stay the night. Always on the go, he is.'

Eustacia said faintly, 'Yes, isn't he? Do wait until he is gone if you can do so without spoiling anything. The boys will still have to go to bed…'

She went back to the drawing-room and found that the game was finished and Colin was standing with his back to the fireplace, his hands in his pockets. 'Ah, there you are,' he observed cheerfully. 'I'll be off again.'

'So Mrs Samways has just told me,' said Eustacia waspishly.

'The hospital board of governors are meeting this evening and they have asked me to look in—'

'Oh, yes? Where will you dine?'

'Rosie will find something for me.' He was still infuriatingly cheerful. He bade the boys goodnight, reminded them that he would be back on Friday evening, wished Mr Crump goodnight too and went to the door, sweeping her along with him. In the hall he asked, 'You're cross—why?'

'I am not in the least cross. After all, there is no reason why I should be told of your plans.' She made the remark with a cold haughtiness which would have shrivelled a lesser man.

He actually laughed. 'Oh, I am sorry, Eustacia. I am so used to a bachelor's way of living. I promise you I'll try to remember that I'm married now. No hard feelings?'

'No,' said Eustacia, loving and hating him at the same time, wondering if it would be possible to be out of the house with the boys when he got back on Friday evening. Serve him right. What was sauce for the goose was sauce for the gander.

'Expect me on Friday evening.' He gave her an avuncular pat on the shoulder and went out to his car and drove away with a wave of the hand as he went.

Standing in the doorway, she waved back, quite unable to see him clearly through the tears she was doing her best not to shed. She wiped them away roughly; the boys would have to be put to bed and they had sharp eyes.

It was during dinner that her grandfather asked, 'What's the matter, Eustacia?'

'The matter? Nothing, Grandpa.' She smiled at him. 'I expect I'm a bit tired—it was quite a long day and I went shopping and then Colin took me to his consulting-rooms…' She enlarged upon this for some minutes and her grandparent said,

'I dare say it is as you say, my dear. It is so peaceful here after Kennington, although I dare say Colin's house is quiet enough.'

'Oh, it is, not at all like the London we lived in.' She began to tell him about the house there and presently they parted for the night.

She was still determined to be out of the house when Colin got home on Friday evening. She was being unreasonably unkind, she knew that, but she wanted to do something to make him aware of her and chance was on her side. There was a bazaar in the village in aid of the church and at the end of the afternoon there was to be a conjuror, a treat the boys didn't want to miss.

'But will it be over before Uncle gets home?' asked Oliver.

'I'm not sure, but I don't think he will mind if we're home a bit late.'

Sir Colin got back earlier than he had expected; indeed, he hadn't stopped for the usual cup of tea after his list, aware of a desire to get to Turville as quickly as possible. He had told his registrar to phone him if it was necessary, made his excuses to Theatre Sister who had a tray of tea waiting in her office, and had driven himself off.

'Well, I've never known him miss his tea,' said Sister, much aggrieved.

'He's never been married before,' observed his registrar. 'She's a beauty—you'll see her on Saturday.'

The house was quiet as Sir Colin let himself in, and the drawing-room was empty. Mr Crump was in the library enjoying a good book, which he put down as Sir Colin walked in. He said in a pleased voice, 'Ah, you are home again. A busy few days, I expect?'

Sir Colin agreed amiably. 'Where is Eustacia? And where are the boys?'

'Oh, I dare say that they will be back at any moment; there was a conjuror's show in the village hall and she took them to see it.' He added, 'A treat, since they have done well at school this week.'

Sir Colin replied vaguely. He had telephoned Eustacia on the previous evening and she hadn't said a word about the conjuror. He began to smile and Mr Crump asked, 'You are pleased that they have done well?'

'Oh, most certainly. You'll forgive me if I go to my study and do some phoning?'

He was sitting in his chair, reading a newspaper with Moses lying on his feet when they got home. He received the boys' boisterous welcome with calm good humour, observing that they appeared to have had a most entertaining evening. 'And you enjoyed yourself too, Eustacia?'

'Oh, very much,' she assured him and smiled for the boys' benefit although her eyes were cool. 'Have you been home long?'

'I was early.' His smile was placid and she reflected that it had been a waste of time planning to annoy him. She doubted very much if she would ever get the better of him, and it was mortifying to realise that he had seen through her efforts to pay him back in his own coin.

The rest of the evening passed pleasantly enough. The boys had their supper, stayed up for an extra half-hour in order to play a boisterous game of Scrabble and went to bed, in due course, nicely tired and looking forward to their weekend in London. As for Eustacia, she entered into the conversation at the dinner table and then sat in the drawing-room, knitting sweaters for the boys while the two gentlemen went away to play billiards.

'For all the world as though we'd been married for half a lifetime,' she muttered to the empty room.

She was knitting, the outward picture of contented composure, when Sir Colin and her grandfather joined her. She looked up as they went in and enquired sweetly if they had had a good game. 'Would you like coffee? I asked Mrs Samways to leave some ready…'

They declined, and after ten minutes or so she stuck her ball of wool on to the ends of the needles and got to her feet. 'Then I'll go to bed.' She flashed them a brilliant smile and made for the door.

Colin got there first and laid a hand over hers. 'Will you spare a moment? I thought we might leave about eleven o'clock, have an early lunch and take the boys to Madame Tussaud's, and then go somewhere for tea. We'll need to leave the house at half-past six for the party—can you get them to bed and dress in an hour?'

'Just about.'

He nodded. 'Good.' He bent and kissed her cheek and then opened the door. 'I am so glad that you enjoyed the conjuror,' he murmured as she went past him.

The next morning went according to plan; a foregone conclusion, reflected Eustacia—plans made by Colin went smoothly and exactly as he wished. A light lunch was enjoyed by them all at the London house and very shortly afterwards the four of them piled into a taxi and were driven to Madame Tussaud's, a highly successful outing despite the frustrated wishes of the boys to view the Chamber of Horrors. The prospect of a splendid tea made up for this and they did full justice to the meal, served with great elegance in Claridge's Hotel; sandwiches, buns and small cream cakes were polished off with the assistance of a sympathetic waiter who produced an unending supply of delicacies and orange squash.

'Did we behave well, Eustacia?' asked Oliver as they got out of the taxi and went indoors.

'You were both quite perfect,' she declared. 'I was proud of you—weren't you, Colin?'

She turned to him and found him watching her with an expression which puzzled her. She forgot it once she was engulfed in the bustle of getting the boys to their beds, arranging for them to have milk and sandwiches once they were there and then going off to dress.

She had ten minutes to spare before they needed to leave; she went along to the boys' room and found them in their beds, demanding their supper. She promised to see Rosie on her way and hurry her up, kissed them goodnight and then, since they wanted it, paraded up and down the room in the new dress, twirling round so that the skirt billowed around her.

'Oh, very nice,' said Colin from the door, 'you will be a sensation.'

She came to a sudden halt. 'Don't be absurd,' she told him severely. 'I shall be very dignified…'

'Why?' He sounded amused.

'Well, consultants are dignified, aren't they? So I imagine their wives are too.' She added slowly, 'I think I'm a little nervous of meeting them.'

'No need. You look exactly as a consultant's wife should look.' He walked towards her and deliberately added, 'Elegantly dressed, beautiful and charming. I shall be the envy of all the men there.'

She blushed charmingly but looked at him uncertainly. He was probably being kind and bolstering up her ego. She said hesitantly, 'As long as I'll do…'

For answer he turned to the boys. 'Will Eustacia do, Oliver—Teddy? Will she be the prettiest lady there?'

They shouted agreement and he said, 'You see? Unanimous. We'll tell you all about it in the morning.'

The party was being held in the large room adjoining the consultant's room, a high-ceilinged apartment used for social occasions, meetings of hospital governors and other solemn events, and as they went in Eustacia had the impression that it was packed to the ceiling with people.

She felt Colin's hand, large and reassuring, on her arm as they made their way to where the hospital governors and his colleagues were waiting. After that, she began to enjoy herself. The men were plainly interested in her and their wives were kind. Presently she found that Colin had been surrounded by a group of older men and she was taken under the wing of the hospital secretary and passed from group to group. There were even a few people she knew: Miss Bennett and Mr Brimshaw and Professor Ladbroke, and in a little while Colin joined her, introducing her to a bewildering number of medical staff as well as the matron and several of the senior sisters. When the medical director called for silence, Colin took her hand and held it fast, which was a good thing, for the medical director, elderly and forgetful and of a sentimental turn of mind, made a long speech about the joys of marriage and young love before presenting them with a wedding gift. A silver rose-bowl which Eustacia received with a shy smile and a murmured thank you. It was left to Sir Colin to reply and anyone listening to him, she thought, would think that he was head over heels in love and blissfully happy. Indignant colour flooded her cheeks and everyone looked at her and smiled kindly, thinking that she was shy.

She smiled in return, while she reflected with something like dismay on a future full of pitfalls.

Marrying Colin for a sensible and good reason was one thing, but to have to enact a loved and loving wife for the rest of her days was suddenly unendurable, since he had shown no desire to have a loving wife, only a surrogate mother for his nephews.

They left soon after with enough invitations for morning coffee and dinner parties to keep them occupied for weeks to come. As they got into the car Eustacia said, 'You're very popular, aren't you, Colin?'

'I have been working at St Biddolph's for years,' he told her, as though that were sufficient answer, and then he added placidly, 'I dare say I should not have received half as many invitations if you hadn't been with me. I can see that you will be a great asset to me, Eustacia.'

She glanced at his calm profile. 'I shouldn't have thought that you needed assets.' She sounded very slightly cross.

'For some reason patients are much more at ease with their medical adviser if he is a married man.'

'What a good thing,' declared Eustacia sharply. 'I must bear that in mind.'

'Yes, do,' said Colin at his most bland.

The boys were still awake when they got back, so they said goodnight for a second time and then sat down to their dinner. 'Would you like to go out this evening?' Colin asked. 'A night-club or dancing?'

She took a mouthful of Rosie's delicious asparagus soup and thought about it. 'Unless you want to, no, thank you…'

'Oh, good. I seldom get a quiet evening at home. I can catch up on my reading, there may be something worth watching on TV, and there are several new novels you may like to dip into.'

But no conversation, thought Eustacia. 'It sounds delightful,' she said with what she hoped was suitable wifely acquiescence, and she quite missed the gleam of amusement in her husband's eye.

They went to the drawing-room and had their coffee and she chose a book and opened it, and Sir Colin, with what she imagined was a sigh of contentment, unfolded the evening paper. She had read page one and embarked on page two when the front doorbell pealed and she heard Grimstone's measured tread crossing the hall and then the murmur of voices. A moment later he opened the drawing-room door and announced, 'Miss Gloria Devlin.'

She came tripping into the room, a brilliant figure in a magenta silk trouser-suit with a black camisole top, and had begun to talk before Sir Colin had cast aside his newspaper and risen to his feet.

'My dears, I heard you were in town for the weekend and after that dreary drinks party at the hospital I knew you would be longing for a lively evening.' She paused as a youngish man came into the room. 'So Clive and I put our heads together and came round to collect you both. We can go to a nightclub…' She looked at Eustacia. 'You haven't met Clive, have you? He's a scream and such good fun.'

'How delightful to see you, Gloria,' Sir Colin was at his most urbane, 'and so kind of you to think of us.' He nodded at her companion. 'Do come in and have a drink. Unfortunately we have other plans for the evening, so we must refuse your invitation, but stay for a while. Sit here, by the fire, Gloria. What will you drink?'

'Oh, my usual, vodka—you surely haven't forgotten after all these months?' She gave a little tinkling laugh and Eustacia wanted to box her ears.

Sir Colin made no answer to this but poured her drink and turned to the man. 'And you, Stevenson?'

'Whisky, thanks.'

'You haven't met my wife, I believe?' went on Sir Colin smoothly. 'Eustacia, this is Clive Stevenson, he runs a clinic for plastic surgery.' He added, 'Would you like a drink, darling?' He smiled across the room at her. 'Perhaps you had better not, since we're going out again.'

She smiled back. 'I don't want anything, thank you, dear.' She turned to Gloria. 'I didn't see you at St Biddolph's this evening.'

'Me? Go there? It's the last place that I'd set foot in. Clive heard about it from one of the doctors there—he anaesthetises for him. Clive has a huge practice making tucks and face-lifting. He alters shapes too…' She gave Eustacia's person a penetrating look, but since there was nothing wrong with it she remained silent, but Stevenson chimed in with a laugh,

'No good looking at our hostess, Gloria, she looks perfect to me.'

Eustacia gave him a look to freeze his bones and

glanced at Sir Colin. His face was without expression but his mouth had become a thin line.

'You must forgive us,' he said in a voice which conveyed the fact that he had not the least interest in their forgiveness. 'We are due to leave in a very short time and I must phone to the hospital first.'

Gloria pouted. 'Oh, Colin, how dull of you to go off on your own, just the two of you—we could have had such a good time.' She cast a sly look at Eustacia. 'As we used to…'

Sir Colin took no notice of this remark and she shrugged her shoulders and got up. 'Oh, well, we might as well go and leave you to your domestic bliss.'

Eustacia got up too. 'So kind of you to call in,' she said sweetly, 'I hope you will have a pleasant evening.'

'I'm sure we shall.' Gloria's voice was just as sweet. 'Though I rather think our ideas of a pleasant evening aren't the same.' She tripped over to Sir Colin and leaned up to kiss him, then grabbed Clive's arm. He had gone over to say goodbye to Eustacia and Gloria gave him a tug. 'Come on, Clive, it's me you are taking out.' She gave another of her irritating trills of laughter. Eustacia watched them go and stood listening to them talking to Colin in the hall, wondering what they were saying. A pity the door was almost closed…

Sir Colin came back presently and picked up his paper. Eustacia addressed the back of it. 'I am sorry if it's inconvenient to you, but I do not like your friends,' she observed waspishly, 'at least, some of them.'

He lowered the paper and looked at her over it. 'Hardly friends—I don't care for Stevenson—'

'She kissed you…' She hadn't meant to say that and she frowned furiously.

'I have yet to meet a man who didn't enjoy being kissed by a pretty woman.' He spoke with maddening calm, but his eyes beneath the heavy lids were watching her cross face with hidden amusement.

It seemed impossible to get the better of him; there was no answer to that. She put down her book and rose with dignity. 'The prospect of looking at the back of your newspaper for the rest of the evening leaves me with no alternative but to go to bed. Goodnight, Colin.'

She sailed to the door and most unfortunately tripped up as she reached it; he was just in time to set her on her feet again, making no effort to let her go. 'Thank you,' she said coldly. He smiled down at her.

'Crosspatch.' The kiss he gave her would, in the right circumstances, have been very satisfying.

Chapter 7

Eustacia lay awake for a long time; a good weep had done very little to relieve her feelings, and the evening's events were going round and round in her head until they were in such a muddle that she had no clear idea of what she was thinking about any more. She slept at last and woke in the morning with the lowering feeling that she had behaved badly. She dressed and went to see how the boys were getting on and presently they all went down to breakfast. There was no one at the table but, looking out of the window, they could see Sir Colin in his small garden. He had Moses with him and Madam Mop was sitting on the edge of a stone bird-bath, watching them. The garden was charming, ringed around by a variety of small trees and a high brick wall, with a patio outside the house, a small lawn in its centre and flower-beds bordering the narrow paths. In another week or so there would be daffodils everywhere and, later, tulips. Sir Colin was crouching over a centre bed, planting bulbs, and the boys lost no time in opening the french window and rushing out to join him.

Eustacia watched while they gave him a hand; they were talking nineteen to the dozen and getting in the way of their uncle, and she very much wanted to join them. She was feeling awkward about meeting Colin again after the previous evening; she had been insufferably rude and, not only that, his kiss had taken her by surprise, leaving her uncertain and more in love with him than ever, a state of affairs which wouldn't do at all. She was roused from her unhappy thoughts by Rosie's voice.

'Catch their deaths out there,' she said, 'and breakfast all but on the table, too.'

'I'll call them in,' said Eustacia hastily, 'but it's not cold, is it?' She turned to smile at the housekeeper.

'Well, not so's you'd notice, my lady, but there's good hot porridge waiting to line their stomachs.'

Eustacia said, 'Oh, good, Rosie,' and opened the french windows again and yelled, 'Breakfast—now, this instant!'

She watched them go in through the garden door and presently they came into the dining-room. 'Did you wash your hands?'

They chorused a yes and Sir Colin said meekly, 'I washed mine too. Good morning, Eustacia.'

Her good morning was drowned by the boys' demands to know what they were going to do all day. 'Sit down, eat your porridge and I'll tell you,' said Sir Colin. 'Church?' He cocked an eyebrow at Eustacia, who nodded without hesitation. 'St Paul's, I think, don't you? And afterwards we'll cross the river and drive and find somewhere for coffee before we come back here for lunch. How about an hour or two at the zoo before tea? And then we'll go back to Turville.'

This programme was greeted with approbation by the boys and, after they had made a hearty breakfast, Eustacia led them away to be tidied and fastened into their coats, while Sir Colin wandered off to appear in a short time suitably attired in a dark grey suit and beautifully polished shoes.

'I like that outfit,' he told Eustacia, who was waiting for him in the hall, and to her great annoyance she blushed.

The vastness and magnificence of St Paul's Cathedral did much to soothe her. She listened to Teddy's shrill voice piping up when he knew the hymns, Oliver's more assured treble and Colin's deep rumbling bass and, since it was expected of her, joined in with her own small, clear voice.

They found somewhere to have coffee after the service, and then went home to Rosie's Sunday dinner of roast beef, Yorkshire puddings, roasted potatoes and sprouts, cooked to perfection, and followed by a trifle which was sheer ambrosia.

They wasted no time in going to the zoo, and Eustacia was glad of that. There had been no opportunity to be alone with Colin, let alone talk to him; they had the boys with them all the time and when they got home they had tea together, a substantial meal of Marmite on toast, sandwiches and chocolate cake.

It was as they were on the point of leaving after this meal that Grimstone asked, 'At what time will you be back, Sir Colin? Rosie will have a meal ready for you…'

'No need,' he replied, shrugging himself into his coat. 'I'll have dinner at Turville. Go to bed if I'm not back, Grimstone, but see that I'm called at seven o'clock tomorrow morning, will you?'

Grimstone inclined his head in a dignified manner, wished them all a safe journey and they got into the Rolls and drove away.

The boys, in the back with Moses, carried on the kind of conversation normal for small boys, but Eustacia sat silent, racking her brains for a suitable topic of conversation and, since the man beside her remained silent too, presently she gave up searching for a harmless subject, so that they gained Turville with no more than the odd remark exchanged. But once in the house there was a welcome bustle and a good deal to talk about for Mr Crump wanted to know about their weekend and Mrs Samways wanted to know about the boys' supper.

That attended to, Eustacia went to her room, tidied herself and went back downstairs to warn Mrs Samways that Sir Colin would be staying for dinner.

'I thought he might, my lady. Me and Rosie, we're used to him coming and going, as it were, though I dare say now he's settled down he'll get a bit more regular in his ways, if you don't mind me saying so.'

Eustacia assured her that she didn't mind in the least. 'Though I dare say it will take a little time to adjust, Mrs Samways.'

'No doubt, my lady, but you'll attend to that, I'll be bound.'

Eustacia agreed, thinking that it would be very unlikely, and went to preside over the boys' supper and then to get them bathed and into their beds. They were tired and went willingly enough after protracted goodnights to their uncle.

Once they were settled she went along to her room and changed her clothes. There was a rather nice Paisley-patterned dress hanging in the wardrobe which hadn't been worn yet. She put it on and was pleased with the result; Colin might even notice...

They had drinks and then dined, the three of them, and the conversation was of nothing in particular; indeed, she had the suspicion that Colin was encouraging her grandfather to reminisce so that conversation between the two of them was unnecessary, and very soon after they had had coffee he declared that he had to get back. 'I've a round at eight o'clock tomorrow,' he explained, 'and a list after that, but I'll try and get down in a couple of days.'

Eustacia went out into the hall with him and stood watching him while he got into his coat.

'We're bound to get some invitations to dine,' he told her cheerfully, 'but I'll ring you each evening and we can decide what to do about them.'

'Very well. And if there are any messages for you?'

'Oh, let Grimstone know, he'll find me and pass them on.' He broke off as Samways came into the hall. 'Samways, tell Mrs Samways that dinner was excellent, will you? Lady Crichton will let her know when I'm coming down again—in a day or so, I hope.'

Samways inclined his head gravely, wished him a good journey and withdrew discreetly.

Eustacia waited until he had shut the door behind him. 'I cannot think,' she declared pettishly, 'how it is that you manage to have such willing staff at both your homes. Some of the wives I met at the party were saying that they couldn't get anyone, not even cleaning ladies.'

He ignored the pettishness and answered her seriously. 'I pay them well, I house them well, I give them due credit for work well done, just as I hope that my patients give me credit when I succeed in making them better.' He grinned suddenly. 'And I inherited Grimstone.'

She felt foolish and muttered, 'Oh, yes, so you did,' and looked away from his amused glance and raised eyebrows. She had been silly to talk like that and now she suspected that he was laughing at her.

'Take care of the boys,' he said gently, 'and take care of yourself.'

She nodded, hoping that he would kiss her, but he smiled again and opened the door and was gone.

She went to bed presently, a prey to highly imaginative doubts as to where Colin had gone and what he was doing. Gloria loomed large, set against a background of exotic night-clubs and restaurants with pink-shaded table-lamps. After all, she told herself worriedly, Colin had never actually said that he hadn't been, at some time, in love with Gloria—he might still be, although she was quite sure that now he was married he would give her up—although in this modern world, she reflected gloomily, it would be quite permissible for him to continue to be friends with the woman. From what Gloria had said, they had known each other for a long time. She went to sleep at last, having convinced herself that the pair of them were in some remote restaurant, looking into each other's eyes and breaking their hearts silently. She woke once in the night and it all came flooding back, more highly coloured than ever. 'I hate the woman,' said Eustacia angrily before she went to sleep again…

The day seemed endless; she did flowers, talked to her grandfather, discussed the meals with Mrs Samways and ferried the boys to and from school. By eight o'clock, she had given up hope of Colin telephoning.

It was almost ten o'clock when he did, and quite forgetful of her role of concordant partner she snapped, 'It's almost ten o'clock—you're late.'

Sir Colin thought of his busy day, not yet over, but all he said was, 'Is there something worrying you?' and that in the mildest of voices.

'No, but you said—'

He said smoothly, 'I am not always able to keep to an exact timetable, Eustacia.'

She said recklessly, common sense quite drowned in vivid imagination, 'I suppose you've been out to dinner with—with someone?'

Sir Colin, who had got through his day on a sandwich and a beer and a cup of tea forced upon him by his theatre sister, said equably, 'If that is what you think, my dear, who am I to deny it?' He laughed suddenly. 'You have Gloria in mind?'

Eustacia put down the receiver with a thump and burst into tears.

She felt terrible about it in the morning; she had been a fool and behaved like a silly, jealous schoolgirl, probably he would never want to see her again, she was utterly unsuitable as his wife and she had made a hash of being married to him. With a great effort she managed to behave normally towards the boys, listening to their ideas about the Easter holidays, now looming. 'It would be nice to go away on holiday,' said Teddy, 'but it might be cold at the seaside.'

She agreed that it certainly would be. 'But there are heaps of other things we can do,' she promised. 'Perhaps your uncle will be able to spare the time to take you to see your Granny.'

Teddy liked that idea. 'But perhaps we'll have to go and stay with Granny and Grandpa Kennedy,' he said worriedly. 'I don't want to.'

'I dare say you would have a lovely time—'

'Only if you and Uncle Colin are there too.'

'Well, no one has said anything about it, my dear, so we don't need to think about it, do we?'

'All right, when is Uncle Colin coming home?'

Eustacia said in an animated voice, 'Oh, he rang up last night, quite late, and he had been very busy—he didn't say.'

'I hope he'll come soon,' said Oliver, 'in time for the end-of-term concert.'

'He'll come just as soon as he can,' said Eustacia, dreading the idea and longing to see him just the same.

He came that evening, between tea and dinner, while Eustacia was sitting at the small table in the sitting-room, helping Oliver with his history and encouraging Teddy to write tidily in his copy-book. The three of them were so engrossed that they didn't hear Sir Colin's quiet entrance until his equally quiet, 'Hello, there.'

The boys flew to greet him, both talking at once, and he listened patiently to a jumble of information about school and the holidays and the last day of term, and would he be there because Oliver had to recite a poem and Teddy was singing a song with six other little boys?

Eustacia had time to look at Colin as he bent his height to the little boys' level. He was tired, and his handsome looks showed lines of fatigue, but he answered the boys' excited questions, came to the table to look at their homework and bent to drop a quick kiss on her cheek. 'Perhaps the boys could go and tell Mrs Samways that there will be one more for dinner,' he suggested placidly. 'I don't need to go back until tomorrow morning.'

They pranced off with Moses in close attendance and he sat down at the table facing Eustacia.

'You and I have to talk,' he said quietly, 'but not now. Perhaps we can present a suitable front for the sake of the boys in the meanwhile.' And as they came running back again, 'I shall certainly be here for the end of term and I heard from Mother yesterday—she would like us to spend a few days with her during the holidays. I can manage four or five days.'

Teddy had climbed on to his knee and Oliver had got on to the chair beside him. 'Your Granny and Grandpa Kennedy have asked if you would go and stay with them. I said that I would ask you. I know you don't want to go very much, but it might be fun, and Eustacia and I will drive you up and come to fetch you home, so will you go?'

They looked at him and then at Eustacia. 'Just a week?' she coaxed.

They nodded reluctantly and Sir Colin said, 'Good chaps.' Then he added, 'And when you come home we'll do something really exciting—you shall choose.'

'May we stay up and have our supper with you?' asked Teddy.

'I think that's a splendid idea, if Eustacia agrees.' He looked at her with raised eyebrows and a smile and she said at once,

'Oh, I don't see why not, but it might be a good idea if they have their baths now and get into their pyjamas and dressing-gowns so that they can pop into bed directly after dinner.' She got up. 'I'll let

Mrs Samways know…' She smiled at the three of them, not quite looking Colin in the eye.

Dinner over and the boys in bed and the three of them in the drawing-room, she handed Colin several envelopes. 'These came—invitations—two for dinner and one for drinks; they're all in town. What would you like me to reply?'

'Oh, we'll accept, shall we?' He glanced at them in turn. 'The dates won't interfere with our visit to Castle Cary. I met Professor Ladbroke this morning and I told him that a couple of weeks' time would suit us—the boys will be in Yorkshire and we can stay in town if we feel like it.' He looked at Mr Crump. 'You won't mind, sir?'

'My dear Colin, I am in my seventh heaven here.'

'I'm glad.' He handed the invitations back to Eustacia. 'Will you answer them? I dare say there will be more. It might be a good opportunity to give a dinner party while the boys are in Yorkshire—in town, I think, don't you? You too, of course, sir.'

'That would be delightful, but I wouldn't wish you to feel compelled to invite me.'

'You need have no fear of that; I don't see enough of you—of any of you.'

His glance lighted upon Eustacia who, with her knitting in her lap, had been watching him. They stared at each other for a long moment before she picked up her needles and began to knit furiously.

The house came alive when he was at home, but once he had gone again in the morning it sank back into its peaceful state. Eustacia was glad when the boys were back from school in the afternoon, taking her attention so that she had little time to think.

School was to break up at the end of the week, and the evening before Sir Colin came home. He would have to go again on the Monday morning, he explained, but only for a few days and then they would all go to Castle Cary. His manner towards Eustacia was exactly as usual, placid and friendly, and she did her best to respond for the sake of the boys.

They all went along to the school in the morning, Sir Colin in one of his sober, beautifully tailored suits and Eustacia very smart in a new grey suit and a silk blouse and, since it was an occasion, a grey felt hat with a small brim turned up at one side. Before they left she was inspected by the boys, who pronounced her very nicely dressed. 'You'll be just like all the other Mums,' said Teddy, and his small lip quivered.

Eustacia flung an arm round his narrow shoulders. 'Oh, good, darling, and just look how smart your uncle looks. We both mean to be a credit to you, and I can't wait to hear you sing.'

Teddy sniffed. 'I do love you,' he whispered.

'And I love you, Teddy...'

'And do you love Oliver and Uncle Colin too?'

'Yes. That's what a family is, you see, people living together and loving each other, just like all of us.'

She kissed the upturned face and Sir Colin, who had heard every word, sighed gently.

The day was a great success; Teddy sang in his choir, Oliver recited his poem and they all watched the short play put on by the older boys before the buffet lunch. Once home again, their reports were studied and discussed and suitably rewarded with loose change from Sir Colin's pocket. 'Eustacia and I are very proud of you both,' he told them.

When Oliver asked, 'As proud as Daddy and Mummy would have been?' he answered at once.

'Just as proud, are we not, darling?'

He looked at Eustacia, who blushed because he had called her darling even though he hadn't meant it. 'Oh, rather—I've been thinking, on Monday suppose we drive over to Henley and buy the Easter eggs? We shall need to make a list—a secret list, of course.'

They had tea round the fire for the days were still chilly, and after the boys were in bed they dined and made plans for the next week or two.

'I'll be back here on Thursday,' said Sir Colin. 'We can go to Mother's on Friday and stay until the middle of the week, perhaps a little longer. The Kennedys expect the boys on the Sunday after that, we'll drive them up and have lunch on the way and go straight back home for the night so that I can check on one or two things. Shall we say Monday evening for our dinner party?' He fished in a pocket and studied the list in his hand. 'Eight guests, I thought, if you're agreeable.' He read out names: colleagues and their wives and the hospital matron to partner Mr Crump. Eustacia, who had half expected to hear Gloria's name, sighed with relief.

Sunday went too swiftly and she watched the Rolls slide round the corner of the drive with a pang of unhappiness which she shook off at once. The little boys had had enough unhappiness of their own, and it behoved her to show a cheerful face.

Surprisingly the days went by quickly, and Sir Colin was back once more and this time for a week at least. She packed happily, bade her grandfather goodbye and got into the car with the boys and Moses in the back, and with them there it was easier to be on friendly terms with Colin. There was a good deal of talk and giggling as they travelled and it would have been impossible not to have joined in the fun. They stopped in Hindon at the Lamb Inn for their lunch and, because Colin said it would be good for them to stretch their legs, they walked Moses down the village street and back again before driving on. It was a matter of half an hour later they drew up before Mrs Crichton's house in Castle Cary. Martha had been watching out for them and had the door open before they could reach it, and their welcome from Mrs Crichton was full of warmth. There was a good deal of milling around and happy chatter before Eustacia was led upstairs with the boys darting to and fro and following at their heels.

'You are in your usual room, my dears,' said Mrs Crichton. 'Eustacia, you are next door to them.' She led the way into a charming, moderately sized room overlooking the garden at the back of the house. 'The bathroom is through that door and Colin's dressing-room is beyond that. I do hope you will be comfortable. It's so delightful having you all. Are the boys happier now? Have they settled down?'

Eustacia was looking out of the window; Colin was in the garden with Moses. 'Very nearly. Oliver seems to have got over it better than Teddy, but, of course, Teddy's younger. Sometimes they wake in the night, you know…'

'And what do you do, my dear?'

'Cuddle them and let them cry if they want to, and then we talk about their mother and father and all the nice things they remember.'

Mrs Crichton nodded. 'I understand they are to go to Yorkshire next week. A pity.'

'Mrs Kennedy is anxious to have them. We're going to take them up and then fetch them again.'

'You and Colin will have a few days together—that will be very nice.'

'Oh, very,' said Eustacia, and some of the happiness she felt at the thought bubbled up into her voice so that her companion gave her a quick, thoughtful glance.

The next few days were sheer delight; Mrs Crichton was a splendid granny, mixing mild authority with a grandparent's legitimate spoiling. They all went out every day—Cheddar Gorge and the caves, Cricket St Thomas to see the animals and sample the simple amusements for the children, Glastonbury and its Tor. Mrs Crichton declined to climb its steep height but the boys, with Eustacia and Colin following more sedately, did. When they got home each afternoon Martha had a magnificent tea waiting for them and that was followed by an hour or so in the drawing-room, with Moses dozing at Colin's feet while they played Snakes and Ladders and Beat your Neighbour and the memory games. Sir Colin always won—he seemed to know exactly where the cards were. Eustacia, regrettably, was quite unable to remember where the cards were, but that was because her thoughts weren't on the game but centred on Colin sitting, large and relaxed, so close to her.

The last day of their visit came, and they bought presents for the Samways and the maids, and for Grimstone and Rosie, presented Mrs Crichton with an armful of roses and Martha with a box of chocolates, had a last walk down the high street and got into the car with the promise that they would pay another visit just as soon as it could be arranged. Half-term, as Sir Colin pointed out in his placid way, was a bare two months away, and it would be early summer. The boys brightened at the thought, hugged their grandmother once more and settled down in the car with Moses perched between them.

They were home in time for tea, and Eustacia, mindful of their trip to Yorkshire in three days' time, disappeared as soon as the meal was over to confer with Mrs Samways about washing and ironing and the clothes the boys should take with them—something which suited her very well, for she was becoming far too fond of Colin's company.

He drove himself up to the hospital the next morning, saying he would be back that evening. But five o'clock came and then six o'clock, and just as she was getting the boys ready for bed he telephoned. Something had come up, he told her; he would be delayed, and it might be better if he stayed in town for the night.

'Very well,' said Eustacia in a matter-of-fact voice which hid her disappointment, 'I'll explain to the boys.'

'And you?' enquired Sir Colin gently. 'Am I to explain to you, Eustacia?' And when she remained silent, 'Or don't you want to know why I'm staying here?'

She said primly, 'I'm sure if it is necessary for you to stay that is sufficient reason—you have no need to tell me anything you don't wish to.' Upon which unsatisfactory conversation she hung up, after wishing him goodnight in a voice straight from the deep-freeze.

The unwelcome shadow of Gloria hung over her as she prepared for bed and caused her to lose quite a lot of sleep so that she was hard put to it to be her usual cheerful self in the morning. Luckily she was fully occupied for most of the day, seeing to the boys' clothes ready for their journey to Yorkshire, and they spent a good deal of their time with her grandfather, but by teatime there was nothing left to do and she was sitting with them in the drawing-room, watching Samways setting out the tea, when Sir Colin walked in.

He crossed the room to her chair and bent to kiss her cheek before returning to the boys' excited welcome and her grandfather's sober one.

Eustacia was grateful for the excited talk from the boys so that there was no need for her to say much, which was a good thing for she could think of nothing to say. She had been longing for Colin to come home and, now that he was here, she was dumb. She thought with excited pleasure of the week ahead—a whole week, the greater part of it in London. She would have the opportunity of getting to know him, perhaps.

They had tea, had a rousing game of Scrabble with the boys before the youngsters went off for their supper and bed and then she went back to the drawing-room. Sir Colin was alone.

'Can you spare half an hour?' he asked her. 'About tomorrow—it will take about five hours to drive to Richmond. We'll go up on the A1, I'll cut across country to Bedford and pick it up a few miles further on from there. The M1 would be quicker but it's very uninteresting for the boys to be on it all day. We'll stop for lunch on the way and get there around tea-time. Would you be too tired if we drove back that evening? We can come back straight down the M1 and be home by midnight. We can stop on the way for a meal.'

Eustacia agreed quietly and hoped she didn't look as excited as she felt. He poured drinks and came and sat down again. 'The dinner party is on Monday, isn't it? We'll fetch your grandfather up to town in the afternoon, and if he doesn't want to stay I'll drive him back the same night. I dare say you might like to stay in town for a couple of days? I have a list on the Tuesday, one I can't put off, but I thought we might go to a theatre on the Wednesday if you like and drive back to Turville that evening and stay there until we fetch the boys back on Sunday.' He was watching her carefully. 'Unless there's anything else you would rather do?'

'It sounds delightful, and I shall enjoy a day's shopping.' She added silently, But not half as much as I shall enjoy being with you, my dear.

They were away before nine o'clock the next morning, stopping for coffee just before they joined the M1 and then driving fast up the motorway. They stopped in Wetherby and had lunch at the Penguin Hotel and, since the boys had grown a little silent at the idea of parting, the meal was a leisurely one with the talk centred on what they would all do when they got back home again, with a few tactful remarks about the pleasures in store for them with their grandparents.

The children had been there before with their parents, brief visits of a day or so, but they had no lasting memories of them.

'Isn't there a castle there?' asked Eustacia. 'A ruined one, I mean. Did you go there?'

Oliver nodded. 'We went twice. I liked it...'

'So did I,' said Teddy. 'Mummy and me found a little hole like a cave and we hid.' He gave a prodigious sniff and Eustacia said cheerfully,

'It sounds fun. Will you buy a postcard and write to us? There'll just be time before we come again. I'm sure your granny will help you with the address. I dare say she will have all kinds of surprises for you.'

The Kennedys lived in a Victorian redbrick house

on the edge of the town; it had high iron railings and a short drive to the front door, and the curtains at its sashed windows were a useful beige of some heavy material. The front door was large and had coloured-glass panels and was opened by a thin woman with an acidulated expression who gave them a grudging good-day and led them across the dark brown hall.

The Kennedys were waiting for them in a large, high-ceilinged room, as brown as the hall and filled with heavy furniture. Eustacia, snatching a quick look, thought that everything had cost a great deal of money and was of the very best quality even if gloomy.

They were welcomed with meticulous politeness before Mrs Kennedy swooped upon the boys to hug and kiss them and then burst into tears. Eustacia stole a look at Colin's face and saw that he was angry, although he said nothing, only when there was a chance suggesting that the boys might like to see their rooms before they had tea. 'Eustacia will unpack for them,' he added. 'I'm sure that you have enough to do, Mrs Kennedy.'

Mrs Kennedy wiped her eyes with a wisp of handkerchief. 'Oh, indeed I have; the planning and shopping I have had to do, you have no idea. The boys are in the room at the back of the house if you'd like to take them up…'

They were shown the way by the thin woman, who opened a bedroom door for them and went away again without a word and Eustacia, making the most of things, went over to the window and said, 'Oh, look, what a lovely view of the town, and surely that's the castle? And what a lovely big room.'

She sounded enthusiastic but her heart sank at the sight of the two small faces looking up at her. She sat down on one of the beds and caught them close. 'Darlings, this time next week we'll be in the car and Uncle Colin will be driving us all home. Don't forget to write, and do you suppose you could send a postcard to Grandfather Crump?' She opened her handbag. 'And here's some pocket-money; I know Uncle has given you some already, but you'll want to buy presents—don't forget Mr and Mrs Samways and Rosie and Grimstone.'

They helped her unpack and then the three of them went downstairs again.

Tea had been set on a table on Mrs Kennedy's right, and her husband and Sir Colin were sitting opposite her. Colin got up as they went in and Mrs Kennedy uttered an awkward little laugh. 'Oh, I hadn't expected Oliver and Teddy to have tea with us, but of course they shall if they like to. I'm not used to small children. Come and sit down, dears.' She looked at Eustacia. 'Perhaps you would ring the bell there by the fireplace and we'll have more cups and plates.'

The boys sat one on each side of Eustacia, balancing plates on their small, bony knees, and she was thankful that they had had a hearty lunch, for tea was a genteel meal of thin bread and butter and slices of madeira cake.

'The boys will have their supper before they go

to bed,' observed Mrs Kennedy. 'I'm sure Cook has something special for them.' Eustacia hoped so too.

They said goodbye presently with a false cheerfulness on Eustacia's part and near tears on the part of the boys. Sir Colin put a great arm around their shoulders. 'Look after each other,' he begged them, 'and remember about all the things you see so that you can tell us next week.'

His goodbyes to the Kennedys were very correct and he listened with every sign of attention to Mrs Kennedy's gushing account of the pleasures in store for the boys. 'They won't want to leave us,' she cried playfully, and then said a cold goodbye to Eustacia. Her husband had very little to say; Eustacia hoped that he would let himself go a bit and be good company for the boys.

She sat very still beside Sir Colin as the Rolls slid out of the drive. She hated leaving the boys and she wanted quite badly to cry about it.

She said in a rather shaky voice, 'They're not going to like it there. I do hope their granny doesn't keep crying over them, and the house is so—so very brown.'

Sir Colin laid a large hand briefly on the hands in her lap. 'I know. I hate the idea of their being there, but we have no right to prevent them going to stay with their grandparents; they must get to know them as well as they know my mother.'

'Yes, but she loves them and they love her, you know they do.'

She sniffed dolefully, and he said comfortably, 'A week soon passes, my dear.'

They were on the A1 again and then the M1, travelling fast. At Lutterworth they stopped at the Denbigh Arms and had dinner, then they drove on. The motorway was fairly empty and they made good time; well before midnight he stopped the car outside their home and Samways, appearing silently, opened the door and offered hot drinks and sandwiches.

Sir Colin glanced at Eustacia. 'Ah, Samways, good of you to wait up. A pot of tea, I think, and one or two sandwiches. We'll be in the small sitting-room.'

Samways made his way to the kitchen where Mrs Samways was waiting, ready dressed for bed in a red woolly dressing-gown. 'Tea,' said Samways, and gave his wife an old-fashioned look. 'Mark my words, Bessie, Sir Colin's head over heels even though he may not know it. Tea—I ask you—him drinking tea at this hour of the night?'

'And very right and proper too,' said Mrs Samways, arranging sandwiches on a plate. 'It's time he was a family man.'

Sir Colin put an arm round Eustacia's shoulders. 'Tired? It has been a long day.'

'I enjoyed it, though I hated leaving the boys. Do you suppose they'll be all right?'

They sat down opposite each other with Moses in between them.

'Provided Mrs Kennedy doesn't weep all over

them. I know she must miss her daughter and grieve for her, but it is hardly fair to inflict her grief upon the two small boys.'

They drank their tea, not talking much, and presently Eustacia said goodnight and took herself off to bed. 'It was a lovely day,' she told him. She would have liked to have said a great deal more than that, but the bland look upon his face stopped her just in time.

They drove up to town after lunch the next day and after they had telephoned the Kennedys. The boys were out walking, they were told, and had settled down very well.

'They slept well?' asked Eustacia.

'Of course they slept well.' Mrs Kennedy sounded quite put out and Eustacia felt it necessary to make soothing sounds by way of apology. With that they had to be content.

Grimstone admitted them, assured them that everything was in train for the dinner party and bore Mr Crump off to his room while Sir Colin disappeared into his study and Eustacia, after tidying herself and unpacking her overnight bag, went to talk to Rosie in the kitchen. They had discussed the menu at some length and now she was assured that everything was going well. The sorrel soup, the grilled trout with pepper sauce, the fillets of lamb with rosemary and thyme and the chestnut soufflé with chocolate cream were in various stages of cooking and Rosie herself would see to the dinner table. In the meantime tea would be taken into the drawing-room whenever it was wanted.

'Oh, then now, I think, Rosie, and you and Grimstone have yours before you have to go back to the cooking.'

The guests had been bidden for eight o'clock. Eustacia, wearing a new dress—a pleasing mixture of blues and greens in soft silk—went downstairs to check the dining table and then join the men in the drawing-room.

'Nervous?' asked Sir Colin as she went in. 'You shouldn't be, you look quite delightful.'

A remark which seemed a good augury for the evening. As it was, Eustacia went to bed that night feeling pleased with herself; it had been highly successful, conversation had never flagged and she had liked her guests. Moreover Colin had been pleased with her and her grandfather proud of her. The two gentlemen had driven off to Turville after the guests had gone and she had waited up until Colin had come back. His casual, 'Still up?' rather dampened her good spirits, but she said in her usual quiet way, 'I was just going to bed. Will you be at the hospital all day tomorrow?'

'Yes, it's quite a heavy list and I've one or two private patients I must see first.'

She nodded and smiled in what she hoped was a wifely fashion. She had hoped that he might have remembered his promise to take her round the hospital one day, but obviously that wouldn't be possible. She wished him goodnight, agreeing pleasantly that if he found himself unable to get home in time for dinner she was to dine alone.

'You won't mind too much?' he wanted to know.

'Me, mind? Not at all.' She smiled charmingly as she escaped upstairs, but he didn't miss the sharp edge to her voice.

She went shopping in the morning and got home for a late lunch. She had put away her purchases and sat down with a book until teatime when the phone rang. Mrs Kennedy's voice, thick with emotion, shrilled in her ear. 'He's run away, the silly child—you should have sent a governess or someone with them, I've never—'

Eustacia cut her short, ice-cold fingers running up and down her spine. 'Teddy or Oliver? And when? Mrs Kennedy, pull yourself together and tell me plainly what has happened.'

'That is no way to speak to me… Teddy, of course—oh, some time this morning, he had been rude and I corrected him,' her voice rose, 'and Oliver slapped me—he's in his room, the naughty boy.'

'Who is looking for Teddy?'

'My husband is searching the streets. Of course the child isn't far—he can't be, probably he's just hiding.'

Eustacia choked back a rage she didn't know she possessed. 'You are to let Oliver out of that room at once, Mrs Kennedy. Tell him I'm on my way to you and so is his uncle.' She put down the receiver since there was no point in wasting time with Mrs Kennedy, and then she dialled St Biddolph's. Sir Colin wasn't available, she was told, he was in theatre, but the porter obligingly put her through to the theatre block. A rather timid voice answered her and, when she said who she was, vouchsafed the information that Sir Colin had just started to operate and was expected to be in theatre for at least another three hours.

'The same case?' asked Eustacia.

'Yes, Lady Crichton. Do you want me to get hold of someone? I mean, I'm only a first-year student.'

'He mustn't be disturbed, but when he is finished I want you to tell him to ring his home the minute he is free, tell him it's urgent. Don't forget, will you?'

She went in search of Grimstone next and thanked heaven that he was quick to understand. 'I want a car,' she told him, and, 'When Sir Colin rings please tell him exactly what I have told you. If he wants to call the police he'll do that. Now, a car—'

'The Mini is in the garage, my lady, I'll fetch it round while you collect up your things. Which way will you go?'

'Up the M1 as far as possible.' She flew up to her room and found a coat and stuffed money into her handbag, and when she got down to the hall there was Rosie with a Thermos flask and some scones in a bag. 'No time for any sandwiches,' she explained as Eustacia got into the Mini. Eustacia glanced at her watch as she drove away. She had only one thought: to get to Richmond.

Chapter 8

Eustacia concentrated on getting out of London as quickly as possible, not allowing herself to think of anything else, but once clear of the city she had time to reflect. She began to wonder if she had done the right thing. Should she have told the police? But surely Mr Kennedy would do that? And would Colin be angry with her for not letting him know immediately? On the other hand, he couldn't stop in the middle of an operation and just walk away from the patient, and it must have been major surgery if it was going to last for so long. In any case, there was no point in indulging in hindsight now; she was committed to drive to Richmond and find Teddy, and hopefully Colin, when he learned of what had happened, would know exactly what to do. 'Oh, my darling, if only you were here,' she said loudly. 'And I'll shake that awful Mrs Kennedy until her dentures rattle when I see her—shutting Oliver up. She has absolutely no idea how to be a granny.'

The Mini scooted along and thankfully the tank was full; upon reflection she decided that Colin's cars would always be ready to get into and drive. A splendid man, she thought lovingly, only she wished she knew what he was thinking sometimes behind that calm face of his. Perhaps it was as well that she didn't.

She was on the M1 now, keeping the little car at seventy but driving carefully too. She glanced at the clock and was surprised to see that it was almost six o'clock—it had been some time after half past three when Mrs Kennedy had telephoned and it would be another hour before Colin came out of theatre, and in that time she would be well on her way. If she could keep up the pace until she reached Leeds she had a good chance of getting to Richmond soon after dark. The thought cheered her and she began to think about Teddy. He might, as his grandmother seemed to think, have hidden in some nearby garden or shed, or he could have wandered into a shop... She frowned—as far as she could remember there had been no shops close to the house. At least it wasn't on a main road and the traffic along it had been light. The moment she got there she was going to question Oliver, since he was the most likely to know where Teddy had gone. A faint memory stirred at the back of her head and became all at once very clear. They had been talking about the castle at Richmond and Teddy had told her about a cave there where he and his mother had been. If he was lonely and unhappy, might he have tried to find it? It was a shot in the dark but at least it was something to start with. Possibly the police would have found him by now, in which case should she take the boys back with her? But then Colin would have telephoned… She had told Mrs Kennedy that he would drive up to Richmond, but that had been a spur of the moment remark as much to give herself comfort as Mrs Kennedy. If he were free he would have come, she was sure of that, but he had a responsibility to his patients too.

It had been a dull day and dusk was falling early, but she was nearing Leeds and there were only around seventy miles left to go. She had to slow down now for it had begun to rain from low-lying clouds, but it was no good getting impatient; she kept on steadily, watching the miles go by with what seemed like maddening slowness. When she reached the outskirts of Richmond it was nine o'clock and quite dark. She couldn't remember exactly where the Kennedys lived—she had to stop twice and ask the way, and it was with a great sigh of relief that she finally turned into the short drive and stopped before the door. There were lights on in the downstairs rooms but the curtains were drawn. She thumped the knocker and the thin woman came to the door.

Eustacia walked into the hall. 'Where is Mrs Kennedy? Is Teddy found?'

'In the dining-room.' The woman opened a door and ushered her in.

Mr and Mrs Kennedy were seated at the table, eating their supper. There was no sign of Oliver. It was no time for good manners. 'Where is Teddy? And Oliver…?'

Mr Kennedy had got to his feet but his wife remained seated. She said, 'Oliver is in bed, of course. Teddy hasn't come back yet but he can't be far away—several people have seen him during the afternoon. Mr Kennedy has been out all day looking for him—he is exhausted, and although I mustn't complain I am severely shocked.'

Eustacia let that pass. 'The police? Are they searching for Teddy?'

'We thought we would wait until the morning,' said Mr Kennedy. 'After all, they can't do much now that it is dark, and since Teddy has hidden away twice already in the garden and across the road in the house opposite, that's where he'll be now.'

'How can you sit there—?' Eustacia choked back rage and walked out of the room and upstairs to the room where the boys slept. Oliver was there, a small, wretched heap in his bed, and she went straight to him and put her arms around him. 'It's all right, love, I'm here and I'll find Teddy and I'm quite sure that your uncle will be here just as soon as he can. Have you any idea where Teddy could be?'

Oliver shook his head, and his voice was tear-sodden. 'He ran away and hid twice and Grandmother was very cross…'

'Why did he run away, darling?'

'Grandmother keeps talking about Mummy and crying and saying how we couldn't have loved her because we're happy with you and Uncle Colin. We do love her, but we love you too.'

'You can love any number of people for the whole of your life, that's the nice thing about it. So, now we know why he ran away—you were shut up, weren't you? Was that after he disappeared?'

'I tried to go after him, but you see Grandmother was so unkind to Teddy and I smacked her, so I was shut up here and then someone came and unlocked the door.'

Eustacia got off the bed. 'Now, love, I want you to be very brave and stay here and if—no—when your uncle comes tell him that I've gone to the castle. I've an idea, perhaps it's a silly one, but it's worth a try. Don't tell anyone else where I've gone.' She kissed him. 'Are you hungry?' and when he nodded, 'So am I—famished. As soon as Teddy and Uncle Colin are here we'll find something to eat.'

She tucked him into bed and slipped quietly out of the house. Apparently no one was in the least interested in her movements. She didn't take the car—it was a small town and it didn't take her long to walk to the other end and take the path to the castle, a gloomy pile against the cold night sky. She had had the wit to take the torch from the car, and she was glad of its cheerful light as she approached the ruins. Nasty ideas concerning ghostly figures, tramps and thieves on the run flitted through her head but she kept on, moving into the shadow of the ancient walls.

She hadn't the least idea where to look. She crept around, her teeth chattering with cold and fright, and finally came on to an outer wall overlooking the river below. There was a railing, but she swallowed panic and started to walk its length. Halfway along, a narrow opening led to an inner wall and then a whole series of ruined walls, and she stood there still shining her torch and calling Teddy softly by name. There was no answer and she stood irresolute, wondering what to do next, where to go. She swept the beam of her torch around her and then held it steady. A little to one side of her there was a low opening, and through it she could just glimpse a small foot clad in a red sock and a stout little shoe. Teddy.

He was asleep, the deep, sound sleep only small children enjoyed—she could have walked round blowing a trumpet and he wouldn't have stirred. But he was cold and he had been crying. She wedged herself in beside him and put a careful arm round him while she thought what to do.

She would have to wake him up and probably carry him to start with until he had warmed up a little. When she got him back to the Kennedys, should she put him to bed? And would they let her stay the night? And perhaps give her some supper? Her insides were woefully empty.

She caught her breath at a whisper of sound somewhere out there in the ruins and clutched Teddy more tightly. It could be a tramp, a desperate man hiding, a ghost—there must be hundreds in a place as old as this, she thought wildly and then gave a great gulp of relief as a voice she longed to hear said placidly, 'Hello, my dear. Oliver gave me your message.' He crouched down beside her and dropped a kiss on her cheek and laid a gentle hand on Teddy.

Eustacia sniffed away a great lump of tears in her throat. 'They said you'd be hours in theatre…didn't you operate after all?'

'Oh, yes. I flew up here.'

Her tired, grubby face broke into a wide smile. 'Oh, Colin…'

He smiled slowly. 'Yes, well—later. Let us get this young man into his bed and reassure Oliver.'

'Can't we go home?'

'In the morning, my dear. There is a good deal of talking to be done first. We must talk too, you and I.' He scooped up the sleeping Teddy. 'Can you manage? Take the torch and go ahead of us.'

Going back was easy because Colin was there. They left the dark ruins behind them and went through the quiet town until they were back at the Kennedys' home.

Mrs Kennedy met them in the hall. 'Well, where did you find him? Not far away, I'll be bound. Bring him in here—'

'He needs to go to bed at once,' said Sir Colin in a firm, detached voice which Eustacia had never heard before. 'Will you send someone up with warm milk for the boys? Are there electric blankets? No? Then hot-water bottles if you please.'

He went upstairs with the sleeping Teddy and Eustacia trailed behind. Oliver was awake, sitting on top of his bed wrapped in a blanket.

'You said Uncle Colin would come and he did,' he told Eustacia. 'Can we have supper now that Teddy's back? He must be awfully hungry.'

'He will be when he wakes up. I'll find something as soon as I can, my dear.'

Sir Colin had put Teddy on his bed and was taking off the boy's shoes. Teddy began to sit up and stir and then whimper, and Eustacia said matter-of-factly, 'Hello, there. Wake up, darling, we're all dying for our supper.'

Someone knocked on the door and the thin woman handed her a tray with two glasses of milk on it.

'Well, it's a start,' said Eustacia and gave one to Oliver before starting to undress Teddy.

There was another knock on the door; this time it was Mrs Kennedy. 'There's nothing wrong with him, is there? He ran away to annoy us, I have never been so upset—'

'Could we have something to eat?' asked Eustacia baldly.

'It's gone ten o'clock, Cook will be in her bed and Mary only stayed up to oblige me—just in case you came back, as I knew you would. Such a fuss—'

'We shall do our best not to inconvenience you, Mrs Kennedy. Eustacia and I will sleep here with the boys and leave in the morning, for that seems the best thing to do, does it not? Perhaps later, in a month or two when you feel stronger, they can pay you another visit.' Colin spoke pleasantly but Mrs Kennedy took a few steps back to the door. 'Don't worry about food, we shall be quite all right.'

When she had gone Eustacia said with a hint of peevishness, 'It may be all right for you, but the boys and I are starving— '

'So am I. Get the boys sorted out, I'm going off to buy fish and chips.'

He was a man in a thousand, she reflected, watching his broad back disappear through the door. She had the two boys in their beds by the time he returned, carrying a large newspaper parcel and with a bottle under one arm. He sat down on Teddy's bed and portioned out the food, found two tooth-glasses in the bathroom and opened the wine. Eustacia gave a rather wild giggle. 'If you read this in a book you wouldn't believe it...'

'Who wants books?' Sir Colin handed her a glass. 'Drink up. The boys can have some too.'

She ate a chip with enormous pleasure. 'Look, what do we do? I mean, tonight? And isn't anyone going to explain anything?'

He waved a fishy hand. 'You are, for a start. Try and begin at the beginning and tell me everything.'

Between mouthfuls she gave him a brief and sensible account of what had happened. He nodded when she had finished. 'Now, you, Oliver, tell us just what went wrong.'

Oliver was sleepy, but he managed very well. Eustacia kissed him and told him what a good, brave boy he was and he fell asleep with the suddenness of a child. Teddy, awake now and eating his supper with gusto, was rather more difficult to understand but presently Sir Colin said, 'I think I have enough now. I'm going downstairs to talk to Mr Kennedy.' He put a hand on Eustacia's shoulder. 'I'll be back.'

Teddy was asleep before she had tidied away the fishy newspaper. She perched on his bed, leaning her head against the headboard, and since she was tired out she closed her eyes.

It was almost an hour later when Sir Colin returned. He stood looking down at Eustacia, dead to the world, her head lolling sideways against the bedhead, her pretty mouth half open. He put out a hand and shook her gently awake and she shot upright at once, letting out a protest at a stiff neck and a stiff shoulder.

'Sorry,' said Sir Colin, 'but you can't sleep like that all night. I've had a talk with Mr Kennedy; he agrees with me that perhaps the best thing is for us to take the boys home in the morning.' His voice was dry and she wondered what had passed between the two men. 'I suggested that we might all come up again later in the year,' and at the look on her face, 'Yes, I know, but we have to try again. In the meantime that sour-faced woman has been prevailed upon to make up the beds in a guest room. I'll sleep there with Oliver, you stay here with Teddy.'

'Yes, but I haven't anything with me—no toothbrush, or soap or nightie…'

He brushed this protest to one side. 'There will be soap in the bathroom, you can clean your teeth with the children's toothpaste and your finger and you don't need a nightie…' He bent down and kissed her cheek, a light, comforting kiss. 'Get to bed, my dear, you've had a worrying time. You'll feel better in the morning and we'll all be laughing about it.'

He scooped up Oliver and went away without another word, leaving her to undress slowly, and after a sketchy wash she got thankfully into Oliver's bed, intent on sorting out her muddled thoughts. She was asleep within a couple of minutes.

She could have slept the clock round, but Teddy woke at around six o'clock and promptly burst into tears. She got into bed with him and cuddled him close. 'She said we didn't love Mummy any more, she said we'd forgotten her and Daddy, but we haven't, and she smacked me and Oliver tried to explain and she took him away so I ran out of the house… I went to the castle…'

'Yes, darling, I know. I guessed you would go there and that's why I came to find you, and Uncle Colin brought us both back here.'

'He's here, Uncle? May we go home?'

'As soon as we've had breakfast. Now, will you go to sleep for a little while? I'll be here; I'm going to get dressed presently and then you shall dress too.'

Teddy slept then and in a little while she got up, swathed herself in the coverlet off Oliver's bed and went in search of a bathroom. The house was quiet and she ran the bath stealthily, did the best she could with her teeth and, feeling guilty, dried herself on a splendid towel which she rather thought was there on display rather than for use. Wrapped once more in the coverlet, she stole back to the bedroom, dressed and did her face and hair and, since it was well after seven o'clock, wakened Teddy.

Oliver and Sir Colin were in the bathroom, Oliver in the bath and his uncle at the washbasin, shaving himself. Eustacia said good morning, urged Oliver to get out to substitute Teddy in the bath, then wrapped Oliver up in the towel, now very damp, and asked, 'Where did you get that razor?'

'From my bag. You're up early.'

'I've been up since before seven o'clock—I had a bath. Isn't there another towel? This one's sopping.' She rubbed Oliver briskly before turning her attention to Teddy, reflecting that it was all so extraordinary, like *Alice in Wonderland*, and yet she didn't feel that everything was unusual, just quite normal.

She got Teddy out of the bath and rubbed him as dry as she could and Sir Colin observed, 'Do I have to dry myself on that towel? You'd better wring it out first.' He let the water out of the bath and turned on the hot tap, sitting on the side of the bath in his trousers and nothing else, quite at ease. Eustacia caught his eye and began to laugh.

'It just isn't true,' she gurgled, 'I mean, things like this just don't happen.' She put toothpaste on the children's toothbrushes and stayed sitting on the side of the bath beside Colin. 'How will you get home?'

'In the Mini, of course.'

'Four of us and the luggage?'

'Why ever not? It will be a trifle cramped, but I

don't suppose the boys will mind.' He turned off the tap and she got off the bath, collected the boys and marched them off to get dressed. They were in high spirits, and presently when Sir Colin joined them, looking as well turned out as he always did even though there were tired lines in his handsome face, they all trooped downstairs. Mr Kennedy came into the hall as they reached it.

His good morning was stiff. 'Our housekeeper has very kindly risen early and has prepared your breakfast.' He looked at the two boys. 'I'm afraid that your grandmother is so upset by your behaviour that she is forced to remain in bed; she is a very sensitive woman and the shock has been great.'

Eustacia had her mouth open to ask what shock; Colin's firm hand, pressing her shoulder gently, stopped her in time.

'I think we have all had a shock,' observed Sir Colin in what she privately called his consultant's voice, and just for a moment Mr Kennedy looked embarrassed. She wondered what Colin had said on the previous evening.

They went into the dining-room, which was brown like all the other rooms, and heavily furnished, sparing no expense, with dark oak. The table had been laid and they sat down to boiled eggs, rather weak tea and toast. The sour-faced woman was doubtless glad to see them go, but she wasn't going to speed them on their way with bacon and eggs.

The boys bade their grandfather a polite goodbye and he shook their small hands, observing that he hoped that the next time they met it might be in happier circumstances. 'Your grandmother is going to take some time to recover…'

Eustacia went very red in the face with rage—her wish to comment upon this was great, but she had once more encountered a glance from Colin. It was a speaking glance and she closed her mouth firmly and choked back the words she had wished to utter. It was a relief to get outside and get the boys settled in the back of the Mini while Colin saw to their luggage. Mr Kennedy stood in his doorway, making sure that they were going, she thought, and an upstairs curtain twitched. Mrs Kennedy was making sure too.

She got into the car and Colin got in beside her.

'Rather a tight fit,' he said. 'Fortunately we're all on speaking terms.' A remark which made the boys laugh their heads off, but they waved obediently to their grandfather as they drove away and Eustacia had a pang of pity for him; Mrs Kennedy wasn't the easiest of wives to live with.

'I hope I never get like that,' she said, speaking her thoughts aloud.

'You'll not get the chance,' said Colin, uncannily reading her mind. 'Have you enough room?'

She said yes happily, although his vast person had overflowed on to her. She would get cramped before long but she really didn't mind. She turned her head to look at the boys. They beamed back at her and Oliver said, 'That was a beastly breakfast—we're hungry.'

'We'll stop at the service station at Ferrybridge

before we get on to the M1.' Sir Colin glanced at Eustacia. 'Comfy?'

She nodded. 'It's fun, isn't it? I shall have very hot coffee and hot buttered toast.' She sighed. 'There's such a lot to explain it's hard to know where to begin.'

'Time enough when we get home,' he said comfortably. 'Let's have a day out.'

They were on the A1 now, and she had to admire the way he handled the car, keeping up a steady pace, taking advantage of any gap in the stream of early-morning traffic. The boys kept up a constant stream of talk and she hardly noticed the miles passing until she was aware of him slowing into the service station and parking the car.

The Little Chef was half full, warm and welcoming. They sat round the table, contentedly drinking their coffee and orange juice and eating hot buttered toast, and presently Sir Colin got up. 'I'm going to telephone your grandfather,' he told Eustacia, 'and Samways and Grimstone. We'll go back to the town house this evening and go on to Turville in the morning.'

Eustacia, who would happily have spent the rest of her life in a high-rise flat with him, nodded happily.

The boys had recovered completely. 'We knew you'd come,' sighed Oliver, 'only Teddy couldn't wait...'

'That's all right, love, we quite understand,' said Eustacia, 'and you see how quickly Uncle can get to you when you need him. I should never have thought of hiring a plane.'

'That's because you're a girl,' said Oliver. 'Did you mind driving the Mini all by yourself?'

His uncle had sat down again and passed his cup for more coffee. 'I dare say she minded very much, but she was anxious to get to you. When you have to do something important you don't think about anything else.' He smiled at her. 'We shall have to think of something nice to do by way of a thank you.'

'A day at Cricket St Thomas,' said Teddy eagerly, 'you'd like that, wouldn't you, Eustacia?'

'Or Longleat with the lions,' suggested Oliver.

Sir Colin was looking at Eustacia intently. 'That sounds splendid,' he observed, and unusually for him he hadn't heard a word the boys had said. Nor had Eustacia—she was far too busy trying to look nonchalant even while the colour flooded her face. There was something in his look which had set her heart thundering against her ribs in a most unsettling manner.

They packed themselves back into the Mini presently and drove on.

'Since we're having a day out we might as well have lunch somewhere,' observed Sir Colin, a suggestion with which they all agreed enthusiastically.

They stopped in Madingley, a charming little village of thatched cottages not far from Cambridge. The restaurant was housed in an oak-panelled and beamed cottage and the food was England's best—steak and kidney pie, vegetables from the garden and apple tart and cream for a pudding. Over a large pot of coffee Eustacia said, 'That was a gorgeous meal—what a lovely day we are having.'

She had addressed the boys but she was conscious of Colin's eyes on her.

'We must do this more often,' observed Sir Colin. 'Supposing we drive over to Castle Cary and see Granny—we'll go to Turville tomorrow and go the day after, just for lunch and tea. How would you two like to have her to stay for a week? I'm going over to Holland in two weeks' time and I thought I'd take Eustacia with me. We can stay with friends and she can see something of the country while I'm lecturing.'

The boys chorused their approval and Eustacia said primly, 'If that is an invitation, yes, I shall enjoy going to Holland.'

They were getting into the car again and Colin turned from fastening the seatbelts. 'Haso and Prudence are looking forward to seeing you again, and I promised I'd bring you with me next time I went to Holland.'

A remark which effectively quenched any ideas she might have had about him wanting the pleasure of her company.

A dignified Grimstone was waiting for them when they reached London. And for once he was smiling broadly. 'There's tea ready for you,' he told them. 'Rosie's been cooking and baking…' His elderly face creased suddenly. 'A nasty shock it was, to be sure.'

Eustacia took his hand. 'Grimstone, you have no

idea how lovely it is to be home again to such a welcome. We can't wait for Rosie's tea…'

She led the excited boys up to their room, tidied them up and sent them downstairs, then went along to her own room. She looked awful, she decided, examining her face in the looking-glass—no wonder Colin hadn't had much to say to her; her face was pale with worry and lack of sleep, and her hair needed attention. She washed her face and put on make-up again and brushed her hair and then, suddenly impatient, went downstairs.

Sir Colin came in from the garden with Moses as she went into the drawing-room and thought that she had never looked so beautiful…

They ate a splendid tea with Moses, pressed against Sir Colin's leg, gobbling up odds and ends of cake and sandwiches, and Madam Mop enjoying a saucer of milk under the table. By common consent they didn't talk about Yorkshire; Sir Colin had telephoned Mr Crump and told him what had happened with the promise that they would all return to Turville in the morning and, since the boys were tired now, Eustacia got them ready for bed and then sat them down to their supper. She was tired herself; once they had had dinner, she would go to bed. Colin was already immersed in the various letters and messages that had arrived for him; he wasn't likely to miss her.

The boys tucked up and already half asleep, she had a shower and changed into a dress and went downstairs to find that Colin had changed too. He put down the letter he was reading and fetched her a drink before sitting down by the log fire.

'There hasn't been the time or the opportunity to tell you how grateful I am to you for your part in this unfortunate incident. You must be tired and quite worn out with the worry of the whole thing. Do you feel you can tell me about it? Mr Kennedy wasn't very forthcoming yesterday evening; according to him, Teddy had been a little monster and Oliver not much better. I don't believe that, of course…'

Eustacia took a very large sip of sherry. 'They didn't have their meals with Mr and Mrs Kennedy; they had to have them in the kitchen, and each morning Mr Kennedy took them for a walk and then they went back to spend half an hour with their grandmother, who talked about their mother all the time, telling them that they must never forget that she was dead… How could she?' Eustacia polished off the sherry and set the empty glass down on the table beside her chair. Sir Colin got up and filled it again without a word and she went on. 'Of course they won't forget their mother and father and they'll go on loving them, but they can be happy too—how could she be so unkind, loading them down with her own grief? And why can't she love them? As your mother does…she's a wonderful granny.'

Eustacia drank the sherry at one go and sat back, a little bemused from the two glasses one on top of the other. Sir Colin watched her with hidden amusement. 'Indeed she is. Tell me, Eustacia, will you enjoy coming to Holland with me?'

'Oh, yes, only don't you think I should stay with the boys?'

'No. My mother and your grandfather will enjoy being in charge. I phoned her just now, and she's delighted with the idea. She is also looking forward to seeing us all tomorrow. Have the boys all they need for school next term? Do you want to bring them up to town to buy things? They're due back on Thursday next week, aren't they? I've a list on the following day—you said you wanted to see round St Biddolph's, so you can visit the wards while I'm in theatre.'

'Oh, may I?' She sat up, happy that he had remembered after all. 'And may I go into the operating theatre so that I know where you work?'

'No. You can look through the door but no more than that. Here is Grimstone to tell us that dinner is ready.'

Very soon after their coffee she pleaded tiredness and he showed a disappointing lack of desire to keep her from her bed. She wished him goodnight in a chilly voice and cried herself to sleep.

In the morning she took herself to task—she was allowing her dreams to cloud reality and she would have to stop. She was brisk and chatty at breakfast so that Sir Colin glanced at her once or twice in a thoughtful fashion; he had never known her any more than quiet and matter-of-fact with an occasional flash of temper. But this wasn't temper, he decided, it was an act she was, for some reason best known to herself, putting on for his benefit.

He sighed, for once unsure of himself.

The visit to Castle Cary filled the next day most successfully; the boys, once they were there, had a great deal to tell their grandmother and she listened carefully before summoning Martha. 'Will you take the boys across the street and let them choose some sweets?' She handed over some money. 'And they might like to buy a comic each.'

When they had gone she settled back in her chair. 'Now let me hear the whole story,' she begged. Sir Colin told her, with Eustacia sitting quietly, her hands in her lap, saying nothing at all.

'Very unpleasant,' commented his mother finally. 'Poor children. It was splendid of you to go after them, Eustacia, and to find Teddy.'

Eustacia spoke then. 'With hindsight, I can think of lots of ways of getting them back. It would have been just as quick to have waited for Colin to finish in the theatre; he got there almost as soon as I did.'

'Just as quick, but without heart. You knew he would follow you?'

'Oh, of course.' Eustacia smiled at Mrs Crichton and the older lady nodded and smiled too.

'Just so.'

They left soon after tea, racing smoothly back to Turville, and Eustacia allowed her mind to brood over the evening ahead. Grandfather would be there, which would make it easier to ignore the invisible barrier which had reared itself between her and Colin. She tried to think how it had happened, but she couldn't put a finger on the exact moment when she'd realised that it was there. Had she said something, she wondered, or far worse, had she allowed her feelings to show?

She was aware of it during the evening; Colin was friendly and perfectly willing to talk, but only about things which had nothing to do with them personally, and so it was until he went back to London on Monday, reminding her laconically that he would be at her disposal on Friday. 'I shall start my list at eleven o'clock—I'll come for you about half-past nine, if you can be ready by then?'

'Of course I can,' said Eustacia loftily. 'The boys have to go to school at half-past eight.'

They parted coolly, although Eustacia didn't remain cool for long; Gloria telephoned during the day, intent on seeing Colin. 'That Grimstone of his says he doesn't know where he is—I suppose he's there with you?' complained Gloria.

'No, he isn't. Probably he's operating at another hospital if he's not at St Biddolph's. Can I give him a message?'

Gloria chuckled. 'You sound too good to be true! Don't worry, I'll find him.' There was a little pause. 'I always do.'

Eustacia was ready and waiting when Colin arrived on Friday morning. She had dressed with care: a leaf-brown suit, a silk blouse the colour of clotted cream and simple but perfect gloves, shoes and handbag. She thought for a long time about a hat, and in the end she settled for a supple, small-brimmed felt, worn quite straight. It gave her dignity, or she hoped it did.

Colin wished her good morning pleasantly, took in her appearance with one swift glance, remarking that she looked just the thing, and swept her into the car. 'No time to waste,' he pointed out as he called goodbye to Mr Crump, who had come to wave them off.

'Which reminds me,' said Eustacia with icy sweetness. 'Your friend Gloria telephoned yesterday. She assured me that she would find you. I hope she did.'

'Do you really?' He sounded interested and amused. 'I must disappoint you. What did she want?'

'You,' said Eustacia waspishly.

He said nothing until he came to a lay-by, where he stopped the car and turned to look at her. 'You have allowed your imagination to cloud your good sense,' he told her calmly. 'I have taken Gloria out once or twice but no more than other women of my acquaintance—that was in my bachelor days and a perfectly normal thing to do, you must allow. I am not in love with her, nor have I ever been. Satisfied?'

She wanted to say no, but she said yes instead and they drove on, she a prey to unhappy thoughts, he apparently perfectly at ease.

As they entered the hospital he took her arm. He was a rather grave, well-dressed man, self-assured without being pompous about it; she couldn't fail to see the deferential manner with which he was greeted as they made their way to the theatre block. They went through the swing-doors and he stopped for a moment, looking down at her. 'You were in a bunched-up pinny,' he observed, 'you were very earnest and I suspect a little scared. You were beautiful, Eustacia, just as you are now.'

She gaped up at him, her eyes wide. 'Well—' she began and was interrupted by Sister's approach.

'There you are, sir,' said that lady briskly, 'with your lady wife too. Shall we have a cup of coffee before you start your list? I've got Staff Nurse Pimm to take Lady Crichton round the hospital. If you haven't finished shall she go to the consultant's room or come back here?'

'Oh, here, I think, Sister.'

She nodded. 'They've slipped in that case who wasn't fit for surgery yesterday—you might be a little later than you expect.'

'That can't be helped, can it?' he said pleasantly as they wedged themselves into Sister's office to drink Nescafé and eat rich tea biscuits and talk trivialities.

Presently a head appeared round the door to utter the words, 'Your patient's here, sir,' and Sir Colin got up.

'I'll see you presently, darling,' he said and followed Sister out and away through another door, leaving Eustacia in the care of a small, plump girl who beamed at her widely and asked where she would like to start.

The morning went swiftly; Eustacia poked her pretty nose into one ward after another, visited the canteen, the hospital kitchens, spent a long time in the children's ward, was introduced to a great many people who appeared to know all about her and was finally led back to Sister's office. 'It's only an implant,' said her guide, 'Sir Colin won't be long now. You don't mind if I go? It's been nice…' She beamed once more.

'Thank you very much, you've been wonderful, I've really enjoyed it,' said Eustacia. And she had, as she could imagine Colin at work now.

He came ten minutes later, in rubber boots and his theatre garb, his mask pulled down under his chin, a cotton cap on his head. 'Hello, been waiting long?'

'No. I had a lovely time. Have you finished?'

'Yes. Sister and my registrar will be along in a moment and we'll all drink tea. I'll need to take a look at my patients and then we'll go.' He glanced at the clock on the wall. 'I've a couple of patients to see at two o'clock—we'll have time for lunch first.'

That night, getting into bed, she reflected that it had been a lovely day. She was, she had discovered, slightly in awe of him, but she loved him too. She would have to try very hard to be the kind of wife he expected: well dressed and pleasant to all the people he worked with, a good hostess to his friends, and, above all and most important, take care of the boys. He had married her for that, hadn't he? she reminded herself.

He came to Turville for the weekend and they all went walking and spent a good deal of each day in the garden. There was a gardener but there was always a lot to do—weeds to pull and things to plant. Monday came too soon but she consoled herself with the knowledge that he would be back on Wednesday and they would be going over to Holland on the Thursday night ferry. 'And I'll drive down on Tuesday and fetch Mother,' he told her as he was getting ready to leave after breakfast. 'I'll stay here for the night.'

He bade the boys goodbye, dropped a kiss on to her cheek and drove himself off.

'You look sad,' said Teddy, and Oliver said,

'Well, of course she does, silly, Uncle Colin's gone and they like to be together like mothers and fathers do. Don't you, Eustacia?'

'Yes, oh, yes,' said Eustacia and sniffed down threatening tears.

Chapter 9

Eustacia had plenty to occupy her after Colin left. Mrs Samways wanted advice as to which room Mrs Crichton should occupy, and there was a serious discussion as to the meals to be cooked and eaten while Eustacia and Colin were away. Then there was her packing to think of; Colin had said nothing about taking her out, and she supposed that he would be occupied the whole day and probably wouldn't be anxious to go out in the evening, but for all she knew Haso and Prudence might have quite a busy social life. She added a couple of dresses suitable for the evening and, just to be on the safe side, a black chiffon skirt and a glamorous top to go with it. That done, she turned her attention to the boys' cupboards, making sure that there was enough of everything until she got back. She strolled in the garden with her grandfather after lunch and presently fetched the boys from school. She felt restless and unhappy, and when Colin rang up later that evening she had a job not to beg him to come home, even if it was only for an hour or so. She was glad that she hadn't given way to anything so silly, for he was at his most casual, and after a minute or two she handed the phone to the boys.

The next day was better—after all, Colin would be coming home that evening. She busied herself arranging flowers, shopping in the village for Mrs Samways and attending a meeting of the church council. She felt rather at sea doing this but it was something that she could do for Colin, who wasn't always free to attend. She listened to plans for new hassocks, the church bazaar, the possibility of getting more people to sing in the choir and whether the steeple would hold out until there was money to repair it. She had plenty of good sense, and the other members of the council, all a good deal older than she, were kind and friendly. She offered to provide the material for the hassocks and went back home in time to fetch the boys from school.

Sir Colin arrived about eight o'clock with his mother, greeted Eustacia in his usual calm manner, handed Mrs Crichton over to her with the remark that they hadn't kept dinner waiting for too long, and went upstairs to say goodnight to the boys.

Eustacia led Mrs Crichton up to her room. 'I do hope you'll be comfortable,' she said, 'and it is so very kind of you to look after the boys. You will find Grandfather a great help; he plays chess with them and keeps an eye on their homework.'

'We shall manage very well, my dear,' said Mrs Crichton comfortably. 'You and Colin deserve a week together. I know he will be busy during the day but you will have your evenings free.'

'Oh, yes,' agreed Eustacia brightly. 'I dare say we shall go out quite a lot.' A remark made for the benefit of her mother-in-law. She had no idea what plans Colin had made, and he certainly hadn't told her about them.

They went back downstairs presently and she was able to tell him about the church council. 'I promised to get the material for the hassocks,' she finished, 'I hope that was the right thing to do…'

'Oh, undoubtedly.' He turned to his mother. 'You see what an invaluable partner I have found myself!' he remarked. He spoke pleasantly, but Eustacia found herself blushing, wondering if she had sounded boastful.

Mrs Crichton gave her a quick glance and saw the blush. 'More than a partner,' she said, 'someone to love the boys and someone to come home to each evening.'

Only he doesn't, thought Eustacia, smiling brightly.

Sir Colin went back to London directly after breakfast the next morning, and after taking the boys to school Eustacia sat down with his mother and discussed the following week.

'I'll keep to your routine, my dear, as far as possible, and your grandfather will put me right if I slip up. Is Colin lecturing every day or will you be able to spend some time together?'

'I'm not sure…'

'He works too hard,' said his mother. 'You cannot imagine how delighted I was when you married, my dear, I was beginning to think that he would remain single for the rest of his days. But now he has another interest in life and later, when you have a family, he will discover that life isn't all work.'

Eustacia refilled their coffee cups. 'For what reason did he receive his knighthood?' she asked, and missed Mrs Crichton's surprised look.

'He hates to talk about it. For outstanding work in the field of surgery. Two—three years ago now.'

'You must be very proud of him,' said Eustacia.

'Indeed I am, my dear. He is a good son and I have no doubt that he will be a good husband and father. His dear father was, and he is fond of children.'

'Yes,' said Eustacia faintly, 'he's marvellous with Oliver and Teddy.'

Sir Colin came home late that evening. He looked tired, as well he might, but he was as placid as usual, answering the boys' questions with patience before Eustacia hurried them off to bed.

'We shall miss you and Uncle,' said Teddy, 'but you are coming back, aren't you?'

'Of course, darling. And you're going to have a lovely time with Granny and Grandfather Crump. What shall we bring you back from Holland?'

They slept at once, for they had been allowed to

stay up to say goodnight to their uncle, and Eustacia went back downstairs, to spend the rest of the evening taking part in the pleasant talk and stealing glances at Colin from time to time, until he looked up and held her gaze without smiling.

She saw little of him the next day; although he didn't go up to the hospital he went to his study and spent a good deal of time on the telephone and dictating letters. Eustacia strolled round the gardens with Mrs Crichton and her grandfather, to all appearances a contented young woman with no cares, while all the while she was wondering why Colin was avoiding her. He had taken the boys to school and had said that he would fetch them that afternoon and, with the excuse of the pressure of work, had shut himself in his study. It didn't augur well for their trip to Holland.

They were sailing from Harwich and left in the early evening amid a chorus of cheerful goodbyes and hand-waving. Eustacia, in a jersey outfit of taupe and looking her best, got into the car beside Colin and wondered just what the next week would bring. Sir Colin, having emerged from his study the epitome of the well-dressed man, appeared as placid as usual; if he was anticipating a pleasurable few days ahead of him, there was no sign of it. He could at least pretend that he's going to enjoy himself, she reflected peevishly, and then went pink when he observed, 'I'm looking forward to this week; there should be some time between lectures when we can go sightseeing.'

She mumbled something and he cast a quick look at her. 'I'm sure that Haso and Prudence will have plans for our entertainment.'

The Rolls swallowed the miles in a well-bred manner and they were on board with half an hour to spare. 'Too soon for bed,' Colin said. 'I'll collect you from your cabin in ten minutes and we'll have a drink before we sail.'

The ship was full; they sat in the bar surrounded by a cheerful crowd of passengers which, as far as Eustacia was concerned, was all to the good. Conversation of an intimate nature was out of the question—not that Sir Colin gave any sign that he had that in mind, which puzzled her, for he had said several times that they needed to have a talk together.

She went to her cabin as soon as the ship sailed and slept soundly until she was called with tea and toast just after six o'clock. She got up and dressed and left her cabin, and found Colin waiting for her.

'Would you like breakfast before we go ashore,' he asked, 'or shall we have it as we go?'

'Oh, as we go, please. Is it far?'

'About two hundred and fifty kilometres—around a hundred and ninety miles. We shall be there by lunchtime.'

They reached Kollumwoude, the village near Leeuwarden where Haso and Prudence lived, shortly before noon, having stopped on the way and eaten a delicious breakfast of rolls and butter and slices of cheese and drunk their fill of coffee. It had been a delightful drive too; Colin knew the country well and was perfectly willing to answer Eustacia's questions. The country had changed now that they were in Friesland, and she exclaimed with delight as they drove through the village and turned in through high wrought-iron gates and stopped before a three-storeyed house, its windows in neat rows across its face and with small, round towers at each end of it. The walls were covered with creeper and there were a lot of open windows, and one had the instant impression that it was someone's well-loved home.

They got out of the car and an earnest, elderly man opened the door, to be followed at once by Prudence and, more slowly, Haso.

Their welcome was very warm. Prudence kissed Eustacia and then Colin, and Haso kissed her too before shaking Colin's hand. 'Welcome to our home,' he said and added, 'Eustacia, this is Wigge, who looks after us.'

She shook hands with him and went with Prudence into the house. It was as charming inside as it was from the outside. The hall was rather grand and the room they entered was large and lofty and splendidly furnished, but all the same it looked comfortably lived in—there was knitting cast down on a table, newspapers thrown carelessly down on the floor by a vast wing-chair and a great many flowers in lovely vases. There was a dog too, a Bouvier who lumbered to meet them and was introduced as Prince. Two very small kittens, asleep in an old upturned fur hat, completed the reassuringly cosy picture to Eustacia's eye.

'Come and see your room,' said Prudence presently. 'Lunch will be in half an hour, so there's time for a drink first.'

She led the way upstairs and into a room at the end of a corridor. 'Nice and quiet, it's at the back of the house,' said Prudence. 'Here's the bathroom,' she opened a door in the further wall, 'the dressing-room's on the other side. I'll leave you to do whatever you want to do, but don't be long.' She smiled and whisked herself away, leaving Eustacia on her own to survey the room, large and light and furnished with great comfort, with gleaming walnut and pale curtains and bedspread. The bathroom was perfection with piles of fluffy towels and bowls of soap and a white carpet underfoot, and from glass shelves there were trailing plants hanging. She paused just long enough to admire them and opened the other door. The dressing-room was a good deal smaller than the bedroom but well furnished, and Sir Colin's luggage was there. She went back to the bedroom, did her face and hair and went downstairs.

The rest of the day was taken up with an inspection of the house and garden, which was large and beautifully laid out, and in the evening there was a good deal of talk as to what they might do to amuse Eustacia.

'I don't need amusing,' she protested. 'It's lovely just being here…'

'It is nice, isn't it?' said Prudence happily. 'We'll go into Leeuwarden and spend some time shopping and the country around is worth looking at. Oh, and we must go to Sneek and Bolsward and Dokkum—'

'My love,' said Haso, 'they're only here for a week and Colin will be lecturing each day. I might even do some work myself…'

'Oh, well, I'll drive Eustacia round and perhaps we could go out one evening? There's Cremaillere in Groningen—'

'Or the Lauswolt in Beesterwaag—'

'We can dance there.'

Eustacia went to bed, convinced that no stone would be left unturned in the attempt to keep her amused during the next week. It was to be hoped that Colin would be amused too.

She saw little of him during the days which followed, although he returned in the late afternoon, when they would sit around over their drinks, talking over their day, and after dinner more often than not friends would call in, and on the second evening that they were there Prudence gave a dinner party for their closer friends and Haso's mother. Eustacia liked her at once, just as she liked his sister when Prudence took her to Groningen to meet her. Her days were full, but disappointment mounted as each day passed and Colin, kind and attentive as he usually was, made no attempt to be alone with her.

Her hopes rose when Haso announced that they would all go to Beesterwaag that evening for dinner and dancing. The hotel was some twenty miles away and they used Colin's car, the two girls sitting in the back, Prudence in russet taffeta and Eustacia in silk voile patterned in pink roses. The two men had complimented them upon their charming appearance when they had joined them in the hall, and Haso had given his wife a long, loving look which spoke volumes. Eustacia had had to be content with Colin's quiet 'charming, my dear', and when he had looked at her it was from under drooping lids which had allowed her to see nothing of his gaze.

The evening was a great success; they dined deliciously on lobster thermidor after a lavish hors d'oeuvre, and finished their meal with fresh fruit salad and lashings of whipped cream, and since it was a party they drank champagne.

They danced too; Eustacia floated round with Colin, conscious that she looked her best. He was a good dancer and so was she, and she could have gone on forever. 'Enjoying yourself?' he asked her.

'Oh, so much, Colin. Only I wish you didn't have to be away all day.' To which he made no reply.

It was Haso, dancing with her later, who suggested that she might meet Colin for lunch in Groningen. 'Prudence can drive you there and you can come back with him later.'

He broached the subject later as they sat over their coffee, and Colin agreed placidly. 'Why not? The day after tomorrow, if you like, Eustacia, if Prudence doesn't mind driving you in.'

'A chance to do some last-minute shopping, since you'll be going the next day.'

It was when they were back home again and Prudence and Haso had gone into the garden with Prince that Eustacia found herself alone with Colin.

'You don't mind if I come to Groningen?' she asked.

'My dear girl, why should I mind?' he asked casually.

'You didn't suggest it yourself,' she told him angrily. 'We've been here for four days and you've never once wanted to—'

She paused, and he prompted, 'Wanted to what, Eustacia?'

'Be alone with me,' she muttered.

'True enough,' and at her sharp, angry breath, 'But I think that we must agree to Haso's suggestion, don't you? For the sake of appearances.'

She took a steadying breath. 'What have I done, Colin?' and then with a flash of rage, 'Oh, why did I ever come here with you, why did I ever marry you…?'

'As to that, my dear, we still have to have that talk, do we not? But somehow the right moment hasn't presented itself.'

'There is nothing to talk about,' said Eustacia icily, and when he put a hand on her arm, 'Let me go…' She darted away from him and up the staircase just as the others came back into the house.

Crying herself to sleep didn't improve her looks; Prudence took one glance at her slightly pink nose and said nothing, and after breakfast she suggested that they might drive over to Dokkum and have lunch there. 'The men won't be back until teatime and tomorrow you'll be in Groningen for most of the day.'

In the evening, when Haso and Colin came in, Eustacia was quite her usual self, rather more so than usual in fact. She wasn't a talkative girl usually, but this evening she excelled herself. When they parted for the night and Haso mentioned that she would be lunching with Colin the next day, she replied with every appearance of pleasure that she was simply delighted at the prospect.

'Well, you haven't seen much of each other,' said Prudence.

The men had gone by the time Eustacia and Prudence got down for breakfast. They ate unhurriedly and presently got into Prudence's car and drove to Groningen. Eustacia, listening to Prudence's chatter, was thinking hard. The time had come to tell him her real feelings. She felt quite brave about it at the moment, but probably by lunchtime her courage would have oozed out of her shoes.

They had coffee at Cremaillere before Prudence walked with Eustacia to one of the two central squares in the city. 'Go down there,' she advised, pointing to a crowded, narrow street, 'keep on for a few minutes and then turn to the right. Take the first turning on the left and the hospital's about five minutes' walk away. You are sure you want to walk? I could drive you there in no time at all…'

'I'd like to walk; it's my last chance to see the city and I've heaps of time.'

'Well, yes, you have—Colin's sure to be a bit late. You know what these lectures are—someone always wants to ask questions when he's finished. Have a nice lunch together.' She took Eustacia's parcels. 'I'll take these back with me—see you later.'

Eustacia started walking. It was really the first chance she had had of talking to Colin alone for any length of time, and she intended to take full advantage of it; there was such a lot she wanted to say and it was time it was said. She wondered if she could pluck up the courage to say that she loved him and ask what they could do about it, and as she walked she began composing various speeches on the subject. She would be cool and very matter-of-fact, she decided, and match his own bland calm. She was pleased with the speeches she was making up in her head, although it wasn't likely that he would reply as she imagined, which was a drawback. All the same, she had rehearsed what she would say, and was so engrossed that she didn't turn to the right but walked briskly over the crossroads and found herself in another busy main street. Another few minutes brought her to more main roads, and this time she remembered that she had to turn right—or had Prudence said left? She stood undecided on the pavement, and since she couldn't make up her mind which way to go she stopped a passer-by and asked.

'The hospital?' said the man in English. 'Cross over and take the left-hand road, walk for five minutes and then turn right. The hospital is in that street.'

He raised his hat politely and walked on and Eustacia, very relieved, did as he had bidden. She was already ten minutes late and she hurried now; it had taken her longer than she had expected but she consoled herself with the thought that Prudence had said that Colin would be late anyway.

The street was shabby, with run-down shops between small brick houses and here and there a warehouse, and the hospital loomed large halfway down it. She went through the swing-doors with a sigh of relief and approached the man sitting behind the reception desk in the gloomy hall.

She tried out her, *'Goeden morgen'* on his rather cross face and added, 'Sir Colin Crichton?' He stared at her without speaking so she added, 'Seminar, conference?'

He nodded then, said *'Straks,'* and, seeing that she didn't understand, pointed to the clock. 'Late,' he managed.

She smiled at him and asked, 'May I wait?' and took his silence for consent, and went and sat on a hard chair against the opposite wall. She was hungry and on edge and she hoped she wouldn't have to wait too long. It was half an hour before the lifts at the end of the hall began to disgorge a number of soberly clad gentlemen, none of whom bore the least resemblance to Colin. She watched the last one disappear into the street, waited for five minutes and then got up.

The man at the desk wasn't very helpful—he shook his head repeatedly at her attempts to make him understand until finally he picked up the telephone, dialled a number and handed her the phone. 'I speak English,' said a voice. 'You wish to enquire?'

'Sir Colin Crichton—I've been waiting for him. Is he still in the hospital?'

'There is no one of that name here. He was not at the meeting held here this morning. I am sorry.' The voice ended in a smart click as the receiver was put down.

There was nothing for it but to retrace her steps, and once she got to the square she had started from she would see if Prudence was still there; she had said she had more shopping to do and Eustacia knew where the car was.

She thanked the man and made for the door. It swung inwards as she reached it and she came to a halt against a massive chest.

'Where the hell have you been?' asked Sir Colin, and when she looked up into his face she saw that he was angry—more than angry, in a rage.

How nice it would be to be six years old again, she thought, then she could have burst into tears in the most natural way and even screamed a little...

'Here,' she said in a voice rendered wooden with suppressed feeling. 'Waiting for you.' She drew an indignant breath. 'You weren't here.'

'Of course I wasn't here, you silly little goose. You are at the wrong hospital. Although how you managed to go wrong when it was less than five minutes' walk from the square is something I fail to understand.'

'Understand?' said Eustacia pettishly. 'You don't understand anything—you're blind and wrapped up in your work and—and...'

'And?' prompted Colin, dangerously quiet.

'Oh, go away!' said Eustacia, and was instantly terrified that he might just do that.

But all he said was, 'The car's across the street. Come along.'

He shoved her into her seat with firm, gentle hands, got in beside her and drove off. 'Hungry?' he wanted to know.

'Not in the least,' said Eustacia haughtily.

'Good, in that case we might as well go back to Kollumwoude.'

And that was exactly what he did. And if he heard her insides rumbling he said nothing.

Prudence, standing at the window, saw the Rolls turn in and stop by the door. 'They're back,' she told Haso urgently. 'Something has gone wrong—just look at Eustacia's face, she can't wait to get into a dark hole and have a quiet weep. And just look at Colin…'

Haso came to stand beside her. 'Perhaps that's what they need—rather like a boil that needs to come to a head before it bursts.'

'Don't be revolting,' said Prudence and kissed him. 'What shall we do?'

'Why, nothing, my love. But we might have tea a little earlier than usual, as it is just possible that they've had no lunch.'

The blandness of Colin's face gave nothing away and Eustacia, never a talkative girl, gabbled her head off; the weather, Groningen and its delights, the splendour of its shops, the charm of the countryside all came in for an animated eulogy which continued non-stop until it was time for them to go to their rooms to change for dinner. Since it was the last evening of their brief visit there were friends and colleagues coming and Eustacia, quite exhausted with so much talking, came back from her shower and looked longingly at her bed, but the evening wouldn't last forever and she wouldn't need to talk to Colin; there would be enough guests to make that easy. She studied her two dresses and then decided on the black skirt and the top, which was a glamorous affair of cream satin exquisitely embroidered. She surveyed her person with some satisfaction when she was dressed, and went downstairs to find the men already in the drawing-room. Prudence followed her in, looking her magnificent best in a taffeta dress of hunter's green.

'That's nice,' she declared, studying Eustacia, 'and such a tiny waist.' She beamed at her. 'We're big girls, aren't we? And I'm going to get bigger…'

'I hope we shall be invited to be godparents,' said Colin.

'Well, of course you will. Haso wants a boy, I'd like twins…'

They drank a toast with a good deal of light-hearted talking and presently the first of the guests arrived.

It was after midnight when Eustacia got to bed; she had managed very well, hardly speaking to Colin during the evening but taking care that when she did she behaved like a newly married girl, very much in love with her husband. Which she was.

They left shortly after breakfast the next morning after a lingering goodbye to Prudence and Haso, and Eustacia, determined to preserve a nonchalant manner, made polite conversation all the way to Boulogne where they were to board a hovercraft. She hardly noticed that Colin answered her in monosyllables, she was so intent on keeping up a steady flow of chat. It did strike her just once or twice that when he spoke at all he sounded amused…

Their journey was uneventful, accomplished in great comfort and with a modicum of conversation. As they neared London Eustacia asked, 'Do you have to go to St Biddolph's tomorrow?'

'It depends. If you want to go to Turville you can take the Mini if I'm not free.'

She said, 'Very well, Colin,' in a meek voice; he sounded preoccupied, and if he didn't want to talk neither did she, she decided crossly.

Grimstone welcomed them with stately warmth, removed coats, luggage and Sir Colin's briefcase, ushered them into the pleasant warmth and a hectic greeting from Moses in the sitting-room and produced tea.

It was nice to be home, thought Eustacia, and was surprised to find that was how she regarded the house now. She poured tea and handed cake and Colin, with a word of apology, read the letters and messages with which Grimstone had greeted him.

'Nothing that can't be dealt with later,' he observed. 'Shall we phone Turville?'

The boys took it in turns to talk on the telephone, and then Mr Crump and Mrs Crichton detailed the week's happenings. Which all took some time, so that Eustacia had only a short time in which to tidy herself for dinner and have a drink with Colin, and even then there was no chance to talk even if she could have thought of something to say for Prudence rang up to see if they had arrived safely. Eustacia was glad of that for it gave her something to talk about while they sat at the beautifully appointed table, eating the delicious meal Rosie had cooked.

'Would you like coffee in the drawing-room?' she asked, conscious of the enquiring look Grimstone directed at her.

'Just as you like, my dear.' Colin sounded placidly uninterested, but he crossed the hall with her and sat down in his chair while she poured their coffee. They drank it in silence while she sought feverishly for something to talk about and, since her mind was blank, she poured more coffee.

'We have had very little time together,' said Sir Colin quietly, 'and, when we did, we have been at cross purposes. I think that it is time that we understood each other. Do you know why I married you, Eustacia?'

She put her cup and saucer down and looked at him thoughtfully. 'You wanted someone to look after the boys and love them and take care of them. Circumstances rather forced you into choosing me, didn't they? I don't suppose you had any intention of marrying me until it was—was thrust upon you…'

'But I had already asked you to come and live with us, had I not?'

She was a little bewildered. 'Well yes, as a kind of governess…'

'Would it surprise you if I told you that—' The telephone on the table at his elbow shrilled and he frowned as he picked it up. 'Crichton.' He spoke unhurriedly and listened patiently to whoever was at the other end. Presently he said, 'I'll be with you in ten minutes or so. No, no—not at all, you did right to call me.'

He got up and stood towering over her. 'I'm sorry, I have to go to the hospital. Fate, it seems, isn't going to allow me to tell you something I have wished to say for a long time.'

He was already at the door, but in the hall she caught up with him.

'What was it, Colin? Please tell me.'

He opened the door. 'Why not? I've been in love with you ever since I saw you that first time.'

He had gone. She stood at the open door watching the tail-lights of the Rolls disappear down the street until Grimstone, coming into the hall, saw her there and closed the door. He gave her a curious look as he did so. 'You feel all right, my lady?'

She gave him a bemused look. 'Oh, yes, thank you, Grimstone. Sir Colin has had to go to the hospital—I'm not sure how long he'll be.'

She went back to the drawing-room and sat down

again with Moses and Madam Mop. 'Did you hear what he said?' she asked them in a whisper. 'That he was in love with me. But he never… I had no idea.' She drew an indignant breath. 'And fancy telling me like that just as he was going away.' The little cat got on to her lap and stared into her face. 'Yes, I know, he hadn't time to explain and I did ask him…'

She glanced at the clock—if it was just a case of examining a patient and giving advice he would be home soon. She put an arm round Moses, who had climbed up beside her, and fell into a daydream.

It was after eleven o'clock when Grimstone came into the room to tell her that he had locked up and ask, would she like him to wait up for Sir Colin?

'No, thank you, Grimstone, you go to bed. Rosie has left coffee on the Aga, I expect? I'll give Sir Colin a cup when he gets in.'

'As you wish, my lady. Shall I mend the fire?'

'No need. He won't be much longer and the room's warm. Goodnight, Grimstone.'

He gave her a grave goodnight, and went away. The house was quiet now save for the gentle ticking of the bracket clock and she sat, half asleep, waiting for the sound of the key in the door. The long-case clock in the hall chimed midnight and she got slowly to her feet. Surely Colin would be coming soon? He could have phoned, or was he regretting what he had said and deliberately staying away? She took the animals to the kitchen and settled them in their baskets and went back to the drawing-room. The fire was smouldering embers now and the room would soon be chilly. She put the fireguard before it, turned out the lights and went back into the hall, turned off all but one of the wall sconces and started up the stairs, to pause and then sit down on one of the lower treads, facing the door. If she went to bed she would only lie awake, listening for him…

The slow ticking of the clock was soothing, and after a few minutes she leaned her head against the banisters and closed her eyes.

It was half an hour later when Sir Colin let himself into his house. He stood for a moment, looking at Eustacia bundled untidily on the staircase, her head at an awkward angle, her lovely face tear-streaked, her softly curved mouth a little open. Being very much in love with her, he didn't notice the gentle snore. He closed the door, shot the bolts soundlessly, put his bag down and crossed the hall to stand looking down at her.

She woke then, stared up at him for a moment and then said, 'Would you say that again?' It wasn't what she might have said if she had been wide awake, but it was the first thought that entered her sleepy head.

He smiled slowly and the smile soothed away the tired lines of his face. He said very clearly, 'I have been in love with you ever since that first time—you wore a most unbecoming overall and I gave you a kidney dish. I didn't know it at the time, of course, I only knew that I wanted to see you again, and when we did meet I knew that I loved you, that you were part of me, my heartbeat, my very breath. It seemed that fate was to be kind to me when circumstances made it possible for us to marry, but then I began to doubt… You are so much younger than I, my darling, and somewhere in this world there must be a young man only waiting to meet you…'

Eustacia was wide awake now. 'Oh, pooh,' she said strongly. 'In the first place I don't much care for young men, and in the second place I love you too.' Quite unexpectedly two large tears rolled down her cheeks. 'I thought you didn't care tuppence for me, so I tried to be what I thought you wanted me to be.' She sniffed and he proffered a snowy handkerchief. 'We've never been alone…' she added dolefully.

'I didn't dare to be. But we are now.' He swooped down and plucked her to her feet and swept her into his arms. 'My dearest darling, we are now.' He kissed her in a slow and most satisfying manner, and then quite roughly so that she found it impossible to speak, and when she would have done, 'No, be quiet, dear heart, while I tell you how much I love you.'

'Oh, how very nice,' said Eustacia, managing to say it before he kissed her again. Then, 'I am so glad that we're married…'

She looked up into his face. His heavy lids had lifted and his blue eyes blazed down into hers. 'So am I,' he told her softly.

* * * * *

A GENTLE AWAKENING

Chapter 1

The hot June sunshine of a late afternoon bathed the narrow country road in warmth, and the only traveller on it dawdled along, pedalling slowly, partly from tiredness after a day's work, and partly from a reluctance to arrive at her home.

The village came in sight round the next curve: the bridge over the river, leading to the road which would eventually join the high road to Salisbury, and then the cottages on either side of the lane. They were charming, tiled or thatched, their red bricks glowing in the sunshine, their porches wreathed with clematis and roses. The cyclist came to a halt before one of these, and at the same time a silver-grey Bentley swam to a soundless halt beside her.

The girl got off her bike. She was small and thin,

with gingery hair plaited into a thick rope over one shoulder, green eyes transforming an ordinary face into something which, while not pretty, certainly lifted it from the ordinary.

The car driver got out: a very large man, towering over her. Not so young, she decided, studying him calmly, but very good-looking, with dark hair sprinkled with grey, a formidable nose and heavy-lidded blue eyes. He smiled down at her, studying her in his turn, and then dismissing her from his thoughts. None the less, he smiled at her and his deep voice was pleasant.

'I wonder if you could help us? We wanted to stay the night in the village, but the Trout and Feathers can't put us up and we would rather not drive back to Wilton or Salisbury.' He glanced over his shoulder to where a small girl's face was thrust through the open window of the car. 'Just bed and breakfast—we can get a meal at the pub.'

He held out a hand. 'The name is Sedley—William Sedley.'

The girl offered a small brown hand and had it engulfed. 'Florina Payne, and yes, if you go on as far as the bridge, there is a farmhouse facing it; they haven't got a board up, but I'm sure they would put you up.' She wrinkled her ginger brows. 'There isn't anybody else in the village, I'm afraid. You would have to go back to Burford St Martin on the main road.'

She was thanked politely, and the child in the front seat waved to her as they drove off. She wheeled her bike along the brick path at the side of the cottage and went in through the kitchen door, thinking about the driver of the car, to have her thoughts rudely shattered by her father's voice.

'So there you are—took your time coming home, didn't you? And then wasted more of it talking to that fellow. What did he want, anyway?'

The speaker came into the kitchen, a middle-aged man with an ill-tempered face. 'You might at least get home punctually; you know I can't do anything much for myself, and here I am, alone all day and you crawling back when it suits you…'

He paused for breath and Florina said gently, 'Father, I came just as soon as I could get off. The hotel is very busy with the tourist season, you know, and that man only wanted to know where he could get a room for the night.'

Her father snorted. 'Pah, he could afford a hotel in Wilton, driving a Bentley!' He added spitefully, 'Wasting your time and his for that matter—who'd want to look twice at a ginger-headed plain Jane like you?'

Florina was laying the table and, although colour stole into her cheeks, she answered in a matter-of-fact voice. 'Well, it won't be a waste of time if he gets a room at the farm. Sit down, Father, tea won't be long.'

She would very much have liked to have sat down herself and had a cup of tea; it had been a busy day at the hotel. During the summer season, tourists expected meals at odd hours, and she and the other two cooks there had worked all day, whisking up omelettes, steaks, fish dishes, egg dishes and salads, just as fast as they could. They had taken it in turn to eat a sandwich and drink a mug of tea, but it had been a long day. She had worked there for three years now, hating the long cycle ride in the winter to and from her home, as well as the long hours and the lack of free time. But the pay, while not over-generous, was good; it supplemented her father's pension and brought him all the extra comforts he took as his right. That it might have given her the chance to buy pretty clothes had never entered his head; she was his daughter, twenty-seven years old, on the plain side, and it was her duty to look after him while he lived. Once or twice she had done her best to break free, and each time, when she had confronted him with a possible job away from home, he had clutched at his chest, gasped that he was dying and taken to his bed. A dutiful, but not loving daughter—for what was there to love?—she had accepted that after the one heart attack he had had several years ago, he could have another if he became upset or angry; so she had given in.

She was a sensible girl and didn't allow self-pity to overwhelm her. She was aware that she had no looks to speak of, and those that she had were hardly enhanced by the cheap clothes, bought with an eye to their hard-wearing quality rather than fashion.

Her father refused to cook for himself during the day. She left cold food ready for him before she left each morning, and tea was a substantial meal, which meant that she had to cook once more. Haddock and poached eggs, a plate of bread and butter, stewed fruit and custard, and tea afterwards. She had no appetite for it, but the suggestion that they might have salads and cold meat met with a stream of grumbles, and anything was better than that after a day's work.

They ate in silence. Her father had no interest in her day and, since he had done nothing himself, there was nothing to tell her. He got up from the table presently and went into the sitting-room to sit down before the TV. Florina started to clear the table, wash up and put everything ready for breakfast. By the time she had finished the evening was well advanced but still light; half an hour's walk would be pleasant, she decided. She cheerfully countered her father's objections to this and set off through the village, past the cottages, past the Trout and Feathers, past the lovely old house next the pub where old Admiral Riley lived, and along the tree-lined lane. It was still warm and very quiet, and if she stood still she could hear the river beyond the trees.

When she came to a gate she stopped to lean on it, well aware of the beauty of her surroundings, but too busy with her own thoughts to heed it. The need to escape was very strong; her mother had died five years previously and since then Florina had kept house for her father, pandering to his whims, because the doctor had warned her that a fit of temper or any major disturbance might bring on another heart attack. She had resigned herself to what was her plain duty, made the more irksome since her father had no affection for her. But things could be different now; her father had been for a check-up in Salisbury a week or so previously and, although he had told her that there was no improvement in his condition, she had quite by chance encountered the doctor, who had told her that her father was fit enough to resume a normal life.

'A part-time job, perhaps?' He smiled at Florina, whom he thought privately had had a raw deal. 'He was in a bank, wasn't he? Well, I dare say he could get taken on again. He's only in his mid-fifties, isn't he? And if he can't find something to do, I've suggested to him that he might take over the housework; a little activity would do him good. Give you a chance to have a holiday.'

She mulled over his news. Her father had flown into a rage when she had suggested that he might like to do a few chores around the house. He had clutched his chest and declared that she would be the death of him, and that she was the worst possible daughter that any man could have.

Florina, having heard it all before, received his remarks with equanimity and said no more, but now she turned over several schemes in her mind. A different job, if she could find one and, since her father no longer was in danger, preferably away from home. Something not too far away, so that she could return for the weekends… She was so deep in thought that she didn't hear anyone in the lane until they were almost level with her. The man and the little girl from the car, walking along hand in hand. When she turned to see who it was, the man inclined his head gravely and the little girl grinned and waved. Florina watched them walk on, back to the village. Presumably they had found their bed and breakfast, and tomorrow they would drive away in their lovely car and she would never see them again.

She waited until they were out of sight, and then started back to the house. She had to leave home just after seven each morning, and tomorrow it would be even earlier, for there was a wedding reception at the hotel.

She went back without haste, made their evening drinks, wished her father goodnight and went to her room, where she wasted five minutes examining her features in the looking-glass. There was, she considered, very little to be done about them: sandy hair, even though it gleamed and shone, was by no means considered beautiful, and a slightly tip-tilted nose and too wide a mouth held no charm. She got into bed and lay wondering about the man in the car. He had been very polite in a disinterested way; she could quite see that there was nothing in her person to attract a man, especially a man such as he, used, no doubt, to enchanting girls with golden hair and beautiful faces, wearing the latest fashions. Florina smiled at her silly thoughts and went off to sleep.

It was the beginning of the most gorgeous day when she left early the next morning. Sir William Sedley, standing at his bedroom window and drinking his early morning tea, watched her pedalling briskly along the lane. The sun shone on her sandy head, turning it to gold, and she was whistling. He wondered where she was going at that early hour. Then he forgot her, almost immediately.

It was a splendid morning and there was almost no traffic. Florina, going at a great rate on her elderly bike, wished that she could have been free to spend the day out of doors. The hotel kitchens, admirable though they were, were going to be uncomfortably warm. She slowed a little as she went through the small town, still quiet, and passed the nice old houses with the high walls of Wilton House behind them. The hotel was on the other side of the road, a pleasant building, surrounded by trees and with the river close by. She paused to take a look at the green peacefulness around her, then parked her bike and went in through the kitchen entrance.

She was punctual, as always, but the place was already a hive of activity; first breakfasts being cooked, waiters loading trays. Florina called 'good morning' and went over to her particular corner, intent on icing *petits fours*, filling vol-au-vents and decorating the salmon in aspic designed for the wedding reception.

She was a splendid cook, a talent she had inherited from her Dutch mother, together with a multitude of housewifely perfections which, sadly, her father had never appreciated. Florina sometimes wondered if her mother had been happy; she had been a quiet little woman, sensible and practical and cheerful, absorbing her father's ill-temper with apparent ease. Florina missed her still. Whether her father did so too, she didn't know, for he never talked of her. When, from time to time, she had tried to suggest a holiday with her mother's family, he had been so incensed that he had become alarmingly red in the face, and she had feared that he would have another heart attack.

Her thoughts, as busy as her fingers, darted to and fro, seeking an escape from a home which was no longer a home. Interlarded with them was the man in the car, although what business of his it was eluded her.

He wasn't thinking of her; he was strolling down the village street, his daughter beside him. His appointment was for ten o'clock and it wanted five minutes to the hour. The church clock struck the hour as they turned in through the open gates leading to the house where Admiral Riley lived.

It was a delightful place, L-shaped, its heavy wooden door half-way down one side. It stood open, and there was no need to thump the great knocker, for the old man came to meet them.

'Mrs Birch from the village, who looks after me while my wife is away, has gone to Wilton. So I'm alone, which is perhaps a good thing, for we can go round undisturbed.'

He led the way through the hall and into a very large room with a window at its end. There were more windows and an open door along one side. It was furnished with some handsome mahogany pieces, and a number of easy chairs, and there was a massive marble fireplace facing the windows. The admiral went across the room and bent down to roll back the carpet before the hearth.

'I don't know if the agent told you about this?' He chuckled and stood back so that his visitors could see what he had laid bare. A thick glass panel in the floor, and under it a steady flow of water. 'There used to be a mill wheel, but that's gone. The water runs under this room…' He led the way through the doors on to a wide patio and leaned over a stone balustrade. 'It comes out here and runs through the garden into the fields beyond.'

The little girl caught her father's hand. 'Swans, Daddy!' Her voice was a delighted squeak. 'Do they live here, in this garden?'

'Not quite in the garden,' said the Admiral. 'But they come for bread each day. You shall feed them presently, if you like.'

The kitchen wing was in the other side of the L-shape, a delightful mixture of old-fashioned pantries, with everything that any housewife could wish for. There were other rooms, too: a dining-room, a small sitting-room, a study lined with bookshelves. Upstairs, the rooms were light and airy; there were five of them and three bathrooms, as well as a great attic reached by a narrow little stair. 'My playroom,' whispered the little girl.

They went back to the drawing-room presently, and the Admiral fetched the coffee tray and bread for the swans. 'I've been here for more than twenty years,' he observed, 'and we hate to leave it, but my wife has to live in a warm climate. She's been in Italy for a couple of months and already she is greatly improved. May I ask where you come from, Sir William?'

'London—Knightsbridge. I'm a paediatrician, consultant at several hospitals. I want Pauline to grow up in the country and, provided I can get help to run the house, I can drive up and down to town and stay overnight when I must. There's a good school, I hear; Pauline can go by the day.'

'Too far for her to cycle.'

'Yes, whoever comes here to look after us will have to drive her in and fetch her each day. A problem I'll deal with later.' He smiled suddenly. 'I should like to buy your house, Admiral. May our solicitors get to work on it?'

He sat back in his chair, very relaxed, a calm man who had made up his mind without fuss. 'They'll take three weeks if we bully them,' he said. 'May I come again with someone to advise me about cooking stoves and so on?' He added, 'I'm a widower, but I have plans to re-marry.'

'Of course. I shall probably be ready to move out before the solicitors fix a date. Feel free to arrange for carpets and curtains and so forth. Wilton is small, but there are a couple of excellent furnishing firms.'

They finished their coffee in companionable silence; two men who arranged their lives without fuss.

Walking back through the village, presently, Sir William asked, 'You're pleased, darling? You'll be happy here? I'll get Nanny to come and live with us for a time...'

'Until you marry Miss Fortesque?' said Pauline in a sad voice, so that her father stopped to look down at her.

'Look, darling, I know it's a bit difficult for you to understand, but Wanda is very fond of you, and it'll be nice for you to have someone to come home to and talk to...'

'There's you, Daddy...'

'I shall be in town for several days in the week. Once Wanda's here she will be able to get to know everyone about, and you'll have lots of friends.'

Pauline's small, firm mouth closed into an obstinate line. 'I'd be quite happy with Nanny.'

'Yes, love, but Nanny retired last year, she won't want to start working all over again. If she comes for a few months...'

'Until you get married?'

'Until I get married,' repeated her father gently, and then, 'I thought you liked Wanda?'

Pauline shrugged her small shoulders. 'She's all right, but she's not like a mother, is she? She fusses about her clothes!'

'I imagine you'll fuss about yours when you're older. Now, what shall we do with the rest of our day?'

He drove her to Stourhead and they had lunch at the Spread Eagle pub. Then they wandered right round the lake, and on the way back in the afternoon they stopped in Shaftesbury and had a cream tea. It was well past six o'clock before they got back to the farm. It was a warm evening and the country was very beautiful; they wandered over the road to the bridge and leaned over to watch the river, waiting until their evening meal would be ready. The church clock struck seven as they left the bridge and strolled to the road. They had to wait a moment while a cyclist went by.

'That's the nice girl we saw yesterday,' said Pauline.

'Was she nice?' asked Sir William in an uninterested manner.

Pauline nodded her head vigorously. 'Oh, yes. When we live here I shall ask if I may be her friend.'

'A bit old for you, darling?' He had no idea of the girl's age, and he wasn't interested. 'You must go to bed directly after supper. We're going to make an early start in the morning.'

They were driving through Wilton when Pauline saw the small, ginger-haired figure getting off her bike as they passed the hotel. 'Oh, there she is!' she cried excitedly. 'Daddy, do you suppose she works there?'

Sir William glanced sideways without slackening speed. 'Very likely. I dare say you'll see more of her when we come to live here.'

It was July when Admiral Riley left, and after that there was a constant coming and going of delivery vans, carpet layers, plumbers and painters. The village, via the Trout and Feathers, knew all that was going on and, naturally enough, Florina knew too. The new owner would move in in two weeks' time, his small daughter was going to school in Wilton, and there was a housekeeper coming. Also, Mrs Datchett from Rose Cottage, and Mrs Deakin, whose husband was a farm worker, were to go to work there four times a week.

'Disgraceful,' grumbled Florina's father. 'That great house, with just a man and child in it…'

'But there's work for Mrs Datchett and Mrs Deakin, close to their own homes, as well as for old Mr Meek, who is seeing to the garden. And the tradespeople—it's much better than leaving the house empty, Father.'

'Don't talk about things you don't understand,' snapped Mr Payne. 'It's bad enough that you go gallivanting off to work each day, leaving me to manage as best I can…'

Florina, laying the table for their meal, wasn't listening. She had heard it all before. It was wicked, she supposed, not to love her father, but she had tried very hard and been rebuffed so often that she had given up. Once or twice she had questioned the amount of her wages which he told her were necessary to supplement his income, only to be told to mind her own business. And she had done so, under the impression that his health would suffer if she thwarted him. Now according to the doctor, there was no longer any fear of that.

She went into the kitchen to cook the liver and bacon. Moments later her father poked his head round the door and demanded to know if he was to get anything to eat. 'I dare say you'd like to see me dead,' he grumbled.

'No, Father, just a bit more cheerful,' said Florina. At the same time, she resolved to start looking for another job on the very next day.

As it happened, she had no need. She was getting on her bike the next morning when Mrs Datchett came out of Rose Cottage, just across the street, and accosted her.

'Eh, love, can you spare a minute? You've heard I'm to go up to the Wheel House to work? Well, the housekeeper who took me on asked me if I knew of a good cook, and I thought of you. Lovely kitchen it is, too, and a cushy job as you might say, with that Sir William away most of the time and only the little girl and that housekeeper there. I don't know what he'll pay, but you'd not have that bike ride every day. Why don't you have a go?'

Florina cycled to work, thinking hard. By the time she got there she had made her mind up to apply for the job; it could do no harm and it seemed to her that it was a direct sign from heaven that she should look for other work… To strengthen this argument, it was her half-day; usually spent in cleaning the house.

She got home about two o'clock and, instead of getting into an apron and getting out the vacuum cleaner, she went to her room, put on a clean blouse, brushed her blue skirt, did her hair in a severe style which did nothing for her looks, and went downstairs.

'Why are you going out?' enquired her father suspiciously.

'Don't worry, Father, I'll be back to get you your tea.' She skipped through the door before he could answer.

It was barely five minutes' walk to the Wheel House and Florina didn't give herself time to get nervous. She thumped the knocker, firmly, and then took several deep breaths. She had read somewhere that deep breathing helped if one felt nervous.

The door was opened and there was a tall, bony woman with grey hair and faded blue eyes. She looked stern and rather unwelcoming, so that Florina was glad of the deep breaths.

'Good afternoon. Mrs Datchett told me this morning that you were wanting a cook…'

'Sir William is wanting a cook. I'm the housekeeper. Do come in.'

She was led into a small sitting-room in the kitchen wing. 'Why do you want to come?'

'I work at a hotel in Wilton—I've been there for several years. I cycle there and back each day. I'd like to work on my own.' Florina added, anxiously, 'I'm a good cook, I can get references.'

'You live here?'

'Yes, just this side of the bridge.'

'You'd have to be here by eight o'clock each morning, make out the menus, keep the kitchen clean, cook lunch if Sir William is here, and dinner as well. You'd be free in the afternoons. You'd have help with the washing up and so on, but you might have to stay late some evenings. Do you want to live in?'

'I live very close by and I have to look after my father…'

The housekeeper nodded. 'Well, you're not quite what I had in mind, but I dare say you'll suit. You can come on a month's trial. There's Sir William at weekends, his daughter, Pauline, living here with me, and you must be prepared to cook for guests at the weekends. You do know that Sir William intends to marry?'

Florina shook her head. She hadn't realised until that moment that Sir William loomed so large in her life. The idea of him marrying left her with a feeling of disquiet, but she had no time to wonder about it, for the housekeeper said, 'Sir William will be moving in at the end of next week. Can you start then? A month's trial and, mind, he expects the best.'

She had to give a week's notice. She would go and see the hotel manager in the morning, for that would give him ten days in which to find someone to take her place.

'You haven't asked what your wages will be,' said the housekeeper, and mentioned a sum which sent Florina's ginger eyebrows up.

'That's a good deal more than I'm getting now,' she pointed out.

'Probably, but you'll have to work for it.'

'I'd like to work here,' said Florina. She would see Sir William sometimes, even if he never spoke to her.

'Very well, you'll get a letter in a day or two. My

name is Frobisher, Miss Martha Frobisher. If you have any problems you'll bring them to me. Sir William is a busy man, he hasn't the time to bother with household matters.' She eyed Florina's small, neat person. 'What is your name?'

'Payne—Florina Payne.'

They wished each other goodbye with guarded politeness.

Mr Payne, apprised of his daughter's astonishing behaviour, called upon heaven to defend him from ungrateful daughters, painted a pathetic picture of his early death from neglect and starvation, since there would be no one to look after him. Finally he declared that he might as well be dead.

'Nonsense, Father,' said Florina kindly. 'You know that's not true. I'm likely to be at home more than I am now. You've had to boil your kettle for breakfast for years now, and I'll leave your lunch ready just as usual…'

'The housework—the whole place will go to rack and ruin.'

'I shall be home each afternoon, I can do the chores then. Besides, the doctor said it would do you good to be more active now you're better.'

'I shall never be better…'

Florina said cheerfully, 'I'll make a cup of tea. You'll feel better then.'

The manager was sorry that she wished to leave, but he understood that the chance of a job so close to her home wasn't to be missed. He wrote out a splendid reference which she slid through the letter-box at Wheel House, together with her letter accepting the job. If she didn't suit, of course, it would mean that she would be out of work at the end of a month; but she refused to entertain that idea, for she knew she was a good cook.

She went to the Wheel House the day before she was to start work, so that she might have a good look round her kitchen. It had everything, and the pantry and cupboards and fridge were bulging with food. She spent a satisfying afternoon arranging everything to her liking, and then went home to get her father's tea, a meal she sat through while he grumbled and complained at her lack of filial devotion. It was a relief, once she had tidied their meal away, to walk back to Wheel House and put the finishing touches to the kitchen. Miss Frobisher was upstairs somewhere, and the old house was quiet but for the gentle sound of running water from the mill. She had left the kitchen door open so the setting sun poured in, lighting the whole place as she made the last of her preparations for the morning. Sir William and Pauline would be arriving after lunch; she would bake a cake and scones in the morning and prepare everything for dinner that evening. She would have all day, so she wouldn't need to hurry.

She crossed to the door to close it and, with a final look round, went down the passage to the front hall. Sir William was standing there, his hands in his pockets, his head on one side, contemplating a large oil painting of a prissy-looking young lady in rose-coloured taffeta and ringlets, leaning over a gilded chair.

He glanced over his shoulder at her. 'Hello. She doesn't seem quite right there, does she? One of my more strait-laced forebears.' He smiled. 'I expect you're here for some reason?'

At the sight of him, Florina was experiencing a variety of sensations: a sudden rush of delight, peevishness at the thought of her untidy appearance, a deep sadness that he hadn't a clue as to who she was, which of course was ridiculous of her. And woven through this a variety of thoughts…suitable food which could be cooked quickly if he needed a meal.

He was watching her with faint amusement. 'Have we met?' He snapped a finger. 'Of course! You were so good as to tell us where we might stay when we first came here.'

'Yes,' said Florina breathlessly, 'that's me. I'm the cook. Miss Frobisher engaged me, but only if you approve.' She added to make it quite clear, 'I'm on a month's trial.'

'You don't look much like a cook.' He stared rather hard at the ginger plait hanging over one shoulder. 'But the proof of the pudding…as they say.'

He turned round as Miss Frobisher bustled in. 'Nanny, how nice to see you. I'm here a day too soon, aren't I? I've left Pauline with her aunt, but I'll drive back tomorrow and fetch her after lunch. I had a consultation in Salisbury and it seemed a good idea to come on here instead of driving back to town. Is everything just as it should be?'

'Aye, Sir William, it is. You'll be tired, no doubt. Cook will get you a light meal…'

'No need. I'll go to the Trout and Feathers. And I can't call you "cook", not with that pigtail. What is your name?'

'Florina Payne.' She caught Mrs Frobisher's stern eye, and added, 'Sir William.'

'Not an English name, but a pretty one.'

'My mother was Dutch, sir.'

'Indeed! I go to Holland from time to time.' He added kindly, 'Well, Florina, we'll see you in the morning—or do you live in?'

'In the village.'

'I'll need to leave early,' he observed, and strolled away towards the drawing-room.

Mrs Frobisher said, in a warning voice, 'So you had best be here at half-past seven, Florina, for he will want his breakfast at eight o'clock. You can have your own breakfast with me after he has gone.'

Florina glanced at the broad back disappearing through the open door of the drawing-room. She found the idea of cooking his breakfast positively exciting; an idea, she told herself sternly, which was both pointless and silly.

All the same, the thought of it sustained her through her father's diatribe when she got back home.

She made tea before she left in the morning, and took a cup up to her father, bade him a cheerful good morning, reminded him that everything was ready for his breakfast, just as usual, and walked quickly through the still quiet village. Wheel House was quiet, too. She went in through the kitchen door, using the key Mrs Frobisher had given her, and set to work. The kettle was boiling and the teapot warming when Sir William wandered in, wrapped in a rather splendid dressing-gown. She turned from cutting bread for toast and wished him a polite good morning. 'Where would you like your tea, sir?' she asked him. 'Breakfast will be in half an hour, sooner, if you wish.'

'Half an hour is fine. And I'll have my tea here.' He fetched a mug from the dresser, poured his tea and went to stand in the open doorway. 'What's for breakfast?'

'Bacon and eggs, with mushrooms, fried bread and tomato. Then, toast and marmalade, tea or coffee, sir.'

'Where did you learn to cook?' he asked idly.

'My mother taught me and I took a cookery course in Salisbury. I worked at the hotel in Wilton for several years.'

He nodded. 'I shall have guests sometimes. You could cope with that?'

She said seriously, 'Oh, yes.' She put a frying pan on the Aga. 'Would you like more tea, sir?'

He shook his head. 'Why not have a cup yourself?' He wandered to the door. 'Pauline will be glad to see you—she'll be here this afternoon.'

She set the table in the dining-room, and was making the toast when Miss Frobisher came into the kitchen. She eyed the laden tray with approval and her greeting held more warmth than usual. 'Sir William always likes a good breakfast; he's a big man and needs his strength for his work.' She shot a look at Florina. 'He's a doctor, did you know that? A very well known one. He was a dear little boy, I always knew he'd be successful. You'd better take that tray in, I can hear him coming downstairs.'

Florina laid the food on the table before him, casting a motherly glance at him hidden behind the morning paper. She had liked him on sight, she remembered, and that liking was growing by the minute. She would very much like to know all about him, of course, though she had the good sense to know that she never would.

Chapter 2

There was plenty to keep Florina busy that morning. After breakfast, shared with Mrs Frobisher, there was the menu to put together, the cake and scones to make and everything to prepare for the evening. That done, there was coffee to make for Mrs Frobisher, Mrs Deakin and Mrs Datchett, who came to sit around the kitchen table for a short break from their polishing and dusting. The latter two ladies were inclined to gossip, but received short shrift from the housekeeper, who didn't answer their questions about the new owner and silenced them with an intimidating eye.

'But he is going to marry?' persisted Mrs Deakin, not easily put off.

'It seems very likely,' conceded Mrs Frobisher,

and Florina thought that there was a trace of disquiet in the housekeeper's voice.

Florina left an excellent light lunch ready for the housekeeper, and took herself off home to get a meal for her father and herself. The breakfast dishes were still on the table and he was sitting in a chair, reading the paper.

He greeted her with a disgruntled, 'So there you are, and high time too!' Then he picked up his paper again, leaving her to clear the table, wash up and get a snack meal.

They ate in silence and Florina made short work of tidying everything away. Cleaning the house, dusting and carpet-sweeping took her another half an hour; there was an hour of leisure before she needed to return to Wheel House. She spent it in the big garden behind the cottage, weeding and tying back the clumps of old-fashioned flowers her mother had planted years ago, and which Florina tended still. She made tea for her father before she went, drank a cup herself, tidied her already neat person and returned to Wheel House. She had left everything ready for tea, and as she went round the back of the house to the kitchen wing she could hear the little girl's excited voice from the drawing-room, the door of which was open as she passed. Her hand was on the kitchen door when she was stopped.

The girl rushed at her from the room. 'I'm Pauline—oh, isn't this fun? Have you seen my room? It's pink and white! We've eaten almost all the scones and half the cake. Daddy says you must be a treasure in the kitchen.'

'Hello,' said Florina, and beamed at the pretty little face grinning at her. 'I'm so glad you enjoyed the cake. I'm going to get dinner ready now.'

'I'll help you.'

Pauline danced into the kitchen, examining the pots and saucepans, opening the cupboards and peering inside, peeping into the fridge. Florina, changing out of her dress into the striped cotton frock and large white apron which was her uniform while she was working, called from the little cloakroom leading from the kitchen, 'Put everything back where you found it, won't you, Pauline?'

She reappeared to collect the ingredients for the watercress soup, *boeuf en croûte*, and the chocolate sauce to go with the profiteroles.

Florina worked steadily, undeterred by Pauline's stream of excited chatter. She was chopping mint and Pauline was sitting on the table, running a finger round the remnants of the chocolate sauce in the pan, when Sir William wandered in.

'Something smells delightful. Is it a secret?'

'Watercress soup, *boeuf en croûte*, potatoes with mint, courgettes, new carrots, spinach purée, profiteroles with chocolate sauce, cheese and biscuits and coffee,' recited Florina, finishing the last of the sauce.

'It sounds good. Are you cordon bleu trained, Florina?'

'Yes, but I think I learnt almost everything from

my mother—the cordon bleu just—just put the polish on.'

She had washed her hands, and was piling profiteroles into a pyramid on a china dish. It crossed her mind that she felt completely at ease with Sir William, as though she had known him for years… She really must remember to call him Sir William. 'Dinner will be at half-past seven unless you would like to change that, Sir William?'

He said carelessly, 'Oh, no, why should I change it? I'll take Pauline off your hands—we'll go for a stroll.'

Without Pauline's pleasant chatter and her father's large presence, the kitchen seemed empty and quiet. Florina went to and fro, putting the finishing touches to the food. She was a little warm by now, but still very neat. Mrs Frobisher, coming into the kitchen, nodded approvingly.

'You certainly know your work,' she allowed. 'Sir William is a very punctual man, so have the soup ready on the dot. I'll carry in the food.'

The meal over and the last of the dishes back in the kitchen, Florina put the coffee tray ready to be carried in, and started on the clearing up.

The china, glass and silver Mrs Deakin would see to in the morning, but she did her saucepans and cooking utensils. It had been a strict rule at the hotel and one she intended to continue. She had just finished burnishing the last pan when Mrs Frobisher came back with the coffee tray. 'Sir William is very satisfied with your cooking,' she told Florina, 'I'm to pass on his compliments. He wants to know if you can cook for a dinner party next weekend. Eight sitting down to table, and Miss Fortesque, his fiancée, will be staying for the weekend.'

'No problem. If there is anything special Sir William wants, I'll do my best.'

'I'll ask him. You're finished? Did you put everything to keep warm in the Aga? Good. I'll lay the table and you dish up. It's been a busy evening, but you've done very well. I've suggested to Sir William that we get a girl from the village to come in in the evenings and help you clear up and see to the vegetables and so on. Do you know of one?'

Florina thought. 'Yes, there is Jean Smith at Keeper's Cottage—she's left school, but she's got to wait a month or two before she can start work training as a nurse. She will be glad of the money.'

'I'll leave you to ask her to come along and see me. Now, let's have dinner. I've seen Pauline safely up to bed, and Sir William has got all he wants. Your father knows you won't be home until later?'

'Oh, yes. I left his supper ready for him.'

'You're kept busy,' observed Mrs Frobisher. 'Mind you, during the week it will be midday dinner and a light supper at seven o'clock. You'll have most of the evening free. It is a pity that you can't live in.'

'Oh, I don't mind working late or coming early in the morning,' said Florina, and tried not to sound anxious.

She did not quite succeed, though, for Mrs Frobisher said quickly, 'Oh, don't worry about that dinner, Sir William won't want to lose you on any account. I was only thinking that it would be much easier for you; there's a nice little room at the top of the back stairs with its own bathroom, and nicely furnished, too. Still, I dare say your father would miss you.'

Florina, serving them with the last of the profiteroles, agreed quietly.

She faced a long-drawn-out lecture when she got home. She listened with half an ear while she washed up his supper things and put everything ready for the morning. When her father paused at last, she surprised him and herself by saying, without heat, 'Father, the doctor said that it would be good for you to do a few things for yourself. There's no reason why you shouldn't clear away your meals and wash up. You could make your bed, too, and get your own tea. I'm really working hard for most of the day, and I give you almost all my money. You could even get a part-time job! Then you would have more money and I could have some money of my own.'

She waited patiently while he gobbled and snorted, and told her several times that she was a wicked and ungrateful girl.

'Why?' asked Florina. 'It's not wicked to get you to help a little, especially when the doctor says it would be good for you. And what do I have to be grateful for, Father?'

'A roof over your head, and food and a bed!' he shouted very angrily.

She could get those if she lived in at Wheel

House… 'I'm thinking of leaving home,' she told him. 'I'll stay until you can get someone to come in and keep the house tidy and do the washing. You said a few days ago that a cousin of yours—Aunt Meg, was it? I don't remember her very well—had been widowed. She might be glad to come and live here with you…'

'You would leave your home? But you were born here, your mother lived here.'

'Yes, I know, Father, but now she isn't here any more it isn't home, not to me.' She added gently, 'You'll be happier if I'm not here, won't you?'

Her father's face turned alarmingly red. 'To think that a daughter of mine should say such a thing…'

'But it's true, isn't it, Father? And if Aunt Meg were here, she would be at home all day and be company for you. You wouldn't miss my money because she would pay her share, wouldn't she?'

He agreed in a grumbling voice. 'And, since you are determined to leave home and leave me to shift for myself, I'll write to her, I suppose. But don't you think you can come sneaking back here if you're ever out of a job.'

'There is always work for a good cook,' observed Florina.

Sunday was very much like Saturday, except that there was hot lunch and cold supper, which gave Florina a good deal more leisure. She left everything ready for tea and, intent on striking while the iron was hot, asked Mrs Frobisher if she had been serious when she had suggested that for her to live in would be more convenient for everyone.

'Yes, of course I was,' declared that lady. 'Why do you ask?'

Florina explained, leaving out the bits about her father's bad temper.

'A good idea. Come and see the room.'

It was a very nice room, its windows overlooking the river running through the garden. It was well furnished, too, with a small writing desk and an easy chair with a table beside it, and a divan bed along one wall with a fitted cover. There were pictures on the walls and a window-box cascading geraniums. There was a cupboard in one wall and a small bathroom, cunningly built into the roof. A minuscule kitchen contained a sink and a minature gas cooker, capable of turning out a meal for one, as well as an electric kettle.

'Why, it's perfect! Whoever thought of it?'

'Sir William. He enjoys comfort, and wants everyone around him to be comfortable, too. I believe that he will be pleased if you were to live here, Florina, but of course I'll say nothing until you've decided.'

She had a good deal more leisure for the rest of the week. Sir William left early on the Monday morning, but that leisure was very much encroached on by Pauline, who attached herself to Florina at every possible moment. Though Florina, who had perforce led a somewhat solitary life, enjoyed her company; it was fun to show the child where she could find mushrooms and wild strawberries, sit by the river and watch for water voles, and feed the swans. Pauline, who had spent almost all her life in London, loved every minute of it. But, if life was pleasant while she was at the Wheel House, it was uncomfortable at home. Her father had indeed written to her aunt, and received a reply, full of enthusiasm for his scheme and suggesting that she would be ready to join him in a couple of weeks' time, news which apparently gave him no pleasure at all. Not that he wanted Florina to change her plans. Indeed, she had told him Mrs Frobisher knew that she was willing to live in, providing Sir William agreed. Cutting sandwiches for Pauline's tea, she had never felt so happy.

It had to be too good to last. On Friday morning she began her preparations for the weekend. She and Mrs Frobisher had decided on a menu, and the housekeeper had gone to Wilton and bought everything for Florina on her list, so it had only remained for her to assemble them ready for Saturday evening. Mrs Frobisher, who seemed to like her, in a guarded manner, had taken her upstairs in the afternoon to show her the guest room.

'Miss Fortesque is used to town ways,' she explained. 'She'll expect her breakfast in bed…' She sniffed. 'She'll not want me here when they're married.'

'But were you not Pauline's Nanny?'

'And Sir William's before her.' Miss Fortesque forgotten momentarily, Mrs Frobisher threw open the two doors close to the room they were viewing. 'Guest rooms,' she pointed out. 'Pauline's room is on the other side of the landing, as is Sir William's. You've noticed that there are more rooms above the kitchen. The housekeeper's—I sleep on this landing at present because otherwise Pauline would be alone… There is another bathroom and a third bedroom. I dare say Miss Fortesque will want someone else to live in. It's a large house and I doubt if she knows what a duster looks like.'

Certainly, dusters were the last things one would think of at the sight of Miss Fortesque, thought Florina, watching from the kitchen window as she stepped from Sir William's car on Saturday morning. She was the picture of elegance, the sort of elegance never seen in the village: a sleeveless dress of what Florina was sure was pure silk in palest blue, Italian sandals and enormous hoop earrings matching the gold bracelets on her arms. Florina sighed without knowing it, twitched her apron so that it covered her small person correctly, and went back to the preparation of *crêpes de volaille Florentine.* She was making the cheese sauce when Sir William wandered into the kitchen.

'Hello,' he said. 'Every time I see you, you're slaving over a hot stove.'

She couldn't prevent her delight at seeing him showing on her face, although she didn't know that. 'I'm the cook, sir,' she reminded him.

'Yes—I seem to have difficulty in remembering that.' He smiled at her and called over his shoulder, 'Wanda, come and meet Florina.'

Miss Fortesque strolled in and linked an arm in his. 'Oh, hello. You're the cook?'

The air positively hummed with their mutual dislike, instantly recognized, even if silent. Sir William watched them from half-shut lids.

'Florina is our treasure—she cooks like a dream, and Pauline considers her to be her best friend.'

Wanda opened large blue eyes. 'Oh, the poor child, has she no friends of her own sort?' She made a small gesture. 'Is it wise to let her live here, William? At a good boarding-school she would make friends with all the right children.'

'Who are the right children?' he asked carelessly. 'Don't be a snob, Wanda. Pauline is happy; she'll be going to day school in Wilton in September, and there's plenty to occupy her here meantime.' He glanced at Florina. 'Does she bother you, Florina?'

'Not in the least, Sir William. She is learning to cook and she spends a great deal of time gardening. She and Mrs Frobisher go for long walks.'

Miss Fortesque turned on her heel. 'Oh, well, if you're quite content to leave her with the servants...' She smiled bewitchingly, 'I shall alter all that, of course. When are the others arriving?'

Florina was left to seethe over the Aga. The horrible girl was quite unsuitable to be Sir William's wife, and she would be a disastrous stepmother. If Sir William was as easy-going as he appeared to be, then Pauline would find herself at a boarding-school, and she and Nanny would be out of jobs. Not too bad for Nanny, for she had already officially retired, but it would mean finding work for herself, and away from home, too.

Despite her rage, she served up a lunch which

was perfection itself, and shared a quick meal with Nanny. When Sir William, with his fiancée and Pauline, had driven off for a brief tour of the surrounding country, Florina arranged the tea tray and then got down to preparing dinner. The house was quiet: Mrs Frobisher had gone to put her feet up before tea, Mrs Deakin was doing the last of the washing up and Florina concentrated on her cooking. By the time she heard the car stop by the house, she was satisfied that there was nothing more to do for an hour or so.

Two other cars arrived then, and Mrs Frobisher, much refreshed by the nap, carried in the tea tray and the assortment of cakes and sandwiches Florina had got ready, before she came back to share a pot of tea with Florina.

The kitchen was warm; she opened the windows wide and sat down gratefully, listening to Mrs Frobisher describing Sir William's guests. Rather nice, she was told, and had known him for years—doctors and their wives, rather older than he was.

'And, of course, Miss Fortesque,' added Nanny, and she sounded as though she had inadvertently sucked on a lemon. 'A well preserved woman, one might say, but of course she spends a great deal of time and money upon herself.'

Obviously Nanny didn't approve of Sir William's Wanda, but Florina didn't dare to say so; she murmured vaguely and her companion went on, 'Had her claws into him for months. I'm surprised at him—she'll be a bad wife for him and a worse stepmother for my little Pauline.' She passed her cup for more tea. 'He's so busy with all those sick children, he only sees her when she's dressed up and all charm and prettiness. Of course, that's very nice for the gentlemen when they've had a hard day's work, but when all's said and done they want a wife as well, someone who'll sit on the opposite side of the fireplace and knit while he reads the papers, listen when he wants to talk, and love his children.' Nanny snorted. 'All she likes to do is dance and play bridge.'

'Perhaps she'll change,' suggested Florina gently, not quite sure if she should voice an opinion. Nanny was obviously labouring under strong feelings, and possibly she would regret her outburst later on.

'You're a good girl,' said Nanny, 'I've wanted to say all that to someone for weeks, and you're the only person I've felt I could talk to.'

To Florina's distress, Mrs Frobisher's eyes filled with tears. 'I had him as a baby,' she said.

'They're not married yet,' ventured Florina. She added, very thoughtfully, 'It just needs someone to give fate a push and change things…'

Mrs Frobisher blew her nose, an awesome sound. 'You're a sensible girl as well as a good one, Florina.'

Florina dished up a splendid dinner: artichoke hearts with a sharp dressing of her own invention, lobster cardinal, medallions of beef with a wine sauce and truffles, and tiny pancakes filled with strawberries and smothered in thick cream.

When the coffee tray had gone in, she and Nanny sat down to eat what was left, before Nanny went away to see Pauline into bed. Mrs Deakin had come back to help with the clearing up, but all the same the evening was far gone, and Sir William seeing his guests on their way, by the time they were finished in the kitchen. Florina set everything ready for the morning, changed into her dress and, with Mrs Deakin for company, locked the kitchen door after her and started for home.

They were at the gate when Sir William loomed out from the shrubs alongside the short drive. 'A delightful meal, Florina! My compliments, and thank you, and Mrs Deakin, for working late.'

Mrs Deakin muttered happily; she was being paid overtime, and generously, for any work she did over and above her normal hours. Florina said quietly, 'Thank you, Sir William. Goodnight.'

He would go into his lovely house presently, she supposed, and Wanda would be waiting for him. Florina had caught a glimpse of her during the evening—a vision in scarlet chiffon. Enough to turn any man's head, even that of the placid, good-natured Sir William.

She was making a salad the next day when Miss Fortesque, in a startling blue jersey dress and a great many gold bangles, strolled into the kitchen.

'Hello, Cook, busy among your saucepans again? It's really surprising that even in the depths of the country it's possible to find someone who can turn out a decent meal.' She smiled sweetly. 'After town standards, you know, one hardly expects it.'

Florina shredded lettuce with hands which shook very slightly with temper, and said nothing.

'That sauce last night,' continued her visitor, 'I fancied that there was a touch too much garlic in it. Sir William didn't complain—he's really too easy-going...'

'When Sir William complains to me, Miss Fortesque, I shall listen to him,' said Florina very evenly.

Wanda's eyes opened wide. 'Don't you dare to speak to me like that, Cook! I'll have you dismissed...' She advanced, rather unwisely, too close to Florina, who had started to whip up a dressing for the salad. She increased her beating with a vigour which sent oily drops in all directions. The blue dress would never be the same again; a shower of little blobs had made a graceful pattern down its front.

Wanda's breath was a hiss of fury. 'You clumsy fool—look what you've done! It's ruined—I'll have to have a new dress, and I'll see that it's stopped out of your wages! I'll...'

Sir William's voice, very placid, cut her short. 'My dear Wanda, if you hadn't been standing so close, it wouldn't have happened. You can't blame Florina, you've only yourself to thank. Surely you know that cooks must be left in peace in their kitchens when they are cooking?'

Wanda shot him a furious glance. She said pettishly, 'I'll have to go and change. I hope you'll give the girl a good telling-off.'

She flounced out of the kitchen and Florina began to slice tomatoes very thinly. Sir William spoke from the door. 'I found the sauce exactly right,' he said gently, and wandered away.

He took his fiancée back to town that evening, leaving behind a rather unhappy Pauline. He sought out Florina before he left, to tell her that for the next few weeks, while the child was on holiday, he would come down each weekend on Friday afternoons, and drive back early on Monday morning.

'Nanny tells me that you may decide to move in with us. Your father doesn't object to being alone?'

Her aunt had written to say that she would be arriving at the end of the week. She told him this, leaving out the details. He nodded pleasantly. 'I'm sure it will give you more leisure. I hope you'll be happy here. Pauline will be over the moon when you tell her.'

She thought wistfully that it would have been nice if he had expressed the same satisfaction, even if in a more modified form. She bade him a quiet goodnight, more or less drowned by Miss Fortesque's voice, pitched high, demanding that they should leave at once.

The week unfolded at a leisurely pace; Florina packed her things, got her room ready for her aunt and moved to the Wheel House. Her father bade her goodbye with no sign of regret, merely warning her again that she need not expect to go crying back to him when she found herself out of a job. She received this remark without rancour, aware that if he should fall ill again the first thing that he would do would be to demand that she should return home to look after him.

She enjoyed arranging her few possessions in her

room at Wheel House, helped by a delighted Pauline. Once settled in, she found that she had a good deal more leisure. Cooking for the three of them took up only a part of her day; she helped Nanny with the ironing and the cleaning of the silver, took Pauline mushrooming in the early mornings, and, with Mrs Frobisher's consent, started to give her cooking lessons. By the time Sir William arrived on Friday afternoon, there was a dish of jam tarts and a fruit cake, a little soggy in the middle but still edible, both of which Pauline bore to the tea table with pride. Sir William, a kind and loving parent, ate quantities of both.

The weekend was one of the happiest Florina had spent for a long time. For one thing, there was a peaceful content over the old home. Sir William insisted that they all breakfast together in the kitchen, a meal which Florina cooked with an almost painful wish to serve up something to perfection, just to please him. She succeeded very well; he ate everything put before him, carrying on a cheerful conversation meanwhile, even making Nanny laugh, something she seldom did. They were at the toast and marmalade stage on Saturday morning, when Pauline said, 'I wish it could be like this always—just us, Daddy—you and me and Nanny and Florina. Must you marry Wanda? She wouldn't sit at the kitchen table, and she's always fussing about eating in case she gets fat.'

Florina saw the look on Sir William's face. There was a nasty temper hidden away behind that calm exterior, and to avert it she got to her feet, exclaiming loudly, 'Shall I make another pot of coffee? And how about more toast?' At the same time she cast a warning glance at Pauline.

The child had gone very red and tears weren't far off. She sighed and said, 'I'm sorry, Daddy.'

His face was placid again. 'That's all right, darling. What are we going to do today?'

The pair of them went off presently, and Florina prepared lunch, decided what to have for dinner, made the coffee and went to help Nanny with the beds. The rest of the weekend was peaceful, and Florina, taking along the coffee tray to the patio where Sir William had settled with the Sunday papers after church, while Pauline fed the swans, thought how delightful life was.

She gave him breakfast the next morning, happily aware that he would be back on Friday afternoon. Wanda Fortesque had gone to stay with friends in the south of France, and Florina allowed herself the childish hope that something, anything, would prevent her from ever coming back from there!

The weather changed suddenly during the day, by the evening it was chilly and grey, and Pauline seemed to have the beginnings of a cold.

Nanny came down to the kitchen after she had seen Pauline to bed. 'The child's feverish,' she declared. 'I think I'd better keep her in bed tomorrow; these summer colds can be heavy.'

But when morning came, Pauline was feeling worse; moreover, she had a pinky, blotchy rash.

'Measles,' said Nanny, and phoned for the doctor.

He came from Wilton that morning, confirmed Nanny's diagnosis, and observed that there was a lot of it about and that Pauline, having had an anti-measles injection when she was a little girl, would soon be on her feet again. 'Plenty to drink,' he advised, 'and keep her in bed until her temperature is down.' He patted Nanny reassuringly on the shoulder. 'Nothing to worry about.'

All the same, Nanny telephoned Sir William in London, only to be told that he was at the hospital and would be there all day. She put the phone down, undecided as to what to do, when it rang again.

Florina, making iced lemonade for the invalid, heard her talking at some length, and presently she came back to the kitchen.

'Sir William's not at home and won't be until the evening, but Miss Fortesque was there. She rang back when I told her I wanted him urgently, said she would tell him when he got back. I would rather have phoned the hospital, but that would be no use if he is in the theatre or the out-patients.'

By the time they were ready for bed, more than ready, for Florina had suggested that neither Mrs Deakin nor Mrs Datchett came to work until Pauline was better, for they both had children, there had been no word from Sir William. Nanny telephoned once more, only to be told by Miss Fortesque that he was still out.

Pauline was much better in the morning and Nanny, while still a tiny bit puzzled as to why Sir

William hadn't telephoned, decided that there was no need to bother him, not until the evening at any rate. She and Florina spent another busy day, for the house was large and there was a certain amount of work to get through, as well as pandering to Pauline's increasing whims. Nanny had a headache by teatime, and Florina persuaded her to go to bed early.

'Only if you telephone Sir William,' declared Nanny.

Florina waited until she had taken up two supper trays, eaten a scratch meal of beans on toast herself, before dialling the number she had been given. Miss Fortesque answered. No, Sir William wasn't at home and wasn't likely to be for some time and was it urgent? He had had a busy day and needed his rest. She slammed down the receiver before Florina had got her mouth open.

Nanny had a rash in the morning, a high temperature, a terrible headache and a firmly rooted opinion that she was going to die.

'Nonsense, Mrs Frobisher,' said Florina robustly. 'You've got the measles. I'm going to get the doctor.'

He wasn't quite as cheerful about Nanny. It transpired that she had never had measles as a child, an illness, which he pointed out to Florina, that could be quite serious in anyone as elderly as Nanny. 'Keep her in bed,' he advised. 'Plenty of fluids, and don't let her read or use her eyes. Keep the blinds drawn and take her temperature every four hours. I'll be out to see her again tomorrow.' He added as an afterthought, 'Can you manage?'

Sir William would be home on the next day, so Florina assured the doctor that, of course, she could manage.

It was hard work. Pauline had made a quick recovery, although she still needed looking after and had to stay in bed for another day or so, but Nanny, suddenly an old, ill Nanny, needed constant attention. Not that she was a difficult patient, but she was feverish, her head ached and she fretted at lying in bed.

Florina, trotting up and down stairs with trays and cool drinks, was tempted to telephone Sir William again, but it hardly seemed worth it since he would be home in less than twenty-four hours. She settled her two patients for the night at last, and went to the kitchen to make out a menu for Sir William's dinner for the following evening. It would have to be something quick, and which could be left in the Aga to look after itself. She made a chocolate mousse and put it in the freezer, made a vegetable soup, and then decided that she would make a cheese soufflé—something which could be done at the last minute. She had picked some peas and beans earlier in the day, and there was plenty of fruit and cheese and biscuits. She went to take a last look at her two patients and then went to bed herself, to sleep the moment her head touched the pillow.

Doctor Stone came again the next morning, cautioned her that Pauline should stay in bed for another day or so, declared that Nanny was holding her own nicely, but that she would need careful nursing, accepted a cup of coffee and remarked that Florina was managing very well.

'No need to send you a nurse,' he told her, 'and, since there isn't one available at the moment, that's a good thing. Is Sir William coming down for the weekend?'

Florina said that, yes, he was, and thought tiredly of all the extra cooking there would be. She was, after all, the cook, and he had every right to expect well prepared meals to be set before him. Doctor Stone went, and she made a large quantity of lemonade, then made herself a sandwich and started to get a light lunch for Pauline. Nanny didn't want anything, but Florina made an egg nog and spent some precious time persuading her to drink it.

She spent more time settling Pauline for the afternoon. There was the radio, of course, and her cassette player, and since reading wasn't to be encouraged, a sketch-book had to be found with coloured crayons. Florina, finally free to go to the kitchen, put on a clean apron, tossed her plait over her shoulder and started to shell the peas.

She was very tired; she let the sound of the stream, racing under the house and on into the garden, soothe her. She was disturbed five minutes later by a leisurely tread in the hall, and a moment later Sir William said from the kitchen door, 'Hello! The house is very quiet.'

When she turned to look at him he saw her white, tired face.

'What's wrong, Florina?'

She heard the sudden briskness of his usually placid voice. 'Measles,' she said. 'Pauline started on Monday and now Nanny has it… Yesterday—I've had the doctor. Doctor Stone, from Wilton.'

'Why wasn't I told?'

'Nanny telephoned you on Monday night, and then again on Tuesday. I rang again on Thursday evening…'

Sir William didn't answer. He went to the telephone on the wall by the Aga, and dialled a number. Florina went back to shelling her peas and listened.

'Jolly? Get hold of our Shirley and bribe her to sleep in for a few nights with Mrs Jolly. Then pack a bag and drive down here as soon as you can. Take the Rover and make all speed. We have a problem on our hands. Measles, no less!'

'On your own?' he asked, as he put back the receiver.

'Well, yes. You see, Mrs Deakin and Mrs Datchett have children.'

'Very wise. I'm going to take a look. Is Pauline on the mend? She had her jab when she was small.'

'Yes, she's over the worst. Mrs Frobisher is really quite ill, though…'

She heard him going upstairs two at a time.

By the time he returned she had finished the peas, had the kettle boiling for tea and had laid a tray with the tea things and a plate of scones.

He sat down at the kitchen table and told her to get another cup. 'Very spotty, the pair of them. Nanny's going to take a little while to get over it, but Pauline's well out of the wood.' He shot the next question at her so fast that she answered it without once pausing to think. 'Who answered the telephone when you and Nanny telephoned?'

'Miss Fortesque...' She went red because he would think her sneaky. 'I'm sure it was a misunderstanding...'

He didn't answer that. 'You've had your hands full—up for a good deal of the night, too?'

'Well, yes. Nanny felt so hot and ill, but Pauline slept well.'

His rather sleepy gaze swept round the kitchen. 'You've been running the place, and cooking, as well as looking after Pauline and Nanny?'

She misunderstood him completely. 'Oh, but I had all day. Dinner will be ready at half-past seven, but I can put it forward half an hour if you wish. I don't settle them for the night until about nine o'clock. Pauline likes her supper about eight o'clock and Nanny doesn't want to eat at present—I've been giving her egg and milk and tea and lemonade.'

He smiled at her suddenly. 'My poor dear, you are tired to the bone, aren't you? You've got dinner fixed already?' When she nodded, he continued, 'We'll eat here together, then you can get supper for Pauline and I'll take it up; I'll see that Nanny takes her fluids, too, and then I'll wash up while you get Pauline ready for bed.'

She opened her mouth to protest, but he lifted a large hand to stop her. 'I'm going back to take another look at Nanny and then to phone Doctor Stone. Which room should Jolly have when he comes?'

'There is the small guest room at the end of the passage where Nanny is—I'll make up the bed…'

'Put the bed linen out; I'll see to the bed, you stay here and get on with dinner.'

Florina, whose father had always considered the making of a bed to be a woman's work, was surprised, but Sir William had spoken in a voice which, while quiet, obviously expected to be obeyed. She cleared away the tea tray and set the kitchen table for the two of them before getting the ingredients for the soufflé.

Sir William was as good as his word; she was ready soon after seven o'clock, and he fetched the sherry decanter from the dining-room and poured each of them a glass, and then sat down opposite her and ate dinner with a splendid appetite, talking about nothing much. When they had finished, he sent her upstairs to Pauline. 'I'll fetch the tray down; you tidy her up for the night and then come back here.'

It was pleasant to have someone there to arrange things; Florina did as she was told and half an hour later went back downstairs to find Sir William, one of Nanny's aprons strained around his person, making the coffee.

'Sit down and drink it,' he ordered her, 'then, if you'll see to Nanny, I'll finish up down here and say goodnight to Pauline.'

Nanny was quite willing to be settled for the night. Everything, she told Florina, would be quite all right now that Sir William was home. 'You cooked him a good dinner?' she demanded.

Florina said that yes, she had, but she didn't mention that she had shared it with him at the kitchen table. There was no sense in sending Nanny's temperature up! She wished her goodnight and went yawning down the staircase; bed would be delightful, but first she must make sure that the kitchen was ready for the morning. Sir William would want his breakfast, and there was early-morning tea, and what about Jolly—who was Jolly, anyway?

The kitchen door to the garden was still open and Sir William was out on the patio, leaning over the balustrade, watching the stream below him.

'Come and have five minutes' peace,' he advised and she went to stand beside him, hot and dishevelled and very tired. He glanced sideways at her smiling faintly, surprised that it worried him to see her looking so weary. He didn't say anything and she was glad just to lean there, doing nothing until a car turning into the gates roused her.

'That will be Jolly,' said Sir William, and went round the side of the house to meet him.

Chapter 3

Florina was still standing on the patio when Sir William returned, with Jolly beside him. Jolly was the antithesis of his name. He had a long, narrow face, very solemn and pale, dark eyes, and hair greying at the temples, smoothed to a satin finish. He was dressed soberly in a black jacket and striped trousers, and wore an old-fashioned wing-collar and a black bow-tie.

Sir William halted in front of Florina. 'This is Jolly, who runs my home. Jolly, this is Florina, who cooks for me and has been coping on her own for the last couple of days. I think we'll send her to bed and we'll discuss what's best to be done. Off you go, Florina, sleep the clock round if you want to.'

She was quite shocked. 'Breakfast…'

'Ah, you don't really trust us with the frying-pan. I dare say you're right. Breakfast is at half-past eight. You do the cooking, we'll clear up. We'll work out a routine in the morning. Now, off with you.'

It was difficult to go against this casual friendliness. Besides, she had had a long day. She said goodnight to them both, and went upstairs to lie in the bath, half-asleep, and think about how nice Sir William was. But the cooling water brought her wide awake, and she tumbled into bed, to sleep soundly almost at once.

She was wakened by Sir William's voice, and shot up in bed, in an instant panic that she had overslept. He was wearing a rather grand dressing-gown, and stood by the bed with a mug from the kitchen in his hand.

He gave it to her and said cheerfully, 'Tea—you've slept well?' Then he sat himself down carefully on the side of the bed. He hadn't appeared to look at her, but he had taken in her face, rosy from sleep, her hair freed from its tidy plait, hanging in a mousy tangle round her shoulders. She looked a different girl from the pale, tired little creature he had found in the kitchen on the previous evening.

He went on easily, 'I've taken a look at our two invalids. Pauline is doing fine; Nanny's still feverish—she'll need a few days' nursing still, but luckily she's decided not to die this time, and is already giving orders about cleaning the bath and getting extra milk. A good sign!' He got off the bed. 'It's half-past seven. When you're ready, would you go along and make Nanny comfortable before breakfast? Jolly will see to the table for you and lay the trays and so forth. We'll eat in the kitchen; that will save dusting the dining-room.'

He smiled and nodded and wandered away, leaving her to drink her tea and then, as quickly as she could, to shower and dress, reflecting as she did so that she had never met anybody quite like him before. She couldn't remember her father ever bringing her a cup of tea in bed; he had always been at pains to point out to her, and her mother while she had been alive, that since a man spent his day working to keep a roof over their heads, it was only right that he should be properly looked after in his own home.

Her hair once more neatly plaited, wearing one of her striped cotton dresses, she went along to visit Pauline first, sitting up in bed and feeling so much better that she demanded to be allowed up.

'Not until your father says so,' said Florina briskly. 'I dare say he'll come to see you when he's had breakfast. What would you like? Are you hungry?'

They settled on scrambled eggs and, as Florina skimmed to the door, intent on dealing with Nanny, Pauline called after her, 'You are nice, Florina—the nicest friend I've ever had. Daddy likes you, too.'

A remark which sent a pleasant glow through Florina's person. It was delightful to be liked and needed. She beamed at Nanny's cross face, coaxed her to have her face and hands washed, smoothed her bed and suggested a pot of tea and some thin bread and butter.

'If you insist,' said Nanny peevishly, 'though I don't say I'll eat it.'

Jolly was in the kitchen, laying the table. He bade her a dignified good morning, expressed the hope that she had slept well, and started to cut bread for toast. Florina busied herself with the frying-pan, bacon, mushrooms and a bowl of eggs. 'Yes, thank you, Mr Jolly…'

'Jolly, miss. I am Sir William's manservant.'

She turned to look at him. 'Well, I'm his cook. I think that's what you should call me…'

His severe expression broke into a brief smile. 'If you don't object, I prefer to call you miss.'

'Well, if you want to, as long as Sir William doesn't mind.'

'What am I objecting to?' He was a large, rather heavily built man, but he moved with speed and silence.

'Mr—that is, Jolly wishes to call me miss, and I'm the cook…' She looked up briefly from scrambling eggs.

Sir William took a slice of bread and buttered it and began to eat.

'You're not Missus, are you?' he asked with interest.

'Certainly not!'

'Engaged or walking out, or whatever?'

'No, Sir William. Would you both like bacon and eggs and mushrooms and tomatoes?'

'Speaking for myself, yes, please, and I'm pretty sure Jolly would, too. Mrs Jolly always gives me fried bread and I dare say she gives it to Jolly, too.'

'Very well, Sir William. I'll just run up with Pauline's tray.'

'Give it to Jolly—what is Nanny having? Is this her tray? I'll take it up when you're ready.' He made the tea, whistling cheerfully, and presently they sat down to breakfast, a pleasant meal, with Sir William carrying on an easy conversation and Jolly, rather surprisingly, contributing his share of the talk. As for Florina, she had little to say. She was shy, for a start, and for another thing, meals with her father had been strictly for eating; no attempt had been made to enliven them with conversation.

Sir William got out the vacuum cleaner after breakfast and, while Jolly cleared the table and washed the dishes, he strode around his house, taking no notice of Florina's attempts to stop him, hoovering like a whirlwind.

'You have a poor opinion of my capabilities,' he observed. 'I think you should go away and shake up pillows and make beds. You can tell Pauline that if she stays quietly in bed, she may come down for tea this afternoon.'

She was half-way up the stairs when he asked, 'What are we eating for our lunch?' He switched off for a moment so that she could hear him. 'Ploughman's lunch? Then you won't need to cook. Is there any Stilton in the house?'

'Of course.' She spoke coldly, affronted that he should doubt her housekeeping.

He didn't notice. 'Good. Do you want any shopping done? I can run into Wilton with the car...' He was at the bottom of the staircase, looking up at her. 'Let me know when you come down.'

While she made the beds and attended to Pauline and Nanny, she reviewed the contents of the fridge and freezer. She would need eggs from the farm and a chicken as well as cream. There was a nice piece of beef in the freezer and vegetables in the garden. When she went back to the kitchen later, it was to find Jolly setting out mugs for coffee and bending in a dignified manner over the coffeepot on the Aga. Smiling widely at him, despite his forbidding appearance, she felt sure he was a very reliable man and, in his reserved way, she felt also that he was disposed to like her. As for Sir William, she didn't allow herself to think too much about him; he resembled a little too closely for her peace of mind the rather vague dreams she had of the man who would sweep her off her feet and marry her and live with her happily ever after. She reminded herself once again that daydreaming got you nowhere. Indeed, it was downright silly when you had your living to earn. She accepted a mug from Jolly, frowned fiercely when Sir William joined them, then she blushed, remembering how she had let her thoughts stray.

He gave her a quick glance and began to talk to Jolly. Presently, when he made some remark to her, she had regained her usual composed manner. The rest of the morning passed busily, and somehow the sight of Sir William standing at the sink scraping potatoes put her quite at her ease with him. The invalids attended to, the three of them sat down at the kitchen table again. She had made a bowl of salad, and Jolly had cut great hunks of bread and arranged the Stilton cheese on a dish flanked by pickles and chutney. Sir William had a tankard of beer beside him, Jolly had made himself a pot of tea and Florina had poured herself a glass of lemonade. Not at all the kind of meal Sir William was used to, reflected Florina, but he seemed happy enough, spreading his bread lavishly with butter and carving up the Stilton. They talked comfortably of small everyday matters and then fell to discussing how she should cook the chicken. *'Poulet au citron?'* suggested Florina, and caught Jolly's approving look.

'Nice,' observed Sir William, 'Mrs Jolly does a very nice *Poulet Normand*.'

This remark instantly put her on her mettle. 'If you prefer that, Sir William, I think I could manage it.'

He laughed. 'Don't be so modest, Florina. You could turn a stale loaf into a splendid meal with one hand tied behind your back!' He watched the colour wash over her cheeks; for a moment she looked quite pretty.

They were sitting at the table drinking their coffee, deciding which vegetables to have, when the front door was banged shut and high heels tapped across the hall's wooden floor. Wanda Fortesque pushed the kitchen door wide open and came to a halt just inside it, looking at them. It was evident that she was in a splendid rage and had no intention of hiding it, but Sir William didn't appear to have noticed that; he got up without haste.

'Wanda, my dear girl, what a delightful surprise!'

'Surprise?' she almost spat at him. 'I'd say it was a surprise! What's this? A *ménage à trois*?'

He said easily, 'Hardly, since there are five of us here. Come and sit down—have you lunched? Or would you like coffee?'

She stared at the table. 'I don't eat in the kitchen, William.' Her very beautiful lip curled. 'I thought you employed a cook.' Her peevish eye settled on Florina, sitting like a mouse, hardly daring to breathe. 'She can make me an omelette and salad and bring it to the dining-room. Oh, and some fruit. Why on earth is Jolly sitting here, doing nothing?'

Sir William put his hands in his pockets; he spoke pleasantly, but there was no expression on his face. 'Jolly is here because I asked him to come and, since you enquire, he has been working flat out since he arrived. You see, my dear, Nanny and Pauline have the measles—Nanny is quite ill. Florina had been managing on her own, deciding, quite rightly, that it was hardly fair to our usual help to expect them to come in from the village—measles is so very infectious…'

'Measles,' repeated Wanda, in a voice that had become a little shrill. She backed away. 'Why didn't you say so in the first place? I've not had them—the place must be full of germs.' She added wildly, 'It's spots, isn't it? Great red blotches, and puffy eyes and headaches.'

She turned on her heel and hurried back through the hall. Sir William went after her.

She turned to face him when they reached the door. 'Why didn't you tell me? You could have telephoned...' It was an accusation.

'I did,' he told her mildly. 'You weren't at home and you had left a message to say that I wasn't to ring you, you would ring me.' He added gently, 'I'm sorry you're upset, Wanda. Why not stay now you are here? You won't have to go near Pauline and Nanny.'

'You must be mad—supposing I caught them? There's the Springfields' party next week, and Mother is giving a dinner—and there is that dress show I simply mustn't miss...'

'Why not?' He was smiling now, but she didn't smile back.

'Don't be an idiot, William—I have to have clothes. I've hardly a rag to my back. I intend to be a wife you can be proud of. Besides, I know so many influential people; it's important to mix with the right people, especially when you're a doctor.'

He was still smiling but his eyes were chilly. 'I already mix with the right people, my dear. My patients.'

'You're impossible. I'll not listen to another word! You can come and apologise when you get back to town on Monday.'

He walked with her to her car. 'It doesn't seem

likely that I'll be back on Monday,' he told her patiently, 'but I'll be in touch.'

Back in the kitchen he said calmly, 'Sorry about that—Miss Fortesque is rather—highly strung is the popular phrase, I believe. Some people are inordinately nervous of catching things.' He took the tea-towel from Florina and began to dry the dishes Jolly was washing.

'Will there be scones for tea?' he asked her. Then, as an afterthought, 'You've had measles?'

Florina said primly, 'No, but I don't in the least mind having them, though I'd rather not, as it would make things so awkward for everyone.'

He shouted with laughter and Jolly allowed himself a dry chuckle.

'Well, that's a bridge we'll cross when we come to it. What a boring job washing up is! Jolly, you should have told me…'

'It was mentioned a year or so ago, Sir William, if you remember, and a dishwasher was installed. A boon to Shirley, if I might say so.'

'Well, we'd better have one here, too. See to it, will you, Jolly?'

Florina, assembling the ingredients for the scones, marvelled at the way some people lived. Shouldn't he have consulted Miss Fortesque first? On second thoughts, no.

She put the scones in the Aga and went to see how the invalids were getting on. Pauline was happy enough, as good as gold in bed, knowing that presently she would be going downstairs for her tea.

Nanny, however, badly needed a great deal of attention. She was hot, she was thirsty, she wanted her bed remade, and who had banged the front door and wakened her from a refreshing nap?

Florina soothed her, sped downstairs to take the scones from the oven, refill the jug of lemonade, and skip back again. Half an hour later, Nanny washed and in a fresh nightie, her bed remade, her hair combed, and sitting up against her pillows sipping lemonade, felt well enough to tell Florina that she was a good girl with a kind heart and she, for her part, was delighted to hear that Miss Fortesque had taken herself off again.

'I cannot think what Sir William sees in the creature,' she declared, and Florina silently agreed. Although perhaps a lovely face, and clothes in the height of fashion and an air of knowing that one was never wrong, could be irresistible to a man. She went down to the kitchen and got tea ready before starting on the chicken.

They played Monopoly after tea, still at the kitchen table, and Florina and Sir William took it in turns to visit Nanny. In between times she saw to dinner. There was a pause while everyone watched her pour the brandy into a skillet and hold a lighted match over it. The flames soared as she tipped the pan from side to side and, when they had died down, she poured the delicious liquid into the bowl of cream and covered the chicken before popping it into a pan and putting a lid on it. There was time for her to make her fortune at Monopoly, which she did while it simmered. Jolly laid the table, and Sir William went down to the cellar to fetch the wine while she made the sauce, cooked the rice and fried the triangles of bread to arrange around the chicken. Pauline had coaxed her father to let her stay up for dinner, and she sat watching Florina as she trotted to and fro between the table and the Aga, peering into the pans holding the baby carrots, the garden peas and the courgettes. Sir William, strolling in with the bottles under his arms, paused to watch her, her hair a little shaken loose from its plait, her small nose shining, intent on her work. A pleasant enough nonentity, he had decided when he had first seen her, but he had been wrong; small, unassuming and nothing much to look at, she still merited a second look. She would make a good nurse, too. He toyed with the idea and then discarded it. She was far too good a cook; besides, Pauline had developed a great liking for her.

'It smells delicious,' he observed, and put the bottles in the fridge. 'If I pour you a glass of sherry, will it upset the cooking?'

Everything was eaten, and Jolly pronounced the chicken every bit as good as that his wife could cook, adding rather severely, 'Although, of course, miss, it wouldn't do to go and tell her so.'

'It shall remain a secret, Jolly,' Sir William had promised. He smiled across the table at Florina. 'Did you conjure the crème caramel out of the air?'

She answered him quite seriously. 'No, Sir William. I baked them in the oven, with the milk pudding for Mrs Frobisher.'

'All of which she ate. Now take yourself off for an hour, while Jolly and I clear up.' When she would have protested he added, 'You need some fresh air, and heaven knows, you've earned some leisure.'

'I'll take a little walk then. Thank you both for washing up. First, I'll make sure that they are all right upstairs.'

She whisked herself out of the kitchen before he could say anything.

It was a light, warm evening for it was full summer. She strolled away from the village, past the outlying cottages, sniffing at the air, fragrant with meadowsweet, dog roses and valerian. She was tired, but she had enjoyed her day, all except the bit when Wanda Fortesque had walked in. Sir William, she reflected, must love her very much to put up with such peevishness. Florina sat on a gate and debated with herself as to whether she would like to go on working as the cook at Wheel House once Sir William had married. Or if, indeed, Wanda would want her to stay. It seemed unlikely; they shared a mutual dislike. On the other hand, if she stayed, Pauline would have someone to talk to. She was a nice child, and Sir William loved her, but she didn't think Wanda would make a good stepmother. From what Pauline had told her, her father had taken her with him whenever he could, and made sure that she had had all the usual treats a child of her age might expect: the circus, the pantomime, museums, sailing, swimming. Florina couldn't see Wanda taking part in any of them.

She wandered back presently, and stopped just inside the gates to look at the house. It was beautiful in the twilight, and the sound of the stream was soothing. The drawing-room curtains hadn't been drawn, and she could see Sir William sitting in an easy chair, smoking his pipe and reading. Jolly came in while she stood there and said something to him, then went away again, and a moment later the kitchen light was switched on. She thought guiltily that she had been away long enough, and went round the side of the house through the patio, past the open drawing-room doors.

'Had a pleasant walk?' asked Sir William from his chair.

'Yes, thank you. Is there anything else you would like, Sir William?' When he said no, nothing, she said, 'Then I'll say goodnight.'

Jolly was in the kitchen, laying the table for breakfast, and she thanked him for his help and added, 'I'll take a look at Pauline and Mrs Frobisher. Can I do anything for you before I go to bed?' She added shyly, 'You've done so much since you came, I'm so grateful…'

Jolly smiled. 'It's been a pleasure, miss. Goodnight.'

Sir William and Jolly didn't leave until Monday evening. Watching the car turn out of the drive, Florina felt a pang of loneliness. Sunday had been a lovely day, with Pauline allowed up for a good deal of it, Nanny feeling better at last, and Sir William and Jolly dealing with the mundane jobs around the house, with a good deal of light-hearted talk on the part of Sir William and an indulgent chuckle or two from Jolly. She had expected them to leave on Sunday evening, but Sir William had gone into the study and spent a long time on the telephone; when he had come out, it was to announce that his registrar would deal with his cases at the hospital. So she had had another lovely day, with Pauline dressed and up, and Nanny sitting out of her bed for a short while, well enough to want to know what everyone was doing and scattering advice like confetti whenever she had the chance.

She was to telephone Sir William immediately if things should go wrong, or if she felt that everything was getting on top of her. Sir William had kissed Nanny's elderly cheek, hugged his daughter and dropped a casual kiss on Florina's cheek as she stood in the doorway to wave them goodbye. When the car had gone, she put a hand up to her cheek and touched it lightly. She was sure that kissing was quite usual among his kind of people and meant nothing other than a social custom; all the same, it had disturbed her.

The house seemed too large and very empty. Sir William and Jolly had left it in apple-pie order, and on Wednesday Mrs Deakin and Mrs Datchett were to return. So, since Pauline was up for most of the day, there would be very little to do. The week slipped by; Sir William telephoned each evening, talking at length to Pauline, after he had had a brief report from Florina. He would be down on Friday evening, he told her, and he would be coming alone.

With Nanny sitting comfortably beside the Aga and Pauline making a cake for tea, Florina bent her mind to food for the weekend. By the time the car came to a quiet halt before the house, she had a vegetable soup simmering on the Aga, *Boeuf flamand*, rich with beer and onions, in the oven and a strawberry pavlova in the fridge. Moreover, she had put on a clean apron, replaited her hair and done her face with the modest make-up at her disposal.

It was, therefore, disappointing when Sir William, his arm round Pauline's shoulders, wandered into the kitchen, and greeted Nanny warmly before glancing briefly at her with a casual, 'Hello, Florina. I hear that Pauline's made a cake for tea.'

She assented quietly; there was, after all, no need for him to ask how the week had gone; he had phoned each evening and she had given him a faithful account of the day. She made the tea and carried the tray out on to the patio while he went upstairs with Pauline. When they came down again she had shut the kitchen door, put a small tray beside Nanny's chair and gone back to her cooking, a mug of tea on the table beside her. She heard them on the patio presently and went to set the table in the dining-room. The cheerful meals in the kitchen had been all very well, but the circumstances had been unusual. She arranged the glass and silver just so on the starched linen cloth, set a bowl of roses in its centre and stood back to admire the effect.

'Very nice,' said Sir William from the door, 'very elegant. You have a talent for home-making, Florina—your husband will be a lucky man.'

He came into the room and sat on the edge of the table. 'I'm taking Pauline back with me on Sunday—she's going to spend a week with my sister's children at Eastdean, near Brighton. I'll drop her off on my way back to town. Nanny will stay here, but she is well enough to leave alone if you would like to take time off to shop or to go home. You don't mind being on your own with Nanny and Pauline? I've never asked you and I should have done.'

'I know everyone in the village,' she told him, 'and I'm not nervous. Will you be bringing Pauline back next weekend?' She added quickly, in case he thought it was none of her business, 'Just so that I can help her pack enough clothes…'

'We'll be back on Saturday morning; I won't be able to get away from hospital until Friday evening. I'll drive down to my sister's and spend the night. Oh, and I dare say Miss Fortesque will be joining us. She'll drive herself down some time on Saturday, but have lunch ready, will you?'

He wandered over to the door. 'You've had more than your share of hard work since you came here—and no free time, let alone days off. If and when you want a week's holiday, don't hesitate to ask, Florina.' He gave her a kind smile as he went.

In her room that night, getting ready for bed, she pondered a holiday. She couldn't remember when she had last had one—when her mother had been alive and the pair of them had gone to Holland once a year to see her mother's family, and she remembered that with wistful pleasure. After her mother's death, her father had said that there was no point in wasting money on visiting uncles and aunts and cousins whom he hardly knew. She wrote to them regularly in her perfect Dutch, for her mother had been firm about her speaking, writing and reading that language. 'For you are half-Dutch,' she had reminded Florina, 'and I don't want you to forget that.' It was so long now since she had visited her mother's family, but she had liked them and had felt at home in the old-fashioned house just outside Zierikzee. She would like to see them again, but it didn't seem very likely.

Sir William took Pauline for a short drive in the morning, and in the afternoon they sat on the patio, watching the swans below them. Florina, making a batch of congress tarts for tea, could hear them laughing and talking. After tea, before she needed to start cooking for the evening meal, she changed into one of her sensible cotton dresses and went home. Her father greeted her sourly and went back to reading his paper, but her aunt was glad to sit down and have half an hour's gossip. She had settled down nicely, she told Florina, and her father seemed happy enough. 'You've got yourself a nice job, love. That Sir William is spoken of very highly in the village. Had a busy time with the measles, though, didn't you?'

Her father didn't miss her, thought Florina regretfully, as she returned to the Wheel House, but at least she thought he seemed content, and Aunt Meg was happy. She went to the kitchen and started on dinner—avocado pears with a hot cheese sauce, trout caught locally, cooked with almonds, and a summer pudding.

After dinner, Sir William came into the kitchen and told her how much he had enjoyed his meal. He was kind but casual; there was none of the friendliness of the previous week.

He went after lunch the next day, taking Pauline with him; a Pauline who was flatteringly loath to leave Florina behind. The warmth of her goodbyes made up for the casual wave of the hand from her father as they drove off.

It was pleasant to have some leisure. Half-way through the week, Florina left Mrs Datchett to keep Nanny company, and took herself off to Salisbury. She had her wages in her pocket and the summer sales were on. The shops were full of pretty summer dresses, but she went straight to Country Casuals where she found a jacket and skirt in a pleasing shade of peach pink and a matching blouse. She added low-heeled court shoes and a small handbag and left the shop, very well satisfied, even if a good deal lighter in her pocket. There was enough money left over to buy a cotton jersey dress, canvas sandals and some undies, even a new lipstick and a face cream guaranteed to erase wrinkles and bring a bloom to the cheeks of the users. Florina, who hadn't a wrinkle anyway, and owned a skin as clear as a child's, could have saved her money, but it smelled delicious and fulfilled her wish to improve her looks. She wasn't sure why.

She showed everything to Mrs Frobisher when she got back, and then hung her finery in the cupboard in her room, got into one of her sensible, unflattering cotton dresses and went to pick the raspberries. On Friday she would cycle into Wilton and get some melons; halved and filled with the raspberries and heaped with whipped cream and a dash of brandy, they would make a good dessert for Sir William and whoever came with him. He hadn't said that he was bringing guests but she must be prepared…

He arrived on Saturday morning, with Wanda beside him and a sulky Pauline on the back seat. Mrs Frobisher, on her feet once more, but not doing much as yet, opened the door to them, and Florina heard them talking and laughing in the hall; at least Wanda was laughing. A moment later, the kitchen door was flung open and Pauline danced in.

'Oh, Florina, I have missed you, it's lovely to be here again! Can I make cakes for tea? My aunt has a cook too, but she wouldn't let me go into the kitchen. My cousins are scared of her. I'm not scared of you.'

Florina was piping potato purée into elegant swirls. 'Oh, good! Of course you can make cakes. Any idea what you want to make?'

'Scones—like yours. Daddy says they melt in his mouth…'

'OK. Come back about three o'clock, Pauline. I'm

going to pick the last of the raspberries after lunch; you can make the scones when I've done that.'

Pauline danced away, and she got on with her cooking, trying not to hear Wanda's voice on the patio, or her trilling laugh. With luck, she wouldn't have to see anything of her over the weekend; Mrs Deakin or Mrs Datchett would be early enough to take her breakfast tray up each morning.

Florina chopped parsley so viciously that Sir William, coming into the kitchen, said in mock alarm, 'Oh, dear, shall I come back later?'

Could she knock up some savoury bits and pieces? he wanted to know. He had asked a few local people in for drinks that evening, and could dinner be put back for half an hour?

On his way out of the kitchen he turned to look at her. 'Quite happy?' he wanted to know.

Her 'Yes, thank you, sir,' was offered without expression. There was no reason for her to be anything else. She had a good job, money in her pocket and a kind, considerate employer. Of course she was happy.

A dozen or so people came for drinks. She knew them by sight; people from the bigger country houses in the vicinity. Doctor Stone and his wife were there too, and the Rector, and the dear old lady from Crow Cottage at the other end of the village whose husband had been the local vet. She lived alone now with several cats and an elderly dog. Florina had made cheese straws, *petits fours* and tiny cheese puffs, while Pauline made the scones. The first batch were a failure; Florina put them into a bowl, observing that the swans would soon dispose of them, and advised Pauline to try again. 'And this time they will be perfect,' she encouraged.

Edible, at any rate! Her father assured her that they were delicious and ate four, and Pauline swelled with pride, although the sight of Wanda taking a bite and then refusing to finish hers took the edge off her pleasure. 'I expect I'm fussy,' said Wanda, laughing gently. Then she shot a look of dislike at Pauline, who wanted to know if she knew how to make scones.

'I have never needed to cook,' she said loftily. 'I have other things with which to occupy my time.'

'It's a good thing that I have the means to employ someone who can, my dear,' observed Sir William, and cut himself a slice of Florina's apple cake. It was as light as a feather and he felt that he deserved it after his small daughter's offering. 'But it is reassuring to know that, should I ever be without a cook, Pauline will at least know an egg from a potato.'

He drove Wanda back to London on Sunday evening, for she refused to get up early on Monday morning so that he might be in the hospital in time for his mid-morning clinic. She was, she declared, quite unable to get up before nine o'clock each morning. Florina heard her saying it and heartily despised her for it. Anyone with any sense knew that one of the best parts of the day was the hour just as the sun was rising. Besides, Sir William was no lie-abed; hospitals, unless she was very much mistaken, started their day early, and that would apply to most of the staff, including the most senior of the consultants.

Pauline came in from the front porch where she had been waving goodbye.

'It's super to be here again just with you and Nanny, only I wish Daddy were here, too.'

'Don't you like your home in London?' asked Florina. She was getting their supper and had made Nanny comfortable in a chair by the Aga.

'Oh, yes, that's super too, only Wanda is always there. She walks in and out as though it were her home, and it isn't, it's Daddy's and mine, and Jolly and Mrs Jolly's of course.' She added, 'Oh, and Shirley, she lives there too. Mrs Peek comes in each day to help, but she goes home after her dinner.'

'It sounds very pleasant,' said Florina a bit absent-mindedly: she was remembering that Wanda hadn't spoken to her at all during the weekend. Sir William hadn't said much, either, but he had thanked her for the bits and pieces she had made for the drinks party, and praised the roast beef she had served up for dinner on Saturday evening. He had also wished her goodbye until the following weekend.

'I'll be alone,' he had told her, 'perhaps we might have a picnic...Pauline has rather set her heart on one. You and Nanny, Pauline and I.'

The fine weather held; the three of them picked beans and peas and courgettes and tomatoes, and stocked up the freezer. And, with Pauline on a borrowed bike, Florina cycled with her to Wilton, and they shopped for the weekend and had ices at the little tea room in the High Street.

It was on the Thursday that she had a letter from her Tante Minna in Holland. Florina's cousin Marijke was going to be married, and would she go to the wedding and, if possible, stay for a week or so? It was a long time, wrote Tante Minna in her beautiful copperplate Dutch, since Florina had been to see them, and, while they were aware that her father had no wish to visit them, her family in Holland felt that they should keep in touch. The wedding was to be in a week and a half's time and she hoped to hear…

A wedding, reflected Florina—a chance to wear her new outfit and, since she could afford the fare, there was no reason why she shouldn't accept. Sir William had told her that if she wanted a holiday she had only to ask. He would be back at home on the next day. She spent the rest of the day and a good deal of the night deciding exactly what she would say to him.

He looked tired when he came, but he still remembered to see her in the kitchen and to ask if everything was all right. 'I see Nanny has quite recovered—I hope Pauline hasn't been too much trouble?'

Florina gave a brief résumé of their week, and took in the tea tray.

'Worn to the bone,' commented Nanny as they drank their own tea in the kitchen. 'What he needs is peace and quiet when he gets home of an evening, but that Miss Fortesque is always on at him to go dining and dancing.'

It wasn't the time to ask about holidays, and Florina went to bed feeling frustrated. Perhaps she wouldn't have the chance to ask him, and if she didn't this weekend it would be too late to make arrangements to go to the wedding. She spent a poor night worrying about it, which proved a waste of time for, as she was boiling the kettle for early morning tea, he wandered into the kitchen in trousers and an open-necked shirt.

'Oh, you're up,' she said stupidly, and then, 'Good morning, Sir William.'

'Morning, Florina—too nice to stay in bed—I've been for a walk. Is that tea? Good.' He sat down on the side of the table and watched her, clean and starched and neat, getting mugs and sugar and milk. 'Have a cup with me, I want to talk.'

Her hand shook a little as she poured the milk. The sack? Wanda and he getting married? Something awful she had done?

'I'm wondering if you would like that week's holiday? In a week's time I have to go to Leiden to give a series of lectures, and I thought I would take Pauline with me. Nanny can stay here, and the Jollys can come down and keep her company. Our Shirley is quite happy to look after the house in town, and Mrs Peek will move in while we are away and keep her company...'

He broke off to look at her. Florina was gazing at him, her gentle mouth slightly open, wearing the bemused look of someone who had just received a smart tap on the head. 'In a week's time,' she repeated, a bit breathless. 'Oh, I'll be able to go to the wedding!'

'Yours?' asked Sir William.

She shook her head. 'No—my cousin—they live close to Zierikzee, and she's getting married, and I've been asked to go and it's just perfect! While you are in Leiden, I'll be able to stay with my aunt.'

She beamed at him and then asked soberly, 'That is, if you don't mind?'

He leaned over and poured the tea into two mugs. 'My dear girl, why should I mind? It's the hand of fate, of course you must go. How?'

'Oh, I'll fly, I did it with Mother several times, when she was alive we went each year, Basingstoke, you know, and then a bus to Gatwick…'

Sir William cut himself a slice of bread from the loaf she had put ready for toast. 'I know a better way. When is this wedding?' When she had told him, he said, 'It couldn't be better. We'll give you a lift in the car and drop you off…'

'It's out of your way,' she pointed out.

'A mile or so, besides I've always wanted to take a look at Zierikzee. Can you stay with your aunt until we pick you up on the way home?'

'Yes—oh, yes!' Her face glowed with delight and Sir William took a second look at her. Quite pretty in a quiet, unassuming way, and she had lovely eyes. He got off the table. 'That's settled, then. We'll work out the details later. Can you really be ready for this picnic by eleven o'clock? The New Forest, so Pauline tells me. She has it all planned.'

Florina nodded happily, in a delightful daze, quite unable to stop smiling. Sir William, on the way upstairs to his room, reflected that she was a funny little thing as well as being a marvellous cook. She didn't seem to have much fun, either, and this cousin's wedding would be a treat for her.

Chapter 4

The Bentley slid with deceptive speed around the southern outskirts of Salisbury, took the Ringwood road and at Downton turned off to Cadnam. Florina and Nanny, sitting in the back of the car, admired the scenery and listened to Pauline's happy chatter to her father. In Lyndhurst, a few miles further on from Cadnam, they stopped for coffee at an olde-worlde tea-shop, all dark oak and haughty waitresses dressed to match. The coffee was dreadful and Sir William muttered darkly over his, only cheered by Florina's recital of what she and Nanny had packed in the picnic basket.

Just outside the little town they entered the Forest, and presently turned off into a narrow lane which opened out into a rough circle of green grass surrounded by trees. It was pleasantly warm and Pauline pranced off, intent on exploring, taking her father with her. He had hesitated before they went, looking at Florina, but she had no intention of leaving Nanny alone.

'We'll get the lunch ready,' she said firmly, wishing with all her heart that she could go with them.

They were back after half an hour or so, and in the meantime she had spread their picnic on the ground near the car. They had brought a folding chair for Nanny, and she was sitting in it, telling Florina what to do, watching as she set out the little containers with sausage rolls, sandwiches, meat pies and cheese puffs. There was lemonade, too, and beer for Sir William as well as a thermos of hot coffee, and apples and pears. Sir William heaved a sigh of contentment as he made himself comfortable against a tree stump.

'The temptation to retire is very strong,' he observed and, at Florina's surprised look, 'No, I'm not sixty, Florina, although I feel all of that, sometimes.' He bit into a pie. 'This seems as good a time as any to plan out our week in Holland.' He glanced at Mrs Frobisher. 'Nanny, I'm taking Pauline over to Holland with me when I go in a week's time—we'll be gone for a week. The Jollys are coming down to keep you company. You'll like that, won't you? Florina is going to Holland too, to a cousin's wedding, and we'll bring her back with us. Now, how shall we go?' He looked at Florina who, having no idea at all, said nothing. 'Hovercraft, I think, and drive up from Calais.' He finished the pie and started on a sausage roll.

'Have you a passport, Florina? No—well go to the post office in Wilton and get a passport from there. There isn't time for you to get a new one through the normal channels; you'll need the old one for details, though. Pauline's on my passport. Let me see, if we leave Dover about ten o'clock, we should be in Zierikzee during the afternoon, and Amsterdam a couple of hours later. I start lectures on the Monday, so that will fit in very well.'

'Will Pauline be alone?' asked Florina.

'We're staying with friends. She'll have a marvellous time, they have four children.'

It was nice to know that Wanda wasn't to be of the party. Florina poured coffee and allowed her thoughts to dwell on the pleasures in store.

The weekend went too quickly. They all went to church on Sunday morning, and in the evening Sir William drove himself into Wilton to a friend's house for drinks. He had a lot of friends, reflected Florina, concentrating on the making of lemon sauce. In the morning he left early, while Nanny was still in bed. Pauline had come down to say goodbye, but she went back to bed again, leaving Florina to clear away Sir William's breakfast things and start the day's chores. He wouldn't be back until the next weekend, and it seemed a very long time.

Actually, the days passed quickly. Florina needed Pauline's help to gather together suitable clothes to take with her, there were beds to be made up and the house to be left in apple-pie order for the Jollys' arrival. There was her own wardrobe to decide upon;

she would be able to wear her new clothes, but they would need to be augmented. Sir William phoned most evenings to talk to Pauline but, although he spoke to Nanny once or twice, he evinced no desire to speak to Florina.

He arrived rather late on Friday evening, and Jolly and his wife drove down at the same time in the other car. Pauline, already in bed, came bouncing down to fling her arms around his neck. 'We're all ready,' she assured him excitedly, 'and Florina is ready too, and she's filled the fridge with food that means Mrs Jolly won't have to bother too much. She washed her hair this afternoon and she did mine last night.'

She skipped away to greet the Jollys. 'There is supper for you and we put flowers in your bedroom.'

'Bed for you, Pauline,' said Nanny severely, appearing to greet Sir William and the Jollys. 'The child is excited,' she told Sir William.

'So am I, Nanny.' He went past her, into the kitchen where Florina was putting the finishing touches to the salad.

'Busy as usual?' he observed kindly. 'All ready for your holiday, Florina? I do wonder what on earth you'll do with yourself without your cooking stove?'

She smiled politely; she wasn't a girl to him, just the cook—it was a mortifying thought. She thrust it from her, and said soberly, 'Well, I haven't seen my family for some time, Sir William. I expect there will be a lot to talk about.'

That sounded dull enough, she thought crossly. If only he could see her, dressed in her new clothes, being chatted up by some handsome Dutch cousin—only all her cousins were either married or with no looks to speak of; and when would he see her anyway?

She wished that he would go away, not stand there looking at her in that faintly surprised fashion. It disturbed her, although she didn't know why.

They left very early on Sunday morning, driving through the still-sleeping village, past the pub, her home, the farm opposite the bridge and along the narrow country lane which would lead them to Wilton.

She had spent an afternoon with her father during the week, but he hadn't been particularly interested in her plans. She could do as she wished, he had observed grumpily, and he hadn't even expressed the hope that she would enjoy herself. Everyone else had; even Nanny, so sparing in her praise, had told her that she had earned a holiday. 'And I just hope you meet a nice young man,' she had added.

Florina, sitting in the back of the car, bubbling over with excitement, hoped that she would too. If she met a nice young man, then perhaps Sir William wouldn't seem quite so important in her life.

They had an uneventful, very comfortable journey. It made a great difference, she reflected, if you had money. You stopped when you wanted to at good hotels for coffee and lunch, with no need to look at the price list outside to see if you could afford it. Moreover you spoke French in France and when you reached Holland you switched to Dutch, which, while basic, got you what you wanted without any fuss. And you did all that with the calm assurance which was Sir William.

They were crossing the Zeeland Brug by mid-afternoon, glimpsing Zierikzee ahead of them. On dry land once more, Sir William said, over his shoulder, 'You must tell me where to go, Florina. It's outside the town, isn't it?'

She leaned forward, the better to speak to him. 'Yes, go straight on, don't turn into Zierikzee, go to the roundabout and take the road to Drieschor; Schudderbeurs is about two miles…'

The road was straight and narrow, snaking away into the distance. The sign to the village was small and anyone going too fast would miss it. Sir William slowed down when she warned him, and turned left down a narrow lane, joining a pleasant, leafy lane with a handful of cottages and villas on either side of it. There was an old-fashioned country house standing well back from the road with a wide sweep before it. As they went past it Sir William said, 'That looks pleasant; it's an hotel, too…'

'Yes. It's quite well known. I've never been there, it's expensive, but I believe it's quite super… My aunt lives just along that lane to the right.'

There were a handful of houses ringing the edge of wooded country, not large, but well maintained and with fair-sized gardens.

'It's this one.'

Sir William stopped, got out and opened her door. A door in the house opened at the same time and

Tante Minna, looking not a day older than when Florina had seen her five years or more ago, came down the garden path. She had begun to talk the moment she had seen them; she was still talking when she opened the gate and hugged Florina, at the same time casting an eye over Sir William and Pauline. Florina disentangled herself gently. 'Tante Minna, how lovely to see you…' She had slipped into Dutch without a conscious effort. 'This is Sir William, I'm his cook, as I told you, and this is his daughter Pauline. They are on their way to Leiden and kindly gave me a lift.'

She had already told Aunt Minna all that in her letter, but she was wishful to bridge an awkward gap.

Tante Minna transferred her twinkling gaze to Sir William. Her English was adequate, about as adequate as his Dutch. They shook hands warmly and Tante Minna turned her attention to Pauline, and then took her by the arm and turned towards the house. 'You will take tea? It is ready. You will like to see my cat and her five kittens?'

They went into the house, light and airy and comfortably furnished. She said in Dutch to Florina, 'Will you explain that your uncle Constantine is in Goes? Marijke and Jan and Pieter are here, though, and Felix Troost—his father is a partner in your uncle's firm. I believe you met him years ago…'

Florina translated, leaving out the bit about Felix Troost, and they went into the sitting-room where Florina was instantly enveloped in a round of handshaking and kissing, emerging to find Sir William talking easily to Felix, whose English was a good deal better than Sir William's Dutch. Pauline had disappeared with Florina's aunt, doubtless in search of the kittens. Indeed, she reappeared a few minutes later with a small fluffy creature tucked under one arm.

Her cousins hadn't changed much, Florina decided; Marijke, a year or two younger than herself, was plump and fair and pretty, good-natured and easy-going, Jan and Pieter, who had still been at school when she had last seen them, were young men now, towering over her, calling her little Rina and wanting to know why she wasn't married. But when the tea tray was brought in, the talk became general, while they drank the milkless tea in small porcelain cups and nibbled thin, crisp biscuits. Not very substantial for Sir William's vast frame, thought Florina, watching him, completely at his ease, discussing their journey with Pieter. He looked up, caught her eye and smiled, and she felt a pleasant glow spreading under her ribs.

He and Pauline left soon, for they still had rather more than an hour's drive ahead of them across the islands to Rotterdam, and then a further hour on the motorway to Amsterdam. But before they went Sir William sat himself down by Florina. 'We'll fetch you next Saturday,' he reminded her. 'I'd like to get to Wheel House in the fairly early evening, so we should leave here not later than two o'clock. Will you be ready then?'

'Yes, of course, Sir William. Would you like coffee here before we go?'

He shook his head. 'No time. We can have a quick stop on the way if we must.' He stood up. 'Have a good holiday, Florina. I envy you the peace and quiet here.'

She had forgotten that he was to give lectures for most of the week, and Amsterdam, delightful though it was, was also noisy. She said quietly, 'Perhaps you will be able to spare the time to spend a few days in the country—somewhere like Schudderbeurs, the *hostellerie* is quite famous, you know.'

'Yes, perhaps one day I'll do that.' He patted her shoulder and went out to his car with Pieter and Jan, leaving Pauline to say goodbye.

'I hope I shall like it,' she said uncertainly. 'Daddy won't be there for most of the day…'

'You'll have a gorgeous time,' said Florina cheerfully. 'We'll compare notes when we meet next Saturday, and think how nice it is for your father to have you for company.'

Pauline brightened. 'Yes, he likes me to be with him, that's why I don't see why he needs to marry Wanda. She hates quiet places, she likes to dance and go to the shops and theatre and have people to dinner.'

'Ah, well, perhaps she will change when your father marries her!' Florina kissed the pretty little face, and then walked out to the car and stood with her aunt and cousins, waving until it was out of sight.

'A very nice man,' commented Tante Minna. 'He is married?'

'No, but he is going to be—to a very lovely girl called Wanda.'

'And you do not like her, I think?' asked her aunt, sharp as a needle.

'Well, I don't think she's right for him. He works very hard and I believe he likes his work; it's a part of his life, if you know what I mean. She enjoys the bright lights and I think she's annoyed because he's just come to live at Wheel House—and you know how quiet the village is, Tante Minna! He has a house in London, too, though I don't know where it is, but he likes to spend his weekends at Wheel House, if he can.' She paused, 'And Pauline doesn't like her.'

'It seems that he needs to be rescued,' observed Tante Minna, and added briskly, 'Come indoors, child, and tell us all your news—it's so long...'

Florina made short work of that for, of course, what they really wanted to talk about was the wedding. Marijke took her upstairs to show her her wedding dress, and when they joined the family again she was regaled with the details of the ceremony, Christiaan's job, the flat they would live in and the furniture they had bought for it. Which reminded Florina to go upstairs to the small bedroom at the back of the house and fetch the present she had brought with her. Place mats, rather nice ones, depicting the English countryside, and received with delight by her cousin. Christiaan came then, and they had their evening meal with Oom Constantine, and when it was finished Felix Troost arrived again. He had been in Goes with Florina's uncle, he explained, but had had to call on someone on the way home. He was a good-looking young man, with blue eyes, set rather too close together, and a good deal of very fair hair. He was obviously at home there, and he greeted Florina with a slightly overdone charm. They shook hands and exchanged polite greetings, and she decided then and there that she didn't like him.

A feeling that she became uncertain of as the evening progressed, for he was casually friendly, talking about his work, wanting to know about her life in England. She must have been mistaken in the sudden feeling of dislike that she had had when they met, she reflected as she got ready for bed. Anyway, she would be seeing a good deal of him while she was staying with Tante Minna, and he would be at the wedding and the reception afterwards at the hotel. She allowed her thoughts to dwell on the peach-pink outfit with some satisfaction. It was a pity that Sir William wouldn't see her in her finery. She wondered what he was doing; dining and dancing probably, with some elegant creature whose dress would make the peach-pink look like something run up by the local little dressmaker. She sighed sadly, not knowing why she was sad.

Everyone was up early the next morning and, although the wedding wasn't until mid-afternoon, there was a constant coming and going of family and friends. Florina, nicely made up and wearing the peach-pink, greeted aunts and uncles and cousins she hadn't seen for years, exclaiming over engagements, new babies and the various ailments of the more elderly. She blossomed out under observations that she had grown into quite a presentable young woman, for, as one elderly aunt observed in a ringing voice everyone could hear, 'A plain child you were, Florina. Your mother despaired of you. Never thought you'd get yourself a husband…engaged, are you?'

Black beady eyes studied her, and she blushed a little and was eternally grateful to Felix, who flung an arm round her shoulders and said, 'She's waiting for a good honest Dutchman to ask her, aren't you, Florina?' And he kissed her on one cheek. Everyone laughed then, and she decided that she had been mistaken about Felix; he had sounded warmly friendly and he had been kind…

With the prospect of the wedding reception later on in the day, no one ate much of the lunch Aunt Minna provided. Guests were to go straight to the *Gemeentehuis*, but even the most distant relations who weren't seen from one year to the next came to the house, so that there was a good deal of good-natured confusion. Deciding who was to go in whose car took considerable time, and presently Florina found herself sitting beside Felix in his BMW with two elderly aunts on the back seat. It was the last to leave in the procession of cars, leaving Marijke, following the time-honoured custom, to wait for her bridegroom to fetch her from her home, bearing the bridal bouquet.

The *Gemeentehuis* was the centre of interest, and the congestion in the narrow street was making it worse than ever to drive through the little town. The guests trooped up the narrow steps into the ancient building and made their way to the Bride Chamber, a handsome apartment at the top of a broad staircase. Florina was urged into a seat in the front row of chairs, since she was a cousin of the bride, while Felix, being a family friend, found his way to a seat at the back, but not before giving her hand a squeeze and whispering that he would drive her to the church presently. She nodded, not really listening, for Marijke and Christiaan were taking their places in front of the *Burgermeester* and the short ceremony started.

Florina, watching closely, thought it seemed too businesslike. It certainly wouldn't do for her. She was glad that Marijke had wanted a church wedding as well, not that she herself was likely to marry, whether in Holland or in England. She didn't know any men, only Felix, and she didn't know him at all really, and Sir William, who didn't count, for he was going to marry Wanda. She fell to day-dreaming of some vague, faceless man who would meet her and fall in love with her at once and they would marry. These musings led, naturally enough, to what she would wear: cream satin, yards of it and a tulle veil. Marijke was wearing a picture hat trimmed with roses, and her dress was white lace. Florina had helped her to dress and had zipped the dress up, only after having urged her cousin to breathe in while she did so, for Marijke was a shade too plump for it. All the same, she looked delightful and her pinched waist had given her a most becoming colour. They were signing the register now, and a few minutes later the whole party followed the bride and groom out to the long line of cars.

The church was barely two minutes' drive, behind the Apple Market, bordering on the big market square, so that the entire wedding party could park in comfort before filing inside. It was a *Hervormdekerk*, and the service was sober and the short homily delivered sternly by the *Dominee*. Florina allowed her attention to wander, stealthily checking on the congregation, refreshing her memory as to who they were. She had forgotten over the years what a very large family her mother had; sitting there in the church she felt more Dutch than English. Her eye, roaming round the church, lighted upon Felix who smiled and nodded. He seemed like an old friend, and she smiled back, stifling the vague feeling of dislike she had for him.

The service ended and the bride and groom got into their flower-decked car and started on their slow tour of the town before driving back to Schudderbeurs, while everyone else went back to the *hostellerie*.

The wedding party was to be held in the large room built at the back of the hotel. It had been decorated with pot plants and flowers, and a buffet had been nicely arranged on a long table at one end. The afternoon was still warm and sunny, and the doors on to the garden had been opened so that the guests could spill outside. Florina, driven back by Felix, stood taking breaths of fresh air, listening idly to his rather conceited talk about himself and his work. He was doing his best to impress her, but she didn't feel impressed; indeed, she was shocked to find that she was bored. Suddenly she wanted to be back at Wheel House, busy at the stove while Sir William sat on the kitchen table, polishing off the scones she had made for tea.

She heard Felix say in a cocksure manner, 'And, of course, I shall be a partner in a year or so.' He gave a self-deprecating laugh. 'You can't keep a good man down, you know!'

She murmured politely and was glad that the bridal pair had arrived and everyone could sit down and eat the delicious food the hotel had provided. There was champagne, of course, and speeches. No wedding cake, for that wasn't the custom in Holland, but little dishes of chocolates and sweetmeats and more champagne. Presently, friends and acquaintances arrived, each with a present or flowers, to wish the bride and groom every happiness, and join in the dancing. It was great fun, reflected Florina, her ordinary face glowing with warmth and excitement, whirling around the floor with cousins and uncles and Felix; Felix more than anyone else, but what with the champagne and the cheerful, noisy party, she was content to dance the night away. She hadn't enjoyed herself so much for years.

Presently, the newly wedded pair disappeared in the direction of the little white house in the hotel grounds, where they would spend the night before driving to their new flat in Goes on the following day. It was only in recent years that newly marrieds had abandoned the custom of going straight to their new home from the wedding reception. The little white house was much in demand among the young people, some of them coming from miles around.

The dancing went on for another hour or more before the guests finally left. Some of the more elderly were staying at the *hostellerie* for the night, the younger ones were either putting up with friends in the village or driving home through the night. Florina walked the short distance to her aunt's house, arm in arm with a bevy of cousins and Felix. He was to spend what remained of the night with friends in the village, and he parted from them on the doorstep, but not before he had asked her to spend the next day with him.

When she had hesitated, he had promised, 'We won't do anything strenuous, and I won't come round until eleven o'clock.'

And when she still hesitated, her cousins joined in. 'Oh, go on, Rina, none of us will want to do anything tomorrow, and you'll enjoy a day out.'

She wasn't too happy about it as she tumbled into bed, perhaps because she was tired. Besides, she could always change her mind in the morning.

She didn't; she was awake only a little later than usual and it was a glorious morning. There were only four days left of her holiday—she must make the most of them. She had a shower and dressed in the cotton jersey and went down to the roomy kitchen. Her aunt was already up; there was coffee on the stove and a basket of rolls and croissants on the table.

'Going out with Felix?' asked Tante Minna.

Florina nodded. 'You don't mind? He's not coming until eleven o'clock—I'll give you a hand around the house—you must be tired…'

'Yes, but it was a splendid wedding, wasn't it, *liefje*? When shall we see you marry, I wonder?'

Florina bit into a roll; Tante Minna was awfully like her mother. She felt her throat tighten at the thought but she answered lightly, 'I've no idea, but I promise that you shall dance at my wedding if every I have one…'

'Do they dance at English weddings?'

'Oh, rather, discotheques, the same as here.' But she wouldn't want that—only a quiet wedding in the church at home, and a handful of family and friends and, of course, the bridegroom—that vague but nebulous figure she could never put a face to. She finished her roll and tidied away her breakfast things and then, armed with a duster, set about bringing the sitting-room to that peak of pristine perfection which Tante Minna, wedding or no wedding, expected.

Presently her uncle appeared to drink his coffee and then go into the garden to inspect his roses, and after him, Felix, flamboyantly dressed, oozing charm and impatient of the coffee Tante Minna insisted on them having before they went. Florina got into the car beside him, told her aunt that they would be back in good time for the evening meal, eaten as was customary at six o'clock, and sat quietly while Felix roared through the tiny village and on to the road to Browershaven, away from Zierikzee.

The day wasn't a success. Felix talked about himself and, what was more, in a lofty fashion which Florina found tedious. He had no clear idea where they were going, but drove around the surrounding countryside in a haphazard fashion, and when she had suggested mildly that it would be nice to go to the coast he said, 'Oh, you don't want to walk on the beach, for heaven's sake.'

'Then what about Veere or Domburg?'

'Packed out. We'll go inland and find a place to eat, and park the car somewhere quiet and get to know each other.'

Florina wished that she hadn't come, but it was too late to do anything about it now. They stopped at a small roadside café, full of local men playing billiards and, unlike most Dutch cafés, not over-clean. She lingered over her *limonade* and kaas broodje, uneasy at the amount of beer Felix was drinking. With good reason, she was to discover, for, once more in the car, he stopped after a few miles and flung an arm around her shoulders.

Florina removed the arm and eyed him severely. 'Tante Minna expects me back before six o'clock, so be good enough to start back now. I'm sorry if I disappoint you, but I came with you for a pleasant day out and that's all.'

She was aware that she sounded priggish, even in Dutch, but she wasn't prepared for his snarling, 'Prudish little bitch—no wonder you haven't got a man. I wish you joy of your cooking. That's all you're fit for.'

Neither of them spoke again until they reached Tante Minna's house, and when Florina said goodbye in a cold voice Felix didn't answer.

'Had a nice day?' asked her aunt. Seeing her stony face, she added hastily, 'We are all going to Goes the day after tomorrow. You'll come won't you, *liefje*? Just the family—Marijke wants us all to see their flat.'

The last day of her holiday was pure pleasure. On Thursday, she joined a happy gathering of family at a proud Marijke's new home, which was smothered in flowers and pot plants from friends and such members of the family who hadn't been able to attend the wedding. Florina admired everything, drank a little too much wine, ate the *bitterballen* served with it, and agreed that the bridal bouquet, hung on the wall at the head of the bed, was the most beautiful she had ever seen. Presently, she sat down with everyone else to *nasi goreng* and an elaborate dessert of ice-cream. A day to remember, she assured her uncle when he wanted to know if she had enjoyed her holiday.

Sir William had said that he would pick her up after lunch on Saturday. She was up early to pack her small case, eat her roll and sliced cheese and drink her aunt's delicious coffee, before wheeling out her aunt's elderly bike from the garage and setting off for a last ride with Jan and Pieter. They went to Zierikzee to start with and had more coffee. Then they went on to Haamstede and cycled on to the lighthouse, where they sat in the sun and ate ice-creams. The morning had gone too quickly, as last mornings always do; they had to ride fast in order to get back to Tante Minna's in time for the mid-day lunch.

It was a leisurely meal, for there was time enough before Sir William would arrive. Presently, Florina did the last of her packing and closed her case. She did her face and hair too, anxious not to keep him waiting. She went to wait downstairs and found, to her annoyance, that Felix was there.

There was nothing in his manner to remind her of their last meeting; he greeted her as though they had parted the best of friends, and began as soon as he could to talk of the possibility of meeting her again. 'Mustn't lose sight of you,' he observed smugly, and flung an unwanted arm across her shoulders.

Florina edged away, and went into the garden on the pretext of saying goodbye to her uncle, but he followed her outside, seemingly intent on demonstrating that they were the best of friends, and more than that. He was standing with her when the Bentley slowed to a silent halt on the other side of the hedge. Florina, talking to her uncle, didn't see it at once, but Felix did; he put an arm round her waist and drew her close, and Sir William, getting out of his car, couldn't help but see it.

He turned away at once to say something to Pauline, so missing Florina's indignant shove as she pushed Felix away. At the same time, she saw the car, and a moment later Sir William, strolling towards her aunt's front door. The wealth of feeling which surged through her at the sight of him took her by surprise. He had been at the back of her thoughts all the while she had been at Tante Minna's but she hadn't understood why, but now she knew. *He* was the vague man of her day-dreams, the man she loved, had fallen in love with, not knowing it, weeks ago; ever since she had first set eyes on him, she realised with astonishment.

She hurried to meet him, thoughts tumbling about her head. It was bliss to see him again, but never, never must she show her feelings, although just at that moment she longed above all things to rush at him and fling her arms around his neck. This last thought was so horrifying that she went a bright pink, and looked so guilty that Sir William frowned at his own thoughts.

He glanced at Felix, decided that he didn't much like the look of him and countered Florina's breathless, 'Sir William…' with a pleasantly cool, 'Ah, Florina, we have arrived at the wrong moment. My apologies…'

This remark stopped her in her tracks. 'Wrong moment? I'm quite ready to leave, Sir William…'

'But not, perhaps, willing?'

She gaped at him, and when Felix sidled up to her and put an arm round her shoulders she barely noticed it. At that moment, Pauline came prancing over to fling her arms around her neck and declare that she was over the moon to see her darling Florina again.

There was a polite flurry of talk, then coffee was offered and refused, and goodbyes said. Presently, Florina found herself in the back of the car, listening to Pauline's chatter. Sir William was, for the most part, silent, but when he did make some casual remark it was in his usual placid manner. He asked no questions of Florina about her holiday and she, suddenly shy of him, sat tongue-tied. What should have been a happy end to her holiday was proving to be just the opposite. Her newly discovered love was bubbling away inside her. Although she knew that he had no interest in her, he had always treated her with what she had thought was friendship and she was willing to settle for that, but now she had the feeling that behind his placid manner there was a barrier.

To brood over her fancies was of no use, so she bestirred herself to listen to Pauline's plans: picnics and mushrooming and cycling with Florina and cookery lessons…

'Wanda will be staying with us for at least a week,' said her father. 'You'll be able to go out with her if I am not at home.'

Pauline made a face over her shoulder to Florina, who smiled in a neutral fashion. The smile froze when Sir William added pleasantly, 'Florina has a job to do, Pauline. You mustn't monopolise her free time.'

That remark, thought Florina, puts me nicely in my place.

Chapter 5

They arrived back at Wheel House to a most satisfyingly warm welcome. The journey had gone smoothly, although Florina, knowing Sir William, would have been surprised if it had been otherwise. She had spent the greater part of the journey alternately day-dreaming and worrying as to why his manner towards her had become so cool—still friendly, but she had to admit it was the friendliness of an employer towards an employee.

They all sat down to supper round the kitchen table, talking cheerfully with Sir William asking questions of Jolly and being given a résumé of the week's happenings. Presently, an excited Pauline was escorted off to bed by Nanny, and Sir William turned to Jolly.

'I'll need to be away by seven o'clock at the latest. I'd like you and Mrs Jolly to drive back at the same time. I've a list for ten o'clock, so I'll offload my bag at the house and go straight on to the hospital. I'll not be back for lunch, and I'm taking Miss Fortesque out to dinner—if there is anything you want me for, I'll be home round about tea time.'

Florina said, in a colourless voice, 'Would you like breakfast at half-past six, Sir William?'

'We shan't need you, Florina. Mrs Jolly will see to that.' He added, in a kind, impersonal voice, '*You* must be tired, why don't you go to bed?'

So she went, exchanging polite goodnights. There had been no chance to thank him for taking her to Holland, and he had evinced no wish to know if she had enjoyed herself, but then, why should he? She was the cook and she had better remember that. Besides, she had no part in his life; Wanda had that. She cried herself to sleep and woke early to listen to the Jollys quietly leaving the room on the other side of the landing. Presently she smelled the bacon frying and the fragrance of toast, and heard the murmur of voices. Her window gave her a view of the road running through the village, providing she craned her neck, and soon she saw the two cars disappearing on their way to London.

Sir William had given her no instructions, but when she went downstairs later and started to clear the table and lay it again for their breakfast, Nanny joined her.

'You didn't have much to say for yourself at supper,' she observed, her sharp eyes studying Florina's swollen eyelids. 'Wasn't your holiday all you'd hoped for?' She added, 'Did you want to stay in Holland?'

'No. Oh, no! And I had a super time. It was a lovely wedding, and it was so nice to see everyone again. It is lovely to be back, though…'

Nanny grunted. 'Well, I missed you, for what it's worth.' She accepted the cup of tea that Florina offered, and sat down by the open door. 'Sir William won't be back until Friday evening, and Miss Fortesque's coming with him. He intends to give a small dinner party on Saturday—six, I think he said, and if the weather is fine he wants to take a picnic up on to Bulbarrow Down. He's asked the Meggisons from Butt House—they've three children, haven't they? Company for Pauline. He said he would telephone during the week about the food.' She passed her cup and Florina refilled it. 'He said to have a quiet week and to see that Pauline got out of doors. If she wants to go to Salisbury she may, he says, provided that one of us goes with her. She will be starting school soon.' Nanny looked round the pleasant kitchen. 'I shall miss this…'

Florina, slicing bread for toast, looked up, startled. 'Mrs Frobisher—you're not going away?'

'Just as soon as that Miss Fortesque can persuade Sir William that I'm not needed.' There was a pause and the stern, elderly voice wavered slightly. 'With Pauline at school, she'll say that there's nothing for me to do…'

'But that's rubbish!' cried Florina. 'You see to the

silver and the mending, and keep the accounts and look after everything.'

'I do my best, but it's my opinion that once they're married she'll pack Pauline off to a boarding-school and come down here as little as possible.'

'But Sir William loves this house. I dare say he has a beautiful home in London, too, but you can love two houses… Besides, he works so hard, and he can do what he likes here.'

If Nanny found Florina's outburst surprising, she gave no sign. She said, 'Well he's old enough and wise enough to know what he wants, but he deserves better. His first marriage wasn't happy—he married too young. I told him so at the time, and I'll make no bones about saying that it was a relief when she was killed in a car accident, gallivanting off with one of her men friends while he worked. A bad wife, and a worse mother, poor young woman.' She gave Florina a quick look. 'I can't think why I'm telling you all this, but you're fond of Pauline, aren't you, and you like Sir William?'

'Oh, yes,' said Florina, putting so much feeling into the two words that Nanny nodded gently, well aware why she had unburdened herself. One never knew, she thought, and there was no harm in spying out the land, as it were. Florina had come back from Holland sad and too quiet, and Sir William had been holding down some problem or other behind that placid face of his—no one was going to tell her different. She had known him all his life, hadn't she?

And she wouldn't let anyone tell her not to interfere if she saw the chance.

'Well, have you any plans for today?' she asked briskly.

'Well, I'll go through the cupboards, then go up to the farm shop if we are short of anything. Perhaps Pauline…'

She was interrupted by the little girl dancing into the kitchen to hug first Nanny and then her.

'It's marvellous to be back!' she declared. 'I want to go cycling—Florina, do say you will, and we can go into Wilton and buy Daddy a birthday present.'

She inspected the table. 'Oh, good, it's scrambled eggs—I'm famished. Daddy woke me to say goodbye. Did he say goodbye to you, Florina?'

'No, dear, but I'm sure he won't mind us going into Wilton. When do you want to go?'

The week passed too quickly. There was so much to do: the swans to feed, the Meggison children to visit for tea, long rambling walks to take and the promised visit to Wilton. Sir William telephoned each evening, but it wasn't until Thursday that he asked to speak to Florina.

He began without preamble. 'Florina, Miss Fortesque and I will be down on Friday evening, so lay on a good dinner, will you? There will be six of us for dinner on Saturday. Any ideas?'

She had been listening to his calm voice, but not his words. With a great effort, she tore her thoughts away from him and mentally thumbed through her cookery books. 'Watercress soup? Grilled trout with pepper sauce? Fillets of lamb with rosemary and thyme and *pommes lyonnaises* and a fresh tomato purée…' She thought for a moment. 'I've got pears in wine or peaches in brandy…'

'My dear girl—my mouth is watering. It sounds splendid. About the picnic on Sunday—shall I leave that to you?'

She said sedately, 'Very well, Sir William. Just lunch?'

'Yes—we'll be back for one of your splendid teas.' He rang off, leaving her quiet, and quite certain that she was going to be so busy at the weekend that she would barely glimpse him, let alone speak to him. Although what did that matter? she reflected sadly. She was the cook and let her never forget it.

With female perversity, she dragged her hair back into a severe plait on Saturday, didn't bother with make-up and, once the serious business of preparing dinner was finished, went to her room and got into a freshly starched dress and white apron. Pauline, prancing into the kitchen to see what there was for tea, stopped short at the sight of her.

'Florina, how severe you look! And you've forgotten your lipstick.'

'No time,' said Florina briskly, taking a fruitcake from the Aga. 'There are some fairy cakes on the table, and I've made strawberry jam sandwiches. Don't eat too much or you won't want your dinner.'

Pauline gave her a look of affection. 'You sound just like a mum,' she observed. 'Do you suppose Wanda will be a nice mum?'

'Oh, I expect so,' lied Florina briskly. She would be awful, she thought, no sticky fingers, no quick cuddles with grubby toddlers. There would be a nursemaid, young and not in the least cosy, and the children would be on show for half an hour after tea. She wondered if Sir William would stand for that; that's if there *were* any more children.

'You look so sad,' said Pauline, 'ever since you left Holland.'

Nanny had said the same thing, reflected Florina. She would have to mend her ways or leave. Unthinkable! 'Well, I'm not.' She made her voice sound cheerful. 'Sit down for a minute and tell me what you would like to have to eat on this picnic.'

Sir William arrived soon after six o'clock, with Wanda exquisite in an outfit in cyclamen and hunter's green; not in the least suitable for a weekend in a small country village, but guaranteed to give its inhabitants something to talk about for a few days.

She got out of the car and went into the house ahead of him, calling in a petulant voice, 'Where's everyone? I want my bags taken up to my room; I'm not fit to be seen!'

She paused by the passage leading to the kitchen and addressed Florina's back, busy at the Aga.

'Cook, leave that, and get my things from the car.'

Florina took no notice; she was at the precise point when the sauce she was making would either be a triumph of culinary art or an inedible failure.

She didn't turn round when she heard Sir William say, 'Florina has her work, Wanda. You can't expect her to leave it to carry your cases. I'll bring them up in a moment.'

Florina heard his laughing greeting to Pauline, their voices fading as they went out to the car. He had always come to the kitchen to ask her how she was, but this evening he didn't, perhaps because he had gone upstairs with Wanda's cases. She knew soon enough that that wasn't so, for she heard him talking to Nanny in the hall. She went about the business of dinner: mushrooms cooked in wine and cream for starters, minute steaks with duchesse potatoes and braised celery, lemon sorbet and Bavarian creams with lashings of cream. She had baked rolls, too, and curled the farm butter and arranged a cheeseboard. To please Wanda, she had made a dish of carrot straws, shreds of celery, slivers of cabbage and apple. She had made home-made chocolates, too, to go with the coffee, something she knew Pauline would like.

There was half an hour before she needed to dish up, so she slipped up to her room and tidied her hair. Then, since there was no one about, she went out to the patio. It was a lovely evening, turning to dusk, and the white swans were gliding away to settle for the night. A bat or two skimmed past, and somewhere in the distance an owl hooted. From the nearby pub there were muted sounds of cheerful talk and laughter. A peaceful rural scene; no wonder Sir William liked to spend his weekends in his lovely country home. Florina fell to wondering about his house in London; in its way it was probably as charming as Wheel House. Well, she would never see it, nor would she know more of his life than she did now, and that was precious little.

She gave a great sigh and then spun round as Sir William said from the drawing-room door, 'Hello, Florina, you look sad. Did you leave your heart in Holland?'

She stammered a little. 'Oh, good evening, Sir William. No no, of course not…' She retreated to the kitchen door. 'I was just waiting here before I dish up—I hope you don't mind?'

He said testily, 'Mind? Why should I mind? You have as much right to be here as I. Has Pauline been plaguing you?'

'Heavens, no, she's a dear child! We've had such fun, biking and walking and she likes to cook.' She hesitated. 'I suppose she couldn't have a dog or a cat? She loves animals—the swans come when she calls, and we were at the farm the other day when the Jersey cow calved—you don't mind?'

'I entirely approve, Florina, and of course we'll have a dog—*and* a cat. She will have to look after them while I'm in London. Of course when she's at school, you will have to do the looking after.'

'I'll enjoy that—she'll be so happy.'

He said thoughtfully, 'I should have thought of it for myself.'

'I think that you have a great deal to think of, Sir William?' She forgot everything for a moment and gave him a sweet, loving look, and he stared back at her without speaking.

'It's time to dish up.' She was suddenly shy, anxious to get back to the kitchen. But presently, through the open door, she heard Pauline come on to the patio and her squeals of delight when she was told about the dog and cat.

Her delight wasn't echoed by Wanda, who had wandered into the drawing-room unsuitably dressed in flame-coloured taffeta. 'I loathe cats, and I detest dogs with their filthy paws. There'll be neither, Pauline, so you can forget it.'

Florina, in the dining-room, setting the soup tureen on the serving-table, stopped to listen.

'I'm afraid you'll have to overcome your dislike, Wanda.' Sir William sounded at his most placid. 'I have promised Pauline that she shall have them.'

'Well, don't expect me to come here…'

His quiet, 'Very well, my dear,' made her pause.

'Oh, darling, don't be unkind—after all, I bury myself down here in this God-forsaken hole just to please you.'

He sounded interested. 'Is that how it seems to you?'

Wanda pouted prettily. 'No decent restaurants within miles, nowhere to go dancing, no shops. You've no idea what sacrifices I'm making for you, my angel.'

'You would like us to live in town permanently?'

Wanda gave a little crow of delight. 'There! I knew you would see it my way.'

'You're mistaken, Wanda. We'll have to talk about it later on.' He put an arm round his daughter's shoulders. 'Next weekend, we'll have a look for a cat and a dog.'

Florina glanced at the clock, and skipped to the hall to tap on the door and sound the dinner gong. It wasn't quite time, but she considered that intervention of some sort would be a good idea. That wasn't the last of it, however. Long after dinner was finished and Pauline was in bed, as Florina and Nanny were clearing away their own meal, Wanda came into the kitchen.

'I suppose it was you who put Pauline up to badgering her father for cats and dogs? Well, Cook, you can take it from me, once Sir William and I are married I'll get rid of them, and you'll go at the same time.'

Nanny drew in a hissing breath, ready to do battle, but Florina forestalled her. 'I should think Sir William will wish to be consulted before you do anything so unwise, Miss Fortesque. And in any case, I've no intention of listening to your threats.'

Wanda glared back at her, her eyes, narrow slits of dislike. 'Wormed your way in, haven't you?' she observed spitefully. 'Just because you can cook—you're only a servant…'

She stopped when she heard Sir William's footsteps crossing the hall.

'I was just telling Cook how delicious dinner was.'

She turned her back on the kitchen and hooked an arm through his. 'How about a stroll before bed, darling?'

'The hussy!' Nanny's rather dry voice was full of indignation. 'If he only knew what was going on...'

'Well, there is nothing we can do about it, Mrs Frobisher.' Florina began to set the table for breakfast and found that she was shaking with rage.

'Huh!' Nanny put a great deal of feeling into the sound. 'But Sir William is no fool and he has got eyes in his head—I'm not despairing.'

But Florina was; she might love him with her whole heart, but she was powerless to do anything about it. Especially now that he had somehow contrived to put a barrier between them. And what could she have done? If she had been as attractive as Wanda and as beautifully dressed and, moreover, living in Sir William's world, she would have made no bones about competing with Wanda. But famous paediatricians didn't fall in love with their cooks, not in real life, anyway. She laid the last plate tidily in its place and offered to make Nanny a cup of tea before she went to bed.

Pauline spent a good deal of the following morning in the kitchen. She had refused to go to Salisbury with her father and Wanda, who declared that she had to do some urgent shopping. Florina suggested that she should make cakes for tea, and went on with her own preparations for dinner. Lunch was to be cold and there was a raised pie she had made on the previous day, and a salad. She would have an hour to spare in the afternoon, and she planned to go and see her father.

With the exception of Wanda, they had shared

breakfast round the kitchen table, and Sir William had gone off with Pauline directly afterwards, to reappear a few minutes before Wanda, who trailed downstairs, declaring that she hadn't slept a wink and demanding to be taken to the shops without delay.

'I'm glad she's gone,' declared Pauline sorrowfully, and burst into tears.

'Hush now, love,' said Florina, 'things are never as bad as they seem.' Then she offered the making of cakes, so that the child cheered up, and presently was laughing with Florina.

Lunch dealt with, Florina changed into a dress and went through the village to see her father. She had paid him a hurried visit soon after they had got back from Holland but, despite her gifts of tobacco and whisky, he had been morose. When she went up the familiar path and opened the door, she saw that today's visit wasn't going to be a success, either. It was with relief that she went back to Wheel House, got back into her overall and apron, and went to work on the dinner.

She knew everyone who came that evening. They glimpsed her as they passed the short passage to the kitchen, and called her a good evening, and after the meal they came to the patio door to tell her what a splendid meal it had been, and ask her how she did it. It didn't seem quite the right thing but, since Sir William was with them and evinced no sign of annoyance, she supposed that he didn't mind. Presently Nanny took coffee into the drawing-room, and then went upstairs to see if Pauline was asleep, while Florina got their own meal.

They didn't linger over it. It was Sunday the next day, and there would be no help from the village and there was the picnic to prepare in the morning. They did their chores, turned out the lights and went to their beds.

Sir William had said that he would drive Wanda back after tea. Florina did her chores and then sat for a while on the patio with Nanny, drinking their coffee in the sun and watching the swans. They had an early lunch and, with Nanny comfortably resting on her bed, Florina got tea ready. Sir William had suggested that they might have it on the patio, since the Meggisons and their three children would return with them. She set out cakes and sandwiches, scones, jam and cream on the kitchen table, then covered the lot with damp cloths, and went to her room to do her hair and tidy. There would still be time to sit in the garden for an hour and leaf through the Sunday papers.

As things were to turn out, there wasn't. The picnic party returned early, making over-bright conversation, while the children looked mutinous. Florina's heart sank when she saw Sir William's face, smoothed of all expression and covering, she had no doubt, a well-bottled-up rage. She had known the Meggisons for years; she greeted them now and led the children away to wash their hands, while Wanda, looking sulky, led Mrs Meggison upstairs.

Back again, with the children milling round her,

Florina took another look at Sir William. He was talking to Ralph Meggison, but he turned to her as she went out on the patio.

'Wanda had a headache,' he told her, in a voice which gave nothing away. 'I'm afraid we've cut your afternoon short.'

Florina gave her head a small shake. 'Tea is quite ready—would you like it now?'

'As soon as we are all here…'

'If Miss Fortesque's headache is bad, would the children like to have tea in the kitchen?'

'That's a very good idea. Could you bear the noise?'

'I shall like it,' she said, and meant it.

The children helped to take some of the food out to the patio, and Pauline took a tea tray up to Nanny before they gathered round the kitchen table to fall upon the food, making a great noise and laughing immoderately.

Florina laughed with them, and saw that they minded their manners and had a good tea. Finally, when they were finished, the eldest Meggison child said, 'Gosh, this is fun! We'd have hated being out there with her.'

'And who is her?' asked Florina. 'The cat's mother?'

They fell about laughing. It was Pauline who whispered, 'Wanda, of course. She grumbled all the while—it was too hot and there were wasps and the grass was damp and the food was all wrong…'

Florina bristled. 'Wrong? What was wrong? I put in everything I thought would make a picnic lunch.'

'It was super,' they hastened to reassure her. 'We ate everything. Only she was cross all the time.'

The youngest Meggison added, in a piping voice, 'She's not a country lady, not like you, Florina. You know where the mushrooms are and the blackberries and nuts. Pauline says you're going to have a dog and a cat…'

They were all shouting out suitable names to each other when Sir William joined them.

He pulled up a chair, stretched out a hand for a cake and observed, 'You *are* having fun! I've been thinking, Pauline. You had better come up to London next weekend. There's an animal sanctuary I know of—we should be able to find something suitable.' He added, as an afterthought, 'Florina, you had better come, too. I'll come down on Friday evening and we can drive back early on Saturday morning. I'll bring you and the animals back here on Sunday.'

Pauline flung herself at him, shrieking with joy. Florina, sitting sedately in her chair, would have liked to do the same. She would have the chance to see his home in London, get a glimpse of his other life, too! She looked up and caught his eye. 'Nanny will be all alone,' she pointed out.

'Mrs Deakin will sleep here. You'll need an overnight bag, that's all.' He took another cake, munched slowly and said, 'I must leave in half an hour.'

He got up, hugged Pauline, nodded to the other children, then smiled a sudden, tender smile at Florina and wandered back to the patio, leaving Florina with a red face, which was viewed with interest by her companions.

'You're very red,' said the youngest Meggison. 'Why?'

Pauline rushed to her rescue. 'It's all the cooking she does. She had to make all the food for the picnic and our tea…'

'Why didn't you come with us on our picnic?' persisted the tiresome child.

Florina had recovered her calm. 'Well, if I had, you wouldn't have had any tea. Now, if you've all finished, do you want to feed the swans? I expect you will have to go home soon.'

They all scampered away, and presently the entire Meggison family put their heads round the door to say goodbye. The youngest Meggison's parting protest that Florina should have gone to the picnic, too, left her feeling awkward, since it was uttered in piercing tones which Sir William and Wanda must have heard.

Before he left, Sir William came into the kitchen. Nanny was sitting at the table stringing beans, and Florina was at the sink peeling potatoes. He kissed Nanny on a cheek and looked across at Florina.

'Thank you for making the weekend pleasant. I'll be down on Friday as soon as I can manage.'

Her sedate, 'Very well, Sir William,' was at variance with her flushed cheeks, and he stared at her for a long moment before turning on his heel and going out to the car.

Wanda was already in it. Florina could hear her

complaining voice and his mild reply as he drove away, pursued by Pauline's shrieking goodbyes.

Friday seemed an age away, but, in fact, the days went quickly. Pauline changed her mind a dozen times as to what she would wear in London, a problem Florina didn't have. If it stayed fine, she would be able to wear her pink outfit that she had bought for the trip to Holland, if it turned wet and chilly it would have to be the rather worthy suit she had had for several years.

When she got up on Friday morning the first thing she did was to hang out of the window and study the sky. It showed all the signs of a splendid day and she heaved a great sigh, for she would be able to wear the pink suit. But, to be on the safe side, she would take the jersey dress and a mac.

Sir William arrived soon after tea, and when Florina offered to make a fresh pot she was rewarded, as he sat down at the kitchen table with Pauline beside him, listening to her excited chatter and eating the buns left over from their own tea. He had given her a casual greeting, kissed Nanny who had come bustling to meet him, and presently declared that he needed some exercise and would take Pauline off for a walk. This was a good thing for Florina's peace of mind; just the sight of him had sent all thoughts of cooking out of her head. She applied herself to that now and, punctual to the minute, dished up an elegant dinner which Pauline shared along with him.

In the evening, after Pauline had gone to bed, he went along to his study, and only emerged just as she was about to go to bed, in order to remind her that they would be leaving at nine o'clock, and could they have breakfast an hour before that? His good-night was casual, rather as though he had forgotten her. It was like looking at someone through a glass window; you could see them but you couldn't get at them, as it were.

There was a good deal of traffic on the road in the morning, but most of it was leaving London, not going into it. The Bentley sped silently up the motorway with Pauline talking non-stop and Florina sitting in the back in a contented haze of happiness, for was she not to spend the next two days in Sir William's house? Probably she wouldn't see much of him, but it was his home… She had worried at first, in case Wanda would be there too, but Pauline had asked her father and he had observed that she was spending the weekend with friends, which meant that Florina could sit back and dream about the weekend. She came awake when they stopped for coffee, joined in the talk without hearing more than half of it, and then climbed back into the car to continue her dreams, hardly noticing when Sir William slowed as they reached the outskirts of London. But gradually she became aware that he had turned away from the main streets and was threading his way through a quieter part of the city, its streets lined with tall Regency houses facing narrow railinged gardens in their centres.

The traffic here was sparse, and mostly private cars. She wasn't sure where they were, but it looked very pleasant. If one could live in such streets, she reflected, then life in London might be quite bearable.

Sir William had turned out of one street into another very similar, and stopped the car half-way along a row of narrow houses, their bow windows glistening in the sun, their front doors pristine with new paint. He got out, as Pauline skipped out on her side and ran up the short flight of steps to the door of the house before them. He opened Florina's door and ushered her out, too.

By the time they had joined Pauline at the door, Jolly had opened it, received Sir William's greeting with dignity, Pauline's delighted outburst with scarcely concealed pleasure and Florina's composed good morning with an almost avuncular mien, before standing aside to admit them.

The lobby opened out into a semicircular hall, with a graceful staircase at one side and several doors leading out of it. Sir William flung one open now and urged Florina to enter. The room was at the back of the house overlooking a small, but delightfully planned garden.

'I use this room when I'm here alone,' he explained. 'The drawing-room is upstairs, and a bit too grand unless I have guests.'

Florina, taking in the elegant furnishings, the portraits on the walls and the generously draped brocade curtains, found the room delightful but grand enough. She wondered what the drawing-room would be like. This room had a pleasant air of homeliness about it. She sat down at his request, drank the coffee Mrs Jolly brought in and, having done so, got to her feet when Pauline suggested that she should show her her room before they had lunch.

They mounted the stairs behind Mrs Jolly, and Florina was shown into a room at the head of the stairs: a beautiful room, all pink and white, with its own bathroom and a view of the street below.

'I'm next door,' Pauline explained. 'Come and see my room when you're ready.'

Warned by Mrs Jolly that lunch would be in fifteen minutes, Florina wasted five of them inspecting her room. It was really a dream, the kind of room any girl would wish for. She wondered who had furnished it right down to the last tablet of soap and matching bath oil. There was even shampoo and hand lotion, all matching. She did her face and tidied her hair, and then knocked on Pauline's door.

Her room was as pretty as Florina's, but here the furnishings were in a pale apricot, and the bed and dressing-table were painted white.

'Do you like your room?' asked Pauline eagerly. 'Daddy let me help him furnish some of the bedrooms. Of course, Wanda doesn't like them. She told Daddy that she was going to do the whole house over.'

'A pity,' observed Florina in a neutral voice. 'I find them delightful, but people have different tastes.'

They went back to the sitting-room and Florina was given a sherry before they crossed the hall to the dining-room. Its walls were papered in a rich red, the mahogany gleaming with polish. Florina, good cook that she was, could find nothing wrong with the shrimp patties, the lamb cooked with rosemary and the fresh fruit salad and cream which followed them.

They had their coffee at the table and, as they were finishing it, Sir William said, 'We will go tomorrow morning and choose a dog and cat. This afternoon I thought perhaps we might go to a matinée: I've tickets for *Cats* which starts at three o'clock. I have some telephone calls to make, then we'll take Florina round the house, shall we, Pauline?'

Florina went to bed that night in a haze of happiness; the day had been perfect, never to be forgotten. They had explored the house at a leisurely pace, allowing her plenty of time to admire everything. It was perfect, she thought, and she said so, forgetting that Wanda was going to change the lovely old furniture and the chintzes and velvets. Afterwards, they had gone to the theatre, and then to tea at the Ritz and finally back home, to sit by the window overlooking the garden, arguing happily about names for the animals.

They would leave at half-past nine the next morning, Sir William had said at dinner. 'For I have to go to the hospital and check on a couple of patients.'

After dinner, when Pauline had gone to bed, Florina sat opposite him, listening to him talking about his work. He had paused briefly to ask, 'Am I boring you? Wanda dislikes hearing about illness, but I think that you are interested.'

She had told him fervently that she was and, being

a sensible girl, never hesitated to stop him so that he might explain something she hadn't understood.

She could have stayed there all night listening to him talking, but remembered in time that she was the cook, however pleasant he was being. So she made rather a muddled retreat in a flurry of goodnights and thanks, and Sir William's eyes had gleamed with amusement. He had made the muddle worse by bending to kiss her as she reached the door, so that just for a moment she forgot that she was the cook.

Chapter 6

They spent almost two hours in the animal sanctuary. Finally, they left with an ecstatic Pauline sitting on the back seat with a large woolly dog beside her, and a mother cat and her kitten in a basket on her lap. The dog was half-grown, his ancestry so numerous that it was impossible to classify him, but he had an honest face and eyes which shone with gratitude and anxious affection. His coat was curly, and once he had recovered his full health and strength its brown colour would be glossy. He had been found by a hiker tied to a tree and left to starve. The cat and kitten had been picked up on a motorway, tied in a plastic bag. They were black and white, the pair of them, and still timid, not believing their luck.

Florina, sitting beside Sir William, listened to the

child talking to her new pets and spoke her thoughts aloud. 'Isn't it nice to hear Pauline happy?'

Sir William threw her a quick sideways look. 'Is she not always happy?'

'Almost always.'

'But she is sometimes unhappy. Will you tell me why?'

'No, I can't tell you that—at least I can, but I don't choose to do so.' She added hastily, 'I don't mean to be rude, Sir William.'

His grunt could have meant anything. Presently he broke his silence. 'I shall be away for the whole of next week, and I think it likely that I shall remain in town over the weekend. Nanny will be with you, of course, but you can always phone if you need anything—Jolly will know where I am.'

She said meekly, 'Yes, Sir William,' and wondered where he would be going. To stay with Wanda? Very likely. She sat silent, brooding about it.

Back at the house, Pauline ran off to the kitchen to show Mrs Jolly her pets, and Sir William excused himself on the grounds of telephone calls to make and departed to his study, which left Florina standing in the hall, not sure what to do. It was Jolly who entered the hall just then and told her that lunch would be in half an hour, and if she cared to go into the drawing-room she would find drinks on the table under the window.

So she went in there and sat down in one of the smaller of the easy chairs. She didn't pour herself a drink, and she was surprised at Jolly mentioning it. After all, she should really be in the kitchen…

The house was quiet. But from the closed door leading to the kitchen came the sound of Pauline's excited voice. The study door was shut, so Florina nipped smartly out of the room, and crossed the hall silently. The dining-room door was half-open; she peeped round it—the table was set for three persons. She took a soft step forward and was brought to a startled halt by Sir William, speaking within inches of her ear. 'Set your mind at rest, Florina, you are lunching with us.'

She had whizzed round to gape up at his amused face. 'How did you know? I mean, I expected to eat with the Jollys,' she added fiercely. 'You forget that I work for you, Sir William.'

'Yes, I do,' he agreed, 'but for quite different reasons than those you are supposing.' He turned her smartly around. 'Shall we have a drink? We shall have to leave soon after lunch—I've a date for this evening. I'll not be down at the weekend, as I've told you already. I've a long-standing invitation I most particularly wish to keep.'

She said nothing to this. It would be with Wanda, of course; even when she wasn't there she made her presence felt, tearing Florina's futile day-dreams to shreds. She sat down in the chair she had just vacated, and sipped her sherry while Sir William began a rather one-sided conversation. It was a relief when Pauline came to join them.

'The pets are having their dinner,' she explained. 'Daddy, what shall we call them?'

Names were discussed at some length during lunch. Presently, they all got into the Bentley to drive back to Wheel House, Pauline in the back with the animals and Florina beside Sir William. It would be polite to talk a little, she reflected, so she ventured a few remarks about the pleasures of the weekend and was answered in such a vague fashion that she soon gave up. Perhaps he didn't like chatter as he drove, although Pauline never stopped talking when she sat with him and he hadn't seemed to mind.

She was taken by surprise when he said, 'Don't stop talking. You have a gentle voice, very soothing. It helps me to think.'

She glanced at his profile. He was looking severe but, when he looked at her, suddenly his smile wasn't in the least severe. She began to talk about the garden and the swans and the delight of the mill stream running under the house, rambling on, speaking her thoughts aloud.

When they reached Wheel House she slipped away to the kitchen after Nanny's brief greeting, and carried in the tray set ready. Then she went to her room and put her things away. By the time she went downstairs tea was almost over, and Sir William was preparing to leave. She bade him a quiet goodbye and he nodded casually. 'Think up some of your super menus, will you? I'll be back with Wanda the weekend after next.'

'I'll look forward to that,' she told herself silently.

The two weeks went quickly, what with walking the dog, and initiating the cat and her kitten into the life of comfort they were undoubtedly going to lead. Pauline had chosen their names—Mother and Child—for, as she pointed out to Florina, that's what they were. The dog she called Bobby, because she found he answered to that name. Florina taught her to whistle, and the dog, while not looking particularly intelligent, was obedient and devoted to her. The days were placid, and even her father's ill humour couldn't spoil Florina's content. True, her thoughts dwelt overlong upon Sir William, and any titbit of news about him when he telephoned Pauline she listened to, and stored away to mull over when she had gone to bed. It was a good thing that towards the end of the fortnight she had to begin in earnest on the weekend's food. She helped around the house too, and made sure that Pauline's school uniform was ready for the autumn term was almost upon them.

Nanny, usually so brisk, looked dejected. 'They'll be married, mark my words,' she observed to Florina, as they sat together after Pauline had gone up to bed. 'The child will be at school, and next term she'll find herself a boarder there, with that woman persuading Sir William that it is just what Pauline longs for. Then it will be me, packed off, away from here. And take it from me, Florina, you won't be long following me! She won't risk having you in the house. You're young—and a nice girl—not pretty, but there is more to a girl than a handsome face…'

Florina murmured a reassurance she didn't feel.

Being young and nice was no help at all against Wanda's cherished good looks.

Sir William arrived in time for a late tea. Florina heard the car draw up and shut the door upon the sound of Wanda's voice, strident with ill temper, raised in complaint as she came into the house.

She heard her say to Nanny, who had gone into the hall, 'Still here, Nanny? There can't be anything for you to do—according to Sir William that cook of his is quite capable of running the place. You must be longing to retire again.'

It augured ill for the weekend and Florina, warming the teapot, wished it over. The less she saw of Sir William, the better for her peace of mind. Even so, she longed to see him. She made the tea, put the tea cosy over the pot and began to butter scones.

'Well, well!' Sir William's quiet voice took her by surprise. 'My own kitchen door shut against me! Pauline has been commandeered to help Wanda unpack.' He took a scone and ate it with relish. 'And how are you, Florina?'

He studied her face carefully, and she reddened under his gaze. 'Very well, thank you, Sir William.'

He began on another scone. 'Jolly is with us. Will you or Nanny see that he is comfortable? He has driven down in a Mini—you can drive? You'll be able to take Pauline to school and fetch her.'

She said faintly, 'Oh, will I?' and passed the plate of scones, since he seemed bent on eating the lot.

'There aren't all that number of people I would trust to drive her. Could you escape from the stove tomorrow morning—before breakfast? We'll go for a run?'

All her resolutions about keeping out of his way disappeared like smoke. 'It's breakfast at half-past eight…'

'Couldn't be better. Seven o'clock be OK?' He didn't wait for her answer, but took another scone and wandered out of the kitchen, leaving her door open.

Which meant that after a few moments she heard Wanda's voice as she came downstairs. She was still complaining and Nanny, coming for the tea tray, had a face like a thunder cloud. 'In a fine temper, she is—wanted to stop at some posh hotel for tea, but Sir William wanted to come straight home.'

She stalked off with the tray and Florina set the table for their own tea, helped by Jolly, who had just come into the house.

It was a pleasant meal, with Jolly and Nanny keeping the conversation carefully to generalities. This was a disappointment to Florina, who had hoped to glean news about Sir William and Wanda. After tea, there was no time to talk. There was dinner to see to which kept her in the kitchen for several hours, aware that Pauline's voice, raised and tearful, interlarded by Bobby's bark and Wanda's regrettably shrill tones, were hardly contributing to a happy evening.

Mother and Child were curled up cosily before the Aga, presently to be joined by a furious Pauline and Bobby, who, being good-natured himself, expected everyone else to be the same.

'I hate her!' declared Pauline. 'If Daddy marries her, me and Bobby will run away. She said he smelled nasty.' She sniffed, 'Daddy said it was time for his supper, and then him and me—I—will take him for his walk.'

Daddy seemed good at pouring oil on troubled waters. Florina watched Pauline feeding the animals. The child was entirely engrossed in this, and happy, but how soon would her happiness be shattered once Wanda had become her stepmother? Sir William, much as she loved him, had been remarkably mistaken in his choice of a second wife. Men, thought Florina, however clever, could be remarkably dim at times.

She was in the kitchen all the evening, so that she saw neither Sir William nor Wanda. It was bedtime by the time they had eaten their own supper and cleared it away. Since Jolly had undertaken to remain up until Sir William retired himself, she and Nanny said goodnight and went to their respective rooms.

It was one o'clock in the morning when Florina woke on the thought that she had forgotten to put the porridge oats to soak. Nanny was a firm believer in porridge, but it had to be said that she insisted it was made according to her recipe—old-fashioned and time-consuming. She got out of bed, without stopping to put on a dressing-gown and slippers, and nipped down to the kitchen. There would be no one around at that hour. She put the exact amount of oats into water in a double saucepan, added the pinch of salt Nanny insisted upon, and stirred it smoothly before filling the steamer with hot water and setting the whole upon the Aga. Having done which, she stepped back and glanced at the clock, and then let out a startled yelp as Sir William, speaking from the door where he had been lounging watching her, observed, 'Such devotion to duty! It's one o'clock in the morning, Florina.'

She curled her toes into the rug before the stove and longed for her dressing-gown. 'Yes—well, you see I forgot the porridge. Nanny likes it made in a certain way, and I forgot to soak it. I'm very sorry if I disturbed you…'

He said gravely, 'Oh, you disturb me, but you have no need to be sorry about it.' He stood looking at her for a long moment, and when he spoke his voice was very gentle. 'Go to bed, my dear.'

She flew away without a word, intent on escape, wishing with all her heart that she *was* his dear. Sleep escaped her for the next hour or so, so that the night was short, but she got up and dressed and plaited her hair neatly at the usual time. Then she went down to the kitchen, intent on making tea before they set out, thankful that it would give her something to do, for, remembering their early-morning meeting, she was stiff with shyness.

Sir William was already there, with the tea made and poured into mugs. His good morning was casually friendly, and he scarcely looked at her, so she calmed down and, by the time they reached the garage, she was almost her usual calm self.

Sir William was hardly the build for a Mini. Florina, despite the smallness of her person, found it a tight fit with the pair of them. To make more room he had flung an arm along the back of the seat and she was very aware of it; nevertheless, she made herself concentrate on her driving, going along the narrow country road to Wilton and then back on the main Salisbury road, and taking the turning to the village, over the bridge opposite the farm.

'Quite happy about ferrying Pauline to and fro?' he asked as she ran the little car into the garage. He got out, strolling beside her towards the kitchen door. 'If Pauline's up we'll take Bobby for a walk.' He turned on his heel and then stopped and turned around to face her. 'You have such beautiful hair—a shining mouse curtain. You should wear it loose always.'

'It would get in the soup,' said Florina.

Wanda came downstairs mid-morning, beautifully dressed and made-up, ready to be entertained. It was a pity that everyone should be in the kitchen with the door to the patio open, milling around, drinking coffee, feeding the swans from the patio, playing with the cats and brushing Bobby. In the middle of this cheerful hubbub, Florina stood at the table making a batch of rolls, quite undisturbed by it all. Nobody else noticed Wanda's entrance, and Florina paused long enough to say politely, 'Good morning, Miss Fortesque. Would you like coffee?'

Sir William looked up briefly from Bobby's grooming. 'Hello, Wanda, Pauline and I are going to her school to see her headmistress—like to come with us?'

Wanda shuddered delicately. 'Certainly not. I can't sleep in this house. I'll rest on the patio, if someone takes that dog away. Cook, you can bring me some coffee once I'm settled.'

Sir William said quietly, 'Jolly will do that. Come on, Pauline, we'll be off.' He whistled to Bobby, remarked that they would be back for lunch, and disappeared in the direction of the garage.

Wanda needed a lot of settling: fresh coffee, more cushions, a light rug, the novel she had left in her bedroom. Nanny, looking more and more po-faced, handed these over wordlessly and then disappeared, and so presently did Jolly, leaving Florina to take the rolls from the oven and then start on lunch.

She was arranging cold salmon artistically on a bed of cress and cucumber, when Wanda called her. It would have given Florina great satisfaction to have ignored her, but Wanda was a guest and, what was more, a cherished one. And Florina, in a mixed-up, miserable way, would have done anything to make Sir William happy, even if it meant being nice to Wanda. She washed her hands well and went on to the patio, prepared to offer cool drinks, more cushions or anything else the girl demanded.

She was completely taken aback when Wanda said, 'Don't think I haven't eyes in my head. I've watched you toadying to Sir William—God knows what crazy ideas you've got in that silly head. I dare say you fancy you are in love with him. Well, you can forget it. The day we marry, and that shall not be too far away, you'll get your notice, so you had better start looking for another job.'

Florina, usually so mild, seethed with a splendid rage. She said in a very quiet voice, 'You have no right to talk to me like this. When Sir William tells me to leave, then I shall go, but not one minute before. I think that you are a rude, spoiled young woman, who has no love or thought for anyone. You don't deserve to be happy, but then, you never will be…' She put her neat head on one side and studied the other girl, who was staring speechlessly at her. 'You may report all that I've said to Sir William, but I wish to be there just in case you forget what you said to me, too.'

'If it's the last thing I do,' breathed Wanda, 'I'll see you pay for this.' She sat up and caught Florina a smart slap.

'Cool off, Miss Fortesque.' Florina, who hadn't realised that she could feel so royally angry, picked up the jug of lemonade on the table by Wanda's chair, and poured it slowly over the top of her head. The rather syrupy stuff caused havoc to Wanda's artlessly arranged hair, and did even more damage to her complexion. She jumped to her feet, shrieking threats as she raced away to her room, and Florina put down the jug and went back to the salmon. She had cooked her goose, but just for a moment she didn't care.

Jolly was in the kitchen. He eyed her with a benign smile and a good deal of respect. 'I saw and heard everything, Miss Florina. If necessary I will substantiate anything you may need to say to Sir William. I was prepared to come to your assistance, but it proved unnecessary.'

The enormity of what she had done was permeating through her like an unexpected heavy fall of rain. 'Oh, Mr Jolly, thank you. You're very kind. It was very wrong of me and I forgot that I was just the cook. She'll have me sacked.'

'I believe that you may set your mind at rest on that score,' observed Jolly, who had had several interesting chats with Nanny and was totally in agreement with her. Florina would be a splendid wife for Sir William—and she was in love with him—although she was unaware of how much that showed. As for Sir William, he was old enough and wise enough to get himself out of the mess he had so carelessly let himself get into. Jolly had no doubt that he would do it in his own good time, and when it suited him, and with such skill that Miss Fortesque would believe that she had been the one to call their marriage off. In the meantime, Jolly made a mental note to call Florina 'Miss Florina'—it would be a step in the right direction.

There was no sign of Wanda until lunch time, a meal she ate in a haughty silence which Sir William didn't appear to notice. When they had finished she said in an unnaturally quiet voice, 'William, I must talk to you—now.'

Jolly conveyed this news to the kitchen and Florina, hearing it, lost her appetite completely. Indeed, she was feeling quite sick by the time they had finished, and when Sir William strolled in, she went so white that the freckles sprinkling her nose stood out darkly.

He crossed to the Aga, stooped so as to stroke Mother and Child curled together in a neat ball, and said in his placid way, 'I'd like a word with Florina, if you wouldn't mind…'

Florina watched Jolly and Nanny go through the door, put her hands on the back of the chair she was standing behind and met Sir William's gaze.

'Miss Fortesque has told me a most extraordinary tale—have you anything to add, Florina?' His voice was kind.

'No.'

'There are always two sides to a disagreement. I should like to hear yours.'

'No.'

He smiled a little. He studied the nails of one hand. 'Pauline was listening at the study door, and indeed Miss Fortesque was speaking so loudly, I was forced to send her to her room so that she could indulge her mirth.'

'Please don't ask me to apologise. I'm not the least sorry for what I did. I expect you're going to give me notice.'

He looked surprised. 'Why should I do that? I had hoped that you knew me well enough to tell me your version, but it seems that it is not so.'

Florina burst out, 'How can I tell you? You are going to marry Miss Fortesque.'

He smiled again. 'That is your reason?' And,

when she nodded, 'I think that it might be better to say no more about the matter.' He started for the door and paused to look back at her. 'It seems that lemonade plays havoc with tinted hair.'

Jolly was in the hall, so obviously waiting for him that Sir William said, 'Come into the study, Jolly. I take it that you wish to speak to me?'

Jolly closed the door behind him. 'I was in the kitchen, Sir William, and, begging your pardon, Miss Fortesque was that nasty—Miss Florina was so polite too, in the face of all the nasty rubbish…'

'Rubbish, Jolly?'

Jolly, who had an excellent memory, repeated what had been said. He noticed with satisfaction that Sir William's face had no expression upon it, which meant that he was concealing strong feelings. He wisely added nothing more.

Sir William was silent for several moments. 'Thank you, Jolly. You did right to tell me. I have told Florina that the matter is to be forgotten.'

'Very good, Sir William. Miss Florina is a nice young lady and easily hurt.'

'Quite so.' He smiled suddenly, and looked young and faintly wicked. 'Will you go to Pauline's room and ask her if she wants to take Bobby and me for a walk? Miss Fortesque is resting in her room, but I dare say she'll be down for tea.'

The rest of the weekend passed off peacefully. Florina kept to her kitchen and tried to expunge her bad behaviour by cooking mouth-watering meals and keeping out of the way of Sir William and Wanda.

Pauline, when she wasn't with her father, spent her time in the kitchen, with Bobby in close attendance, curled up before the Aga with the cats.

'Wanda is so cross, I'd rather be here with you,' she explained. 'Daddy said I wasn't to talk about it, but I laughed and laughed. But she is horrid—I shall run away…'

'Now, love, don't talk like that. It would break your father's heart if you were to leave him. He loves you so much.'

'So why is he going to marry Wanda? He doesn't love her.'

'You mustn't say that, she is a a very lovely lady.'

'With a black heart,' declared Pauline, so fiercely that they both laughed.

The house seemed very empty when the Bentley had gone the next day. Sir William had bade Florina a casual goodbye, kissed Pauline and Nanny, swept Wanda into the front seat before there was time for her to say anything, ushered Jolly into the back of the car and driven off. He hadn't said anything about the following weekend. Perhaps he would stay in town to placate Wanda, take her dining and dancing, so that she could wear her lovely clothes and show off the enormous ring she wore on her engagement finger.

Florina retired to the kitchen and got supper, with a good deal of unnecessary clashing of saucepans.

There was plenty to keep her busy during the next few days: tomato chutney to make, vegetables from the garden to blanch and pack into the freezer, and she had Pauline to keep her company when she wasn't having her sewing and knitting lessons with Nanny, something the old lady insisted upon. It was quite late on Thursday evening when Florina heard a car turn into the drive and a moment later the front door shutting. She went down the passage into the hall and Sir William was there. He was standing in the centre of the lovely old Persian carpet, staring at the wall, but he turned to look at her. He was tired; his face had lines in it she hadn't seen before.

She said at once, 'You'd like something to eat—I'll have it ready in ten minutes. Shall I pour you a drink?' She shook her head in a motherly fashion. 'You've had a very busy day.'

He gave a short sigh and then smiled at her. 'Pour me a whisky, will you? Will Pauline be awake?'

She glanced at the clock. 'Probably not, but she would love you to wake her up.'

She watched him going upstairs two at a time, and then went into the drawing-room to switch on a lamp or two and pour out his whisky. The room looked lovely in the soft light, and the gentle flow of the mill stream under the floor was soothing. She hurried back to the kitchen, to warm up soup. An omelette would be quick, and there were mushrooms she could use. She was laying a tray when he came in, the glass in his hand. 'I'll have it here—anything will do…' He sat down at the table and watched her whisking the eggs. 'I should have telephoned you. I'm examining students at Bristol tomorrow, and on Monday and Tuesday. I'll drive up each day—I don't need to be there until ten o'clock and I can be back here in the early evening.'

Florina poured the soup into a pitkin and set it before him. Her heart sang with delight at the prospect of him being at Wheel House. She said happily, 'Oh, now nice—to have you here...' She paused and then went on quickly, 'Nice for all of us.'

Since he was staring at her rather hard, the spoon in his hand, she added, 'Do eat your soup, Sir William, and I'll make your omelette. There's bread and butter on the table. Would you like coffee now or later?'

'Now, if you will have it with me.'

She got two mugs and filled them from the pot on the Aga, put one before him and then went back to the frying-pan, where the mushrooms were sizzling gently. He began to talk, going over his week and, although for half the time she had very little idea of what he was talking about, she listened with interest, dishing up the omelette and then watching him eat it while she drank her coffee. This was how it should be, she reflected: someone waiting for him each evening to share his day's work with him and see that he ate a proper meal and could talk without interruption...

'Of course, you won't understand half of what I'm saying,' observed Sir William and passed his mug for more coffee.

'Well, no—I wish I did! I can understand why you love your work. I think that I would have liked to have been a nurse and to have known a bit more about all the things that you have been talking about. I'm too old to start training now, though.'

'Old?'

'I'm twenty-seven, Sir William.'

'I'm thirty-nine, Florina.' He leaned back in his chair. 'Is there any of that jam you made last week?'

She fetched it, put the loaf and a dish of butter on the table and watched him demolish a slice. When he had finished, she said matter-of-factly, 'You should go to bed, Sir William. When will you be leaving in the morning?'

'Eight o'clock.'

'Will breakfast at half-past seven suit you, or would you like it earlier?'

'That will do very well. I'll help you with these things. You should be in bed yourself.'

He ignored her refusal of help, but found a tea-cloth and dried the dishes as she washed them. He waited as she saw to the animals and climbed the stairs to her room, and then went back to the hall. But he didn't go at once to his bed, he went into the drawing-room and sat down in his great chair, deep in thought. Presently he got to his feet, stretched hugely, turned off the lights and went upstairs. His thoughts must have been pleasant ones, for he was chuckling as he went.

Florina was dishing up the breakfast when he came into the kitchen with Pauline, dressing-gowned and bare-footed, so she did a second lot of bacon and eggs and, much as she would have liked to have stayed, took herself off on the plea of giving Bobby a quick run in the garden. She didn't go back until she judged Sir William would be ready to leave, but he was still sitting at the table. There was a faint frown on his face, and Pauline's lower lip was thrust out in an ominous fashion. He got up as Florina came in, kissed his daughter, whispered in her ear—something which made her small face brighten—observed that he would be back around six o'clock and went to the patio door, fending off Bobby's efforts to go with him, and passing Florina as he went. His swift kiss took her by surprise, and he had gone before she could do more than gasp.

'Why did Daddy kiss you?' Pauline wanted to know. 'Perhaps it was because Wanda wasn't here—though she doesn't like being kissed. She says it spoils her make-up.'

The child stared at Florina. 'You haven't got anything on your face, have you, Florina? You are awfully red…'

The days went too quickly. The brief glimpses she had of Sir William in the morning coloured her whole day, and in the evenings once he was home, even though he saw little of her, she could hear him talking to Pauline, calling the dog, chattering with Nanny. Once dinner was over and the house was quiet, she listened to his quiet footfall crossing the hall to the study and gently closing the door. She pictured him sitting at his desk, making notes or correcting papers. He might just as easily be writing to Wanda or talking to her on the telephone, but she tried not to think of that.

Tuesday came too soon. He left after breakfast and didn't intend to come back until the weekend, for he would drive straight back to London from Bristol. He mentioned casually, as he went, that probably he would be bringing Miss Fortesque with him at the weekend.

Pauline cried when he had gone, climbing on to Florina's lap and sobbing into her shoulder. 'Do you suppose they'll be married?' she asked.

'Most unlikely,' said Florina bracingly. 'Your father would never do that without telling you, love. So cheer up and wash your face. We'll take Bobby for a nice walk, and when we get back you can go into the garden for a bit and keep an eye on Mother and Child, in case they stray off.'

She had reassured the child, but not herself. She had long ago discovered that Sir William was not a man to display his feelings, or, for that matter, disclose his plans. He was quite capable of doing exactly what he wished, without disclosing either the one or the other, and Wanda was a very attractive girl. Florina went and had a look at herself in the small looking-glass in the downstairs cloakroom and derived no comfort from that. The quicker she erased Sir William from her thoughts, the better. It would help, of course, if she could find a substitute for him, but she had known all the young men in the village since she was a small girl, and they had either got engaged or married or had left home. She didn't know anyone… She did, though. Felix, the only young man to show any interest in her, and one she had no wish ever to meet again.

She went to get Nanny's breakfast tray ready, reflecting that the chances of seeing Felix again were so remote that she need not give him another thought.

Chapter 7

Florina took Pauline and Bobby for short trips in the car during the next few days, and even Nanny consented to be driven into Wilton for an afternoon's shopping. Summer was giving way slowly to the first breath of autumn, and there weren't many days left before Pauline would be going to school. The three of them made the most of it, and it wasn't until Friday morning, when Sir William telephoned, that they remembered that Wanda would be with him that weekend. Reluctantly, Nanny prepared the rooms while Florina bent her mind to the menus for the next few days. She was rolling pastry for the vol-au-vents when she heard a car stop in the drive. Her heart gave a great leap—perhaps Sir William had come early, and, better still, Wanda might not be with him.

She heard Nanny go to the door and the murmur of voices, and then Nanny came into the kitchen.

'Someone for you—a young man—says he is an old friend.' She looked at Florina's floury hands. 'I'll put him in the small sitting-room.'

Florina frowned. 'But I haven't any old friends—not young men…' She remembered Felix, then raised a worried face to Nanny. 'Oh, if it's Felix—I don't want to see him, Nanny.' She added by way of explanation, 'He's from Holland. I met him when I went over there for the wedding.'

'Well, if he's come all this way, you can't refuse to see him. It's only good manners,' declared Nanny, a stickler for doing the right thing.

She went away before Florina could think of any more excuses. Florina finished rolling her pastry, put it in the fridge to keep cool and washed her hands. She didn't bother to look in the looking-glass; her face was flushed from her cooking and her hair, still in its plait, could have done with a comb. But if it *was* Felix, and something told her that it was, then she had no wish to improve her looks for him. She would give him short shrift, she decided crossly as she opened the sitting-room door.

It *was* Felix, debonair and very sure of himself. He came across the room to meet her, just as though they were good friends with a fondness for each other. But she ignored his outstretched hands and said crisply, 'Hello, Felix. I'm afraid I have no time to talk, I've too much to do. Are you on your way somewhere? Tante Minna didn't mention you in her letter.'

'I didn't tell her. I'm putting up at the Trout and Feathers; I thought you could do with a bit of livening up. I've got the car, we can drive around, go dancing, hit a few of the night-spots.'

'You must be out of your mind! I work here, it's a full-time job, and when I'm free I don't want to go dancing or anything else, especially with you, Felix. I can't think why you came.'

'Let's say I don't like being thwarted.' He smiled widely, and she thought that his eyes seemed closer together than she had remembered.

'I don't know what you mean…' They had been speaking Dutch, but now she switched to English. 'You are wasting your time here, Felix. I have neither the time nor the inclination to go out with you, even if it were possible.'

He shrugged his shoulders. 'I've taken the room for a week. There's no reason why I shouldn't spend it here if I wish.'

'None at all, but please don't come bothering me. Now, you will have to excuse me, I'm busy.'

'No coffee? Where's your Dutch hospitality?'

'I'm not in a position to offer that, Felix. I'm cook here.'

She led the way through the hall and opened the door. On the threshold, he paused. 'Just a minute. Doesn't your father live here?'

'Yes, he does, but he has no interest in Mother's side of the family—not since she died.'

'Ah, well, they will know where he lives if I ask at the pub.'

He gave her a mocking salute and got into his car.

She shut the door slowly and found Nanny in the hall beside her. The old lady's stern features were relaxed into a look of concern, so that Florina found herself pouring out a rather muddled account of her meeting with Felix at Tante Minna's house, and her dislike of him. 'I thought I'd been unfair to him,' she explained, 'for he was very nice at the wedding. It was afterwards…'

Nanny nodded. 'A conceited young man, and not a very pleasant one,' she commented. 'Did Sir William meet him?'

'Yes.' Florina went pink, for undoubtedly he thought that she and Felix were rather more than firm friends, even though she had denied it. What was he going to think if Felix came to see her? And he was quite capable of it…

She went back to the kitchen and finished the pastry. She was so worried that she curdled the *béarnaise* sauce, which meant that she had to add iced water, a teaspoon at a time, and beat like mad until it was smooth again.

Preparations for the evening's dinner dealt with, she and Pauline took Bobby for his walk. She expected to meet Felix at every corner, but there was no sign of him. Perhaps he had realised that there was no chance of seeing much of her, and had driven off somewhere where there was more entertainment. She was able to wish Sir William a rather colourless good evening when he arrived, and was relieved to hear Wanda go straight upstairs without bothering to say anything to anyone.

'And how is the village?' enquired Sir William. 'Anything exciting happened since I was last here?'

'Nothing—nothing at all,' said Florina, so quickly that he took a long look at her. Guilt was written all over her nice little face, but he forebore from pursuing the matter. Instead, he sighed inwardly; she was holding something back, and until she had learned to trust him utterly there was little he could do about it. He made some casual remark about Mother and Child sitting as usual before the Aga, then strolled away. He could, of course, question Nanny, but he dismissed the idea at once. Florina would have to tell him herself. Until she trusted him he couldn't be sure…

It was after breakfast the next morning that Felix walked up the drive, rang the bell, and demanded of Nanny, who had answered to door, to see Sir William. He was charming about it, but very determined, and she had no choice but to put him in the small sitting-room and tell Sir William.

So this was Florina's secret, he reflected, shaking hands with Felix, good manners masking his dislike.

'This is a surprise,' he observed. 'You are on holiday?'

Felix gave him a look of well simulated surprise. 'Oh, hasn't Florina told you? I'm staying in the village for a week—so that we can see something of each other. I thought that she would be free for part of each day so that we could be together…'

Sir William said mildly, 'I'm afraid that she doesn't get a great deal of time to herself, especially at the weekends. If you had warned her before you came, something could have been arranged. Perhaps she can manage a half-day after the weekend.'

He got to his feet and Felix, perforce, got to his. 'So sorry,' Sir William said. 'You'll forgive me, I'm sure. I have a guest and have the morning planned.'

He bade Felix goodbye at the door and remained there until he was out of sight, then he shut the door quietly and went along to the kitchen.

Florina was peeling potatoes at the sink, lulled into a sense of false security, so that the enquiring face she turned towards him was serene. But it took only a few seconds for her to realise that something was wrong.

Sir William wandered over to the table and sat on it. 'Your friend Felix has just called to see me. Why didn't you tell me he was in the village, Florina?'

She plunged at once into a muddled speech. 'I don't want to—that is he came yesterday—I didn't think—' She made matters worse by adding, 'I didn't have time to talk to him…'

'But you had time to tell me. Remember? I asked you if there was any news and you said—I quote, "Nothing—nothing at all." Why so secretive, Florina? Did you think that I might not allow my cook to have followers?'

'He's not a follower,' she mumbled.

'He followed you here. I think I'm entitled to…'

He fell silent as the door opened and Pauline came in, Bobby in her arms.

'Daddy, Wanda is still in bed. Could we go for a walk until she gets up? There's a darling little calf at the farm. Florina and I went to look at it and we can go any time we like, so I don't suppose they'll mind you, instead.'

She looked at Florina's pale, strained face and then at her father.

'Are you quarrelling?' she wanted to know.

Sir William put a hand on her small shoulders and went to the door.

'When you are old and wise enough, darling, you will understand that one never quarrels with one's cook.' He sounded savage.

Florina finished the potatoes and started scraping carrots. She felt numb and her head was quite empty of thought. Presently, the whole of the little scene came flooding back, and her eyes filled with tears so that she could hardly see what she was doing. Finally, indignation swallowed up every other feeling. He hadn't given her a chance to explain, he had taken it for granted that the wretched Felix actually meant something to her, and he had been unkind, more than that, utterly beastly. It would serve him right if she were to spend an evening with Felix...

She finished the carrots and started on the salsify, and when Nanny came into the kitchen presently, she left the sink and poured coffee for them both.

Nanny sipped appreciatively. 'You make very good coffee, child.' She glanced at Florina's pink nose. 'What's upset Sir William, I wonder? In a nasty old temper when he left the house. Not that any that didn't know him well would even guess at it, but I've known him since he was a baby!'

She took another quick peep at Florina. 'Had all his plans laid, I dare say, and someone's messed them up. Did I see that young man coming up the drive an hour or so ago? I wonder what he wanted? A trouble-maker if ever I saw one.'

Florina said, 'He came to see if I could go out with him. I imagine that he let Sir William think that I knew he was coming to stay.' She poured more coffee. 'Nanny, I'd rather not talk about it, if you don't mind.'

Nanny nodded. 'Least said…' She didn't finish because Wanda came into the kitchen. 'Oh, there you are—this is the worst run household I've ever had to endure. I want coffee in the drawing-room. I won't wait for Sir William.' She turned on her heel and then paused. 'Who was that young man who called earlier this morning? Rather good-looking, I thought. Why haven't I met him before? Does he come from the village—he looked a cut above that.'

Nanny was silent, so was Florina.

'Well, who was he?' She laughed suddenly. 'Never your boyfriend, Cook? I find that hard to believe.' Her laugh became a snigger. 'It was!' She watched Florina's face glow. 'What a joke! Are you the best he can manage? Does Sir William know?' And, when no one answered, 'Yes, he does. I wonder what he thought of it? His marvellous cook with a boyfriend up her sleeve. Well you'll be free to marry him, if that is what he wants, won't you? For you won't be here much longer, I promise you that.'

She swept out of the kitchen, leaving the two of them silent. Presently Nanny said, 'You did quite right not to say anything.' Her sharp eyes searched Florina's pale face. 'She will use this to her advantage—urge Sir William to let you go, so that you can get married…'

Florina nodded miserably. 'But Nanny, I don't want to marry him—even if he were the last man left on earth.'

'I know that. Is he serious about you?'

Florina shook her head. 'I didn't respond and he expected me to. He got very angry…'

'A nasty type. You had better tell Sir William. He'll see that he doesn't bother you again.'

Florina said quite violently, 'No—no, I don't want to talk about it to him. Please don't say anything to him, Nanny. Promise?'

Nanny said briefly, 'I'll promise, if it will make you happy, though you're making a big mistake.' She wouldn't break her promise, but if she could see a way round that she would take it. If there was a misunderstanding at this stage it would be a great pity. Here was Florina, bless the girl, head over heels in love with Sir William and making no effort to do anything about it because cooks didn't marry their employers, especially when they were wealthy and at the top of their profession. And Sir William already engaged to that awful Miss Fortesque…and he as uncertain as a young man in the throes of his first love affair. Nanny, incurably romantic under her severe exterior, sighed deeply, refused more coffee and went away to tidy the chaos in Wanda's bedroom, bearing a tray of coffee for that lady as she went.

Florina stayed in the kitchen, bent on keeping out of sight. She was putting the finished touches to a trifle when Pauline and Bobby joined her. 'Daddy wants his coffee. I said I'd take it. We had a lovely walk and Bobby ran for miles.'

She peered into Florina's face. 'Darling Florina, you look so sad. Was Daddy angry with you?'

Florina arranged the tray and put a plate of little almond biscuits beside the coffeepot. 'Good gracious, no, love! I'm not a bit sad, only rather headachy. Go carefully with the tray. Shall I put another cup on it, for you?'

'May I have my milk here with you? Wanda told Daddy that she wanted to speak to him seriously. She's being all charming and smiling—I bet she's up to no good…'

Florina agreed silently, although she said firmly, 'Pauline, you mustn't say things like that about your father's guests. It would hurt his feelings.'

Pauline picked up the tray. She said, with the frankness of children, 'But he hasn't any feelings for her, I can tell; he's always so polite to her. I can't think why he's going to marry her.'

'People marry because they love each other.'

Pauline kissed her cheek. 'Dear Florina, you're such a darling, but not always quite with it.' She took a biscuit and munched it. 'If Daddy was poor and just Mr Sedley, she wouldn't want to marry him. She worked on him—you know—all sweet interest and how clever he is and all that rubbish. I suppose he thought she'd make quite a good stepmother for me, and he just let himself be conned.' She kissed Florina again, picked up the tray and skipped off before Florina's shocked rebuke could reach her ears.

She was back quickly. 'Daddy's angry! His face is all calm and his eyes are almost shut. I couldn't hear what Wanda was saying but her voice sounded as though she was in church. You know, all hushed and very solemn.'

Florina muttered something neither hushed nor solemn, and said rather loudly, 'I expect they are discussing their wedding.'

Pauline drank some of her milk and, since Florina wasn't looking, poured some of it into Mother's saucer. 'No, they weren't, because I listened a teeny bit as I was closing the door and she said, "Let's have him for drinks, darling."'

Florina dropped the wooden spoon she was holding and took a long time to pick it up.

'Someone from the village, I expect,' she said, knowing in her heart that it was Felix. Well, if it was, she would keep out of sight. She would be busy with dinner, anyway.

It wasn't until after tea that Nanny came to tell her that someone was coming for drinks. 'Sir William didn't say who it was.' She caught sight of Florina's face. 'That young man…this is Wanda's doing.

She can be very persuasive when she wants; probably painted a pathetic picture of you pining for his company. Did you see very much of him in Holland? And did Sir William see you together?'

Florina nodded dumbly. 'I wish I could run away!'

'Run away? Unthinkable! Besides you're not the girl I think you are if you do. Must I still keep my promise?'

Florina lifted a stubborn chin. 'Yes, please.' She added hopefully, 'Probably he won't come in here. He'll be a guest, after all, and only a casual caller…'

It was worse than anything she could have imagined. She was piping creamed potatoes on to a baking tray when the door opened and Sir William, Wanda and Felix came into the kitchen.

It was Wanda who spoke. 'Oh, Cook—here is Felix.' She paused to give him a conspiratorial look. 'You don't mind if I call you that?' She smiled at Florina with eyes like flints. 'He can't wait to talk to you. You are such a marvellous cook that I'm sure it won't bother you if he stays while you work for a while?'

Florina looked at her and then at Felix, grinning at seeing her cornered. Lastly, she looked at Sir William. He was leaning against the door, apparently only mildly interested. She said in a high voice which she managed to keep steady, 'I'm sorry, I can't work in this kitchen unless I'm alone.'

'In that case,' said Sir William, 'let us leave you alone, in peace. I don't want my dinner spoilt.'

Wanda didn't give up easily. 'Pauline is always here…'

He said mildly, 'Certainly she is, but she helps Florina, fetching and carrying, washing up and generally making herself quite useful. And I entirely approve, I should like her to be as good a cook as Florina. I doubt if—er—Felix wishes to wash the dishes.' He turned politely to him. 'You must have another drink before you go. I'm sure we shall be able to arrange something at a more propitious time.'

The party left the kitchen, leaving her shaking with temper. She attacked the food she was preparing quite savagely, curdling a sauce and burning the *croûtons*. With the kitchen full of blue smoke and the pungent smell of the charred remains at the foot of the pan, she clashed lids, dropped spoons and spilt some clarifying butter on to the floor.

It was to this scene of chaos that Sir William returned.

'Something is burning,' he observed.

'I know that!' she snapped. 'Dinner is ruined.' An exaggeration, but excusable in the circumstances.

His fine mouth twitched. 'I'm sorry that we upset you by coming into the kitchen. Wanda was sure that you would be delighted, and certainly there was no need for you to be so reluctant to mention it to me…'

'Reluctant? Reluctant?' said Florina shrilly. 'And pray why should I be that? In any case, it's my business, Sir William.' Rage sat strangely upon her, her eyes blazed in her usually tranquil face, her soft mouth shook. Sir William eyed her very thoughtfully.

'This Felix,' he said at last. 'Are you in love with him?' When she remained silent, he went on, 'No, don't tell me again that it's not my business. After all, it's my dinner which is ruined. But you're not going to tell me, are you, Florina? I wonder why that is?'

She spoke in a small whispering voice. 'You made up your mind that I was being deceitful about him, you—you said he was my follower—that was to remind me that I was your cook, so if you don't mind I will not tell you anything, Sir William. I will make sure that he doesn't come here again. I'm sorry if it has embarrassed you.'

'Good God, girl, why should it do that? On the contrary, it enlightened me.' He was going to say more, but the door was pushed open with an impatient hand, and Wanda came in. She was wearing a white crêpe dress and her hair was carefully arranged in careless curls; she looked sweet and feminine and most appealing.

'William, I'm so glad you are here, now you can hear me say how sorry I am to Cook. I embarrassed her, but I truly thought she would be pleased.' Her blue eyes swam with tears, as she turned to Florina. 'You must think I'm quite horrid. Don't bear a grudge against me, will you? I told Felix that I was sure that you would have time to see something of him while he is here. After all, you won't have anything much to do once we are gone.'

She tucked a hand under Sir William's arm, and

smiled at him prettily. 'Don't be cross with me, darling, for giving orders in your house. After all, it's soon to be mine as well, isn't it?'

Sir William said nothing to that, only stared at Florina. 'We'll go,' he said briskly. 'Florina has had enough interruptions.'

Alone once more, Florina set about rescuing the dinner from disaster. 'Not that I care if everything is burnt to a cinder,' she said to Mother. 'Anyway, you and Child can have the egg custard—it's not fit to put on the table.'

Sir William made no attempt to seek her out. Indeed, it seemed to her that he was avoiding her. Usually he came into the kitchen with Pauline in the morning while she fed Bobby and the cats, sitting astride a chair, talking to Florina about the village and telling her his plans for the garden, but not any more. Nor, to her relief, did she see anything of Felix. Sunday came and went, there were friends for drinks, and very soon after lunch he drove back to London with Wanda, smiling a small, triumphant smile, sitting beside him. He had bidden Florina goodbye in a pleasant manner, but the easy friendship between them had gone.

She got through the rest of the day somehow, presenting a bright face to Pauline and Nanny, and presently retiring to bed to weep silently for the impossible dreams which would never return. At least she had derived a spurious happiness from them.

It was several days later when Pauline came dancing into the kitchen to tell her that her father wanted to speak to her. Florina lifted the receiver with the air of one expecting it to bite her and said a cautious 'hello'.

Sir William's firm voice was crisp. 'Florina? Jolly will drive Mrs Jolly down tomorrow. They will arrive some time after lunch and he will return here after having tea with you. Mrs Jolly will take over from you for two days so that you may be completely free, so make any arrangements you like with Felix; he told me that he wouldn't be returning until Saturday morning.' He added, in a strangely expressionless voice, 'I hope you will have a pleasant time together.'

He had rung off before she could do more than let out a gasp of surprise. Florina toyed with the idea of ringing him back and denying all wish to see Felix again, but that might make matters worse. She detected Wanda's hand in the business and flounced off in search of Nanny.

That lady heard her out. 'Dear, dear, here's a pretty kettle of fish. Does Felix know about this?'

'I don't know, I shouldn't think so—I'm sure Sir William wouldn't phone him deliberately, just to tell him.'

'Miss Fortesque might,' suggested Nanny. 'You must think of something, so that if he comes round here you are ready for him.' Her stern face broke into a smile. 'I have it! Isn't Pauline to spend the next day or so with the Meggisons? You know them, don't you? Could you not go with her? Heaven knows, they have more than enough room for you in that house of theirs.'

'Yes, but what would I say? I can't just invite myself.'

'You can tell them the truth, the bare bones of it, at any rate. If that man comes, don't say anything about it, but get hold of Mrs Meggison and go there with Pauline—she's to get there early after breakfast, isn't she? He is not likely to call as early as that. Don't worry about him, I'll deal with the gentleman.'

'Won't Jolly tell Sir William?'

'Bless you, child, he'll not breathe a word…'

'I'm deceiving Sir William…'

'He's been deceiving himself for months,' observed Nanny cryptically. 'You can tell him when he comes at the weekend.'

Felix arrived later that day and Florina, bolstered by the knowledge that Nanny was on the landing, listening, admitted him into the hall, but no further.

'So, Miss Fortesque kept her promise. She said she would persuade Sir William to give you a couple of days off. I'll be round for you tomorrow about eleven o'clock, and don't try any tricks. Everyone knows in the village that we are going to be married.' He chuckled at her look of outrage. 'Don't worry, darling, I'll be off and away at the end of the week, but I don't like being snubbed by a plain-faced girl who can't say boo to a goose. I'm just getting my own back.' He made her a mock salute. 'Be seeing you! I've planned a very interesting day for us both.'

She shut the door on him and then locked it. They

had spoken in Dutch and Nanny, descending the stairs, had to have it all translated.

'Conceited jackanapes!' she declared. 'Who does he think he is? Why, he's nothing but a great lout under all that charm. Now, off you go and ring Mrs Meggison, and make sure you'll be collected well before ten o'clock.'

'Yes, but what about Pauline? Won't she think it's strange?'

'Why should she? She knows that the Meggisons are old friends of yours, and she loves being with you.'

Mrs Meggison raised no objections, in fact, she was delighted. 'I have to go to the dentist in the morning and I was wondering what to do about the children—now you will be here to keep an eye on them. It couldn't be better, my dear. Can you stay until Saturday? We'll send you both back directly after breakfast if Sir William doesn't mind.'

'He won't mind at all,' said Florina mendaciously, and put down the receiver with a great sigh of relief.

The Meggisons were genuinely pleased to see her. 'You can't think how glad I am that you came,' declared Mrs Meggison. 'There's a new au pair girl coming next week—Danish—and the boys go back to school then, but with all four of them at home I've been run off my feet. Cook and Meg have enough to do; I can't ask them to keep an eye on the children as well. They are all in the garden. Perhaps Pauline would like to trot out and be with them while I show you your rooms.'

It was a nice old house; a little shabby, but the furniture was old and cared for and the rooms held all the warmth of a happy family life. Florina, safely away from Felix's unwanted attentions, enjoyed every minute of their two days, even though she had almost no time to herself. There was so much to do. The school holidays were almost over and they wanted to extract the last ounce of pleasure from them. They worked wonders for Pauline, too, tearing around, climbing trees, riding the elderly donkey the Meggisons kept in the orchard, eating out-of-doors in the untidy garden at the back of the house. The pair of them, much refreshed, climbed into Mr Meggison's Land Rover with mixed feelings. Pauline sorry to be leaving her friends, but anxious to see Bobby and Mother and Child again. Florina was relieved that Felix would be gone, but panicky about meeting Sir William. She hadn't told Pauline to say nothing about her stay with the Meggisons; she had been deceitful, but she didn't intend that the little girl should be involved, too. For deceit it was, whichever way she looked at it. She got out of the Land Rover when they reached Wheel House, mentally braced against meeting Sir William.

Jolly opened the door, beaming a welcome, and invited Mr Meggison to make himself at home in the drawing-room while he sent for Sir William.

'In the kitchen garden, sir, and if Pauline would go and fetch him…'

Pauline went, dancing away, shrieking with delight as Jolly went on smoothly, 'Mrs Jolly is in the kitchen, Miss Florina—there'll be coffee there and I have no doubt she will wish to have a chat with you. We return to London later this morning, but Sir William and Miss Fortesque are here for the weekend.'

Florina had her coffee and a comfortable chat with Mrs Jolly, and then went to her room to change her clothes; there had been no sign of Sir William, and Miss Fortesque had been driven into Salisbury by Jolly directly after breakfast to have her hair done. Mrs Jolly had cleared the kitchen, but since Jolly and she were driving back to London before lunch, Florina would prepare it.

It was almost two hours later, while she was mixing a salad with one eye on the clock, anxious not to be late with the meal, when Sir William strolled into the kitchen.

'I believe we should have a talk,' he observed, at his most placid.

'Oh, yes, of course, Sir William, but lunch will be late…'

She had gone pale, but she didn't avoid his eyes.

'Never mind lunch! You had two days free so that you might spend them with Felix, instead of which, you chose to go to the Meggisons. Why?'

He had taken one of the Windsor chairs by the Aga, and Mother and Child had lost no time in clambering on to his knee. He stroked them with a large, gentle hand and waited for her to answer.

She said coldly, 'I don't know why you should suppose that I should want to spend my leisure with Felix. I didn't ask him to come here in the first place and, as far as I know, I gave you no reason to suppose that I did.'

She sliced tomatoes briskly, ruining most of them because her hand wasn't steady on the knife.

'You didn't make that clear, and I still wonder why. Am I not to know, Florina?'

She was making a hash of a cucumber. The salad wouldn't be fit to eat.

'No, Sir William. I'm sorry I didn't tell you that I was going to the Meggisons, but I didn't think it would matter...'

'On the contrary, it matters very much, but that's something we need not go into for the moment. So I take it that you have no plans to marry?'

'No.'

He set the cats back in their basket, got to his feet and wandered to the door. 'Good, Pauline will be so pleased. You should be more careful in the future, Florina. I've been quite concerned about you.'

He went away, closing the door quietly behind him, leaving her to start on another salad, which would be fit to put on the table.

She was feeding the swans after lunch was finished, when Wanda came on to the patio. Sir William and Pauline had taken Bobby for a walk, and the house was quiet, Mrs Deakin had gone and Nanny was in her room resting.

'I don't know what game you're playing, Cook,' Wanda's voice was soft and angry. 'Whatever it is, it won't do you any good. By next weekend we shall announce the date of the wedding, and don't think it will be months ahead. Sir William will get a special licence and we can marry within days. You had better start looking for another job.' She sniggered. 'You are a fool! You and your silly day-dreams, did you suppose that a man like Sir William would look at you twice? When he does look at you he is looking at his cook, my dear, not you. You had better go back to your Dutch family and find yourself a husband there—you haven't much chance here, even with the village men.' She turned away. 'Don't say that I haven't warned you. You will not stay a day longer than is necessary once I have married Sir William.'

Florina stood where she was, staring down at the water below and the family of swans gobbling up the bread she was throwing to them still. It was something to do while she tried to collect her thoughts.

That Wanda was going to get rid of her was a certainty, and to go to Holland was surely a way out of a situation which was fast becoming unbearable. On the other hand, she would be running away and, as Nanny said, she wasn't a girl to do that. Would there by any point in remaining in England? It wasn't as if she would see Sir William again.

She threw the last crust and watched the swans demolish it. She couldn't see them very clearly for the tears she was struggling to hold back.

'Why are you crying?' asked Sir William and, since she didn't answer, threw an arm round her shoulders and stared down at the swans, too.

Chapter 8

The urge to put her head on Sir William's vast chest and tell him everything, even that she loved him, was something Florina only prevented herself from doing by the greatest effort. Instead, she sniffed, blew her small red nose and stayed obstinately silent.

Sir William sounded calmly friendly. 'Your father—he lives close by, does he not? Would you like to spend a day or two with him? He could probably dispel the rumours Felix has spread.'

'It's kind of you to suggest it, Sir William, but Father and I…he wanted a son, and he has no interest in the Dutch side of me. He tried to turn Mother into an Englishwoman, but he never succeeded—he didn't succeed with me, either.' Her voice was small and thin.

Sir William, who had heard that before from various sources in the village, said comfortably, 'Well, what would you like to do, Florina? You haven't been happy since we came back from Holland, have you? Did something happen then to upset you—and I don't mean Felix?' He added, 'Would it help if you went back there for a week or two? Not to your aunt, for Felix goes there, does he not? I have some good friends in the Hague and Amsterdam; and in Friesland, too—a temporary job, perhaps?'

She was very conscious of his arm on her shoulders. Did he want to be rid of her, in order to placate Wanda and at the same time to spare her from the ignominy of getting the sack? She didn't know, and did it really matter? she reflected.

'I hope you will stay with us.' He had answered her unspoken thoughts so promptly that for a moment she wondered if she had voiced them out loud. 'At least until Pauline is settled in her new school. Will you think about it for a week or so?'

He gave her a comforting pat on the arm, remarking that he had to work in his study, and he left her there.

They exchanged barely a dozen words before he left for London, and as for Wanda, she behaved as though Florina wasn't there; she ignored Nanny, too, and avoided Pauline, but hung on to Sir William's arm on every possible occasion, the very picture of a compliant, adoring wife-to-be.

They wouldn't be down on the following weekend, Sir William told his daughter; he had a consultation on Saturday in Suffolk and he might possibly need to spend the night there. 'I'll phone you each evening,' he promised, 'and you can tell me all about school.'

The week went quickly but now there was another routine, no longer the easy-going times of the holidays, but up early, school uniform to get into, breakfast and then the drive to Wilton, with Bobby on the back seat of the car. It was Florina who took him off for his walks now during the day, although when Pauline got home each afternoon the three of them went into the fields around the village while Pauline recited the happenings of her day to Florina. She was at least happy at school; she knew some of the girls there and the teachers were nice. She had homework to do, of course, and Florina sat at the kitchen table with her and helped when she was asked, while Nanny sat by the Aga, knitting. It was pleasant and peaceful, but Florina worried that it wasn't the life Pauline should have. She needed a mother; her father loved her but he had his work and she suspected that without Wanda he would have more time to spend with his daughter. When Wanda was his wife, that didn't mean that she was going to be Pauline's mother; indeed, with herself and Nanny out of the way, the child would be packed off to boarding-school. Wanda wasn't the kind of woman to share her husband, even with his own child.

The weekend came and since the weather was still fine, the Meggisons came over for tea on Saturday and played croquet on the velvet-smooth lawn behind the house, until Florina called them in for supper and presently drove them back home in the Mini, very squashed with Bobby insisting on coming, too.

When Florina went to say goodnight to Pauline, the child flung her arms round her neck. 'Such a lovely day,' she said sleepily. 'If only Daddy could have been here too.'

'That would have been nice,' agreed Florina sedately, and her heart danced against her ribs at the thought. 'But he said he'd be home here on Friday.'

It was, however, sooner than Friday when she saw him again.

It was on Tuesday morning, while they were driving along the country road to Wilton, that a car, driven much too fast, overtook them on a bend to crash head on into a Land Rover coming towards it.

Florina pulled into the ditch by the roadside; the two cars were a hundred yards ahead of her, askew across the road, the drivers already climbing out, shouting at each other. Pauline had clutched her arm when the cars had collided and then covered her ears from the thumps and bangs of the impact.

Florina opened her door a few inches. 'I'll go and see if they can move out of the way; if they can't we'll have to go round along the main road.' She glanced at Bobby, barking his head off and shivering. 'Don't get out, darling, and don't let Bobby out; he's very frightened and he'll run away.'

She nipped out of the car smartly and shut the door against the terrified dog, and ran up the road.

No one was hurt, only furiously angry. The two

men were hurling abuse at each other until she took advantage of a pause in their vituperation.

'Am I able to get past you?' She had to shout to make them listen. 'I'm taking Pauline to school...' She had recognised one of the farm hands from the village, standing by the Land Rover. 'Will you be able to move soon?'

'Now, luv, that I can't say—this lunatic was coming too fast—you must have seen him—we'll have to get the police and take numbers and the rest. You'd best go round, and back over the bridge.'

There seemed nothing else to do, and Florina turned to go back to the Mini in time to see the door open and Pauline get out. Bobby scrambled out after her, and then, yelping madly, raced away through a gap in the hedge, into the fields beyond. Within seconds Pauline had gone after him, climbing the five-barred gate in the hedge. She took no notice of Florina's shout, just as Bobby took no notice of the child's cries.

Florina reached the car, snatched up the dog's lead, slammed the door shut and climbed the gate in her turn. The men were still arguing, she could hear them even at that distance, much too taken up with their own problems to bother about hers. Bobby was well away by now, running erratically across a further field, newly ploughed, and Pauline wasn't too far behind him. Florina saved her breath and ran as she had never run before. She knew the country around her well; beyond the ploughed field was a small wood, its heavy undergrowth overgrown with rough scrub and brambles, and beyond that was the river winding its way into Wilton, not isolated but unproductive so that not even gypsies went near it.

Bobby had reached the wood, but Pauline was finding the ploughed field heavy-going. However, she didn't stop when Florina shouted, so she had reached the wood before Florina was half-way there.

The wood was quiet when she reached it, save for the birds and the frenzied distant barking of Bobby. There was neither sight nor sound of Pauline; she was probably on the far side by now, making for the river.

The brambles made speed impossible if she weren't to be scratched to pieces, but scratches were the least of her worries. The wood ran down steeply to the river, which, while not wide or deep, was swift-running and, at this time of the year, cluttered with weeds and reeds; Pauline might rush along without looking and fall into it. Bobby was still yelping and barking and she was sure that she heard Pauline's voice; it spurred her on through the brambles, quite regardless of the thorns.

The wood was narrow at that point, and she emerged finally, oozing blood from the scratches which covered her hands and arms and legs. Her dress was torn, as were her tights, and her hair hopelessly tangled, hung in an untidy curtain down her back. She swept it out of her eyes and paused to look around her. Bobby was whining now, but there was no sign of Pauline. She shouted at the top of her voice and started down the steep slope to the river. There were willows and bushes along its banks; she found the child within inches of the water, lying white and silent with Bobby beside her. He greeted her with a joyful bark, bent to lick the little girl's face, and made no effort to run away as she fastened his lead before kneeling beside Pauline.

There was a bruise on Pauline's forehead and a few beads of blood. Florina, her heart thumping with fear, picked up a flaccid hand and felt for a pulse. It was steady and quite strong, so she put the hand down and began to search for other injuries. There were plenty of scratches but, as far as she could tell, no broken bones. She made Pauline as comfortable as she could, tied Bobby's lead to a nearby tree-stump, and tried to decide what to do. She glanced at her watch; it was barely half an hour since they had started their mad race across the fields. She thought it unlikely that either man would have noticed it, for they had been far too occupied with their argument. Pauline was concussed, she thought, but even if she regained consciousness, she didn't dare to let the child walk back to the car; it must be the best part of a mile away. She could only hope that the farm worker would tell someone when he got back to the village, better still, he might go to the police station. This hope was instantly squashed; there was no room to turn on that particular stretch of the road, and they would have to manhandle the car to one side so that the Land Rover could squeeze past. In the village the police could be informed and someone sent to take the car away; it had received by far the most damage.

She sat down by Pauline and lifted the child's

head very gently on to her lap. They might be there for hours; even if the men noticed that the Mini was standing there and no one was in it, they might have thought that they had walked back to the village.

Which was exactly what they had thought; it was almost half an hour before they had got the car on to the side of the road and the Land Rover proceeded on its way, and it was pure chance that the driver saw Nanny walking down the road to get some eggs from the farm. 'They'll be back now,' he observed. 'I didn't pass them on the road.'

'But they aren't here. Did you see them get out of the car? They weren't hurt?'

'No, luv, but that little old dog was kicking up a fine row, ran off, he did, though lord knows where.' He started the engine. 'They'll turn up, safe and sound, but I'll tell the police—we'll have to go to the station in Wilton, and they'll come out here, I've no doubt of that.'

Nanny went on her way to the farm, collected the eggs, and marched back to Wheel House. There was no sign of Florina or Pauline, so she phoned the school; there was always the chance that they had walked the rest of the way…

They hadn't, and when she phoned the police at Wilton they had no news of them. They would ring back, they told her, the moment they knew anything; they couldn't have gone far…

It was a pity that an elderly woman living half a mile along the road from the accident should declare that she had heard a dog barking behind her cottage, on the opposite side of the road to where Bobby had escaped; she thought, too, that she had seen someone running. She was vague and uncertain as to exactly when she had seen them and the excitement of being the centre of interest for the moment led her to embroider her talk, so that the two policemen who had been detailed to search for Florina and Pauline set off in the opposite direction to the wood and the river.

Sir William wasn't in when Nanny telephoned his house, but Jolly undertook to track him down and tell him. 'He'll be at the hospital,' he told her, 'but he's not operating, he mentioned that at breakfast and he said that he had a quiet morning—just ward rounds. He will be with you in a couple of hours.'

It was less than that; Sir William spent ten precious minutes ringing the police, aware that if he warned them he would be allowed to travel at maximum speed provided they had his car number and he gave his reasons.

The Bentley made short work of the ninety miles, and he walked into his house to find Nanny on the telephone. She said 'Thank you,' and put the receiver down as he reached her. 'Thank God you've come, Sir William, I'm that worried!' She studied his face. He looked much as usual, but he was pale and there was a muscle twitching in his cheek. 'You'll have a cup of coffee,' and when he held up a hand, 'You can drink it while I tell you all that I know.'

She was upset, but very sensible too—time enough to give way to tears when they were safe and sound. Sir William listened and drank his coffee and observed, 'The police have drawn a blank so far in Wilton and the direction of Broad Chalke; I'll try the other side, it's open country, isn't it? Where exactly did the accident happen?'

'The Land Rover driver said on the sharp bend about two miles along the road, almost parallel with that road you can see on the left…'

Florina, with Pauline's head heavy on her lap, glanced at the sky; the clouds were piling up and although it was barely one o'clock, there was a faint chill heralding the still distant evening. Pauline had stirred a little, but she hadn't dared to move. Bobby, quite quiet now, sat beside her, aware that something was wrong, fidgeting a little. She had shouted for a time, but there had been no answer and the trees in the wood deadened the sound of any traffic on the distant road. She had racked her brains to find a way to get them out of the fix, but she could think of nothing. It was unlikely that anyone would come that way, for there was no reason to do so, and who would take a country walk through brambles, anyway, but it surprised her a little that no one had searched for them; they weren't all that far away from the scene of the accident.

Pauline stirred again and this time she opened her eyes. 'Florina?' she stared up in a puzzled way. 'I've got such a fearful headache.'

'Yes, darling, I expect you have. You fell over and you bumped your head. Don't move or it will hurt still more. As soon as someone comes, we'll have you home and tucked up in bed.'

'Bobby—where is Bobby?'

'Right here, beside me. Now close your eyes, my love, and have a nap; I'll wake you when someone comes…'

'Daddy will find us.'

Florina said stoutly, 'Of course he will,' and blinked away a tear. She was thoroughly scared by now, as much by her inability to think of a way of getting back through the wood, as by the fact that no one had come within shouting distance.

It was at that precise moment that someone did shout, and for a few seconds she was too surprised to answer. But Bobby set up a joyful barking and began to tug at his lead. Florina shouted, then set him free and watched him tear up the bank and into the wood, to emerge a few moments later with Sir William hard on his heels.

She was beyond words, she could only stare at him as he came to a halt beside her and squatted down on his heels. He let out a great sigh and said, 'Oh, my dears…' and his arm drew her close for a moment before he bent to examine Pauline.

She stirred under his gentle hand and opened her eyes. 'Daddy—oh, I knew you'd come, Florina said you would. Can we go home now?'

'Yes, darling, but just me take a look and see where you're hurt.'

Florina found her voice. 'She was unconscious

when I found her, that was half-past nine. I didn't move her, she came round about eleven o'clock.'

He nodded without looking at her. 'There doesn't seem to be much wrong except concussion. We'll get you both home and put her to bed—she had better be X-rayed, but I think it's safe to leave that until the morning.' He looked at her then. 'And you, Florina, are you hurt?'

'Only a few scratches. Will you carry her through the wood?'

'The pub landlord and Dick from the farm came with me—they are searching at either end of the wood.' He put his fingers between his teeth and whistled and presently she heard their answering whistles.

'Shall I wait for them here? I'll bring Bobby with me, then you can go ahead with Pauline.'

For the first time he smiled. 'Having found you, Florina, I have no intention of leaving you again.' He watched the look of puzzlement on her face, and added, 'They will be here very soon.'

Going back was easier. The two men went ahead, beating back the brambles with their sticks, with Sir William carrying Pauline behind them and, behind him, protected by his vast size, came Florina, leading a sober Bobby on his lead.

At the roadside she made to get into the Mini, but Sir William said no. 'You will come with us, Florina. Dick had a lift here; he can drive the Mini back, if he will.' He grinned at the two men. 'We'll have a pint together later.'

He laid Pauline on the back seat, swept Florina

on to the seat beside him and drove back to Wheel House.

Nanny was waiting. 'Bed for Pauline, Nanny. I'll leave her to you for a moment; she's been concussed so you know what to do. Florina, get out of those clothes, have a hot bath and come downstairs to me. I must phone the police and Pauline's school.'

He went on up the stairs with Pauline, and Florina went to her own room, undressed slowly and sank thankfully into a steaming bath. The sight of herself in the wardrobe mirror had made her gasp in horror; her hair was full of twigs and leaves, her dress was ruined and her tights were streaked with blood from scratches. She gave a slightly hysterical giggle and then fell to weeping. But the bath was soothing, and then, once more in her cotton dress and apron, her hair brushed and plaited as usual, a dusting of powder on her scratched face, she went back to the kitchen.

Sir William was there, pouring tea. 'I don't know about you,' he remarked cheerfully, 'but when I've been scared I've found that a cup of tea works wonders at restoring my nerve.'

'You've never been scared…' She gasped at him in amazement.

'Just lately, I have, on occasion, been scared to death. Come and sit down and tell me just what happened. I've told the police, and Mrs Deakin kindly called at your father's house and told him all was well.'

'I'm sorry we've been such a nuisance.' She

glanced at Bobby, lying with the cats, fast asleep. 'It wasn't anyone's fault, at least, it was the man who overtook us—he was going too fast, the Land Rover couldn't do anything about it. I shouldn't have got out of the car, only both men were shouting at each other and I had to find out if anyone was hurt and if we had a chance of getting by…'

'Pauline got out with you…?'

'Oh, no, of course not, but I'm sure she was afraid, and Bobby was beside himself; he'd gone in a flash and she left after him. I'm sure she thought that she would be able to catch him easily, but the poor beast was terrified.'

Sir William picked up one of her hands from the table; it was covered in scratches and he examined them, his head bent so that she couldn't see his face. 'My poor dear…' His hand tightened on hers and it was as though an electric current had flooded her whole person. She sought to pull her hand away, but he merely tightened his grip as he lifted his head and looked at her, half smiling, his eyes half hidden beneath their heavy lids. She stared back at him, her eyes wide. It was a magic moment for her, shattered almost before she had realised it by Nanny's entrance. Sir William let her hand go without haste and asked, 'Everything all right, Nanny?' in his calm voice.

Nanny had looked at them and away again. 'The child wants to sit up and she says she's hungry.'

He got up. 'I'll go and take a good look; I don't think there's much damage done, and there's no reason why she shouldn't have a light meal, but wait until I've looked at her.'

He went away and Nanny went to the Aga to see if the kettle was boiling.

'We could all do with something,' she observed briskly. 'Do you feel up to getting a meal ready, Florina?'

Florina gave her a sweet bemused look. 'Of course, Nanny. Soup and scrambled eggs with toast and mushrooms and coffee.'

She went to get the eggs, still in a dream, unwilling to give it up for reality. For his hand on hers and his look, tender and urgent, must have been a dream: a conclusion substantiated by his return presently with the prosaic suggestion that Pauline could have both the soup and the scrambled eggs, and wouldn't it be a good idea if she and Nanny had a meal as well? As for himself, he went on, he would go to the Trout and Feathers and have a drink with the landlord and some bread and cheese.

So she shook the dreams from her head and set about getting lunch. They had finished and tidied the kitchen and Nanny had gone to sit with Pauline when Sir William returned. He came straight into the kitchen and sat down on the table. 'I'll feel easier in my mind if I take Pauline back with me; she can be X-rayed at my hospital and if there is anything amiss it can be put right. I'm almost certain that there's nothing to worry about, but I must be sure. We'll leave after breakfast; you will come with us, Florina?'

Her heart gave a great leap, so that she caught her breath.

'Very well, Sir William. Are we to stay overnight?'

'Yes, pack for two or three days, to be on the safe side. I'm going to Pauline's school now. When does Mrs Deakin come?'

'Not until tomorrow morning.'

'Then will you go and see her and ask if she will sleep here with Nanny? If she can't, perhaps Mrs Datchett would oblige us. They'll be paid, of course.'

He went to the door; stopped there to turn and look at her. 'You're all right? I'll give you something for those scratches; you've had ATS injections?'

She nodded, striving to be matter of fact. 'Oh, yes, I had a booster done about six months ago. I'll go along to Mrs Deakin now. Does Pauline know that she is going back with you?'

'No. I'll tell her when I get back. I'll have dinner here with you and Nanny—shall we say eight o'clock? That gives Nanny a chance to settle Pauline first. I'll go up and see her now before I go out.'

He nodded casually and left her there.

Mrs Deakin would be delighted to oblige; she was saving up for a new washing machine and Sir William was a generous employer. Florina skimmed back quickly, not liking to leave Nanny alone, but Nanny was sitting in the rocking chair in Pauline's room; knitting while Pauline slept. Florina made a cup of tea and took it upstairs to her, whispered about plans for the evening and took herself off back to the kitchen. There was plenty to do; a good thing, for she had to forget about Sir William. She bustled about assembling a suitable meal for him: spinach soup, lamb chops, courgettes in red wine, calabrese and devilled potatoes, with an apricot tart and cream to follow. She would have time to make the little dry biscuits he liked with his cheese; she rolled up her sleeves and started her preparations.

She took up Pauline's supper tray and sat with her while Nanny had an hour to herself. The little girl was apparently none the worse for their adventure; she ate her supper without demur and now that she was safely home and in her bed was inclined to giggle a good deal about their adventure. She submitted to Florina's sponging of her face and hands, declared herself ready to go to sleep and, when her father came quietly in, did no more than murmur sleepily at him.

He felt her head, took her pulse and pronounced himself satisfied, kissed the child and picked up the supper tray and beckoned Florina to go with him.

'I've phoned the hospital,' he told her. 'We'll leave just before eight o'clock. She can travel as she is, wrapped up in a blanket. Pack her some clothes, though.'

He was matter-of-fact—more than that, casual—and she strove to match him. They ate their dinner carrying on a guarded conversation about nothing much, and Nanny, sitting between them, watched their faces and thought hopefully of the next day or two in London, praying that Wanda wouldn't be there, and that they would have time together; that was all they needed. Sir William, she was sure now, had realised that he was in love with Florina, and as for Florina, there was no doubt in Nanny's mind where her heart lay. Things would sort themselves out, she reflected comfortably.

The journey to London was uneventful. Pauline lay on the back seat with Florina beside her, and she was content to be quiet, and Florina had her own thoughts, her eyes on the back of Sir William's handsome head.

There were people waiting for them when they reached the hospital: porters with a stretcher, Sir William's registrar, one of his housemen and the children's ward sister, young, pretty and cheerful. She said a friendly 'Hi,' to Florina, standing a little apart, not sure what was expected of her, before she accompanied the stretcher into the hospital.

It was Sir William who paused long enough to say, 'My registrar, Jack Collins, and my houseman, Colin Weekes.' He caught her by the arm. 'You might as well come along, too.'

She sat when bidden, in the X-ray Department waiting-room, for what seemed a very long time. People came and went: nurses, porters, a variety of persons bustling along as though the very existence of the hospital depended upon them, and presently Sir William strolled in, looking, she had to admit, exactly like a senior consultant should look. He was trailed by a number of people, who stood back politely as he came to a halt beside her.

'No problems,' he told her. 'A few days taking

things quietly and Pauline will be quite well. I'll drive you both home now, but I must come back here for the rest of the day. The Jollys will look after you. Get Pauline to bed, will you? Don't let her read or watch television, but she can sit up a little.' He nodded. 'Ready?'

Jolly was waiting for them. Sir William carried his small daughter up the stairs to her room with Mrs Jolly and Florina hard on his heels, while Jolly fetched their bags. In no time at all, Pauline had been settled in her bed, her few clothes unpacked, and Sir William, with a murmured word to Jolly, had departed again.

Florina found herself in the same room that she had had previously, bidden by Mrs Jolly to make haste and tidy herself, and, since Pauline was a little peevish and excited, would it be a good idea if she had her lunch in the child's room? There was a small table there and perhaps Pauline would settle down and have a nice nap if someone was with her.

Which presently, was exactly what happened. Florina sat quietly where she was for a time, thinking about Sir William. She had been foolish to fall in love with him, although she could quite see that one couldn't always pick and choose whom one loved, but their worlds were so far apart, her visit to the hospital had emphasised that...

She picked up her tray, carried it downstairs and stayed for a few minutes in the kitchen talking to Mrs Jolly. 'You'll need a breath of air,' declared that lady. 'I'll bring you both up a nice tea presently and sit with Pauline while you have a quick walk. Sir William won't be home before six o'clock.'

'That's kind of you, Mrs Jolly; perhaps I'll do that. Pauline mustn't read or watch television. I thought I'd read aloud to her before her supper.'

She went back through the baize door into the hall just as Jolly went to answer the front door. It was Wanda, who pushed past him and then stopped dead in her tracks as she caught sight of Florina.

'What are you doing here?' she demanded. Her blue eyes narrowed. 'Up to your tricks again, are you? What a sly creature you are—the moment my back is turned.'

She had crossed the hall and was standing at the foot of the stairs so that Florina couldn't get past her without pushing.

Florina, conscious that Jolly was hovering by the baize door, kept her temper. 'Pauline had an accident; Sir William has brought her here so that she could go to the hospital for an X-ray—somebody had to come with her. She is upstairs asleep.'

Wanda didn't answer, and Florina said politely, 'I'm going upstairs to sit with her—if you wouldn't mind moving…'

Wanda didn't budge. She turned her head and said very rudely: 'You can go back to the kitchen, Jolly.' But he didn't move, only glanced at Florina. She smiled and nodded to reassure him, and he went reluctantly away.

'How long are you staying here?' demanded Wanda.

'Until Pauline is well enough to go back to Wheel House. Sir William will decide...'

'Oh, Sir William, Sir William!' gibed Wanda. 'He's the top and bottom of your existence, isn't he? You're such a fool too, just because he treats you decently and appears to take an interest in you—don't you know that that is part of his work? Being kind and sympathetic—turning on the charm for hysterical mothers, listening to their silly whining about their kids.'

Florina interrupted her then. 'That is not true and it's a wicked thing to say! Sir William is kind and good and he loves his work. You can say what you like about me, but you are not going to say a word against him.'

Wanda burst out laughing. 'Oh, lord, you're so funny—if only you could see that plain face of yours.' She said suddenly, seriously, 'Do you know that we are to be married next week? Your precious Sir William didn't tell you that, did he? But why should he? You are only his cook, and not for much longer, either.'

She turned away and sauntered towards the drawing-room. 'You'd better get back upstairs and keep an eye on that child before she does something stupid.'

Florina went up the stairs without a word, shaking with rage and misery and, under those feelings, prey to first doubts. Wanda had sounded so sure of herself, and indeed, there was no reason at all why Sir William should tell her his plans. She went into Pauline's room and sat down to think, thankful that

Pauline was dozing. Her head remained obstinately empty of thoughts; it was a relief when the little girl wakened and demanded to be read to. So Florina read *The Wind in the Willows*, until Pauline declared that she would like her tea.

'I'll pop down and get us a tray, love,' promised Florina. The house was quiet when she went downstairs. There was still some time before Sir William would return, perhaps she would be able to think a few sensible thoughts by then.

She was in the hall when the drawing-room door opened and Wanda came out.

'Had time to think?' she wanted to know. 'Not that it will make any difference; only a fool like you would be so stupid…'

The street door opened and Sir William asked quietly, 'Who is stupid?'

Florina had a cowardly impulse to turn and run back upstairs but quelled it; even Wanda had been taken by surprise. 'Wanda, I didn't expect to find you here…'

She shrugged that aside. 'I'll tell you who's stupid,' she said spitefully. 'Your cook.' She laughed. 'She's in love with you, William.'

He didn't look at Florina. 'Yes, I know.' He spoke gently. 'You haven't told me why you are here. Shall we go into my study while you tell me?'

He still hadn't looked at Florina, standing like a small statue, her face as stony as her person.

It was only when the door had been closed gently behind them that she moved. She went to the kitchen and fetched the tea tray, oblivious of the Jollys' concerned faces, and only when Mrs Jolly offered to sit with Pauline so that she might have an hour or two to herself did she say in a wispy voice, 'I'd rather stay with her, thank you so much, Mrs Jolly.'

She carried the tray back upstairs, saw to Pauline's wants and poured herself a cup of tea. Mrs Jolly had gone to a lot of trouble with their tea; little scones, feather-light, mouth-watering sandwiches, small iced cakes—Florina, pleading a headache in answer to Pauline's anxious enquiries as to why she didn't eat anything, plunged into talk. There was plenty to say about Bobby and the cats, and school, and whether would Nanny remember to feed the swans. Once tea was over Florina got out *The Wind in the Willows* again and began to read in her quiet voice.

She was interrupted by Sir William, who sauntered in, embraced his daughter and said in a perfectly normal voice, 'I'll sit with Pauline for a while, Florina. I dare say you would like a breath of air. I have to go out this evening, but I shall be back after dinner—I should like to talk to you then.'

She kept her eyes on his waistcoat. Her 'Very well, Sir William,' was uttered in what she hoped was a voice which showed no trace of a wobble.

She went out because she could think of nothing else to do. A nice quiet cry in her bedroom would have eased her, but if she cried her nose remained regrettably pink for hours afterwards and so did her eyelids.

She marched briskly, unheeding of her surroundings for half an hour, and then she turned round and marched back again. The exercise had brought some colour into her white face, but her insides were in turmoil. She would have given a great deal not to have to see Sir William later that evening; she could, of course, retire to bed with a migraine, only if she did he would undoubtedly feel it his duty to prescribe for her. 'Don't be a coward,' she muttered as she rang the doorbell to be admitted by a silently sympathetic Jolly. 'Sir William has just gone out, Miss Florina; he hopes to be back by nine o'clock. Dinner will be at half-past seven in the small sitting-room. Mrs Jolly would like to know if she can help in any way with Pauline.'

'We've given her a great deal of extra work as it is. I'll go up to her and settle her down before dinner. Wouldn't it be less trouble if I were to join you and Mrs Jolly?'

'Sir William's orders, Miss Florina—I dare say he thinks that after the exciting time that you've had you could do with some peace and quiet.'

Pauline was tired at any rate; she ate her supper, submitted to being washed and having a fresh nightie, and declared sleepily that she was quite ready to go to sleep. Florina kissed her goodnight, left a small table lamp burning and went away to tidy herself. She had no appetite, indeed she was feeling slightly sick at the thought of the coming interview, but she would have to wear a brave face…

She managed to swallow at least some of the delicious food Jolly put before her, and, since there was still some time before Sir William would return, she sat over her coffee, still at the table, so lost in a hotch-potch of muddled thoughts that she didn't hear Sir William's return.

When she looked up he was standing in the open doorway, watching her. She was so startled that her cup clattered into the saucer and she got clumsily to her feet, her head suddenly clear. She loved him; it didn't matter that he knew, for what difference would that make? She had felt a burning shame in the hall listening to Wanda's spite tearing her secret to shreds, but now she merely felt cold and detached, as though she was watching herself, a self who wasn't her at all.

Sir William's eyes hadn't left her face. He said, 'If you've finished your coffee, will you come to the study?'

She walked past him without a word, for really she had nothing to say. He opened the door and she went past him and sat, very straight-backed and composed in the chair he offered her.

Chapter 9

Sir William sat down in his chair behind the desk and rather disconcertingly remained silent. He sat back, unsmiling, apparently deep in thought, which gave Florina time to admire his stylish appearance. He was wearing a dinner-jacket, beautifully tailored, and a plain dress-shirt of dazzling whiteness. Dinner with Wanda, thought Florina; somewhere wildly fashionable where all the best people went. Wanda would have been tricked out in the forefront of fashion—taffeta was in fashion, preferably in a vivid colour like petunia. She frowned—definitely not a colour for Wanda—ice blue, perhaps, or black…

She became aware that Sir William had said something and she murmured, 'I'm sorry…I was thinking.'

Because he had nothing to say to that she gushed on, in terror of a silence between them. 'Wanda—Miss Fortesque, you know—she looks her best in black or that very pale blue…'

Behind the gravity of his face she suspected that he was laughing, but all he said was, 'Just for the moment, shall we leave her out of it?' He leaned forward and put his elbows on the desk.

'I think that you should go away for a time, Florina. You have had a tiresome few weeks.' His eyes searched her face and he went on deliberately, 'That is something which we don't need to discuss. I have a colleague at the hospital, a Dutchman over here for a seminar. He will be returning home in a couple of days' time and it so happens that the English girl who helps to look after his children is anxious to go off on holiday. It might suit you very well to take over from her for a few weeks?'

'You don't want me to be your cook?' said Florina baldly.

He smiled faintly. 'That is a difficult question to answer at the moment. The situation is such that I believe the best thing for you is to accept Doctor van Thurssen's offer.'

Florina was feeling reckless; it didn't matter any more what she said, in a day or two she would be gone and probably he hoped that once back in Holland she would find work and stay there.

'You would like me out of the way?' She spoke with deliberate flippancy.

'Exactly, Florina.' He sat back in his chair, staring at her. 'You have no objection to going?'

'I think it is a marvellous idea.' She met his eyes, her own wide, holding back tears.

'I'll get Jolly to drive you back to Wheel House tomorrow so that you can pack your things; he will fetch you back in two days time so that you can travel with Doctor van Thurssen. Can you be ready to drive to the hospital with me in the morning—just before eight o'clock—so that you can meet him?'

'Certainly, Sir William. Would you be kind enough to write me a reference?'

He looked surprised, so she added woodenly, 'So that I can get another job.' She got up. 'If there is nothing else to discuss I should like to go to bed, Sir William.'

He got up at once and opened the door, bidding her goodnight in a calm fashion, they might have been discussing the menu for a dinner party. She went up to her room and sat down on the bed, a prey to a thousand and one thoughts, none of them at all pleasant. She had been so intent on preserving a cool front that she had forgotten to ask exactly what she would be expected to do—and was she to be paid or was this doctor merely doing Sir William a good turn? And for how long? Until this other girl came back? And then what? She could always go and stay with Tante Minna, but if she did that she would have to see Felix. Supposing she had refused Sir William's offer, would he have given her notice? There was Pauline to consider too; she was so fond of the child and she thought that Pauline was fond of her. Sir William was behaving strangely; not at all what she would have expected of him. Suddenly the realisation that she wasn't going to see him again once she had left the house was too much for her; there was no point in keeping a stiff upper lip with no one to see it; so she buried her face in the pillows and had a good cry.

She was up early after a night which had been far too long and wakeful, but Sir William was up even earlier, going soft-footed to his small daughter's room. She was awake; he drew the curtains back and sat down on the bed.

'Can you keep a secret?' He wanted to know and when she nodded, he continued, 'Florina is going away, and when I've explained why I think you'll be very pleased…'

It didn't take long and when he had finished, 'Not so much as a breath or a hint,' he warned her and submitted to her delighted hug before taking himself off down to his study, where he spent ten minutes or so on the telephone to Nanny. It was breakfast time by then; he was sitting at the table when Florina joined him, to carry on a polite conversation while she pushed food around her plate. He made no mention of their talk of the previous evening, for which she was thankful; she couldn't have borne that.

'I'll drop you off at the main entrance,' he told her as he drove to the hospital, and she nodded silently. In a few minutes now she would bid him goodbye; she had been to Pauline's room before they had left the house but she had said nothing about leaving. She would have to do that presently, after she had seen Doctor van Thurssen, and since she was to leave with Jolly by ten o'clock it would have to be a hurried explanation. Just as well, perhaps.

Sir William drew up at the main doors and got out. 'There's no need…I can find my way…' She was gabbling while she tried to think of something cool and dignified to say by way of goodbye.

Sir William took no notice, he took her arm and ushered her into the entrance hall and over to the porter's lodge. Here he relinquished his grasp. 'Benson will take you to Doctor van Thurssen.' He nodded to the elderly porter, who came out of his lodge to join them. At least it would make her goodbye more easily said. She put out a hand and had it engulfed in Sir William's firm grasp.

Conscious of Benson's sharp eyes, she said gruffly, 'Goodbye, Sir William. Thank you for arranging everything.' It was a great effort to add, 'I hope you will be very happy.'

She even managed a smile, rather shaky at the corners.

'I'm quite certain that I shall be, Florina.'

He looked at Benson, who said at once, 'This way, miss,' and marched away towards a long passage at the back of the hall, so that she was forced to follow him. It took her every ounce of will-power not to turn round for a last glimpse of Sir William. He hadn't said goodbye, she reflected on a spurt of anger; loving him had been a great waste of time and what a good thing that she was going away—right away, where there would be nothing to remind her of him and perhaps in time she would be able to forget what a fool she had made of herself over him. She went pink with shame just thinking about it, so that when Benson opened a door and ushered her into a large gloomy room he paused to say, 'You're out of breath, miss—I hurried too much, quite red in the face you are.'

Doctor van Thurssen was looking out of one of the windows, although there was nothing to see, only the bare brick walls of a wing of the hospital. He turned round as she went in, a man in his late thirties with sandy hair and a pleasant, rugged face. He was tall and stoutly built and his eyes were a clear light blue. He would be from the north, she guessed, and remembered that she still knew no details of this job which had been thrust upon her.

He shook her briskly by the hand and spoke in Dutch. 'This is very good of you, Miss Payne. I hope you don't feel that you've been rushed into this; my wife really needs someone to help out with the children until our Nanny comes back.'

'I'll be glad to help, but I don't know very much. Where do you live?'

'Do you know Friesland? I have a practice in Hindeloopen, I'm also consultant at the children's hospital in Leeuwarden. We have six children; the youngest is almost two years old, the eldest fourteen. Ellie, who looks after them, will be away for two weeks. I shall be driving back tomorrow, taking the car ferry from Harwich, if you could manage to be ready by then? You will, of course be given your air ticket to return, as to salary…' He mentioned a generous sum and looked at her hopefully.

She liked him; six children seemed a lot, but the older ones wouldn't need much done for them, and presumably there was other help in the house. She agreed at once, glad to have something solid to hold on to in a nebulous future.

She took a taxi back, for time was running out. Back at the house she hurried to Pauline's room, rehearsing suitable things to say, but there was no need; Pauline said cheerfully, 'Daddy told me you were to have a holiday and you are going to Holland. Will you bring me back some of those little almond biscuits—your aunt gave me some?' She flung her arms tightly round Florina's neck. 'I shall miss you but Daddy says you must have some time to yourself because you've had too much on your mind. Were you very lost when Bobby ran away? Daddy said you couldn't see the wood for the trees—it was a nasty wood, wasn't it? All those brambles…'

'Yes, darling. You'll look after Nanny and the animals, won't you?' Florina got up off the bed and bent to kiss Pauline. 'Jolly is waiting for me, I must go…'

'Did you say goodbye to Daddy?'

It was difficult to speak. 'Yes.' She managed to smile as she went.

Jolly hadn't much to say during the drive to Wheel House, and the fact that she was leaving wasn't mentioned. He was a loyal old servant and she would have been surprised if he had referred to it. But he was kind and helpful and she believed him when he said that both he and Mrs Jolly would miss her, but that wasn't until the next morning, after she had packed her things, arranged for most of them to be sent to her father's house, and bidden Nanny goodbye. Nanny had had very little to say and Florina had been rather hurt over her lack of concern for her future. She had been kind and had fussed around Florina, and she and Jolly did everything to help her, but they hadn't expressed any interest in her future. She thought sadly that even Pauline hadn't minded overmuch. She had got up early and stripped her bed and left the room tidy, reflecting that she wouldn't be missed and would certainly be quickly forgotten in the bustle of the forthcoming wedding.

Her father, when she had walked through the village to see him, had said in a satisfied voice, 'I told you so, didn't I? But you knew best, and look where it's landed you. You'd better find yourself work in Holland, for I can't afford to keep you.'

They were to drive to the hospital where she was to meet Doctor van Thurssen, and as Jolly helped her out of the car and carried her case into the entrance hall she looked around, longing to see Sir William just once more, but no one was there. She said goodbye to Jolly and sat down to wait.

Doctor van Thurssen came presently and they went out to his car. It was parked in the consultants' car park and the Bentley was beside it; there was no one in it, of course. If she had turned her head and looked up at the windows of the children's ward she would have seen Sir William standing at one of them, watching her. It was only when Doctor van Thurssen had driven away that he turned back to resume his round of his little patients.

If Florina had been happier, she would have enjoyed the journey to Hindeloopen. They had caught the midday ferry, arriving at the Hoek in the evening, and then driving north, to arrive some four hours later at his home. It was dark by then and she was hungry, for they had stopped only long enough to eat a sandwich and drink coffee, and the sight of the brightly lit house on the edge of the little town was very welcome. A welcome echoed by Mevrouw van Thurssen, who greeted her warmly, took her to her room, bade her take off her outdoor things and return downstairs for her supper.

The room was pleasant, nicely furnished and large and the bed looked inviting. She was very tired, but she was hungry too. She went back downstairs and was ushered into a lofty dining-room, furnished with a massive square table and solid chairs, given a glass of sherry and told kindly to sit herself down at the table. Supper was all that a hungry girl could have wished for, and while they ate Mevrouw van Thurssen outlined her duties.

'Of course, the older children go to school, but Lisa, the youngest, is at home. Saska—she's five—goes to *Kleuterschool* in the mornings, and Jan and Welmer go to the *Opleidingschool* here—they are seven and ten—and then Olda and Sebo both go to

Bolsward each day. Either the doctor or I drive them there and back—' she hesitated. 'I don't suppose you drive? Of course, Ellie has a licence, so she was able to take them sometimes…'

'Yes, I've an international licence and I brought it with me. I drove quite a bit when I came to Holland with my mother, although that is some years ago.'

They beamed at her. 'How fortunate we are in having you, Florina—may I call you that? Now, I am sure that you are tired. In the morning you shall meet the children, and perhaps if you come with me to Bolsward you can see where the schools are? Lutsje can take Saska to school and look after Lisa while we are away. Perhaps we could do as Ellie and I do? One of us goes to Bolsward and the other takes Saska to her school and takes Lisa at the same time in the pushchair.'

In bed, Florina closed her eyes resolutely. She had plenty to think about until she went to sleep, and in the morning she would feel quite different; she had turned a page in her life and she wasn't going to look back at it. After all, she was quite at home in Holland; Friesland was a little different perhaps, but she had slipped back into Dutch again without any effort, it should be easy enough to get a job and it didn't matter where… Here her good resolutions were forgotten; she went back over her day and wished herself back in England, at Wheel House, cooking something delicious for Sir William who would come into the kitchen and say hello in his calm fashion. She wondered if he had missed her—just as a cook, of course—but probably by now Wanda had already engaged a French chef…

He had seemed almost relieved to see her go. 'Oh, William,' she mumbled into the pillow. She cried a little then, until at last she slept.

There was little time to think in the morning; the entire family breakfasted together before Doctor van Thurssen went to his surgery, and then, with Lisa left in the care of Lutsje, who would take Saska to school, Florina got into the family estate car with the two elder children and was driven to Bolsward. Olda and Sebo were at different schools; their mother dropped them off and turned for home. 'If you take them tomorrow,' she suggested, 'I could to go to Sneek in the morning. And perhaps you would fetch Saska at midday?'

After that the day flew past. The household was well run; Mevrouw van Thurssen had plenty of help, but there was always something or someone in need of attention, and the day had a certain routine which had to be kept. The family was a happy one and close-knit, and she was kept busy until she had helped put Lisa and Saska to bed. After supper, she helped Welmer with his English lessons. When the children were in bed, she sat for a while with the doctor and his wife, drinking a last cup of coffee before going to her own bed. She was tired by then, too tired to think clearly about her own affairs. In a day or two, she promised herself, she would decide what she was going to do. She slept on the thought.

A week went by and she was no nearer a decision;

by now she had become involved in the life of the Thurssen family; the children liked her; she worked hard, cooked when there was no one else to do it, sewed, bathed the smaller children, ferried the older ones to and from school and helped out with their homework in the evenings. But it wasn't all work; at the weekend they had all crammed into the estate car and spent the day on board the doctor's yacht which he kept moored at Sneek—the weather had been fine, if a little chilly, and Florina had enjoyed every minute of it.

On the way back, Olda, sitting beside her, said, 'We like our Ellie, but I wish you could stay with us too.'

It brought Florina up with a jolt. Ellie was due back in a week and she had done nothing about her future. It was a question of whether she should stay in Holland, get a work permit and find a job, or go back to England. She had a little money saved, enough to live on for a week or two while she found work. London, she supposed, where there were hotels and big private houses where cooks were employed; it seemed sensible to go there. At the very back of her mind was the thought that if she went there to work, she might, just might, see Sir William; not to speak to, of course. She was aware that this was a terribly stupid wish on her part; the quicker she forgot him the better. If she went to see her father she would have to take care to do so during the week when Sir William wouldn't be at Wheel House.

It was all very well to make good resolutions, but

she was never free from his image beneath her eyelids and, however busy she was, he popped up in the back of her head, ready to fill her thoughts. All day and every day she was wondering what he was doing, and that evening, pleading tiredness after their outing, she went to bed as soon as the last of the children had settled down for the night. But she didn't sleep, she lay picturing him at Wheel House, sitting in his lovely drawing-room with the mill stream murmuring and Wanda with him, looking gorgeous and dressed to kill.

She was quite wrong; he was indeed in his drawing-room and Wanda was with him, not sitting but storming up and down the room, stuttering with bad temper. He had, for his own purposes, taken her for a walk that afternoon; a long walk along bridle paths and over fields of rough grass, circumventing ploughed fields and climbing any number of gates. All the while he had talked cheerfully about the pleasures of the country. 'We'll come every weekend,' he assured her, 'and spend any free days that I have here. I must get you a bike, it's marvellous exercise. You'll feel years younger.'

Wanda, her tights laddered, stung by nettles and unsuitably shod in high heels, almost spat at him; she would have argued with him but she had needed all her breath to keep up with his easy stride.

'Just wait until we get back,' she told him furiously. And she had had to wait until they had dined—rather sketchily because Nanny and Mrs Deakin were good plain cooks with small repertoires. Wanda had suggested getting a cordon bleu cook, but Sir William had said easily that there was no hurry, and when she had pointed out that there was no reason why they shouldn't marry within the next week or so, he hadn't been in a hurry about that either; he had a backlog of theatre cases and an overflowing outpatients' clinic. An unsettling remark, since she had spread it around that they were marrying shortly.

Wanda glared at his broad back now and wondered if it was worth it—he was successful and rich and handsome, everything a girl such as herself expected of a husband; he was also proving tiresomely stubborn. She allowed herself to reflect upon the American millionaire William had introduced her to only that very week. Now, there was a man eminently suitable; possessed of oil wells that never required his presence, able to live wherever fancy took him; a real lover of bright lights. He had sent her flowers and she had half promised to see him again; after all, William was so seldom free and, if he was, he liked to have a quiet evening at home.

In the drawing-room, drinking Mrs Deakin's instant coffee, she allowed bad temper to get the better of her good sense. 'This is the worst weekend I've ever had to spend,' she raged. 'This coffee is unspeakable and I'll tell you now, William, I will not live here, not even for weekends. You can sell the place, I hate it.'

Sir William swallowed some more coffee and thought of Florina. 'No, I don't wish to see it sold,

Wanda. In fact I'm thinking of taking on less work and spending more time here.'

She came to a halt in front of him. 'You mean that? You really mean it?'

'Oh, yes, I would like to enjoy my wife and children, and I would need to have more time for that.'

'But you're at the top of your profession—you're well known, you know everyone who matters.'

'I begin to think that the people who matter to you aren't those who matter to me, Wanda.'

She stamped her foot. 'I want some fun, I want to go out dancing and have parties and buy pretty clothes.'

He said thoughtfully, 'When we first met, you told me that you wanted to have a home of your own—you even mentioned children…'

'Well, I found you attractive and I wanted to impress you, I suppose. I must say, William, you have changed. If I marry you, will you send Pauline to boarding-school and get rid of that awful old Nanny and give up this dump? We could have such fun in London; you would have much more time to go out if you didn't have to come racing down here all the time.'

He looked at her from under half closed lids and said mildly, 'No, Wanda, I won't do any of those things.'

'Then don't expect me to!' she shouted at him, as she tugged the diamond ring off her finger and threw it at him. 'I'm going to bed and you can drive me back in the morning. I never want to see you again! All these months wasted…'

She flung out of the room and Sir William went to the side table poured himself a whisky and sat down again. He was smiling to himself—quite a wicked smile. Presently he went into his study and picked up the telephone.

It was Florina's last day; Ellie would be back in the morning. She had packed her case, telephoned a surprised Tante Minna, done the daily chores she had come to enjoy so much and now she was sitting on the side of Lisa's cot reading her a bedtime story. It was when the child gave a sudden chortle that she paused to look up from the book. Doctor van Thurssen had walked into the night nursery and with him was Sir William.

Florina's voice faltered and died. She made no answer to the doctor's 'Good evening' as he picked his small daughter up from her cot and sat her on his lap. She had no breath for that. She could only stare at Sir William and gulp her heart back where it belonged.

'Is it not convenient?' observed Doctor van Thurssen cheerfully. 'Here is Sir William come to fetch you home.'

She was on her feet, wild ideas of escape mixed with delight at seeing him again. She must be firm, she told herself, and cool and matter-of-fact. She said, in a voice she strove to keep just that, 'I have arranged to go to my aunt.'

Sir William crossed the room towards her and

she retreated a few steps, which she realised, too late, was silly; the door was further away than ever. Moreover, there was only the wall behind her and he had fetched up so close to her that she had only to stretch out her hands to touch him. She clasped them prudently and kept her eyes on his waistcoat.

He said in his placid voice, but this time edged with steel, 'I shall take you home, Florina, where you belong.' And Doctor van Thurssen, who had been tucking his small daughter back into her cot, capped this with a brisk, 'Most satisfactory—it could not be better for you, Florina.' And while she was still trying to frame a watertight argument against it, he swept them both downstairs.

Somehow, for the rest of the evening, Florina was thwarted from her purpose to be alone with Sir William; she had to tell him that nothing on earth would make her go back to Wheel House with him, but there was no chance, even when, in desperation, as she and Mevrouw van Thurssen were on their way to bed, she tried to interrupt the men's learned discussion about the treatment of childish illnesses; they barely paused to listen to her request for five minutes of Sir William's time. He simply smiled kindly at her and pointed out that they would have plenty of time to talk as they drove back the next day. She had bidden them a stony goodnight and gone upstairs with Mevrouw van Thurssen, fuming silently.

Everyone was at breakfast and everyone talked; there was not the slightest chance of being heard above the cheerful din. She glowered at Sir William, who apparently didn't notice, although his eyes gleamed with amusement behind their lids. It wasn't until goodbyes had been said and she was sitting beside him in the Bentley that she had her chance at last. She had rehearsed what she was going to say for a good deal of the night. Clear, pithy remarks which would leave him no doubt as to her intention to remain in Holland. Unfortunately not one single word came to mind. She blurted out instead, 'I wish to go to Tante Minna…'

'A bit out of our way, but I think we could squeeze in an hour or so—I'd like to get home latish this evening.'

'I'm not going back with you, Sir William,' her voice was waspish and she was horrified to know that she was near to tears.

'For what reason?' He sounded mildly curious.

'You know perfectly well what the reason is.' She felt quite reckless, what did it matter what she said now? He already knew that she loved him. She pursued her train of thought out loud. 'Wanda told you…'

'Why yes, she did, but she told me something I already knew, Florina.'

Florina sniffed. 'Well, then, why do you persist… She won't have me in the house.' She stamped a foot in temper and he laughed softly.

'And you can stop laughing, you know quite well I wanted to get you alone yesterday…'

'Oh, yes, it needed a lot of will-power on my part to prevent it, too.'

'What do you mean?' He skimmed past a huge articulated lorry. 'You are driving very fast.'

'The better to get home, my dear.'

'I'm not your dear.' Really, the conversation was getting her nowhere. 'Sir William, please understand this, I will not come back to Wheel House—Wanda...'

'Let us leave Wanda out of it, shall we? She is not at Wheel House and I think it enormously unlikely that we shall ever meet again—she is enamoured of a wealthy American and they are probably already married!'

Florina digested this in silence. 'You sent me away—' she began.

'My darling girl, consider—it was obvious to everyone—the likelihood of my not marrying Wanda once I had met you became a foregone conclusion. To everyone but you—if I had not sent you away you would probably have spent your time in earnest endeavours to get us to the altar.'

'You mean Wanda doesn't want to marry you? She jilted you?'

'Yes, with a little help from circumstances.'

She cast a quick look at him; he looked smug. 'What did you do?'

'Oh, nothing really—a long country walk, rather a muddy one, I'm afraid—and the nettles at this time of year. Nanny and Mrs Deakin cooked dinner, and I refused to sell Wheel House and live for ever and ever in London.'

They drove for some miles in silence while Florina sorted out her thoughts. There was no reason why she shouldn't go back to Wheel House now. Just once or twice she had felt a rush of pure excitement wondering what he would say next, only he hadn't said anything, and by that she meant he hadn't said that he loved her. But for what other reason would he take all the trouble to fetch her back? Because she was a good cook?

She frowned, staring ahead of her as the car tore along the motorway. Perhaps it would be wiser if she were to stay in Holland. Perhaps he thought that she was suffering from an infatuation which would pass once she was back in her kitchen. She became aware that he was slowing the car into the slow lane and she looked at him.

'If I tell you that I love you—am in love with you, and have been since the moment I saw you, my darling, will you be content to leave it at that until we are home? I can't kiss you adequately in the fast lane, and nothing else will do!' He smiled at her with a tenderness which made her gulp. All she could do was nod, and he reached out and caught her hand for a moment. 'We will marry as soon as it can be arranged. Now sit quiet and think about the wedding cake while I drive.'

She said, 'Yes, William,' in a meek voice, and then, 'I'm sure Tante Minna would understand if we don't go to see her.' Then, because her heart was bursting with happiness, 'I do love you very much, William.'

He was steering back into the fast lane, but he put out a hand and caught one of hers and kissed it.

She was caught up in a lovely dream. They stopped for coffee and a quick lunch and Sir William maintained a gentle flow of talk, although afterwards she was unable to remember a word which had been spoken. When at last he drew up before the door of Wheel House and she saw the lighted windows, she heaved a great sigh of joy. It wasn't a dream, it was all true; she turned a face alight with love and happiness to him as he opened the car door for her. There was such a lot that she wanted to say but all she managed was 'Oh, William!'

He bent and kissed her and then glanced at the house. 'They will be waiting for us,' he observed, 'but first…' He kissed her again, this time at length and lingeringly. 'You'll marry me, my dearest? I can't imagine being without you—you'll have no peace, for I'll want you with me all the time—we'll live in London during the week and come here each weekend…'

'Pauline?'

'I've talked to her; she likes the idea of being a weekly boarder and she can't wait to be your stepdaughter. Nanny will stay here.' He kissed her once more. 'You know, I thought just for a while that you had fallen for Felix. I could have killed him with my bare hands…'

She reached up to kiss him in her turn. 'I dislike him intensely,' she assured him vigorously, 'and always did—only it was rather difficult to talk about.' She smiled up at him and his arms tightened around her.

'You're the one I've been waiting for,' he said softly, 'all my life—and now I don't need to wait any longer.' He put up a gentle finger and stroked her face. 'Such a beautiful girl…'

She had thought that she would never be happier, but she saw that she had been mistaken; she was bursting with happiness. William had called her beautiful and, what was more, he meant it.

He opened the door and they went into the house together.

* * * * *

HARLEQUIN®
A Romance FOR EVERY MOOD™

SPECIAL EXCERPT FROM

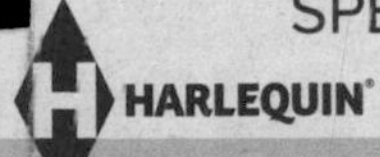

Romance

Read on for an exclusive sneak preview of INTERVIEW WITH A TYCOON by Cara Colter…

KIERNAN WAITED FOR it to happen. All his strength had not been enough to hold the lid on the place that contained the grief within him.

The touch of her hand, the look in her eyes, and his strength had abandoned him, and he had told her all of it: his failure and his powerlessness.

Now, sitting beside her, her hand in his, the wetness of her hair resting on his shoulder, he waited for everything to fade: the white-topped mountains that surrounded him, the feel of the hot water against his skin, the way her hand felt in his.

He waited for all that to fade, and for the darkness to take its place, to ooze through him like thick black sludge freed from a containment pond, blotting out all else.

Instead, astounded, Kiernan became *more* aware of everything around him, as if he were soaking up life through his pores, breathing in glory through his nose, becoming drenched in light instead of darkness.

He started to laugh.

"What?" she asked, a smile playing across the lovely fullness of her lips.

"I just feel alive. For the last few days, I have felt alive. And I don't know if that's a good thing or a bad thing."

HREXP0814

His awareness shifted to her, and being with her seeme to fill him to overflowing.

He dropped his head over hers and took her lips. H kissed her with warmth and with welcome, a man who ha thought he was dead discovering not just that he lived but, astonishingly, that he wanted to live.

Stacy returned his kiss, her lips parting under his, her hands twining around his neck, pulling him in even closer to her.

There was gentle welcome. She had seen all of him, he had bared his weakness and his darkness to her, and still he felt only acceptance from her.

But acceptance was slowly giving way to something else. There was hunger in her, and he sensed an almost savage need in her to go to the place a kiss like this took a man and a woman.

With great reluctance he broke the kiss, cupped he cheeks in his hands and looked down at her.

He felt as if he was memorizing each of her features: th green of those amazing eyes, her dark brown hair curlin even more wildly from the steam of the hot spring, th swollen plumpness of her lips, the whiteness of her skin.

"It's too soon for this," he said, his voice hoarse.

"I know," she said, and her voice was raw, too.

Don't miss this heart-wrenching story, available September 2014 from Harlequin® Romance.

HREXP081